W9-ASK-625

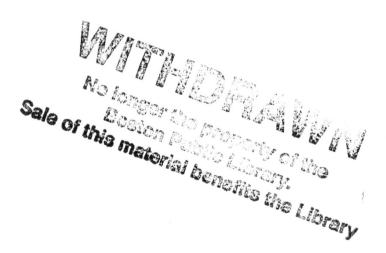
WITHDRAWN
No longer the property of the
Boston Public Library.
Sale of this material benefits the Library

VALLEY

OF

REFUGE

ALSO BY

JOHN TESCHNER

Project Namahana

VALLEY
OF
REFUGE

A NOVEL

JOHN TESCHNER

TOR PUBLISHING GROUP
NEW YORK

This is a work of fiction. All of the characters, organizations, and events portrayed in this novel are either products of the author's imagination or are used fictitiously.

VALLEY OF REFUGE

Copyright © 2023 by John Teschner

All rights reserved.

A Forge Book
Published by Tom Doherty Associates / Tor Publishing Group
120 Broadway
New York, NY 10271

www.tor-forge.com

Forge® is a registered trademark of Macmillan Publishing Group, LLC.

The Library of Congress Cataloging-in-Publication Data is available upon request.

ISBN 978-1-250-82735-7 (hardcover)
ISBN 978-1-250-82736-4 (ebook)

Our books may be purchased in bulk for promotional, educational, or business use. Please contact your local bookseller or the Macmillan Corporate and Premium Sales Department at 1-800-221-7945, extension 5442, or by email at MacmillanSpecialMarkets@macmillan.com.

First Edition: 2023

Printed in the United States of America

0 9 8 7 6 5 4 3 2 1

Dedicated to my mom and dad.
Your unconditional love made everything possible.

VALLEY

OF

REFUGE

PROLOGUE

Sunlight from the doorway fell across the concrete floor of the living room. The pink polyester curtains rippled their familiar pattern high against the concrete wall. Dalton hadn't seen the room this bare since his first weeks, when he had nothing but a plastic chair and a stack of books plucked hastily from a pile in the Country Office—*The Scramble for Africa, Pathologies of Power, Moby-Dick*—the kinds of titles volunteers brought from America and didn't take home.

He remembered how he used to watch the shadow of the curtain climb the concrete wall.

Then he shut the wooden door and swung the barred steel grate across it. For the first time in two years, he left the padlock hanging open. Piled in his dusty yard were six half-liter bottles, two cardboard boxes, one backpack, and an enormous duffel. The rest had gone to Gideon, his counterpart in the computer lab. The school was on holiday. The only people he passed on his way out were two boys steering hand-made wire cars around the dusty bougainvillea beds. They stopped to watch him.

"Tutaonana," said Franky Dalton, without breaking stride, though he knew it wasn't true. He would never see these boys again.

At the Posta, he mailed the boxes and said goodbye to the clerks behind the counter and the kids clustered around the two computer kiosks, part of a UN project bringing Internet to rural Africa. He'd spent hundreds of hours in front of those terminals, half of them debugging. To pay himself back, he'd hacked the log-in. He'd shared the backdoor with two of his favorite students, and now a crowd of teenage boys was always waiting to look up their favorite Premier League players or stare solemnly at American pornography.

His final stop was the Grassland Savanna, the only bar in town that always had cold beer, to return his empty bottles and get back the deposit he'd left two years earlier. There were no more loose ends. The week before, he'd said goodbye to Gideon, Samuel, Mwangi, Wamai, Njoroge, Lampat—men whose formal British English and naked curiosity about America had once felt so alienating; who'd come to this town to work as teachers, clerks, gardeners, cooks; who saw their families on holidays—or didn't—and gathered every night in the lantern-glow of a small hoteli where the food was cooked in fire-blackened pots by a Luo woman who made the best ugali in the majengo, it was widely agreed.

On their last night together, they got very drunk. At one point, Dalton felt a gratitude so piercing it made his vision blur. He listened to the familiar rhythm of mock pronouncements and raucous laughter and realized the barrier that was always there between himself and other people did not exist among these men, his friends. He realized he didn't have to leave. Then his eyes cleared, and he looked around the room again, and the difference was plain. All of them were far from their homelands, but only he would never be at home.

Dalton found his van at the matatu stage, paid the tout, and took the center seat in the second row, the one he'd used since seeing his first wreck on the highway, two matatus twisted open like soda cans, bright pools of blood spreading like syrup across the asphalt.

A young couple was the last to board. The woman held the smallest baby Dalton had ever seen, swaddled like a fuzzy pink pill. They lingered outside the door until Dalton understood and slid over against the window. The young man grinned up at him, then took the baby so his wife could board. Dalton was amazed a man his own age could hold such a thing with so much assurance. The father blew in the baby's face and made her laugh until his wife clucked and he reluctantly handed her up and climbed in behind.

Once the tout had filled the thirteen seats with paying adults and squeezed in four children, plus the baby, he climbed into the footwell and rattled the door shut. The driver sped out of the yard, only to take an unexpected turn away from the highway, into the alleys of the majengo.

"Tunaenda wapi?" Dalton asked.

"Polisi," the tout answered without looking up.

They pulled into the station and disembarked. A female officer gestured impatiently, and a mama unknotted her bright kanga to reveal a pile of cabbages. Next, an old man in a pin-striped suit lifted his ragged lapels and announced something in Kikuyu that made the other men laugh. There was a square of dust on his back from the ground where he'd been sleeping. When it was Dalton's turn, he led the officer to the back of the van and unzipped his bags. The woman glanced inside, then stared at him with a sad expression. Dalton kept his eyes fixed on his Chaco sandals. They were interrupted by a heavy, very black policeman with gold epaulets on his shoulders. "Tumesikia taarifa za wezi kwenye barabara ya Nairobi," he announced, then noticed Dalton and switched from Kiswahili into English. "There are thieves on the Nairobi Road. We have searched you all for weapons. You go at your own risk."

The young father in Dalton's row said something in Kikuyu. The tout answered him curtly. The mama with the cabbages leaned toward Dalton and whispered, "That new baba has requested an officer to accompany us. The tout has asked, can he pay for the seat? Of course he cannot. But it is all right. These thieves are very violent, but they are not so, so clever."

The van raised a plume of dust that drifted over the savanna. Gazelle and zebra grazed in the pale grass. Darkness fell.

In the distance, headlights. High beams flashing urgently. Another fourteen-seat matatu like their own. The drivers stopped to exchange words. Immediately, a debate began inside the van among the tout, the driver, and the young father. Dalton tapped the shoulder of the old man in the pin-striped suit. "Mzee," he said, using the term of respect, "wanasema nini?"

The mzee looked at him in confusion. Then laughed, releasing a sugary cloud of alcohol. "Here is a white man speaking Kiswahili!" he announced to everyone on board. Then he fixed Dalton with his bloodshot eyes. "Mzungu," he said. "There are wezi up ahead. Bandits. This other driver has just escaped."

"Escaped them how?"

"By driving *very* fast."

"And our driver, anasema nini?"

"He says we also will drive fast."

The other matatu roared away. Dalton gagged on the invisible dust. A new smell slowly filled the van. The sweaty, sour odor of fear.

Everyone saw the boulders at the same moment: three black shadows in a line across the road. The driver swerved. The van bounced into the ditch. The young woman fell onto Dalton. The baby slid into his lap. The van swayed. The driver shouted. They bounced back onto the road. White light illuminated everything: the bared teeth of the tout, the puckered scowl of the baby, the father's eyes—bright with something Dalton would never forget—the old man in the pin-striped suit, unaccountably laughing. A truck had swerved onto the road behind them.

The mother snatched her baby back. Everyone was shouting but the driver, who stayed reassuringly silent as he swung around the largest potholes and barely braked for the rest. Dalton was sure they'd blow a tire or crack an axle. But the van held, and the headlights grew fainter until the only light inside the van was the dim orange glow of the instrument panel.

Dalton looked over his shoulder and saw two bright points in the distance. He touched the money belt where he'd hidden six one-hundred-dollar bills.

He looked again. The lights were gone. They proceeded to Nairobi.

He walked quickly and with purpose down Ronald Ngala Street, the way he'd been taught in Peace Corps training, forcing others to swerve around him. Erin was waiting at the hostel on Tom Mboya Street. When she put her arms around him, everything went still. Their mingled breath made a calm, warm space in the chaos of the city. They climbed the four flights of stairs, dropped his bags on a bunk, and walked out to the balcony, where a dozen other Tech Extension volunteers sat at a table covered with every local brand of beer and whiskey: Tusker, Ice Cap, Pilsener Lager, Hunter's Choice, Bond 7.

A heavy bottle found its way into Dalton's hand. He took a long sip, feeling uncharacteristically giddy as he told the story of his trip, feeling Erin's cool gaze from her place in the darkness. She wasn't the type to gasp or squeeze his hand, highjack his feelings for herself. She could, of course. She could have anything she wanted. Only an extremely limited dating pool could explain how he had ended up with her. And even that didn't seem sufficient.

Suddenly, he was on his third bottle, or his fourth, with a few shots of Bond mixed in. "I took my counterpart to the food court at Sarit Center Mall," someone was saying. "He told me, *So this is what America is like? No wonder you are so eager to return.*"

"Are we fucked?"

"Obviously."

"This is the twenty-first century," someone said. "Why are we saying goodbye at all?"

"Because the UN didn't fund ongoing maintenance for all those kiosks at the Posta."

"Fucking classic."

"It wouldn't matter," said Erin. She was the only female Tech Ex in their training class.

"You don't think *having Internet* helps people stay connected?"

Dalton had tried bringing it up with his colleagues, the sneer that wormed its way into their tone whenever they addressed his girlfriend regarding anything remotely technical. They claimed he was imagining it. Had *she* ever complained? He had to admit, she never had.

"You're saying you still email everyone you knew in college?"

She never complained, and she never backed down.

"I'm just lazy."

"Of course you are," said Erin. "But that's the point."

"What point?"

"We all say we want to stay in touch. But when it actually comes to writing an email or dialing a number, it's too much effort."

"So what are you saying?" Dalton asked.

"As long as the Internet is just *connecting* people, it's failing. Because human nature proves that's not enough. We won't follow through. The Internet needs to *be* the place. Like market day in the village. Everyone you know is already there. All you have to do is show up."

"How can the Internet be a place?"

No one was sneering.

"You have a website with a buddy list, like Instant Messenger. Except it's not private. Everyone on your list sees all your updates, and you see theirs. You open one page and see what's new with everyone you know."

"Your personal village," said Dalton.

"What's that in Kiswa?"

"Kijiji?"

"It's called Sokoni," said Erin.

A Public Health volunteer leaned over from another table. "What are you nerds talking about?"

"Just solving loneliness."

"Well, can y'all contribute to a real conversation for once? We're trying to figure out who's had the shits in the worst place. Don't bother telling a matatu story. Everybody has one."

Eventually, Dalton and Erin were alone. They leaned over the rail, looking down four stories into City Center. This hostel wasn't recommended by any of the guidebooks. It was small and shabby and had no private rooms. But it was cheap and convenient, and it had this balcony, where they could watch the ongoing dramas of daily life in this country without any risk of being caught up in them.

Erin took his hand. In a few weeks, she was starting classes at Wharton. He was flying to Oakland to crash with two frat brothers who claimed they could find him an entry-level software engineering job. It seemed impossible that in a few hours, this life he'd built—the only real life he'd ever experienced, the only real friendships, the only real love—would begin the process of receding until the last two years were nothing but a few bright links in a long, gray chain.

Somewhere in the city, a matatu honked. Dalton remembered the helplessness he'd seen in the young father's eyes—someone his own age, already capable of losing so much. Erin squeezed his hand. Instead of squeezing back, he slipped free, flexing his fingers in the cool air high above Tom Mboya Street. He couldn't believe he was about to do this.

"Neither one of us will have any money," he said, "the next few years, to fly back and forth."

Erin stared into the empty street.

"So what are you saying?" she finally asked.

DAY 1

1

The bassline vibrated the walls of the hallway. She was leaving the bathroom, adjusting the hem of her shirt self-consciously. Had she forgotten a zipper? How much had she had to drink?

Why was it so bright?

She had to shoulder her way through the crowd. People gave her dirty looks. They weren't dressed for the club. They wore uniforms, or joggers with hoodies, or shorts with ugly patterned shirts. But beyond them, she could see the oval doorway that led to the wide-open space of the dance floor.

They were talking about her, their voices barely audible above the noise. It would feel so good, to make it to that high, bright space and have room to move.

And to be with her, the woman dancing with her eyes shut.

She was in a dream, she knew that. But she wanted so badly to be back on the dance floor. No reality could be more important than that. She was pushing more frantically now. But the harder she pushed, the more they pushed back. Someone was shouting in her face. She craned her head to find the exit, to be anywhere but in this bright, narrow hallway.

She opened her eyes.

"Ma'am!" A wild-eyed woman was practically in her lap. She tried to kick but hit something hard, and pain exploded in her shin.

"Ms. Diaz!"

Her name?

The woman was wearing a uniform. A cop? A nurse?

She looked up and saw two circles dancing in and out of focus in an oddly low and curving ceiling. To her left, a portal, beyond it, blue.

She was on an airplane.

There were two other flight attendants standing in the aisle. And two men, one Black, one white. Big men.

She was on an airplane. And there was a problem. She was the problem.

She closed her eyes and held up her hands. "Okay," she said. "Okay."

"Ma'am, there is a team of emergency responders waiting for us at the airport. They want to know, have you taken any drugs or medications?"

She began to answer. Opened her mouth. Shut it. Tried again.

"What's my name?"

The flight attendant glanced back at her colleagues.

"Your name is Janice. Janice Diaz. According to your boarding pass."

"How did I get here?"

"Just like everyone else, ma'am. You boarded in Seattle."

"And where are we landing?"

"LIH. Lihue Airport. Hawaii."

Janice Diaz leaned back. "That sounds nice."

The flight attendant stepped back into the aisle, whispered to her co-workers.

"Ms. Diaz, what is the last thing you remember?"

She almost told her about the woman on the dance floor. Then she pictured the Seattle airport. Escalators and empty glass hallways. She knew it well. She tried filling it with people. Faceless, hurrying bodies. She tried to remember the bench she'd chosen at the gate, where she'd bought coffee, the line for security. There was nothing there. Her mind was clear and bright.

She took a deep breath, waited for the never-ending stream of images and mental chatter that constituted who she was.

She took another breath.

"Ma'am?" The flight attendant was in the seat beside her. "I'm going to sit right here until we land."

Without thinking, Janice Diaz clasped the flight attendant's hand. "Am I all right?"

"Oh, honey." The woman lifted a strand of hair from her face. One fingertip brushed her forehead, and the full arc of her skull fluoresced with pain. "I don't think so."

2

Nalani Winthrop took her eyes from the road long enough to dial her mother's number for the fourth time. A few seconds later, the tone cut off mid-ring.

"All right, you fackah, I no want none of your—"

"What? Hey. It's me, Nalani." She grabbed the sheets of paper sliding around the passenger seat.

"Nalani! Honey! It's so good to hear from you! I thought you was one spam caller."

"I only had the same number ten years already."

"Sorry, you know I had get one new phone and lost all my contacts? I lent it to that bitch—"

"Are you suing our family?"

"What? Of course not."

"I have a piece of paper right here that says—"

"Oh, I'm not *suing* the family. I'm just helping—"

"I got *served*. And I know who you're helping. It says right here, you're suing us for title of Uncle Solomon's property. I had a notary at my door telling me to certify this paper saying I give up any standing in the case of Maile Kanahele Winthrop versus—"

"Oh, I never like think of it like that. *Lawsuit* just one technical term for what they need do, *legally*, for, um, consolidate the ownership of . . . something . . . Listen, honey. I like see you!"

"Oh, you going see me. I just like know how I'm supposed to get in now. I hear they get security guards blocking—"

"Don't trust everything you see on social media. Just tell 'em at the gate you're one guest of the Kanaheles and you'd like permission to visit—"

"I'm no *guest*. I *am* a Kanahele. And til you take me to court, I own that land, too."

She jabbed the red button on her screen a few times before the music came back on her car stereo. A local boy's new song was on the radio. *What do you do when no one's there? What do you do when no one cares?*

Nalani realized she was crushing the papers around the steering wheel. She tried to flatten them against the leg of her jeans, then gave up and tossed them on the seat.

She caught herself and took a deep breath, the way her therapist had shown her, from the bottom of her diaphragm. Of course her mother was mixed up in all this.

It had started a few days ago with an unknown number from a California area code. She'd let it ring to voice mail and only got as far as, *How would you like to earn hundreds of dollars for something you don't even know you own?* before she'd hit Delete.

The guy had tried a few more times over the next three days. He even sent a text message: *Aloha, Nalani, I'm a lawyer representing a local nonprofit. Please call for a great opportunity.*

Then she got an email. It had a few more details. She had inherited a plot of land that was of scientific interest to a nonprofit that wanted to study coral reefs on the North Shore. This was her opportunity to help protect vulnerable native species and receive a tax-free incentive.

How did you get my email? she wrote back, then looked up the nonprofit AinaKai Alliance. It had a website, at least: a few pictures of generic coral reefs and something about the promise of artificial intelligence to protect biodiversity. When she clicked on *About Us,* the page said, *Under Construction.*

She was expecting a callback from the hairdresser, so she answered the call from an 808 number that rang a few minutes later.

"Hello. Nalani Winthrop?"

"Yes."

"Well, first off, aloha! So wonderful to meet you."

"Aloha. Who's this?"

"Oh! Ha ha. My name's Samantha Rittenheimer."

"Okay."

"I'm an agent with 'Ohana Executive Properties. I believe an associate of mine has been in touch with you? About an opportunity to support the 'āina?"

"I'm not sure."

"Oh, hmmm . . . So funny. You had expressed an interest in helping the mission of AinaKai Alliance? They're an exciting new nonprofit using the latest Silicon Valley technology to mālama the health of our oceans. And their first project is actually right here on our island."

"I'm sorry. How did you get this number?"

"We're very excited to inform you that you appear on public records as a co-owner of a unique marine environment. In fact, this is such an exceptional opportunity, AinaKai Alliance is actually prepared to generously compensate you for your stake in this very small parcel."

"If you want to buy land, you need to call our family's law firm. That all goes through the trust."

"Oh, ha ha. This isn't *that* side of your family. You are the granddaughter of Lydia Kanahele?"

"I don't know about owning any property."

"No surprise there! This is a *very* small property with honestly really little value—except to science, of course. It's actually unimproved. You are one of hundreds, practically thousands, of owners. In fact, your share is just six-tenths of one percentage point. But through the extraordinary generosity of their donors, AinaKai Alliance is actually prepared to offer you eight hundred dollars cash for your interest!"

"Um, so you're saying this nonprofit wants to pay one-point-three million for a piece of land with no value?"

"Wow. Excellent math. Well, as I said, it is valuable to them, for science."

"Where is this property?"

"It's in a remote area of the North Shore."

"But it must be oceanfront, if they want to study the reef?"

"Yes, it does have access to the ocean. Unfortunately—or fortunately for science, I should say—it is not accessible by road."

"You're talking about Momona Bay?"

"That's right, though technically the beach—"

"No need *technically* me. I know where that money coming from."

"So can I send you some paperwork?"

"Go ahead, send 'em. But if you think I'm going—"

"Wonderful!" Samantha cut her off. "You'll be hearing from us soon. Mahalo!"

And that morning, a notary had shown up at her door, expecting her to sign a legal document. Nalani had taken the paperwork, thanked the notary, and shut the door in his face. Ten minutes later, she was in her Tacoma, heading to Momona.

She felt stupid she hadn't seen through it at once. People had been posting about the situation there for months. They'd all been convinced their messages would be taken down, so whether they were complaining about the construction traffic, or the gatehouses going up on old farm roads, or the public beaches he was supposedly blocking access to, every post always started with an all-caps warning to screenshot and pass it on before it disappeared. Now that they'd all been shared hundreds of times and were still up, those warnings were looking pretty stupid.

Nalani hadn't followed any of it that closely. The legal stuff was confusing, and some of the complaints just seemed petty. The guy had a right to buy property, just like anyone else. She hadn't even looked that closely at exactly which old farms had been involved. Of course, she'd known it must be near Tūtū's kuleana land, but it had been years since she'd been down there.

She felt unexpectedly intimidated when she pulled up to the guardhouse. She'd expected a local boy in a security uniform. But the man behind the glass did not look local, and he wasn't wearing a cheap uniform with a fake badge. He was wearing a black polo shirt, and she couldn't help but be impressed by his obvious and utter lack of interest in making an impression on her.

"Can I help you?"

"My name is Nalani Winthrop. I'm here to visit my family."

The man scrolled his finger down the face of a tablet. "Did you have an appointment?"

"I'm visiting my family's land. The Kanaheles? It's makai of this property. I just need to pass through."

The man stared past her car. "I'm sorry, ma'am, but I don't know anything about other properties. You're going to have to—"

"We have an easement." Nalani was getting heated. "We have a right—"

She heard the shriek of air brakes, and a dump truck pulled in behind her Tacoma.

"Ma'am, I'm going to need you to pull over to the side and turn around."

What was she thinking, believing her mother? Nalani backed her truck onto the grass and did a U-turn to clear the way for the dump truck.

She parked on the shoulder, a few feet from the black metal fence that traced the rising and falling land as far as she could see. There was a horse pasture across the road. Two mud-spattered duns stood flank to flank, whisking flies from each other's faces. She punched her mother's number. Straight to voice mail. Network was still terrible down there, apparently.

The posts popping up on her Sokoni commons had made it sound like a small city was being built out here. But all she could see were pastures and fields, and, in the distance, a few metal barns surrounded by construction equipment. It was hard not to wonder what all the pilikia was about.

She tried again.

"Hello?"

"This your daughter."

"Nalani! Where you stay?"

"I stay beside the road is where. Why you tell me these security guys would let me through?"

"What? They never let you in? And you told them you was one Kanahele? Who's there? That boy Kaulana?"

"There's no Kaulana. It's one haole."

"Ah. You know why? The guy, Dalton, him and his family stay on island. Everything change up when he come. Sit tight. I going check my cousin Solly."

3

Madeleine was in the living area, holding her phone at arm's length toward one of the bare walls. "Que pence tu?" she asked her husband as he walked past.

Frank Dalton stopped and looked over her shoulder. The screen displayed an inscrutable entanglement of crudely painted naked people with various expressions of surprise, fear, and pleasure. "Are they all . . . falling?"

Madeleine cocked her head. "Peut-être," she said as if noticing for the first time. "That's not the point. You see the use of color?"

"I see colors."

"We can preempt an auction if we decide today. No one we know has one of these yet."

Through the floor-to-ceiling windows, Dalton could see two staffers wheeling out the portals. "How much?"

"Three million."

The number made Dalton feel better. It had been a while since Madeleine had acquired anything for only seven digits. "It's fine, I guess."

"You guess?"

"Of course. That's what all of you are doing, right? Speculating?"

"This is my profession."

"You're an expert speculator."

This was a habit he was trying to break: saying something only because it was true. Besides, he appreciated Madeleine's observations. Just because they didn't have utility didn't mean they couldn't be interesting. He was about to say this, but she spoke first.

"You're always so grincheux on Wednesday mornings."

She followed his eyes out to the lanai. There were faces on the screens now. "Do you really have to do this every week?"

He shrugged. It bothered him a little—more than a little—that his wife treated all this like some indulgence. Of course he would love to skip these meetings, to let someone else take responsibility, or, better yet, not have the responsibility in the first place. He couldn't comprehend how she spent hours every day deciding how to invest in contemporary art but couldn't understand why he spent a few hours a week deciding how to invest in their family's security.

They were waiting for him now. He picked a lamp off the kitchen island. It was surprisingly heavy, a column of richly veined wood topped by a lattice of loosely woven bamboo strips. "I like this."

"Moi aussi! It's going in the rec room. I want a Polynesian theme."

"Like, tikis and hula girls?"

Madeleine wrinkled her nose. "Of course not. I'm sourcing everything from indigenous art collectives. That's koa from Lanai. Richard introduced the artist last time we were there."

Dalton set down the lamp and glanced out the window. The giant faces in the portals looked studiously blank. Madeleine was still talking. "He makes traditional Hawaiian weapons, too. Very striking. I commissioned a couple, just for you."

"Sounds great," said Dalton. "Sorry. You know how I am about art."

Madeleine smiled. She did know how he was. "You can't crowdsource taste," she said. "Unless you want to end up paying ten times as much for something once everyone discovers it."

He wanted to point out this math only worked in your favor if you were right more than 10 percent of the time—a mark that she had yet to hit, judging by what they were paying for climate-controlled storage—but he bit his tongue.

The lanai hadn't existed their last time on island. The stainless steel railing wires had been strung the day before, the furniture unboxed that morning. He'd been curious how his security lead would handle the informality but wasn't surprised that, even when sinking into an oversize teal cushion, Colonel Hart was completely at ease.

He couldn't say the same for his lead architect and engineer, who'd been invited to sit in on the macro portion of the security briefing. He'd hoped the builders of his Sanctuary would feel inspired by a glimpse of the full scope of their responsibility, but, glancing at their stiffly attentive expressions, he had no confidence much of it was sinking in.

On one screen, his climatologist offered new calving assessments from their expedition to the Thwaites Glacier. The projections were grim for most of the globe, but updated Coriolis simulations still forecast local rainfall within the lower range of the Sanctuary's ten-year ag plan. On the other screen, Dalton's geopolitical analyst wanted to talk about uncertainty in Indonesia's presidential race. Sokoni's internal analytics now favored a disgraced minister of defense accused of human rights abuses toward indigenous tribes. "Even the local media are writing him off. But he's backed by the oil palm and logging—"

Hart cut him off. "How is this relevant to our *macro* security framework?"

Geopolitics laughed nervously. "Given that the archipelago holds the world's third-largest acreage of rain forest canopy and a deforestation rate that makes it one of the highest carbon emitters, the possibility of reaching a tipping point in moisture feedback loops—"

"All right," said Dalton. "You and climate put your heads together and come up with a model. Any other changes in the macros?"

Hart shook his head. "That's all from Anthropogenics. Astronomy and Tectonics have nothing."

Dalton turned to his building team. "Now that you've seen how we approach these issues, I hope you can understand why our tolerances are so tight. Thank you for joining. The rest of this meeting is privileged."

A staffer emerged to escort the architect and engineer. New faces appeared in the portals.

"Let's move on to local threat assessment," said Dalton. "Colonel?"

Hart made an almost imperceptible grimace. He hated it when Dalton used his former rank. He launched into the usual list of cookie-cutter security issues, which interested Dalton much less than the existential updates. His earbud chimed. Dhillon's jet had just touched down in Princeville. The entire board was now on island. He brought his attention back to Hart.

"And we believe we're close to identifying the source of the Phoenix leaks. As you know, their info-sec protocols have been quite effective against our internal resources. However, we enlisted the services of a specialized contractor, who just informed me they've developed an asset with access to the highest levels, including the whistleblower him- or herself."

Dalton's earbud chimed again. An email with a draft of his remarks for the board. On his tablet, he tapped rapidly across the blanks they'd left for him to personalize. Normally, he wouldn't bother vetting anything as tedious as a welcome to his board. But this gathering had a personal motive.

The Sanctuary was going to be the most state-of-the-art refuge on the planet, regardless, but there were additional layers of security that could be tapped by a collective effort. About 150 people on the planet were capable of investing in their family's future at the scale he envisioned. Five percent would be on his land that afternoon. Few titles in the world were more prestigious than a board seat at Sokoni, the world's largest social network by a factor of one hundred. Dalton had meticulously planned his board's introduction to the island, concluding with a tour of his property and a catered picnic on the bluff. They all thought they'd done Hawaii; most of them owned properties already. He needed to show what these islands offered when you looked with fresh eyes.

4

The flight attendant held her hand until the plane touched down.

Janice Diaz never opened her eyes. Since the first flash of pain across her skull, she'd cataloged more areas of concern: a throbbing jaw, a crusty itch across her collarbone, a migraine: currently knotted at one temple, but sending out curious tendrils. She had an urgent feeling that if she held her head at a very particular angle, she could maintain whatever fragile barriers were holding back the flood. Then the wheels bumped and bounced, the attendant gave her fingers a final squeeze, belts unclicked, bins dropped, and Janice Diaz entered a new level of pain.

Dimly, she heard her flight attendant telling everyone to clear the aisle for the first responders. Then she heard a man's voice—musical, urgent, and kind—asking whether she had any concerns about her neck or spine. She answered honestly, "I don't know."

The flight attendant: "She walked right onto the plane."

"Looking like this?"

"Some of those bruises may be darker."

She still hadn't opened her eyes. She felt someone intimately close. "It's okay if I assess you?"

She nodded, or thought she did. She was so tired. She felt herself sinking right through the fire into the warm, dark space beneath.

Fingers lightly touched her jaw, gently tilting. "Any pain?"

She shook her head.

Talk she could not decipher.

"Ma'am, we're going to try to move you now."

Hands cupping her armpits, an awkward lurch.

"Can you stand?"

She tried and found she could. She let herself be pulled out of the tight row into the aisle and took a peek, for just a moment. Eyes, all on her. Concerned. Irritated. Curious. She pressed hers shut and wobbled in darkness, grateful for the guiding touch. Heat and humidity. The familiar airport smell. Then she was sitting again but still in motion. She opened her eyes and saw the silver arms of the wheelchair. She relaxed back into darkness.

She was in a hospital bed. She was alone. She had a clear head. She attempted to piece together memories and rebuild the bridge back to herself. She remembered the airplane, the flight attendant, the firefighters. Beyond that. Nothing.

The feeling was so strange it punched through the pain and absorbed her full attention. Her mind was working now in a way that felt familiar, chattering to itself, summoning images, seeking answers. She was an adult; that was clear from looking at her white arms stretched beside the mound of her body beneath the blanket. But where were the years?

A nurse came in, tall and round and creamy brown, the most beautiful person she had ever seen. For whatever that was worth.

"You're awake!"

She nodded, tried to smile. The ache in her jaw.

"Do you remember how you got here?"

She opened her mouth experimentally. "I was sick. On a plane."

The nurse smiled and nodded. "Can you tell me your name?"

She knew it. She knew she knew it. "Jennifer?"

"According to your passport, your name is Janice Diaz?"

She nodded. Okay.

"I'm going to let the doctor know you're awake."

A few minutes later, an Asian man stepped into her room. He made no effort to get her attention. He opened the door silently and swung it just wide enough to slip through, then stood against the wall, consulting his notes. But he wasn't shy, she thought, or insecure. He was considerate. And competent. She felt sure of these conclusions. The way she'd known the flight attendant was an ally from the moment she'd spoken. These instant judgments on the character of strangers were—so far—the only certainty she had experienced.

The doctor told her she had a laceration on her chest, bruising on her arms and abdomen, a slight dislocation in her jaw, significant bruising to her skull. They were still waiting on some other tests. Most likely, she'd had a concussion. Did she have any recollection of receiving these injuries?

She shook her head.

He seemed unsurprised.

"The good news is, while you may be in some discomfort for a while, there's no need to keep you overnight. I'm going to begin your discharge process."

This did not seem like good news.

"I understand you just arrived," he said. "Were you traveling alone?"

"I think so."

The doctor nodded. "And where were you planning to stay?"

"I don't know."

Again, the doctor seemed unsurprised. "Your memory issues should clear up in a couple of days. They usually do."

"What's causing it?"

Now the doctor looked impatient. He wasn't an impatient person. He was busy. But he'd be used to that. He worked in an ER. So it was something about her particular situation. Or it was something about her.

"Could have been the concussion," said the doctor. "Or something in your system. We haven't got the labs back yet. Maybe a case of psychogenic fugue. We've assigned your case to our social worker. He should be in shortly."

He slipped out as unobtrusively as he'd arrived, before she could ask another question.

Later, a knock. A chubby brown man stuck his head beyond the door, then stepped in. He was dressed in loose-fitting jeans and a cheerful floral shirt. An overstuffed computer satchel was slung over one shoulder. Someone dressed to spend time with people he did not need to impress. The social worker.

He smiled. "I'm Arnel. I'm here to help with your discharge."

He sank onto the couch and pulled the satchel onto his lap. He was a kind person. That was obvious. Well meaning. But as he paged through a disorderly stack of documents, a judgment arrived from a part of her mind she had no access to: he could not help her.

He smiled excitedly when he found the file he was looking for, then looked up. "So, you're from Seattle?"

She looked at him blankly.

"Are you having any trouble with your memory?"

"Yes."

He smiled again, reassuringly this time. "Don't worry. That's not uncommon. We find people's confusion usually diminishes quite a bit within a few hours. I know it can be a little scary, though."

She nodded again.

"So I want to make sure you get all your things." He opened a ziplock bag and placed a cell phone and a passport on the table beside her.

She stared at them. "That's all?"

He'd presented these items as if it were perfectly normal to travel with nothing but a phone and passport. But her question seemed to give him permission to acknowledge the reality. He looked at them again, drawing his lips tight while continuing to smile with his eyes.

"This was all you had."

"What about my luggage?"

"Oh? Did you have luggage? What did it look like?"

She said nothing.

"I could call the airline?"

"That would be great." She felt defeated. She had no idea what airline she'd arrived on.

"In the meantime, did you have a reservation somewhere, or a friend?"

She looked at him blankly.

He smiled again. It was a thin, practiced smile, meant to offer sympathy, not hope.

"I may be able to find you a voucher. Unfortunately, our shelters are currently full."

"I can't stay here?"

"You've been discharged."

"Ah."

"But I believe the doctor said you could use the room a few more hours."

There was something she wanted to tell him.

"I don't know who I am."

He nodded sympathetically.

"You don't think that's strange."

"Can you tell me about your drug use?"

"My drug use?"

Arnel spread his arms. "This is a safe space."

"I don't know what you're talking about."

"The doctor didn't tell you? You had extremely high concentrations in your system."

"Concentrations of what?"

"Amphetamines."

"Amphetamines?"

"It's all right. This confusion usually passes very quickly."

"I don't know who I am. I don't remember."

"That's a scary feeling."

"But isn't it . . . strange?"

Arnel smiled. "Not in my line of work."

"It's not strange for someone with *amnesia* to land at your airport with no luggage and no money or anything?"

"It happens a few times a week. I mean, usually they have *something* in a bag. But not always. And your confusion *does* seem to fall on the more extreme end of the spectrum. I believe amnesia would require a clinical diagnosis. We can help you with that, once we get you in the system."

"What system?"

"Well, it's still called Homeless Aid, unfortunately. But we prefer to think of it as Houseless Resources."

She stared at him.

"The system is a bit complicated. I'm going to get you registered, and you'll be assigned a case manager to help you navigate it."

She kept staring.

"Is there anyone we can call?"

She shook her head. "I don't know."

"Do you still have family in New Mexico?"

"I'm sorry?"

"Your passport lists your place of birth as New Mexico."

She said nothing.

"Maybe there are some helpful numbers in your phone?"

She glanced at the phone on the table, reached out, tapped the screen. A number pad appeared below six blank spaces.

"I don't know the combination."

He nodded reassuringly. "Try your fingerprint!"

She pressed her thumb against the small black circle.

"This feature has not been activated."

He nodded sympathetically. "We'll see what we can do about that. Are you on Sokoni?"

"I'm sorry, is that, uh, is that another drug?"

"Ha ha. No. Well, maybe. The social network? Sometimes it helps our clients reconnect with loved ones."

She shook her head. "I don't know."

"Well, you're probably very tired. I'll make some inquiries, give you a chance to rest, and then we'll check back in before you leave."

She nodded. Her mind was empty again. She stared at the black screen of the phone. Then she picked up the passport. The grainy photo of a pale woman with black hair. Overexposed. Staring impatiently into the camera. Good looking, despite the bad light.

She touched her jaw. A motion caught her eye. The social worker, by the door, hand raised. "I know this is a very difficult time, but it will get better."

She stared at him unselfconsciously.

He pressed his palms together and bowed ever so slightly.

"It was good to meet you, Janice."

5

The horses had wandered apart and were grazing by the fence line. Nalani shut off the truck and rolled down the windows. The trade winds whipped through the cab, even cooler than her AC.

She'd heard her mother was back on island and staying with Uncle Solly. When she and her cousins were kids, he'd been their favorite. They liked how easy it was to make him laugh and how he brought them small things he'd gathered in the forest or caught underwater. He was patient in a way other adults never were, happy to spend hours diving the reef during the long holiday weekends while their other aunties and uncles fished and cooked and drank on the beach.

But as the cousins got older, they noticed Solomon remained as child-like as ever. Quiet, most of the time, with no interest in any of the things that consumed their parents' conversation. Their tūtū was the last of her generation, and when she died, the long weekends ended. Nalani's aunts and uncles and older cousins were busy with other things, and her mother certainly wasn't going to organize anything. She wasn't sure when Solomon had moved in to the old hale. People seemed happy to leave him to it, relieved he wasn't anyone else's problem.

A few times, in high school, she'd invited her friends down to the valley. There was plenty of room on the beach to set up tents and give Solomon his space. Sometimes, if she was still sitting around the embers of the bonfire in the first light of dawn, she'd see him out on the reef, throwing a net or just squatting on his heels, flexible as a child, examining things too small to make out from shore.

She could have joined him, out on the reef. But she stayed in the circle of the fire, as if whatever it was that isolated him might be infectious.

She tried to remember the last time she'd seen any of those friends. They'd drifted out of her life after her uncle disappeared and the stories started coming out. At the time, it was a relief. She couldn't imagine wedging herself into the selfie group shots that filled her commons every weekend with *#luckyweliveKauai*. And as the months passed, she told herself it happened to everyone as they got older, the same way her mom's generation didn't come together like they once had.

There were a lot of families with falling-down hales on kuleana lands. People struggled to care for their own houses. Who had the time or the money to keep up a property they barely had a stake in?

A horn sounded. In the rearview mirror, a vintage F-150, flaking rust. A brown arm waved from the window. The pickup, she realized, was stopped halfway through the security gate, the orange arm frozen above the cab. She grinned and made a U-turn across the road, startling the horses as she swung onto the shoulder before heading back toward the gate.

She saw Solomon dip his head to say something to the guard before throwing his truck into reverse. He used his rearview mirror to back away at speed until he glanced forward and saw she was through. Then he spun the tires and whirled the old truck onto the grass, its bed bouncing on worn struts, until it was facing down the red dirt road toward the distant ocean.

He drove slowly ahead of her, careful not to raise much dust. They passed yellow excavators crawling over huge piles of dirt. The road dropped into the valley, and they entered the ironwood forest. In that cool, rustling world, feelings arrived she hadn't asked for.

Nalani realized it didn't matter how long she had stayed away, the valley still felt like home.

6

It was the magical time in late afternoon when sunlight spread like butter across the landscape. Dalton surveyed the scene with satisfaction. He'd ended the tour at a hilltop vista of mountain ridges rising toward the island's cloud-shrouded summit and the picturesque reef jutting from the base of his acreage. And he'd timed it perfectly; the green of the ridges and blue of the ocean shone more purely than ever through this patina of golden light.

His fleet of Rubicons was lined up in the grass below the hilltop, custom yellow paint jobs glowing in the light, ready to convey the board members up the old farm road and back to their rental villas. The tour had included the future guesthouse—now serving as the residence until the main building was complete—the office complex where they would have their official meeting in the morning, the reservoir, the hydroponic greenhouses, and the biodynamic ag sites. He hadn't taken them into the Sanctuary—access was highly restricted—but from the portals wired into each Jeep, he'd pointed out the excavators crawling across the pile and explained he was using material cleared for the refuge to reinforce the old plantation dam neglected for decades by previous owners.

His pitch had gone well—according to his team, at least. He'd explained New Zealand *might* have a more comfortable climate in fifty years, but this was American soil, a hop from California, an ideal vacation destination—obviously—and an excellent investment. There was enough undeveloped land to support a like-minded community. And the people, or at least their local government, were much more welcoming than the Kiwis. It had taken a relatively modest donation, just a new wing for the hospital and an upgrade to their ICU—investments he would have made, anyway, for peace of mind—to win the necessary zoning exceptions from the mayor and the county council. And the more people who built their refuges here, the more secure it became for everyone. A true win-win situation, his favorite thing.

That had brought a laugh from the fifteen men and women gathered around the white covered tables. *Success is nonzero sum* was printed on the cafeteria wall at HQ. He was glad they were smiling as he walked over to shake hands, and a caterer handed him a glass of vodka soda. He'd never developed a taste for wine, though his vintners were working on something they promised he would like.

He was heading for the cheerful, imperturbable bulk of Raffi Garcia when he felt a hand on his arm. Abhi Dhillon. An early investor and the company's second-largest shareholder. Dhillon was widely considered the most well-liked man in Menlo Park. His broad smile filled Dalton with terror.

"Franky," he said. "What a place. *What* a place. I've already told my assistant to call my Realtor."

Instead of releasing his grip, Dhillon slipped his arm through Dalton's and used the leverage to steer them away from the circle of cocktail tables to the edge of the hill, where they could look down on the reef and the crescent of beach.

"I'm surprised you didn't mention our little issue with the legislative branch."

"I thought I'd save it for tomorrow," said Dalton. "I know you've had long flights."

With his free arm, Dhillon waved this off. "My jet is the only place I can relax. Listen, we all have our little birdies, but the ones I trust say they're serious this time."

"We are going to discuss this tomorrow," said Dalton. "I'm sure your info is as good as mine. The committee is aiming at data collection, privacy, antitrust. Stuff that hits everyone."

"But hits us the worst."

Dalton stared resolutely at the view.

"Why don't the politicians like us?" Dhillon pretended to pout.

Dalton laughed. "You know why. We're their biggest rivals. They're driving people apart, and we're bringing them together."

Dhillon looked at him with a twinkle in his eye. "When I'm not around you, I forget you're still a Peace Corps volunteer at heart."

"And when I *am* around you, I forget you're Sikh."

"How do you think we can afford to give out all those free meals? They send us third-borns to America and tell us to strive!"

"Seriously, though. Are you really thinking about buying a property? My Realtor can point you to some really exclusive estates."

"Just not quite as exclusive as this one, eh?" Dhillon surveyed the hills. Then he pointed toward the farm road, where two vehicles were raising a low cloud of dust that shone red in the sunlight. "Who's that?"

Dalton looked more closely. One was a relatively new Tacoma. The other was a boxy F-150, a common sight in the farm country that still existed in Northern Virginia when he was a kid. But this wasn't vintage. It was just a piece of junk.

"I'll find out," said Dalton.

A brown man with silver hair was driving the Ford. He looked up the hill, raised his hand in a fist with thumb and pinkie extended, and pumped his arm at the two men in emphatic greeting. Dalton glimpsed a sticker centered in the truck's rear window. Four words he could just make out: *Hunt Fish Dive Survive.*

7

By the time Nalani parked behind the old family hale, Uncle Solly was out of sight.

It was a simple three-room house with plywood walls and louvered windows. The paint was peeling. Rot showed on the boards resting on concrete blocks half sunk in the sandy earth. Thick Naupaka bushes grew right up to the walls. The corrugated roof was uniformly orange with rust. But the few holes were neatly patched, and the gutters running into the concrete cistern at one corner of the house were wired neatly into place.

When Nalani came around the corner, the full force of the trades pressed her shirt tight against her. A shallow brown reef jutted into a blue ocean scarred with whitecaps. There was still no sign of Solomon or her mother.

She surveyed the view, savoring a feeling that had been absent a long time. Nostalgia, she guessed she would call it. A sense of connection to the people she had been: the child exploring the reef, the young woman kindling a campfire out of coconut fibers. It didn't matter whether the memories were fifteen years old or five. All the versions of herself felt equally out of reach.

She watched the waves roar messily to the reef, suck white foam up their hollow faces, then flop into smooth ripples that ran across the small lagoon and broke quietly on the dull sand. The tide was low. She loved the sweetly rotten smell of exposed reef and the red limu growing in its crevices. Her tūtū had told her the seaweed of this tiny ahupua'a had been famous across old Hawaii, but she'd never known whether to believe that or not.

Abruptly, she spun around and walked toward the house. She pushed open the door and found her mother lying on a thin old mattress in an iron frame. At first, Nalani wasn't sure if she was asleep or awake; then she saw the glitter of brown eyes below her mother's long lashes.

"Maile?"

"Nalani!" Her mother pushed to her elbows and sat up. She was taller than her daughter, and skinnier. She wore jean shorts and a man's flannel shirt. Nalani hadn't seen her in three years. She still had a junkie's skin. But there were no fake lashes, no over-applied foundation. It was disorienting. Her mother's beauty. It made her feel small again.

So when Maile opened her arms, Nalani stepped into the embrace.

"I need to look at you," said Maile. She pushed Nalani away, held her by the shoulders with her surprisingly strong hands, looked her daughter greedily up and down, hefted a strand of hair where it curled below her jaw-line. "Honeygirl," she whispered, "what happened to your beautiful hair?"

They took a walk down the beach.

"So that's all his?" Nalani nodded at the bluffs. He was one of the richest men in the world, it was hard not to be fascinated. For some reason, the feeling that kept coming up inside her was pride. It was her island he'd chosen, her family's land he wanted.

Her mother only nodded.

From childhood, before she'd understood what was going on, much less the terminology for it, Nalani could tell in an instant whether her mother was on an upper or a downer, coming off a high or getting on one, under the influence or in withdrawal. But she had never met the pensive woman who walked beside her. She didn't know if this was who her mother had once been, or would have been, or simply what she had become. And she didn't care.

"So that's why you came back?" Nalani asked. "To file this lawsuit and kick Uncle Solly off his land?"

"I came here to get my head clear," said her mother. "That lawsuit thing. I never know exactly what it is. They had call me and say this guy like buy this property. I told 'em me and Solly was staying here. They said they could work something out. Give us time for find another place."

"But this is our family's land. How could you make that decision without talking to us?"

"Our family? Girl. This our ancestors' land. They tended it back when there was still one community down here. When they never needed nothing but what grew right here. But those days over. They tell you how many people own one piece of this land? Almost two thousand. You know two thousand people in this family?"

"If they inherited a share, doesn't that make them family?"

"Honeygirl. I know you have the Winthrop name, but look what happened with that side. This is our chance to do right by *our* family. Take what our ancestors passed on to us and make something new. No one getting robbed. Everyone going get their share."

Nalani wrapped her arms tight around herself and shook her head.

Her mother stepped back, spread her arms. "All those people you say care about this land? Our family? Where are they? Where they been? They rather take the money."

"But you're the one suing them. Suing me."

Her mother looked at her slyly. "You saying that's the worst thing I ever done to you?" Then she turned serious. "I swear, I never even knew it was one lawsuit until you had call me this morning. They never say that. They just say for cases like this, for kuleana land, the state get one process, called. What they call it? Silent something . . . quiet title."

"You never even talked to a lawyer?"

"Of course I talked to one lawyer. I know plenty lawyers on this island. More than you ever will. I worked with *all* of 'em. And I know the best. My lawyer, he say go ahead and sign."

"How much are they giving you?"

Her mother was silent for a long time.

"It's not just for me. For Solly, too. None of you get no idea what that man know. Things *everyone* forget already. But he need help. He been left alone too long."

"I wish I could believe you," said Nalani. "But how many times have you come telling me you have a plan that would finally make everything turn out right?"

Maile turned toward the water. She was silent so long, Nalani wondered if she wasn't sober, after all. "Hey!" she said. "You there?"

Her mother turned to her. "Stay here tonight," she said. "You look like you're not getting enough sleep."

8

Janice Diaz lay in bed and sucked cold water from a thick plastic straw. The room wasn't pleasant—the light was harsh, the blinds drawn—but it filled her with bliss. She could stay forever in this quiet place, where the only intruder from the bustling world outside her door was the aide who cheerfully refilled her enormous plastic mug with crushed ice and water.

A nurse with a clipboard and a wheelchair appeared in the doorway.

In the elevator, the issue of her memory began to feel more urgent. She hadn't been anxious as she lay in bed. If anything, her lack of a past had been part of the bliss. But by the time she saw daylight through the glass doors at the end of the hall, the problem seemed acute.

Arnel appeared. The airline had not located any luggage. He walked the final steps down the hall and held the door, smoothly expelling her into a warm and humid evening. Then she was on her feet, and he was pressing a piece of paper into her hand: an address and a phone number for a social services agency.

"The state has a program to send people in your position back home."

She looked down at the address.

"Your caseworker can help. All you'll need is a family member willing to receive you on the other side."

"I don't even know if I have a family."

He looked at her sympathetically. "A lot can change in a few days!"

She was standing in a grassy cul-de-sac encircling a large tropical tree. Behind her was the hospital. Ahead, a busy road. She walked toward the road.

It was a lovely evening. The sun was setting over green mountains. To her right, the four-lane road curved into a steep, forested valley. To her left was a Walmart. Her instinct said go left.

It took her a long time to pass the Walmart. She finally crossed a street and came to a shopping center at a more human scale, with a bar and a few small restaurants. An island planted with grass and trees divided the parking lot. A woman sat under one of the trees, a shopping cart parked in one of the spaces beside her. The cart was overflowing with items covered by a blue tarp. A small white dog lay between the woman's knees. Both appeared to be asleep.

There were no benches, but there was a storefront with brown paper over the windows. Janice Diaz sat on the stoop and tucked her knees. She took the phone from her pocket and tried pressing each of her fingers against the screen. Then she looked at the six blank spaces and tried to pull numbers from the darkness in her mind. Even after she'd given up, she kept looking at the phone. It made her feel less self-conscious.

There were fewer cars on the road now. Deep twilight had arrived. The trees shook gently above the woman and the dog. Janice Diaz felt herself slip back into the mood of the hospital. The movement of the leaves, the lavender sky, the bright windows of a fast-food restaurant, the warm and heavy tropical air all felt so luxurious it was hard to focus on the abstract elements of her situation.

The white dog sat up, and the woman's head jerked. She scooped the dog in one arm and began hurriedly pushing the cart down the sidewalk.

A black-and-white police SUV pulled in. It moved slowly around the island and parked a few feet from Janice Diaz.

As the officer approached, she wondered what to tell him about the woman. She couldn't help but feel sympathetic, whatever she'd done. But it could be useful to help a police officer. She needed to start building some goodwill.

He was a white man, with the familiar cop's expression of boredom, sternness, and concern. He was still wearing his sunglasses.

How could it be familiar?

He removed his sunglasses, looked her up and down. His eyes lingered for a minute on her plastic hospital bracelet.

"It's time to move on, ma'am."

"Time to move where?"

"I don't want to give you a citation."

"A citation?"

For the first time, he actually seemed to look at her. "Have I seen you before?"

She narrowed her eyes and said nothing.

"I guess you're still learning the ropes," he said, no longer looking. "It's illegal to sit or lie on the sidewalk. You're going to have to move on."

He thought he was being friendly.

She had no idea whether she was the kind of person who resisted authority, or meekly went along with it, or appeared to meekly go along with it while craftily subverting it. Maybe she was in this situation because she'd crossed a line she shouldn't have. Or maybe it was because she'd let herself be pushed around.

She didn't know. It didn't matter. Whoever she'd been, this was her chance to start over.

"Thank you, Officer," said Janice Diaz. She stepped off the curb and walked in the same direction as the woman with the little dog.

It was almost dark now.

The trees were still moving. The sky was a heart-wrenching pink above the rooftops. But all she saw were sidewalks. She wanted to be somewhere brightly lit and busy. But those were the places the police would find her. They had to give people somewhere to sit, and think, and be safe. Didn't they?

She'd passed into an older part of town: a fishing gear store, a Japanese noodle shop, a lumber warehouse. The occasional streetlight made the shadows more impenetrable. There was a little park—playground, benches, a cramped basketball court. Someone was already sitting on one of the benches. A Black woman wearing a winter hat, wrapped in a blanket. The woman nodded and watched Janice Diaz walk slowly around the perimeter of the park. She reached the gate, paused, and kept walking.

On the back side of a warehouse was a loading dock under a floodlight. One dark bay sat beyond the reach of the light. Janice Diaz boosted herself awkwardly onto the dock and stepped into the shadows. It was cold against the concrete blocks of the building, but she was comforted by the light outside and the safety of the darkness.

She'd found another space outside the world. The door of the bay was like a frame, and the gravel and weeds of the lot next door, illuminated in the acid yellow of the floodlight, were somehow like a painting. Something surfaced from the dark in her mind: another concrete building in another ugly light. A lot filled with rubble. She was about to go into the building and do something it was better not to remember.

At first, she thought the shouting was part of the memory. Then she heard a man shout back. Then the woman. She couldn't understand the words. But she heard fear.

What kind of person was she?

Not the kind who hid, apparently. She was already striding toward the playground.

The woman in the blanket was still on the bench. Someone stood over her. Trying to drag her to her feet.

The man didn't know Janice Diaz was behind him until she hit him as hard as she could in the kidney. He whipped around, his arm already lifting, eyes raised two inches above her head. When he looked down, he dropped his arm and smiled. "Never mind us. This not your business."

Janice Diaz had been counting on the odds that a person who inserted herself into an assault would be a person who knew how to fight back. This didn't seem to be the case.

The man stopped smiling. "I said leave us alone, or I make you regret it, yeah? This just one lover's quarrel."

He had the same upbeat accent as the people she'd met at the hospital. It made everything sound like it could be a joke. His odd phrasing reminded her of conversations she'd half heard between support staff out in the hall. He wasn't tall, for a man. But he was thick with fat and muscle. She could tell, because he was wearing nothing but sagging board shorts and a pair of rubber slippers.

"I give you one more chance for leave. Then something going get broke."

Would he really hit a woman? Obviously.

"Do not fuck with me," she said.

"Wa's that?"

"I said, do not fuck with me!" she said, more loudly. "Do *not fuck*. With me."

He turned back to the woman on the bench as if seeking her opinion.

When his head was turned, Janice Diaz pushed him with both hands as hard as she could, causing him at least to stumble. Then she stepped closer. "Do not fucking fuck with me! *Do not* fuck with me. You have no fucking idea what I am capable of. No one does! Not even me."

She did not know how loudly she had ever screamed. But it would have been impossible for her to scream louder than she was right now. She could hear the high, jagged tones echo off the warehouse. She stopped using words and simply shrieked, a wail of anger and despair, of waking from a nightmare and finding out reality was worse.

The man had stepped back, almost between the other woman's knees. "She done it now," he said. "Cops coming. I find you later."

Neither of them watched him go.

The woman gathered her blanket, stood, and folded it neatly on the bench. She lifted an enormous shopping bag and laid the blanket inside. Then she turned back to Janice Diaz.

"You saved a man's life tonight."

She reached into her voluminous dress and lifted out a homemade ice pick, a very large nail hammered into a block of wood that fit into her palm.

"Maleko's right. We have to go."

"Where?"

"Anywhere but here, to start."

"We didn't do anything wrong. You could make a report."

The woman laughed. "The less they see you, the better they treat you." For the first time, she looked Janice Diaz over carefully. "Looks like you've already been in a brawl today. You don't want to report that?"

"I don't know who did this to me."

"Or what you did to them I guess. All the more reason to avoid any questions."

The woman shouldered her bag. "Where is your stuff?"

"In my pockets."

She laughed again. "Then help me with this. We'll move faster." She let the bag slip down her arm. One of the handles fell to Janice Diaz. She took it, and the two walked into darkness with the bag dangling between them.

"There's another park not far from here. It doesn't close until 2:00 a.m."

"Then what?"

"My name's Carlotta."

"I'm Janice."

"How long have you been camping?"

"I arrived on an airplane this morning, and they released me this afternoon."

"I saw you walk by in those nice clothes."

Janice Diaz looked down at her outfit: jeans and a halter top. "Are these nice?"

"Not for long. Why'd you go down that alley? It's dangerous in the dark. Especially dressed like that."

"You were safer in the park?"

"That was just Maleko. We have a history."

They had come back out onto a well-lit street. Carlotta pointed at a sidewalk. "Most of this is city property. Some is county. Some state. All of them get you in different ways. But city is the worst. They have the most officers and the most laws. If you sit or lay down on city property, they can cite you. You're new, so you might not get cited right away. But once you become a regular, watch out."

"Do they know you?"

"I'm the pōpolo princess. Everyone knows me. Here's something else. It might not be cold now, but it will be, even in paradise. So you're going to need a blanket and a piece of cardboard you can lay on. And if you have a tarp, that's good. It rains here."

Janice Diaz nodded.

"And a way to keep everything dry. And to pack up quick. The police are supposed to impound your things and take them to the station, but they'll just say they were abandoned and throw them away."

"Okay."

"You keep your valuables on you at all times, so if you have to hustle out, you won't leave them behind. You don't know me, so I won't ask what you have."

"A phone and a passport."

"Okay. But I didn't ask."

The women walked until the road curved downhill and the buildings gave way to dark trees. "That's the beach down there. State land."

They crossed a narrow concrete bridge and entered a potholed parking lot. The ocean was a murmuring darkness. Beneath the trees that lined the parking lot, Janice Diaz could see the dark humps of cars, the glow of cell phones, flashlights, a few small fires.

Carlotta approached a rusted sedan. "Martin," she whispered. "Jade." From somewhere in the car, a large dog growled.

"Hush, Maka," said a man. "Is that Carlotta?"

"Yeah, it's me. How are you all doing?"

"All right. All right." Something flared in the front seat. A blue smell wafted out. A cough. The lighter flared again. Janice Diaz saw the stern, lined face of an old man focused on a loosely rolled joint. A thin flame ran up the side. He licked his thumb and put it out, leaving a glowing ember at the tip. The red glow danced through the window into Carlotta's fingers. She took a long inhale and offered it to Janice Diaz. Instinctively, she shook her head, waved her hand politely. For the first time, she noticed something happening inside her, like thirst or hunger, but deeper in her body. Somewhere, a drain had opened. She felt restless and afraid, but she didn't know why.

"You coming down off something?" asked Carlotta. "You looking jittery."

"I don't know."

"Didn't they tell you anything in the hospital?"

"They found amphetamines," said Janice Diaz, "in my blood."

Carlotta passed the joint back to the car.

"Everything all right with you?" said Martin. "We been hearing some things."

"Just showing a newbie the ropes is all." There was something new in her voice now, impatience, an edge. Maybe it was the weed. "We're going to head down a way," Carlotta said into the open window. "You stay safe."

They passed a few more cars. A bonfire. Then they were alone again. The lights of houses high over the bay reflected on the water. The stars were out.

"We can't stay here?"

"Not tonight. Maybe in a few days."

"Why not?"

"It's the end of the month. Anyone with prescriptions has burned through them by now. People are on edge waiting for their EBT. Better to steer clear."

She led Janice Diaz onto a narrow beach. The angle was steep. The bag was awkward. Janice Diaz stumbled, and Carlotta took the bag from her and hoisted it back over her shoulder. The beach ended at a lawn of springy grass.

"We'll try our luck here," said Carlotta. "Grass is warmer than sand."

Carlotta sat, and Janice Diaz followed her down. She hugged her knees, then sank onto her back. She heard Carlotta rummaging. Then the woman handed her a ghostly shape. A white plastic shopping bag.

"To keep your things dry."

"Thank you," said Janice Diaz. Suddenly, she thought she would cry.

"Best to get some sleep now." Carlotta handed her a beach towel, then pulled the blanket over herself and rolled away. Janice Diaz spread the blanket and soon felt the ground chill seeping through it.

Someone was shaking her. She'd been back on the airplane. Maleko buckled into the seat beside her. "We've got to go," Carlotta whispered.

At the other end of the beach, a flashlight beam illuminated a circle of sand.

They packed their things and hurried toward the seawall.

"State land closes at 2:00 a.m. I was hoping they wouldn't sweep tonight."

"Can't we just hide under the trees?"

"That's hotel property. They program the sprinklers to go off at 3:00."

"Is it this hard every night?"

Carlotta didn't answer.

"So where are we supposed to sleep?"

"Nowhere good. The beaches are the last to close."

They heard a shout and stopped to look back. The light was shining on someone in the sand, one arm shielding their eyes from the glare.

"Looks like you're not the only one learning the ropes."

This time, they crossed the parking lot, swinging wide to avoid the cluster of cars, and began walking down a road with a steep hill on one side and industrial buildings on the other—warehouses and parking lots protected by guard posts, chain-link fences, barbed wire.

"This doesn't seem like a very good place for a resort," said Janice Diaz, gesturing toward a long, white building with hundreds of windows towering over the warehouses.

Carlotta snorted. "That's the cruise ship. It docks here once a week."

Finally, they were past the docks and back in darkness. "Here," said Carlotta. A narrow trail between slim trees. Then a muddy bank and tangled roots. A crescent moon cast a pale line across the still water. "We're on the river now. Over there is the old fishpond. Wait here in the mangroves. And stay quiet."

Carlotta disappeared. Janice Diaz stood alone on the narrow strip of land. She had no idea how she would get back to the road. Minutes passed. A pale shape swooped silently overhead.

"This way."

She followed the sound of Carlotta's voice to where a raft was rocking on the water.

"Manny says we can sleep here tonight."

Carlotta climbed out onto the roots and stepped carefully onto the deck. Janice Diaz moved to follow.

"Wait," said a male voice. A man was sitting in the middle of the raft. "Let her cross, then come. I no like huli this fackah."

When Carlotta was settled on the opposite side of the raft, Janice Diaz stepped. The deck sank, and she nearly lost her balance. The empty feeling was stronger. Not hunger or thirst, but something worse, like part of herself needed to be replenished or would slip away for good. She sank down, pulling the raft closer to the mangrove root, and put both hands on the deck before bringing her second foot with her, not ashamed to crawl. In a moment, the boat stopped rocking.

"Sorry I no get more room," the man said. He held something out. Her towel. She wrapped it around her shoulders and curled up on her side.

The black line of the mangroves separated the stars from the silver water. All around the curve of the fishpond, small lights rocked back and forth. Janice Diaz gazed above the trees. She wondered whether she had ever seen so many stars, so bright.

DAY 2

9

Of the eleven buildings on the property, two were complete: the family residence that would become guest quarters once Phase Two was complete, and the satellite office, which had open-plan office space for twenty workers, a private executive office, and a meeting room overlooking the bay, where the board was now convening.

Erin had flown in that morning. She was the only Sokoni employee on the board, aside from Dalton. The rest were early investors, attorneys, other CEOs and VPs. Their buy-in was important to Dalton, but there were only a few whose opinions genuinely mattered. When you were majority shareholder, power only went one way. They could be replaced, and he could not.

The sun was still low, and the transparent wall was dimmed to the maximum so their VP of public policy would be visible on the portal. He was calling in from the Georgetown office, where he was personally leading outreach to the Capitol. The situation was grim. To avoid the notice of corporate lobbyists, including Sokoni's eighty-person team, a dozen House members had met without staff for two months to hammer out the framework of a bipartisan bill. Now that details were almost complete, news was finally trickling out to their ex-colleagues on Sokoni's payroll. The upside was that the bill would regulate their rivals in each of their biggest sore spots—privacy, data security, tax policy, anti-competitive practice, contract workers. The downside was that only Sokoni was vulnerable in every one of those areas.

"So, it's the worst-case scenario," said Dhillon after he'd heard enough from the VP. "Despite all our investment in your team, we face an existential threat. How many votes can they afford to lose?"

"They've whipped a substantial number on both sides. Technically, it doesn't even need to be bipartisan."

Dalton cut in. He hated the way Dhillon ran every meeting. Even his. "And the president?"

For a moment, Public Policy looked grateful. Then his expression went appropriately remorseful. This was his failure, after all. "From everything we hear, he sees it as a winner."

"So, what are our options?"

"Either we fight it," said Erin, "or embrace it."

"Embrace it?"

This was the CEO of MonkeyWrench, a company that enabled people to bid against each other for the chance to perform menial tasks. Like most startup founders, he managed to be both narcissistic and sycophantic, often simultaneously. Erin had questioned his board seat, but MonkeyWrench had a robust infrastructure for IRL engagement, one of the few areas Sokoni had repeatedly failed to monetize. Seeds were being planted for an acquisition, something this legislation would obviously derail.

"Embrace it," said Erin. "Consolidate. Focus on the core business and the UX."

"That's a nonstarter," said Dhillon. "They would still try to break us up."

"This is a chance for a reset. Maybe our last."

She was talking directly to Dalton, which was for the best. Erin was constitutionally incapable of disguising the fact that she despised nearly everyone else in the room.

Dhillon refused to disengage. "Earnings in our last quarter were the best we've ever had."

"Our current course is unsustainable."

"So we dismantle our core profit drivers to prevent the feds from dismantling them?"

"We take a hit in the short term and emerge stronger in the long term."

"How's that?"

"We go back to our roots. You all remember the days when the web offered everything but a place we could share together. We created that. It's how we beat the Myspaces and the Facebooks in the race for scale. People wanted more than a phone book with pictures."

"Thanks for the history lesson," said Dhillon. "I heard the same pitch when I gave you your first thirty million. But the kids today don't care about community. You know the metrics as well as I do. In an average day, they spend fifteen minutes on friends' content, and seventy-five on brands and influencers."

"Because that's where we're pushing them."

"We're responding to demand."

"That's bullshit," said Erin. "And anyone who won't admit it's bad for the company is either incredibly stupid or looking to inflate our value so they can cash out."

The room was silent. Dalton had heard versions of this argument from Erin in private, but even he was surprised his COO, employee number two, would say this in a board meeting to the most successful angel investor in America.

There was no trace of Dhillon's easygoing smile now. He ignored Erin and spoke directly to Dalton. "You didn't call it the Park or the Bar or wherever people hang out these days. You called it the Market."

Erin addressed Dalton, too. "If I'm wrong, why did user numbers peak two years ago?"

"People like novelty," said Dhillon. "They want something new."

"Markets have been part of society for thousands of years."

"Yeah, and as soon as a grocery store was invented, they started using it. No offense, but you spent a couple of years in Africa with the full backing of the United States government and a free plane ticket home. It's not so picturesque when it's your only reality. The last thing anyone in a village actually wants is to spend their lives in a village. That's why my family put together every rupee it had to send us to school. That's why social engagement isn't a profit-driver. Our users log on to escape reality, not hang out with people they avoid in real life."

Dalton knew Dhillon had nicked her with that one. Her TED Talk a few years before had gotten a hundred million views and a significant amount of backlash, enough that she'd let her moment of celebrity pass without publishing a book.

Chastened, or at least pretending to be, she appealed to the entire board. "Maybe it's time to acknowledge that we're not just a company, we're a public good. The Internet needed a shared space. We provided it. Now we've scaled to the point where there is no viable alternative. We have a responsibility."

Now Dhillon seemed genuinely shocked. "We're not a utility. Or a charity. We're a publicly traded company responsible to our shareholders to maximize their investment."

"Our shareholders have done better than they ever imagined. Now we face an existential threat. And you just want to carry on with this disastrous strategy?"

"I want to earn as much money as I can. That is my right as a shareholder. I'm not responsible for the happiness of the world. I have an obligation to my family to repay their sacrifices and to my nephews and nieces to give them the same opportunities."

"Your net worth is seventeen billion dollars."

"More like nineteen, last time I checked. And do you really want to get personal here? You're COO. You weren't a bystander."

"Are you two done yet?" It was Raffi. He wasn't worth a billion dollars, and he didn't have a college degree. But every coder alive had used a version of something he'd written thirty or forty years earlier. Most of the people around that table considered themselves a philosopher or a visionary. Raffi Garcia was the only one universally acknowledged to be both, as well as the brewer of the finest LSD in California. And he sat on only one corporate board.

"You're both missing the point." He sat with his back to the ocean, his face a silhouette at the center of a glowing corona of curly white hair. "It's not about money, or engagement metrics, or providing a service. We're past all that. If all we are is *neutral space* for people to gather, we might as well be a government agency. We could have a hundred employers caretaking the whole thing. The Bureau of Digital Land Management. This guy"—he cocked his head at Dalton—"has bigger ambitions. Erin's right. Sokoni's become a dump. But Dhillon's not wrong. If you don't evolve to give people what they want, you don't just lose your users, you lose your influence to shape their lives, to shape the future, or at least nudge it in the right direction. We can't abdicate responsibility. We need to be benevolent dictators. The only way to fuck things up worse than we already have is to turn the power over to people even dumber than we are."

"I don't want to be a dictator," said Dalton.

Garcia laughed. "You want to be a god."

"I think we've gotten a little off track," said one of the attorneys.

"Are we going to fight this bill or not?" asked the CEO of MonkeyWrench, who, as far as Dalton knew, employed exactly zero full-time lobbyists in Washington.

10

Nalani couldn't remember the last time she'd fallen asleep by the ocean. The old hale still had a set of bunk beds on its screened-in lanai, the same ones she'd slept in as a girl. Her mother had brought sheets from the closet, musty but clean. She'd even made the bed.

As they'd walked back down the beach the evening before, the smell of frying fish had drifted up. Solomon sat on a cooler in the sand, frying red menpachi in a blackened wok. He waved his tongs but never lifted his head. They ate at the picnic table under the false kamani tree. Solomon had filled a mixing bowl with raw opihi and Samoan crab on a bed of ice. The food was familiar and comforting, but it was strange to eat in silence at a table that had always been crowded with uncles and aunties talking story and drinking beer until late in the night.

Her mother and uncle went to bed after sunset. Nalani's phone had no service, and the only reading materials she could find were a few pamphlets from the Seventh-day Adventists. She sat outside and watched the white rows of foam cross the invisible reef, then she went in, snuffed the kerosene lantern, and fell asleep almost instantly.

She woke after dawn to an empty house, walked down the steps into the sand, and saw two figures far out on the reef. Her uncle with a throw net twisted around his shoulders. Her mother watching as he pointed at something in the water. He unwound the net from his shoulders and gathered it in both hands, one end dangling loose, the other bunched and coiled, the line of weights making a smooth spreading edge by his knees. He crouched, crept forward, and released the net with a short, smooth swing. It whirled out, unfurling. A hollow ring of droplets lifted from the ocean's glassy surface, then the water roughened as the net settled and the weights sank.

Her mother stepped off the reef up to her thighs, slapping the water with her hands while Solomon pulled the net, its center rising, narrowing, and piling on the reef at his feet. Silver scales flashed in the pale monofilament.

Nalani went back into the kitchen and brewed a pot of coffee in the battered percolator.

She brought her mug to the table in the shade. Her family was coming off the reef. Uncle Solly carried a bucket around the side of the house. Maile stepped into the outdoor shower, then joined Nalani with her own mug.

"Mahalo for the coffee."

"Shoots. What you guys had catch?"

"Not much nothing. Just a few manini."

Nalani only nodded. It was hard for her, suddenly, to look at her mother.

"Listen, daughter. All them, who came to me about the land, they showed me their plans. They like build one research center here. They going use some kind radar for map every puka in the reef and track everything that go on inside. All kine animals and how they holo holo. They going learn things no one ever knew before. Might even make one digital reality, so keikis in school can visit our reef on their computers."

"So everyone can visit our land but us?"

"You want to keep it," said her mother.

"Of course."

"'Cause I had talk it over with your uncle Solly. And we had decide you right. I going call that lady today. Tell her I no more like go forward. If they going buy this land, they got to use someone else's name."

"Is that true? You're going to do that? Stop all this bother?"

For the first time that morning, she met her mother's eyes.

"This place was dark for me long time," her mother said. "Things that had happen. Your uncle understand. But since I come back, my head feels clear. I no like leave, not yet. Maybe never. There's healing for me in this place, I know it. And darkness yet I still need face."

Nalani swallowed back something in her throat. She said, "I'm happy for you. I hope it works out. But I think I need to stay away for a while."

Her mother nodded. "It's going cost us plenty money, you know. I had thought I was going be able to leave you something, after all."

"That's all right."

"Well, you know where for find me. And if you do come, and I not here, probably better you never go looking."

As Nalani was climbing into her truck, Solomon came around the corner with a battered cooler. "Can drop this for share with Leilani guys?" he said shyly.

"Can, Uncle."

He hoisted the cooler into the back of her truck and walked around the house without a word. As Nalani climbed the road out of the valley, she got one more glimpse of the bay in her rearview mirror. She'd been so angry at her mother for betraying the family. Now she had to wonder, if Maile held on to this land just to heal herself, which decision was more selfish?

11

Someone was sitting in her lap, arms entwined around her neck, warm breath, the tip of a tongue sliding between her lips. Heat radiated from the spot where the stiff denim of her jeans bunched against her underwear. She ran her hands up her lover's back, then suddenly down, as deep as she could cram them against the smooth, hot skin below the waistband.

She heard a groan. She opened her eyes and found herself looking into the eyes of the flight attendant, affection and desire mingling in the other woman's gaze. It seemed like a miracle, to be looked at like that. Gratitude surged through her. She unwound her hands and crammed them into her own pockets.

"Take this," she said. "It's all I have."

She was holding handfuls of pale blue hundred-dollar bills.

"Please take it," she said. "I need to make things right."

She was being shaken. She was floating in the dark. Blue light glowed above the trees.

"It's time to go. We're late already."

"Late for what? Is something wrong?"

"Everything's all right. But we have to get moving."

"Why?"

"It's recycling day."

As she balanced on a mangrove, waiting for Carlotta to move carefully across the raft and join her onshore, Janice Diaz scanned the other small craft tied up along the trees: simple rafts of plywood and plastic barrels, kayaks bonded together with fiberglass, battered aluminum skiffs.

"There are so many."

"Life's easy if you have a raft," said Carlotta. "Catch fish. Trap crabs. Float downriver when the police run a sweep."

"How do we eat?" she asked as they trudged across the cold gray sand of the beach. The night before, she'd been distracted by the other craving—a pit the exact shape of her body she could fall through forever. She was still falling, but now hunger was carving its own holes.

"Lihue Mission serves lunch at 11:00."

She decided not to ask what time it was.

"Don't worry," said Carlotta. "That's why I woke you bright and early. We're about to earn some money."

"How?"

"I told you. Every can and bottle we redeem is worth five cents."

Janice Diaz was silent.

"It adds up."

"I'm not sure that's the best use of my time."

Carlotta stopped walking and turned around. "Oh yeah?"

Janice slipped the passport from her pocket, looked at her picture. She was forty-two years old. Born in Albuquerque, New Mexico. She tried and failed to picture Albuquerque.

"You still don't remember?"

She flipped the passport shut.

"Listen, honey, from my experience, when people have trouble remembering something, it's probably best forgotten."

"My entire life?"

Carlotta shrugged.

"I'm not a homeless person. I had an airplane ticket to Hawaii."

"You think the rest of us swam?"

"How do people like you—I mean . . ."

"Because when they buy someone like *us* a ticket to paradise, they can tell themselves they're doing *us* the favor."

"You think somebody out there must have helped me."

Carlotta shrugged. "Could have been the government."

"What government?"

"They deny it. But if you end up in jail enough times, or the ER, a lot of cities figure it's cheaper to make you someone else's problem."

"And you think that's what happened to me?"

Carlotta let her eyes travel from Janice's bruised arms to her bruised skull.

Janice Diaz stared at a boil of yellow clouds on the horizon. For a moment, she looked utterly lost. Then she set her jaw, an act that sent a bolt of pain up the back of her skull. "I don't feel that's who I am."

Carlotta shrugged. "Whatever you're feeling, I wouldn't know. I always stayed away from meth, myself."

"What?"

"I live a clean life. I've seen what it does to people. No offense meant."

"What are you saying?"

"I'm not saying. You told me last night. They found it in your body, at the hospital."

"They found amphetamines."

"Honey, what do you think methamphetamine is? You're shaking right now."

For the first time, Janice Diaz paid attention to the tremors she'd been feeling in her hands. She'd assumed it had something to do with her injuries. "No."

"Are you telling me you're not in withdrawal?"

Janice Diaz did not have an answer. She was crying.

Carlotta stepped forward and took one trembling hand in both of hers. For the last few minutes, the light had been rising. Now, orange beams lit the sand, and the long shadows of lapping waves rose and fell the full length of the beach.

"I'm sorry," said Carlotta. "I wish things had worked out better for you."

Janice Diaz used the back of her free hand to wipe the tears off her face. A layer of grit slid down her cheek. She was still holding the passport. She took a final look at the woman in the photo, then slipped it back into her jeans.

12

Dhillon had scheduled himself into Dalton's agenda. Brunch. On his boat. Dalton knew it would become a pitch for his latest project, and he was tempted to cancel, especially after the debacle at the board meeting. But he'd already convinced Madeleine to come along and bring the boys.

She was feeling cooped up. Security insisted on protocols that made her feel conspicuous in public. And, unfortunately, state law made all beaches public. His legislative affairs team was working on some loopholes, but in the meantime, they had to take advantage of more isolated shores, where standard extraction plans weren't feasible, which meant putting a helicopter on standby, which was enough of a hassle that Madeleine usually just stayed on the property.

They didn't even have Momona Beach to themselves. He'd been told the final easements would be resolved by now. But the road was still open, a fact he'd had to learn for himself the previous evening. So in the middle of a corporate crisis, he'd spent precious minutes on the phone with his Realtor, extracting a promise that she would fix the situation by end of day.

At two and a half, the twins were too young to remember the last time they'd been on a boat. They ran up and down the long leather benches of the limousine tender, kneeling to peer through the portholes as they planed across Hanalei Bay. The purity of their enthusiasm—the way they put everything inside themselves on full display with no self-conscious knowledge that the world could judge or shame them—sent a blade of joy slicing through him and left behind a raw wound, exquisitely sensitive to his sons' vulnerability.

They pulled alongside the boarding deck. Each boy in his high-visibility life vest was handed from a well-muscled crewman on the tender to a well-muscled deckhand on the yacht. The twins laughed as they chased each other around the glass walls of the resistance pool and screamed when

Madeleine and Pilar herded them to the safety of the upper decks, where the chief stewardess led away boys and nanny with the promise of grilled cheese sandwiches in the movie theater.

Dhillon didn't bother giving Dalton and Madeleine a tour. He was between yachts; this was just a charter. "The flying bridge is decent," he said, leading them up a flight of external stairs to a cantilevered platform upholding a dining booth with seating for twelve and a hot tub for at least as many. An Asian woman of indeterminate age in mirrored glasses and a skintight pink suit was seated at the table.

"This is Sonya Park. She's in aerospace."

Park smiled coolly, raising a hand in greeting without getting up.

Dhillon spent the meal ignoring Park and Dalton and relentlessly quizzing Madeleine on the twins' developing personalities and her latest acquisitions for SFMOMA. His strategy was easy to intuit. Dalton was happy when his wife was happy, and Park would sit through anything for the chance to make her pitch. Finally, Dhillon reined in one climactic belly laugh and said to Madeleine, "Would you and the boys be interested in a short excursion? I hear the Napali coast is spectacular from the water."

Madeleine glanced at Dalton, turned on her own smile, and said, "We would *love* that."

"Let me escort you to our tender."

Dalton and Park were left alone.

"So how do you know Abhi?" Dalton asked.

"We met socially. And he funded our Series B."

"Congratulations. He said you were in aerospace?"

She shrugged. "That's what he calls it. We're a bit hard to classify."

"Sounds interesting."

There was no point avoiding flattery during these pitches; he'd learned that sharing his real thoughts just made them talk twice as much.

Park rearranged herself in her chair, squared her shoulders, and straightened her spine. She placed her sunglasses on the table, crossed her legs, and leaned toward him. It was impossible for Dalton not to imagine the mirror she had clearly done this for dozens of times.

Her eyes were blue.

"Why do people die in war?"

"Because otherwise it wouldn't be war."

She smiled, slightly. "We prefer Clausewitz's definition. War as politics by other means. The United States talks about surgical strikes. But it's married to a framework that is essentially medieval."

"Hmmm."

"They wait for an enemy to become a threat, then use human judgment to decide what form of violence will resolve it, often ineffectively. We are going to disrupt this model."

Dalton smiled tightly. "I have the highest security clearance possible for a civilian. We collaborate with DARPA, DOD, DHS. The military's AI capabilities are significantly more advanced than that."

For the first time, Park allowed herself to look annoyed. "We understand the capabilities. But what good is all that hardware if it can't work together? We are offering a *platform* capable of integrating up-to-the-nanosecond hyper-spectral imagery, artificial tactical decision-making from billions of conflict simulations, and an arsenal of ground-, sea-, and air-based weapons systems deployable around the globe. This is the iPhone of war fighting—a stable, intuitive operating system to integrate capabilities currently siloed. Commanders running our tech will make decisions at every level of the chain of command in seconds, not minutes or hours: everything from inserting a special ops team to launching a hypersonic warhead."

"That doesn't sound like a war without casualties."

"That's where you come in."

"Ah."

"Obviously, in the short term, we need AI capable of identifying any individual target in the world. Other companies will sell us the top layer of your database, but we need more than scrapings. And, to be honest, we need your reputation. Obviously, your user data is the gold standard in the industry."

Now, Dalton was ever-so-mildly irritated. Of course, he did not show it. He was well known for being as cool an executive as he was a coder. The legend of his ability to spend days debugging spaghetti code while sitting on the same couch as the person who'd just written it—without ever showing the least hint of impatience or frustration—was what had drawn the first real talent to the company when it was only a handful of people in a rented first-floor office.

"If you're looking for a data contract, Dhillon can direct you to someone in sales."

Park smiled thinly. "Our goal is to end wars before they start. That means the ability to identify specific individuals who pose a threat to our national security. Imagine if we'd identified the virus that mutated into HIV and eliminated it before it ever leaped to humans? What if we could have identified Gavrilo Princip before he shot Franz Ferdinand? Our platform is capable of launching tactical nuclear warheads as easily as firing a single round from an autonomous sniper system, but that doesn't mean we *ever* want to launch one. What if you could prevent a war, or a terroristic attack, with a swarm of nano drones capable of penetrating even the securest bunker?"

"I read that novel. It was dystopian."

Park leaned back with an expression he wasn't used to seeing. "This is not a congressional oversight committee," she said. "You can be honest. We're on the same side."

"Honestly, I find this entire pitch morally obtuse. Besides, we're not a defense contractor."

Park laughed. "Then why did you buy Stellar Avionics?"

"R&D."

"I hope you understand," Park said, "we want you. But we don't need you." She shifted her tone, from determination to vulnerability. "This project is personal for me. My family still lives in South Korea. My nephews and nieces wake every day under the shadow of annihilation."

"I empathize with your family," said Dalton. "But this is not—"

"Sorry to interrupt," said Dhillon jovially. "Were you discussing anything important?"

Park rose. "We're just wrapping up." She shook Dalton's hand, nodded at Dhillon, and strode down the stairs.

"What did you say?"

"I told her it wasn't a fit. Which shouldn't have been a surprise to either of you."

"You realize there's more opportunity out there than selling ads. What are we using, ten percent of our capabilities? Why are we still sitting on the rest of it?"

"Did you tell her about Falkor?"

"Of course not. But I didn't have to. Everyone knows we have more than—"

"If anyone *really* knew, we'd be in a lot more trouble right now."

"Well, if we don't get to the source of these Phoenix leaks, it's going to be out there soon enough. And by the way, we're *still* in a lot of trouble. And I haven't heard your plan to get us out of it. You were conspicuously silent in the meeting this morning."

Dalton hesitated. Time to rip off the Band-Aid. "We need to strip down to battle stations. Give them some of what they want. Shed divisions. Absorb the blow. We refocus on mission and UX, build back our users. And our reputation."

For a moment, Dhillon's incredulity was genuine. Then he smiled slyly. "You're backing Erin."

"Maybe Erin is backing me."

Dhillon laughed at that. "Look, I recognize everything she did to get your company off the ground. But you can't let your history with her cloud your judgment. It's one thing putting her on *60 Minutes* to paint her special vision of the global commons. But you can't let her drive real decisions. That's not what Sokoni is anymore. We swim in different waters. Bringing people together, or whatever, that's not a mission, it's a means to an end."

"So, what's your end game? We get regulated out of existence?"

"First, we double campaign giving. Let it be known our PACs are primed and ready for the next election cycle. Pair that with a three-sixty PR push around how these regulations will hurt people of color and small businesses. I'm talking ad buys in every congressional district. Create a permission structure for members to start jumping ship. Carrot and stick. The usual playbook."

"The usual playbook," Dalton said. "We're losing users, bleeding talent, and the regulators come back harder every time. There are more and more legislators we can't win over. They're angrier, and smarter, and now it's bipartisan. I'm tired of kicking the can."

Dhillon was thinking hard. "I don't care if you own fifty-one percent of shares, the board won't go along with this. There's only so much value this company can lose and remain viable."

"We've got cash reserves for years."

"It's more complicated than that."

"That's why we need to present a united front."

"Whose buy-in have you got? Am I outnumbered yet?"

"I haven't even told Erin. It starts with you. Honestly, you're the only one with the vision to understand."

"And the charm to sell it. But this is a huge mistake. I know you've never been wrong. But it's impossible to be right forever."

"Actually, it's inevitable. If ten thousand people have a coin-flipping tournament, one of them has to win every toss."

Dhillon gave the obligatory smirk of acknowledgment. "Well, I'm not wrong often, either. If we start stripping ads and pushes, we're going to need another income stream."

"I'm open to ideas."

"My idea just walked away."

"It's repugnant."

"I introduced you for a reason. People accuse us of enabling genocide. This is our chance to end war."

"I don't see it. Our market cap is already two-thirds the size of the entire domestic defense industry."

"You have to think bigger."

"Explain."

"Forget all that prediction mumbo-jumbo. This is what happens. Of course, we beta test in the U.S. Then license to allies. But the vision is to get every nation on the platform. Replace mutual assured destruction with mutual assured compatibility. We move war onto our servers. Countries learn the outcome of a conflict before they even have to fight it."

"We turn war into Risk."

Dhillon nodded.

"You know that sounds even crazier. Can we buy them?"

"Park thinks they'll be buying us in a few years. Anyway, we can't scare the regulators. It'll be a plain-vanilla licensing agreement. We get a stake in exchange for our data and a few algorithms, make some promises, and include some very fine print. The only difference is this time, they get full access, to everything."

"You want to give Falkor *to them*?"

Dhillon only smiled wider.

"And if I agree to this, you back me with the board?"

Dhillon, still smiling, raised his mimosa. The bridge rocked with the gentle swells rolling from the blue horizon. Waterfalls tumbled from the green ridges encircling the crescent beach. Hanalei. An ancient paradise, subject of countless chants and songs. And some of the most exclusive property any-where in the world, where a surf shack on a quarter acre could sell for ten million dollars.

Beyond a black point of rocks, Dalton watched the launch returning from its jaunt.

"I'd rather burn our servers to the ground," he said to Dhillon.

13

Carlotta made it sound simple. Aluminum cans, plastic bottles, all five cents. Glass was a bit more complicated—there were no redemption fees on wine or liquor bottles.

They started with a row of dumpsters behind a shopping center. Carlotta began handing down the bags. Janice Diaz tore them open, trying to push aside the rubbish without smearing sticky foulness across her clothes, glancing up every few seconds to make sure no one was watching. Finally, it was time to leave the alley. Carlotta pointed down the line of shaved ice stands, T-shirt shops, tour operators, and convenience stores to the green metal receptacles spaced evenly outside the storefronts.

"Take your time with these. The cruise ship is in port. Tourists toss a lot of bottles."

A flickering cloud of panic enveloped Janice Diaz as she approached the first bin. The lid was heavy. A family stepped from a doorway as she set it on the sidewalk. Both adults averted their eyes. The mother's hand shot toward her girls, whose eyes, above their scoops of rainbow-colored ice, were fixed on Janice. They wanted to see what she'd do next. She bent over the bin and reached both arms into the plastic liner. She learned there was a place inside herself that remained still and cool, no matter what. She dug to the bottom of the bin, handed up the plastic bottles to Carlotta, then went on to the next.

But Carlotta must have seen something in her face. Or maybe she just wasn't that good at picking out recyclables. Regardless, when they reached the park, she was placed on permanent lookout while Carlotta methodically searched each bin, even though most already had a collection of cans and bottles piled neatly on the ground beside them.

"Why aren't they in the bins?"

"Local courtesy," Carlotta said. "For folks like us."

"So why do we need a lookout?"

"Because people can be territorial. Especially at the end of the month."

No trouble came. After a few hours, their bag of cans was getting hard to close, and the bag of glass was almost tearing.

But Carlotta wasn't smiling. "We've got to try something else."

"Really?"

"We worked all morning and we've only got nine dollars to show. Let's take a break."

They sat on a bench with a view of the harbor. The green water sparkled below the cliffs.

"Let's say we earn nine more dollars after lunch," said Carlotta, "which we won't. Can we live on eighteen dollars a day?"

Janice Diaz started calculating. Subtracting rent, insurance, car payments, cable bills. Suddenly life seemed very cheap.

"It was a rhetorical question," said Carlotta. "I've been thinking. You aren't ready to go it alone. You haven't even gone through withdrawal."

"Isn't that what I'm doing?"

"You're on honeymoon, sister. You're going to need me. And I might need you. It's been a time since I was on the street alone."

For the first time in a long time, Janice Diaz felt grateful for something.

"We could spend a hundred and fifty dollars a night on a room," said Carlotta, "once you start getting your assistance. But we won't get halfway through the month that way. No matter what hustle we come up with. Do you have any skills?"

"Maybe."

Carlotta laughed. "Play guitar? Make jewelry? You must have been doing something." She glanced at Janice Diaz's jeans and shirt. "You really don't remember how you got those?"

She smoothed the fabric of her shirt across her stomach. Her clothes were exactly what someone like her would wear. They were who she was.

"I don't remember."

"Maybe someone was taking care of you."

Janice Diaz touched her bruise. "If they were, they didn't do a very good job."

"They usually don't."

"I don't think that's how things were. I don't think that was my life."

"Well, maybe there's something you can do, eventually. But we can't use EBT at restaurants. Which means cooking. Which means we need a stove and fuel. And if we want to live within our means, we'll need our own shelter. And some way to stay warm. And it's all got to be portable."

"You're talking about camping?"

"Walmart has everything we'll need."

Carlotta glared up at the sky, then opened the bag of plastic and rummaged until she pulled out a two-liter Sprite bottle. "This is yours now. Rinse it, then fill it whenever you can. Dehydration can become an ambulance ride real quick, and you want to avoid that mess for as long as you can."

Janice Diaz took the empty bottle. "How much will we need, for supplies?"

"Two, three hundred dollars."

"That much?"

"Being homeless isn't cheap."

"How do we get it?"

"First of the month is just a week away. We've got to get you in the system. It's 11:30. Let's drop these at Reynold's, then stop at the Mission, and head up to the county building after lunch."

As Janice Diaz was standing, a faint chime tripped something in her brain—curiosity/pleasure/guilt/annoyance strung together in a bland, familiar zap of habit that caused her to reach instinctively for the device in her hip pocket—an unexpected echo from another life. The screen was dark. But when she pressed it, a rectangular bubble materialized.

A message. From a contact labeled Alpha. *Team en route.*

She showed Carlotta the message.

"You think that's for you?"

She looked again. If the familiar chime had opened the thinnest linkage to her past, it had closed just as quickly. "I don't know."

"I've personally never been part of a team," said Carlotta. "I was into solitary sports. Chess and tennis and whatnot."

14

The only way in or out of Hanalei was a one-lane steel bridge from the plantation era with a small brown sign on each end: *Local Courtesy is 5–7 Cars.*

Dalton's security team hated it. He could feel the anxiety emanating from the men in the front seat as they idled in the long line of traffic. Six cars passed them, heading into town. Their own line moved. He counted the vehicles crossing the bridge. Three, four, five.

He hated this.

The first black Suburban would be number eight. He knew it would follow the bumper of the car ahead, and the next three in his motorcade would come right after. He and his family were in number three today.

As they rolled over the uneven wooden planks, he glanced at the driver waiting on the other side. The one who'd stopped. It was an older Asian man in a pickup. Probably a farm vehicle. He stared ahead, resigned to the situation. That was worse than being flipped off.

If it was up to him, they'd get something inconspicuous—a Tesla or a Benz—and drive themselves, at least on island. But how would they feel, Madeleine always pointed out, if something did happen and they hadn't done everything in their power to prevent it?

He glanced over his shoulder at the two boys, asleep in their car seats. Madeleine caught his eye, smiled, then looked back down at her phone.

His own phone chimed.

"Hart?"

"Your ETA is seventeen minutes."

"I guess so."

"We just had another vehicle traverse the compound."

"Isn't it your responsibility to control all entries and exits?"

"I've been told it's a legal issue. You have an easement holder with movement rights across the property."

"I thought they'd taken care of that."

"Apparently not. And as long as the integrity of the perimeter is compromised, I'm not comfortable authorizing free movement around the property. I want to add personnel and create an inner layer of security."

"Sounds expensive."

"As long as unauthorized, unvetted vehicles can enter and exit, I believe it's a necessity."

"You're saying my family isn't safe?"

"Not that I can guarantee."

Dalton let his head fall back on the headrest. He felt Madeleine's eyes on him. She'd put her phone away.

He called his Realtor.

"Update me, Samantha."

"I am *so* sorry, sir. We're working to resolve it."

"You've been telling me that for six months now."

"We had a setback. Our family representative in the lawsuit called this morning. She's pulling out of the contract."

"What does that mean?"

"We need someone with standing to consolidate the property claims."

"You're saying I've bought seven hundred million dollars' worth of property, and I can't prevent the public from driving in and out as they please?"

"We're going to resolve it. I'll bring her back on board. Or find a new option."

"I'm beginning to worry you're in over your head. We aren't talking about a golf course here. This is the safety of my family. Do you need me to explain how seriously I take that?"

He glanced at Madeleine. She was staring out the window, absorbing every word.

"It's understood," said Samantha. "Very well understood. We are going to resolve this before the deadline passes."

"The deadline? My deadline was weeks ago."

"I mean the legal deadline."

"What is that?"

"We started a process to sell the property at auction on the courthouse steps, open to anyone with an existing stake in the land. On Tuesday, it will go to the highest bidder, whether we have a claim holder to represent us or not."

"You're saying that in six days, if we don't have a family member ready to place a bid for us, we will lose the opportunity to buy this land?"

"Ummm . . . in the short term, yes."

"And the security integrity of this entire project goes to zero."

"That's not really my area—"

"I know what your area is! And you need to take care of it."

He punched his thumb into the red circle and the screen went blank.

Through the tinted windows, the midday pastures glowed hallucinogenic green. Roadside hedges blurred. Trees in middle distance moved at a stately pace. The mountains rose immobile.

The convoy traveled twenty-five miles an hour above the fifty-mile-an-hour limit. The police wouldn't intervene. Every officer with a clean record had pulled off-duty shifts for him by now. Support positions only, of course: checkpoints, crowd control, gate duty when the family was off island. Hart didn't hire local cops for close protection. The men who staffed the black Suburbans had more interesting backgrounds. He'd been instructed not to ask about them.

He knew what they called people like him: high-net-worth individuals. And those who worked for HNWIs were supposed to be the best of the best at whatever they did—driving point in a motorcade, pouring concrete, transacting real estate. These were people who made more in service professions than his parents had as physicians in family practice. Yet no matter how much he paid them for their expertise, there was always a ceiling to their competence. The ability of even the best of the supposedly best to screw things up was a constant in his life, usually, as a mild irritant—a series of frustrations so particular he hesitated to voice them, even to Madeleine. But sometimes, they mattered.

They were still five minutes from the refuge. He set down his phone, relaxed his neck into the headrest—vegan suede—and closed his eyes. He let himself imagine how it would feel to check on his sleeping kids and lie beside his sleeping wife, secure in the knowledge that by locking his doors, arming his security system, paying his life insurance premiums, and replacing his smoke alarms every ten years, he'd done everything within his power to keep his family safe.

15

Nalani stopped at the homeless village to drop the manini and ended up talking story with Aunty Lei for most of the morning. She was never in a hurry to walk into her empty condo.

She'd been there only a minute when the doorbell buzzed, a sound she wasn't sure she'd ever heard before. She opened to a blond woman jabbing at her phone, lips pinched sourly. The woman lifted her head, and the lines around her eyes and mouth smoothed into a smile that made Nalani, for a moment, proud to be the kind of person who could make someone so happy.

"Aloha! I'm Samantha. Call me Sam."

"Aloha."

"You must be Nalani Winthrop!"

Nalani nodded.

"Wonderful. May I come in?"

Nalani glanced down the third-floor balcony, with its glimpse of ocean to the right and a panoramic view of Kuhio Highway and the busy Kapa'a strip to the left. No one else in sight.

The woman wore a tropic-print jacket and matching slacks. Not quite a suit but definitely professional. A reporter? It had been months since any of them had tried to find her.

"I was actually about to go surfing," she said. "What is this about?"

Now the woman looked up and down the balcony. "It's actually a sensitive matter? I think it's best we talk in private."

"Concerning what?"

Sam pursed her lips and wrinkled her forehead, dramatizing the deep challenge of putting something so sensitive into words. "It concerns *your mother*," she said. "And a *significant opportunity* for you and your family."

Out of curiosity or impatience, Nalani swung the door wider. Sam examined Nalani's apartment with what seemed to be real interest. "So, it's a studio?" she said. "And this is a pullout in the living room?"

"I guess," said Nalani. "I've never used it."

"Garden-view balcony, I see. Very cute!"

Nalani looked around. She'd bought it fully furnished eighteen months ago. All she'd added was a stack of surfboards in a corner.

Her family's financial advisor hadn't been enthusiastic when she told him to liquidate her investments, but she'd felt a need to own something no one could take from her. It meant putting her plans for grad school on hold, something she knew she should regret, but she couldn't muster up the energy.

"It's a *nice* building." Samantha waved her hands. "I managed two lockouts here, *long* ago."

"Is that what you do?"

"Not anymore. Well, for certain clients, I do oversee . . . You don't remember me? Sam Rittenheimer. We spoke on the phone. About the parcel . . ."

"Yeah. The eight hundred dollars. I just discussed it with my mother."

"You did? She didn't mention that."

"She's been talking to you?"

"She sent me a text message? This morning. That's the reason I'm stopping by, actually. You see, I'm a little concerned about her. She's behaving a little . . . erratically?"

"The story of her life."

Sam Rittenheimer smiled tightly. "Mm-hmm. Well. We had an understanding."

"I know. I got served."

"Ah, yes, um. Well, not exactly *served*."

"You sent a notary."

"You see, Nalani . . . Do you mind if I sit down? You see, my client and our team, we are trying to preserve the legacy of your family's land. Malama 'aina? We want to *keep things pono* in perpetuity."

"You explained all that."

Sam Rittenheimer smiled. "We're trying to *rescue* the title of this land. With so many descendants claiming a share, who knows what could happen to it in the future? State law provides a process—the technical term is *quiet title*—once started, it's a very strict deadline."

"Are you talking about the *lawsuit* you served me with yesterday?"

Sam Rittenheimer grimaced. "We're just following the law."

"You're helping Frank Dalton sue my family for our land."

"Ha! *Frank*. You know he actually likes to be called Franky? He's very casual like that. You two would get along!" She glanced at Nalani and changed her tone. "I'm here because your mother suggested she *might* break her contract with us. But she's not picking up her phone."

"Network's no good down there."

"We just want to make sure she's okay."

"She's fine."

"I'm *so* glad to hear that. But *time is running out* for your family to gain financial security and preserve the land you've tended for so long."

"Eight hundred dollars barely covers my HOA fee."

Samantha fluttered her fingers, then pulled her palms together to form an arrow, pointed at Nalani. "Obviously, the finances are quite complex. Franky has created a very unique structure tailored to this situation. He established a *nonprofit organization* to oversee and protect these lands. But for this *nonprofit* to succeed, it will require a consultant, from *your* family, willing to purchase the land—with our help, of course—and *donate* it to the organization. We are prepared to compensate this service with two million dollars."

"This is how you tried to buy my mother?"

Samantha parted her hands and spread them wide, encompassing the women and the land around them. "I understand your hesitation, Nalani. As kamaʻāina of this special island, we both appreciate the mana of the ʻāina. We're all protective! But I want to assure you, this is more than a vacation property for Franky and his family. They feel a call to this island, a connection. No one knows this yet, but he and Madeleine are about to announce an *extremely* generous donation to the hospital. On his land, he's building a biodynamic organic farm. And your family's parcel will be home to the most advanced marine research station *on the planet.* His goal is to offer this island a path back to the self-sustainability your people practiced for thousands of years. Isn't that something you want to be a part of?"

Sam was still perched on the edge of the couch. But it felt like she had spent the last fifteen minutes inside Nalani's head, deftly rearranging. Nalani knew it, and resented it, but couldn't seem to stop it. And she did have to admit, the space did feel more bright and open.

And two million dollars.

It had to be considered. Not accepted on a whim and rejected just as quickly. The family needed someone to evaluate this properly, a person who

could make the decision from a rational perspective, who wasn't emotion-
ally attached, who wasn't literally living there, and who wasn't an addict
with a lifelong history of making terrible decisions for herself and everyone
around her.

"I'll need something to show my lawyer."

Sam Rittenheimer couldn't hide the endorphins that had just flooded her
brain. "Of course," she said. "Of course. Of course. I'll have it all drawn up."

Then her whole face brightened. She leaned forward and placed her hand
on Nalani's. "You know, I really enjoyed meeting you. I'd love to get to
know you better. And I want you to know you can trust me."

Nalani found herself nodding along. It was nice, having her hands held.
It had been a long time.

Sam increased the pressure, ever so slightly.

"Tomorrow I'm showing an amazing property to a celebrity client. It's all
very top secret. And I'd *love* for you to join."

16

The Mission served cold macaroni with canned peas in mayonnaise, fried Spam in sweet yellow rolls, and a sugary pink liquid they called POG—the best meal Janice Diaz had ever eaten. Afterward, Carlotta walked her to the county building, where they shuttled between offices, attempting to get certain papers stamped, only to be told they needed to visit another office for a different stamp before returning. When they were sent back to the same office for a second time, Carlotta loudly demanded to know why they were being sent in circles. At that point, a smiling young woman emerged from a cubicle, took all of their paperwork, made photocopies of Janice's passport, and promised to have everything ready in the morning.

"They're trying to get rid of you," Carlotta told her. "That nice lady is the one they send out when they think you're broken."

"I just need fresh air."

They wandered onto the broad green space beyond the courthouse. There were people scattered here and there amid the monuments and flagpoles. Most sat alone on benches or lay beside their shopping carts or camping packs. A group played drums and guitars, their bare feet stained mud-orange. It was a diverse crowd, at least. White, brown, young, old. She and Carlotta would fit in.

Janice's jeans were stained. Her shirt smelled like stale beer. But her hands and face were freshly scrubbed. Her stomach was full. The black hole inside her was—for the moment—less a sucking drain than a cosmically heavy sphere. Gravity dragged her toward the grass. She understood now how the sprawling nappers slept so deeply, so exposed. She started looking for an unclaimed spot.

"You up for a walk?" said Carlotta. "Beach is just a mile away."

Kalapaki Beach was a small crescent, half a mile wide, ending at a cliff with tall houses clinging to its face and golf flags fluttering at its crown. A resort hotel ran the length of the beach, separated from the sand by a perfect lawn covered with broad trees, lounge chairs, and pavilions. The two women crossed a public beach park with a deteriorating concrete bathroom and a simple shower, where surfers rinsed themselves and their boards under an iron pipe.

Beneath the ironwood trees, brown men and women played horseshoes or tended coolers at collapsing picnic tables. Janice realized that, since the hospital, she'd been sorting everyone she encountered into two categories. These were the first people she'd seen whose status wasn't obvious. If they did have homes, they weren't trying to demonstrate it. And if they didn't, they made no effort to pretend otherwise. They occupied this little bay and pleasant beach as if it was exactly where they belonged.

Carlotta gestured sharply for her to move along.

The sand was hot on the soles of her feet.

"Dig your feet in," said Carlotta. An inch below the surface, the grains were heavy and cool. But it was tiring, shuffling her feet through the sand.

Carlotta finally sighed, dropped her bag, and spread a towel sideways so they could share it. She opened a wide golf umbrella. In silence, they watched the turquoise waves roll in from the point. Children chased each other in the hissing shore break. Young white men and women lay on matching towels side by side, tanning their backs as they squinted at their cell phones.

"This is what it's all about," said Carlotta.

Janice Diaz looked up and down the beach. There were women in bikinis and topless men, of course. Most of the kids wore long-sleeved swim shirts. Heavier men swam in water-stretched T-shirts. A few older women wore pastel outfits, loose slacks and blouses. One middle-aged couple strode across the wet sand in athletic boots and hiking poles. But no one was fully dressed, like she and Carlotta. The two women were painfully conspicuous, huddled under a golf umbrella, sharing a faded towel.

"You've got to relax when you've got the chance," Carlotta said. "Enjoy! This is why you came here, isn't it?"

"Why didn't we sit back there, with the people at the picnic tables?"

Carlotta didn't turn to look. "Best not do that."

"They looked friendly."

"They are. Good people. Mostly. They don't judge, and they'll help you in a pinch. But you don't want to push it."

"Push what?"

"You're a guest on their island. They see people like you coming every day. And if you show respect, they'll give it back. But how many people do you think come here with respect? Tourists, houseless, most of them treat this island the same way, to be honest. And at least tourists come with money to spend."

"Is it because I'm white?"

"Yes. But just try being Black!"

"It's like that, out here?"

"No, not like the mainland. People here are real with you, at least. And like I said, show respect, they give it back. We're good. But I don't need to bring you around on day two."

"Are they homeless?"

Carlotta thought before she spoke. "You can't think that way. Making everybody *this* or *that*. What's a home to you? A four-bedroom house with mom and dad and two kids? By that measure, half the people on this island you could call homeless, with housing the way it is now. Is it having a family around that loves you? Plenty of millionaires don't have that. Many people you call homeless don't want to be anywhere else, at least not at that point in their lives. You see plenty of that here, if you start poking around in the forest and down by the beaches. But how do you tell a Hawaiian he's homeless? They'll tell you themselves, if that's how they feel. But if you see a person fishing on the beach all night, you'd better not assume anything. Like I said, you've got to come with respect."

Janice Diaz nodded.

Carlotta looked up the beach in the other direction, toward the lounge chairs and cabanas. "These people, they can be kind, too. But by and large, they are hostile to us, even if they don't know it. They have paid a lot of money to be on this beach, with the coconut trees and the surfing and the boys in white shirts bringing cold drinks. And right now, they are getting everything they imagined except for a fat Black lady and an ice head with two black eyes sitting their asses down for everyone to see. They think we got some nerve being homeless in the middle of their vacation—You think that's funny?"

Carlotta wiped her eyes. "I've had people call me the foulest things. Some of them try to get the hotel staff to kick me out. But even the police can't touch us here. We have a right to be on this beach, just like everyone else, 'til 2:00 a.m."

"Then the sprinklers come on."

Carlotta nodded. "Now you're getting it. Look. This beach is state land. The park across the stream is county. It closes at midnight, so everyone comes over here to buy themselves a few more hours."

"Are we going back to the boat?"

Carlotta shook her head. "Manuel needs his space."

"So, what are we going to do?"

"I'm working on that. I had a good place for a long time. I'm a little out of pocket now, to be honest."

"You can't go back?"

"Not while Maleko's there. Maybe one day. For now, you and me are going to make our own way."

Time was moving strangely for Janice Diaz. It seemed to her she'd just been sitting on a sunny, crowded beach. Now, she shivered. When she looked up, the ocean was gray and heavy, the sand brown in the shadow of the distant hills. The sky was still bright but seemed farther away. The beach was almost empty.

Carlotta was furling her umbrella.

"Where are we going?"

"They used to call it Wiliwili Camp."

"You have friends there?"

"Ghosts can't be your friend."

17

Madeline and the contractor discussed showerheads as Franky Dalton attempted to distract Lionel and Marc from the rainbow of exposed wiring running from stud to stud in the unfinished master bedroom. The twins screamed as he hoisted each by an armpit, carried them back to the center of the room, stood them on their feet, and let them wobble on his arms until they were stable. As soon as they were free, they headed in opposite directions.

By the time Dalton had chased down Marc, Lionel was leaning all his weight on a taut green cable. "Maddy!" he shouted.

She and the contractor looked up.

"You can't let him do that, Franky!" she said. "It's not safe."

She pounced on Lionel and tried to pry his fingers off the cable. "Si forte. Come help, Franky!"

Marc squirmed up Dalton's shoulder and wrapped his arms around his father's face.

"It's only fiber," said the contractor. "It won't hurt him."

Madeleine pried Lionel free and hugged him around the waist.

"We need to make a decision," she said, grimacing as Lionel hooked each hand into a hair bun, "between the Grohe or the Rohl. I know we were talking about designing something custom." Her voice was continuously rising to compensate for the screaming growing steadily louder. "But everyone says you get better results if you just go with an established—"

"What?!" Franky shouted. "I can't—"

"I said—"

Dalton gave up and set Marc down. Madeleine did the same with Lionel. Together, they tried to pen the twins between their arms.

"I don't care," said Dalton. "I don't care if they're rain showers or pressure heads or whatever. All I want—"

"I know," said Madeleine, "you want a shower that feels as good as a shower you took in Africa."

"It wasn't the shower itself. It was the feeling of taking one after three months of bucket baths."

"Chouchou, we are *all* trying to get you your shower. But you need to tell us what you like! Rain or pressure? It matters!"

"Most of them were just a pipe in a cinder block wall with a sketchy electric heating coil above your head."

The boys were both on their backs now, sobbing. The contractor was looking grim.

Madeleine had reached her limit. "Just choose! The Rohl, the Grohe, a pipe in the wall, whatever you want! Peut-être some things you cannot have. Or maybe taking a hot shower every day while everyone above us is *dying* will make it—"

He glanced at the contractor. "Maddy, that's—"

She caught his look. "He does this for a living, Franky." She turned to the contractor. "Is the recreation area safe?"

"The basketball rims are up. We're just waiting on the parquet. And the climbing walls are still in pieces."

"We'll be there," she told Dalton, sweeping the boys into her arms.

The two men watched her march down the dim hallway, the boys letting their heads rest on each shoulder.

"Enjoy these years," the contractor said. "They go by fast."

Everyone said this. Literally everyone. The P value was essentially zero. So no matter how implausible it seemed in the second-by-second maelstrom of adoration, gratitude, rage, and despair that defined the twins' waking moments, Dalton had to believe it must be true, at least in hindsight. Parenthood was the most challenging thing he'd ever done. The most challenging thing he could *imagine* doing. Less than .01 percent of his users had run an ultramarathon or climbed one of the seven summits. Yet 64 percent had accomplished something he rated to be even more difficult. It was almost enough to give him optimism about the future of humanity.

"Sorry to schedule these tours during family time," he told his contractor. "It will be easier once my wife okays the nanny."

Best practice strongly recommended barring staff from access to a family shelter unless they were assigned a berth. It was bad for day-to-day morale and could present life-threatening complications in a survival situation, since most shelter-owning families were significantly outnumbered by their employees. Madeleine liked to call the Sanctuary a waste of money, or—more often recently—a symptom of acute anxiety disorder. But she still hadn't offered Pilar a spot, even though the woman had a PhD in humanities from the Universitat de Barcelona and was practically a member of the family.

Madeleine was sensitive about their nannies. She said she'd been raised by the house help in Dakar while her parents were in Paris, and she'd vowed she wouldn't do the same to her own kids.

"Let's hold off on the showerheads," he told the contractor.

The two men strolled through the rest of Suite A. The quartz countertops and cabinetry were in place, with raw-looking niches for the Wolfs and Sub-Zeros. "Every appliance will be fully concealed, of course," the contractor mentioned in passing. He knew Dalton could not care less. They paused in the living room, where the contractor gestured at the french doors framing a cinder block cavity eight inches deep. "The 8K screens will be installed next month. They say the landscape renderings are syncing seamlessly in the factory right now."

The windows were operating. They'd been able to buy those on spec. All four displayed the views from the residence: the inland mountains nearly silhouetted against the sunset, the ocean reflecting pale pink clouds, the glowing crescent of Momona Beach in the shadow of the bluff. The contractor tapped his phone. The Golden Gate Bridge and the Marin Hills appeared, white clouds rising from the valleys. He clicked again: a panoramic cityscape of jeweled lights: the view from the royal suite at the Signiel Seoul, one of Dalton's favorites. He watched the red and yellow lines of traffic stop and start one hundred floors below.

They ascended to the rec area, passed the weight room/cycling studio, pool, cinema, and library, which would double as a classroom, and stopped outside the gymnasium. Dalton listened for a moment to the sound of bouncing balls and happy babbling. He was about to push open the door, when laughter turned to wails.

"Let's see how the ops deck is coming along."

One level up, the medical suite and the brig were framed out, bare studs over concrete. Only the armory was finished and fully stocked, at Hart's insistence. Eventually, the halls and common rooms would be paneled with polished white pine. Unfinished, it felt like touring a diamond mine.

The steep, spiraling staircases, on the other hand, felt like a submarine. They reminded him of the stacks in his favorite college library, which were also underground, connected by tight stairs in claustrophobic steel tubes painted a tarnished nautical teal. Most students avoided them, but he had loved to descend floors, immersed in information in a way that seemed old-fashioned, even then, wandering rows of metal bookshelves until he chose a table to boot up his Inspiron 7000 and replace the must of old books with the cool, condensing tingle of a five-milligram bump of Adderall, with no responsibilities for the rest of the night except to load the code space into his brain.

His life was good. That was certain. But he could still be nostalgic for that time. Not only when no one had cared what he coded—or depended on it—but when there'd still been mystery: things he was glimpsing six, seven hours into a session, strange flickers of *something* emerging from unintended intersections of commands and 0–1 switches. If he'd had to describe it, he'd have called it a mind, which was why he'd described it to exactly no one. Eventually, he would find the chat rooms where such things were discussed. But in those early days, the only place to go was deeper into the mystery, at the command line, night after night, writing chains of words and symbols that did more than represent the world, they changed it. His words made things happen. *Hello, World.* As if, in those silent rooms under the ground, he was a wizard or a god.

When the family emerged into the cool, humid night, the boys were subdued. Marc's small legs were wrapped around Dalton's hips. He interlaced his fingers behind his father's neck and let the weight of his head rest against his father's collarbone. Soon his breathing evened out, and his head nestled even heavier. Dalton felt his son's warm breath on his neck. The sweetness of these moments was almost unendurable. This was what went by so fast. The boys would always rebel, but they would never snuggle so trustfully in his arms again, never have the perfect faith that nothing could harm them under their parents' watch.

The contractor was trying to tell him something about the old reservoir. For op sec reasons, they were concealing the extent of the Sanctuary by using the excavated soil to shore up the aging dam. The contractor was trying to explain why this approach was suboptimal, from a civil engineering standpoint, but Dalton's mind was on other things.

"Sounds like an issue for Engineering," he told the contractor. "Work it out with them."

"But—"

"Remind me again," said Dalton, "what are our deterrents to a swarm of nano drones?"

18

They walked a steep road curving away from the beach, up the flank of a jungle valley that split the city. There were no sidewalks. Cars sped past, slipstreams tugging at the women's clothes. Carlotta turned and slipped through a hole in a chain-link fence. They crossed a fading parking lot, following the fence line. The forest bulged against the wire. When they came past the corner of the cinder-block building at the center of the lot, Janice Diaz saw the dwellings built against its long back wall. From a distance, in the dusk, they looked organic, like a row of wasp's nests or beaver lodges. Gradually, she noticed the diversity of their construction: tarps, blankets, bedsheets, flattened cardboard boxes, garbage bags, tentpoles, two-by-fours, plastic netting, galvanized pipes.

In view of the encampment, Carlotta moved more quickly. It was dinnertime. People cooked over stoves and fire barrels. Others rested in plastic chairs or squatted on their heels, chatting and laughing. Janice Diaz swerved toward the smell of woodsmoke and frying meat.

"What are you doing?"

She stopped. "This isn't where we're going?" Her craving made her cunning.

Carlotta didn't answer, just beckoned impatiently and kept moving.

Someone shouted, "Hey, Carlotta! What you doing trying sneak away like that?"

Carlotta stopped. She turned and began walking toward a courtyard created by a blue tarp strung between shopping carts. Two older women sat side by side in folding camp chairs. Below their jackets, bright flowered dresses came down to their ankles. A man tended a grill, obscured by white smoke. A chubby boy sat cross-legged on the pavement, intent on his phone. Two young women entertained a toddler, supporting its hands as it stumbled between them.

One of the old women laughed. She had close-cropped gray hair and many missing teeth. "You must owe somebody money."

Carlotta smiled warmly. "It's good to see you, Mata."

Janice Diaz sank onto the ground beside the boy, the spot, she calculated, where she was most likely to be ignored. Mata was introducing Carlotta to someone. Something about dialysis treatment. Thyroids. She couldn't follow. Someone tapped her knee. She wasn't sure how long she had been sitting when a young woman handed her a Styrofoam plate. Yellow oil dripped from rectangular slices of meat. Crispy outside, soft and salty when she bit. Yellow chunks of something like a potato were piled by the meat. She burned her mouth. The boy, she realized, had looked up from his phone to watch her.

"Thank you," she said to no one in particular.

Soon she was dragging the plastic fork across the plate, collecting orange beads of oil and sucking the tines between her lips.

"We ought to be going," said Carlotta.

"Kasian," said one of the seated women, "help Aunty."

The boy set down his phone, pushed himself to his feet, and held out his hand. Janice Diaz set down the plate, wiped her fingers on her jeans, and took it.

"Thank you," she said again. "It was delicious. What was it?"

"Just Spam and kón," said the man at the grill. "Breadfruit, from the tree. Simple food."

Carlotta was holding a plate, too. But the food was untouched.

"Good luck with your treatment," said Carlotta. "And thank you for dinner."

She slipped her plate to one of the young women, who quietly moved it to her lap and let the toddler grab a handful of breadfruit and palm it into his mouth.

"Such nice people," said Janice Diaz.

"Yes."

"Why were you avoiding them?"

Carlotta only shook her head.

"Do you really owe money?"

Carlotta stopped so abruptly Janice Diaz bumped into her.

"I *tried* to avoid them because I knew this would happen."

"That they would feed us and be friendly?"

"Exactly."

"What's wrong with that?"

"They're Micronesian."

Janice Diaz was silent, choosing her words carefully. "That doesn't bother me."

Carlotta shot her an exasperated look. "Did you notice we were the only ones eating?"

"I thought they were being polite."

"They were."

"So?"

"So they don't get assistance."

"Neither do I."

"That's temporary. And you're not supporting anyone. You heard Mata. Her cousin just flew over for dialysis. They don't have anything like that over there. Their islands are spoiled."

"What does that mean?"

When Carlotta spoke again, she sounded more patient. "I guess you forgot your history, too. They used those islands for nuclear tests and let the people stay, to see what would happen."

"Who did?"

"Government scientists pulled Mata's teeth when she was a girl. They wanted to measure radiation in her bones. Her brother was born with half a skull. Her mother held his brains and nursed him one full week until he died."

"What government?"

"Our government. Those that lived, most of them have cancer. They can get visas to come here. But they can never be citizens. And they can't get any services. No Medicare, no EBT. That's whose food you were eating. Mind you don't tear your shirt."

They'd reached the end of the lot. Carlotta squeezed through another hole in the chain-link and disappeared into the darkness on the other side.

Janice Diaz stooped and followed her into the forest.

"Where are we?"

"Plantation land. Once they stopped growing sugar, they let the woods grow up."

Janice Diaz tapped her phone to turn on the flashlight. It illuminated a narrow red path between forking roots.

"Save your battery," said Carlotta. "I can't see with that thing on."

Janice Diaz shuffled forward, following the sound of Carlotta's steps.

"Tracks ahead. Don't trip."

Loose gravel shifted underfoot. A silver line of train tracks slipped into the gloom. They walked awkwardly on the ties until Carlotta stopped again. "Here it is."

The clouds had come on thicker, and the forest was darker than ever.

"Where are we?"

"An old sugar camp. Not much left of it anymore. The forest is taking it."

Now she could make out concrete pads and skeletal studs in the glow of the invisible city. There were staircases to nowhere. Corrugated metal roofs gleamed like water. Glass glinted in the shadows of walls that hadn't yet collapsed. They walked deeper into the village. "Here we go." Carlotta mounted a set of creaking steps. Janice Diaz followed her into the darkness of an empty doorway. Inside, faint light from the windows fell into the two small rooms.

"Let's see that light now."

Janice Diaz shone her phone around the house. The light flickered over walls covered in spray-paint graffiti. A mattress lay on the floor, one corner burned away, exposing soot-blackened springs.

"Home sweet home."

Janice Diaz heard a click. An orange glow sprang from Carlotta's cupped hands. She set a small white candle on the floor. Then she laughed. "If you could see your face."

Janice Diaz felt tears coming. She was sure this wasn't like her.

"You're in another country now." Carlotta sounded sympathetic.

"I'm sorry," said Janice Diaz. "I don't want to be rude."

"You're free here. You can be whatever you like."

Reality was getting slippery again. Carlotta flickered in and out of view. How long had she been tending to that fragile light?

The darkness pressed against the thin walls of the house the way the jungle pressed against the fence. It was trying to meet another darkness. Something she'd brought with her, growing in her center, an emptiness that would take and take until she gave it what it wanted.

"Here."

Carlotta handed her some kind of bar. Sweet and salty. Chocolate and peanut.

"Cheap calories," Carlotta said. They'd stopped at a convenience store after lunch. Janice Diaz had forgotten all about it. She didn't remember eating the bar. But now she held an empty wrapper. She chugged water from a plastic bottle.

Carlotta was crouched beside her.

"You're stronger than you know. Come back to me."

She came back.

"You okay?"

"I don't know."

The women watched the small flame and its double in the clear wax below the wick.

"Why are you here, Carlotta?" Janice Diaz asked.

"It's where I choose to be."

"On the beach, you talked about people who camp to be free. But you never said you were one of them."

Carlotta laughed. "I'm not free. I'll never be. As long as I can see the truth."

"What is the truth?" Janice Diaz asked.

The light was dimming. The flame glowed fat and orange. "They test you," said Carlotta. "With symbols and signs. The difficulty keeps accelerating. You think you've reached your limit, then discover you can go a little further. And there is always more to learn."

She reached into her bag and handed Janice Diaz a spiral-bound notebook. Its pages were covered with tiny, careful, looping handwriting. Only here and there was a word crossed out neatly and replaced. The words were familiar, most of them, placed in sentences that seemed to be grammatical. But the sense of it all seemed to shift like the shadows of the candle on the dim page. *The following story is a formula of awakening, a template of knowing that comes with a power of natural perfection, the keys to unlock the bondage of the beast machine to recapture our lost connection with the Nephilim, children of Sirius A, who came into the orbit of Earth via the Battlestar Niberu, not only a space platform but, at times, a portal.*

Janice Diaz flipped respectfully through the densely written pages before handing the notebook back across the flame.

"I'd like to read more, when I have more light."

Carlotta nodded quickly, placed the notebook carefully inside her bag, and began pulling out supplies. "Will you be all right with just this towel?"

The floor smelled like mildew and mouse shit. Janice Diaz listened to the darkness outside the house. Insects and leaves. Tapping and knocking. Quiet voices, peaceful as a stream.

"Are we the only ones out here?"

"Oh, definitely."

"How do you know?"

"The Night Marchers keep them away."

"Ah."

Janice Diaz pushed her back into the wall. She felt the darkness press against her eyes.

Just as the dark within and the dark without were merging warmly into rest, she was startled by a buzz against her leg.

She slipped the phone from her pocket.

Team assembled, read the message. *Where R you?*

DAY 3

19

It was still dark when Nalani forced herself out of bed. She'd woken at four a.m. to find her mind still crowded with the ideas Sam had left in there. She was going to see her again that afternoon. She needed to get her head back.

Nalani stared at the quiver of boards in the corner. The last time she'd surfed Momona's awkward right-hand break, she'd been a kid. And she'd been with her mother. There had been a year or two when Maile stayed clean long enough to teach her daughter to surf. For years, Nalani had held on to the memory of the young Hawaiian woman waist-deep in the bay, pushing her into one wave after another. Eventually, she'd forced herself to forget it.

She grabbed a Terry Chung swallowtail and headed down to her car. She thought about the wave as she drove north. It reared up quickly and precisely and closed just as abruptly. The ride was fast and extremely short. If you tried to enjoy it and bailed too late, you'd take a piece of the reef back out with you.

Maile had told her generations of their ancestors had surfed this break. Maybe. But it was a terrible place to teach a kid. It was called No Mistakes.

At the security gate, the haole guard shuffled papers, spoke into his radio, stared into space. Nalani honked just long enough to be impolite. She was a Kanahele. This was still their land. The guard looked down the road, held up his palm. Then he pressed a button and motioned her ahead. She rolled forward as the gate lifted. A pair of headlights was coming up. She passed a black Suburban and watched the mirror as it swung a U-turn and trailed her down the red dirt road. The ocean rose high and silver in her windshield. A white line of cattle egrets flapped across the fields. Light rays fanned from a molten golden cloud on the horizon.

The Suburban halted at the edge of the property. She descended through the ironwood forest, parked in the sand, tugged a wetsuit over her bikini, grabbed her board from the bed. Then she stopped to watch the ocean. It was smooth and glassy, silver where it caught the sun and black where it didn't. She watched the water lap the reef edge, then looked farther. A bump on the horizon, a silver swelling, nothing major, four-foot, Hawaiian scale. But rideable. She grabbed her board in both hands, ran down the cold sand, and skimmed into the water. She still knew where to find the current that would suck her out through the gap in the reef.

Cool water slipped through the cuffs of the wetsuit. Cold, bright drops landed on her face and arms, beading the tip of her board, catching the first light. She sat up and looked back at shore as she waited for the next set: the tiny cottage, the crescent of white beach, the dark forest rising up the slopes, the bright green mountains sheltering her kulāiwi, the land of her ancestors' bones. There was no sign of the plain beyond the bluff. From this perspective, it didn't exist.

Her board rose and fell under a gentle bump. She swiveled toward the rising sun, let another swell pass, lay down, paddled out a few feet, waited, stroked over a steeper face, sat up and swiveled back toward shore. The next time the ocean opened under her, she dropped prone, the shape of the trough revealing all she needed to know about the wave. Her feet rose over her head. She grabbed one handful of water, one more, then pressed upright. For a moment, she was weightless, then she sank her heel and caught the face of the water, feeling its pressure against the rail as if the board were an extension of her own body.

She was almost on the brown reef, sparkling streams of water pouring from its cracks. Faint seaweed smell. She twisted her hips and reversed direction, climbed the wave, tipped over, bent her knees, let the board sink into the calm water on the back side. She could hold her line an extra second next time, now that she had a feel for it.

She remembered how it had felt the last time she'd surfed this wave. She took a moment, between sets, to savor how far she'd come.

After four more rides, she noticed someone else on the water with her—a man in a kayak paddling around the next point.

It was her uncle Solomon, his knees propped high on a banged-up plastic sit-on-top, a speargun poking beyond the prow. She dropped onto her board and paddled to meet him outside the breaking sets. In the hull below his knees was a pile of pale fish with thin black stripes.

"Those cannot be manini."

"Shoots. Why not?"

"I never seen 'em grow so big."

He slipped his hand carefully into the pile and picked one up by the lip.

"Noho," he said. "I been tracking 'em."

"What, all night?"

He laughed. "For weeks already. At low tide, I like walk the reefs an' look the limu. You know we get one special limu here? Anyone in Hawaii tastes our limu kohu, they know it come from this ahupua'a. Even the manini love it."

"But how did you track them?"

"I seen how the limu that side stay real short. So I know manini was there. But only da small kalaka kine stay on da reef. I had for wait one wave li'dis come drive the big noho inside."

"And you going eat all those?"

Now Solomon turned shy. "Going salt some," he said, so quietly she could barely hear him above the water lapping his hull. "Share the rest."

It had been so long since she had talked to Solomon like this. It made her sad, how eager he was when someone showed an interest in the things he loved. Nalani gripped the kayak, and the two spun slowly as they talked. Now they faced the beach and hills. The reef was hidden by the blue-green backs of the waves. She felt her uncle Solly's rough, strong grip around her fingers. He lifted her hand, gave it a squeeze, and gently pushed her away. As they parted, he met her eyes, then dipped his head. A stream of clear water fell from the blade of his paddle.

She watched the sun-dark Hawaiian skirt behind the break and slip across a keyhole in the reef. She tried to catch a few more waves, but missed one, then another, and finally gripped the point of the surfboard and rode the whitewash across the reef into shore.

20

Dalton woke in a good mood. He'd been dreading the conversation with Dhillon, and now it was over. The poison pill had been planted.

The workday had already begun in California. In the kitchen, he punched the touch screen of their Breville and waited for the hissing to stop. As he walked barefoot across the floorboards, he inhaled the bitter aroma from the tiny mug. A sensor detected his approach, and the glass door slid silently, releasing the cool, thick morning air into the room. A teak staircase led up the bluff to the office suite. Halfway, there was a small lanai with a wraparound bench. He sank down and took his first hot sip of the espresso. The ocean mirrored the orange clouds as they caught the day's first rays of light.

These moments were what it was all about.

He didn't know what would become of his company, but at least the course had been set. Now that Dhillon had been informed of Dalton's plan, he could complain all he wanted, but he couldn't crater the company's value, not without great legal and financial risk. Any attempt to sell off his shares would trigger accusations of insider trading. Dhillon had nothing to gain—financially—from a bitter, value-destroying shake-up in the board and every incentive to maintain investor confidence and frame the new strategy as favorably as possible.

And if Dhillon did fight, the short-term unpleasantness would still further Dalton's long-term plans, with a rebuilt board, a streamlined org, and renewed focus on the goals he and Erin had founded Sokoni to achieve. Finally, everyone would be rowing in the same direction. And in a few hours, he was going to give Erin the news.

The sun was up; his espresso was gone. He lingered on the bench, thinking about the meeting. He would hold it right here, keep it casual: a conversation between old friends.

Dalton's daily security stand-ups were early and intimate. Usually just himself and Hart. In Palo Alto, he held them in a secure room where the only data in or out was a dedicated fiber-optic line. Security on island was not as sophisticated yet, but the cell network was spotty and the Wi-Fi not much better, so it seemed secure enough to meet in Dalton's office: a glass cube cantilevered over the bluff.

This morning, Hart was bringing in a third party for an update on the Phoenix whistleblower. Dalton had objected when he saw it on his schedule. The issue was old news, and he had bigger security concerns. But Hart had insisted.

The first Phoenix releases had been in the headlines for weeks and led to a summons before a congressional subcommittee. Erin was the face of that. She was excellent at contrition. She'd acknowledged the company was experiencing growing pains in certain areas—securing private data, targeting ads to juveniles, banning hate speech. No one on the committee brought up the most sensational Phoenix revelation—the existence of a secret list of high-value users exempt from content moderation—until after the hearing, when multiple members asked in private to be added. After the news cycle moved on, they designated a forensics team with unlimited resources to hunt out the whistleblower. That, of course, was an HR matter, and not even under Hart's purview.

A bell chimed on the touch pad built into his desk.

For someone who'd spent a career in uniform, Hart had an uncanny ability to dress for his environment. In Washington and New York, that meant tailored suits. In California, vaguely nautical blazers over a white shirt and khakis, a subtle nod to his former life in the Navy. Here, apparently, it meant a blue polo tucked into the same khakis, mirrored aviators dangling from the placket. The man who slipped in behind Hart was wearing a blazer, maybe a suit? Something pale. Dalton didn't get a good look and immediately lost interest.

"Isn't this an issue for Erin?" he asked rudely.

Hart was unfazed. "It was reclassified under my command, at least until you tell us otherwise."

"All right." Dalton sighed.

Hart cleared his throat. "As you know, initial metadata traced the leaked materials to an outsourcing facility in Phoenix, Arizona. Forensics has been unable to narrow a time-access matrix past a pool of two thousand current and former employees. For that reason, we've switched to a focus on HUMINT." Hart paused. "Human intelligence."

"I know what it means," Dalton said.

"Of course."

"But, um, what does that mean, in this case?"

"We developed a list of targets with potential connections to the whistleblower—such as members of the news media—and put them under multi-spectrum surveillance, as well as other methods."

"Such as?"

"Best not to go into details. Suffice to say, the person we call Phoenix, and we *are* convinced it is one person, has been extremely rigorous in their security protocols. We're not sure *anyone* actually knows this individual's identity, even the intermediary or intermediaries who serve as his go-betweens to the media."

"Didn't you tell me two days ago you were close to identifying him?"

"I should mention that because of certain legal liabilities associated with these methods, we brought in a third party with specialized capabilities. I'd like to introduce you to Ariel Raz."

The second man stepped forward. Dalton tried to form an impression of him, but it was difficult. Except for possibly being a little on the short side, he was average in almost every way. Skin pale but not pasty, fit but not muscular, attractive but not handsome, blond hair, almost brown, or maybe brown hair almost blond.

"It's very good to meet you, Mr. Dalton."

He spoke with an accent. But from where? Eastern Europe?

"As Mr. Hart kindly explained, we've developed a source within Phoenix's inner circle. The operation has reached an *extremely* sensitive and dynamic moment. Although our source had a long working relationship with Phoenix, it was anonymous. He or she is very, very careful. Only in the coming days were they going to meet for the first time and initiate a new phase of their campaign."

"That's great news. When do you expect to identify the whistleblower?"

For the first time, Raz betrayed an emotion: slight discomfort. Hart seemed to edge away.

"Unfortunately, we have temporarily lost contact."

"With Phoenix?"

"With our source."

"That is unfortunate. Do you think he had second thoughts?"

"I can't speculate at this point."

"And you said Phoenix is about to *initiate a new phase*?"

"Yes," said Raz. "And we have laid the groundwork for a countermove we believe will fatally discredit their entire endeavor and neutralize any information they release."

"Do you have any idea what this information is?"

Raz shook his head. "Unfortunately, our source—"

"Sorry, another question." Dalton looked to Hart. "Why is this a *personal* security issue? Any leaked data would be organizational, yes?"

"I can explain that," said Raz, taking a slight step between Hart and Dalton, like a bodyguard shielding his client. "The last communication we had from the source was that Phoenix was planning to fly here."

"To Hawaii?"

"To this island, sir."

"Why?"

"We understand Phoenix was dissatisfied with the impact of the last release. They plan to pair their next information drop with an action that will capture media attention."

"He's coming *here* to perform an *action*?"

Hart stepped forward and Raz faded away. "I see this situation as an excellent reminder of the need to maintain the same level of security at this site as we do on the mainland. While the contents of this briefing may feel disturbing to you, from my perspective, there is nothing we don't deal with every day, in terms of perceived threats to your safety."

Dalton stared through the walls of his office at the whitecaps rushing toward them.

"Sir." There was a tiny hint of pleading in Hart's voice now. "In California alone, we track over five hundred groups and individuals who have expressed antagonism toward you or your company. This is not to minimize the situation but to put it in perspective. I wish you could travel to Hawaii and experience a carefree vacation just like everyone else. Unfortunately, that will never be your reality. There will always be threats, even in paradise. It's why you hire us."

21

Janice Diaz and Carlotta were in line for a hot shower. More precisely, Carlotta was in line. Janice Diaz was cradled in the roots of a large ficus tree, shivering uncontrollably.

This was how she'd woken an hour earlier, on the floor of the plantation house. In the night, a faceless woman had tried to stab her. They ran in circles until she couldn't run any longer and the woman had lowered her knife and exhaled a cold wind into her mouth. She'd woken screaming in the dark. But that must have been a dream, too, because she woke again in daylight to find Carlotta spreading another blanket across her shoulders.

"They're setting up the shower at the park today," Carlotta told her. "It will help you feel better, and we'll get a solid meal in you."

Janice Diaz nodded. Her hunger was a roar, hollowing what was left of her hollowed body.

They left the camp in the forest. The world slid by in a blur of glare and heat, the stink and whir of traffic. When she recalled her situation, her strength failed, and the ground rose toward her. But even her short-term memory was slipping now, and she always found herself walking again. Finally, Carlotta led her to the ficus and let her sink into the cool embrace of its roots.

The phone was buzzing in her pocket. She sank deeper into the shadow. It was cold in the bare dirt between the roots.

A shadow fell across her.

"Aloha, Miss Janice?"

A small brown woman with gray-streaked hair and wide glasses was leaning over her. "Miss Janice? It's your turn at the shower. Your friend Carlotta asked me to come help you."

"Is it safe?"

The woman smiled. "Very safe! The mobile shower is handicap accessible and cleaned between uses. No one causes any problems."

The tiny woman clenched Janice Diaz's forearm firmly between her elbow and her ribs and led her to the head of the line.

"Can you make it up the stairs, or would you like to use the ramp?"

"I'll help her," said Carlotta.

She gripped Janice Diaz's arm, led her up three steps, and opened the door.

Janice Diaz gripped Carlotta's wrist. "Come with me."

Carlotta glanced down at the attendant, then escorted Janice inside.

"Help me undress."

The room glowed green from the sunlight shining through the plastic roof. Water pooled on the floor. She felt Carlotta's hands at her waist. When she felt her shirt coming up over her head, she raised her arms.

"Lean forward."

Carlotta's fingers were on her back. Her bra slid off her shoulders. Her breasts sagged. How long had it been since she'd taken off her underwear?

"Can you do your own buttons?"

She leaned back against the warm plastic wall of the trailer.

"We've only got ten minutes, honey. You need help with your jeans?"

She reached down and felt for the button and the short zipper.

"Now stand up and slide them down."

Janice Diaz stepped out of her jeans and panties. She looked down at the body below her.

"Your phone rang," said Carlotta. "Want me to check it for you?"

Janice Diaz nodded.

Carlotta lifted the jeans, removed the phone, and set them on the bench. "More messages. Should I read them? Girl, you're shivering! Go start the water."

Janice Diaz looked up from her body and stepped across the room. She turned the handle. The water was hot. She felt it trickling through her hair, then pulsing against her scalp. The scratches on her arms and legs burned. She lifted her hands and ran her fingers against her skull, separating the greasy strands so the warm water sluiced through.

"Oh my god," she said.

Carlotta laughed. "I told you it would be worth it."

"What do they say, the messages?"

"Well, someone called *P*, the letter P, says, *Head Count,* and your friend Alpha says, *4 of us here.* P guy says, *Any word from Agile?* Alpha says, *No.* P says, *Are you secure?* Alpha says, *Yes.* P says, *No sign of a breach?* Alpha says, *Affirmative. No concerns.* Twenty minutes later, P says, *Can you proceed with 4?* Alpha says, *Yes.* And P just wrote, *Stand by.*"

Janice Diaz pulled her hair aside so the water could jet directly onto her neck.

"What are you mixed up in?" Carlotta asked.

There was a pump bottle of body wash mounted to the wall. It foamed as she rubbed it across her chest and stomach. It wasn't just the feel of the hot water on her skin, the knowledge that it was rinsing away the salt and sand and mud, the beer stink from the empty bottles, the sticky sugar from their cheap snacks. For the first time, Janice Diaz felt like an ordinary person.

Carlotta was still staring at the phone. "Someone is missing," she said. "And everyone's got code names. They haven't heard from someone called Agile. Is that you? Are you Agile?"

Janice Diaz stood under the showerhead, circles of foam smeared across her belly and thighs. The water had stopped. She hadn't noticed. The woman with the knife, chasing her around the old plantation house. The black-haired woman dancing in the club. She had a face.

There was a quiet knock against the plastic.

"Someone tried to kill me," Janice Diaz told Carlotta.

22

Samantha met Nalani at an Asian fusion restaurant. Nalani ordered the special, which turned out to be a cube of barely seared ahi, four spoonfuls of rice pilaf, and a dozen spinach greens drizzled with a Z of purple dressing.

"What do you think?" Samantha asked eagerly.

"The dressing is delicious," Nalani told her.

Samantha grinned. "House made. It's the reason I come here."

Nalani had wondered what a forty-eight-dollar plate of ahi tasted like; now she knew: almost as good as the trays of sashimi her cousins made whenever they had a successful catch.

They drove north in Samantha's pearl-gray Range Rover. A bucket of waxy white tuberoses filled the vehicle with their fragrance.

"I drive the Tesla whenever I can, of course," Samantha said, apologetically, as if this topic had been hanging awkwardly between them. "But so many of my clients are taller than you would expect, and not even just the athletes. Some of them haven't ridden in a sedan in years."

Nalani watched the familiar buildings on the edge of town go past. Then the clinic on the hill, the firehouse, the Catholic cemetery. She had the uncanny feeling of seeing her hometown from a remove, as if the Realtor's SUV was a submersible descending to the depths of an environment whose atmosphere would crush her if she got out.

"This is so much fun," said Samantha.

Abandoned cars, red dirt, guinea grass, dense thickets of koa haole.

"I think you're going to love this house. They're selling as is, and the décor is so authentic. And the view of Hanalei from the infinity pool is priceless."

Nalani nodded.

"They're asking nine million, but I think we can offer eight point three."

"So not priceless, exactly."

Samantha glanced at her with a flirtatious smile. "Everything has a price."

"You said the client was some kind of celebrity?"

"Oh, I forgot to tell you! You know Dwayne Johnson?"

"The Rock? Oh my god."

"This client funded *five* of his pictures."

"That's amazing."

"He's got such a lovely place in Malibu."

"I bet."

"He's the nicest man. He really feels a connection to this community."

They had passed the turn for Momona. Kilauea Town was coming up. And Namahana. Nalani tried to remember the last time she'd traveled this far north.

"How did you become a Realtor, Sam?"

"My father was in commercial real estate, and a developer, too. Nothing major, just some shopping malls, when those were exciting. He built the first indoor mall in Chula Vista."

"So you learned from him?"

"He thinks I did! But residential is so much different. At least it used to be. Now you spend more time talking to accountants than to clients." For the first time, Samantha sounded a note other than pure, bubbly joy for life. "Don't get me wrong," she said, brightening up. "We still get clients who fall in love with a place and won't take no for an answer. But it isn't always about the view these days. Modern buyers are very interested in sustainability. Like Franky."

"Aren't there places in California for them to sustain?"

They were passing the familiar mountain, its sweeping green shoulders bright and close in the midday sun.

"Funny," said Samantha. "You know you're right. There are. Or at least there used to be. So many scenic areas are burning now. And I think his generation is looking for a new challenge. It was their fathers who made their names with the Sierra Club and whatnot. Some of them are going out west, which is east for us, of course. Teton County is *very* popular. The conservation easements are hard to compete with. Preserve nature *and* cut your taxes? The funny thing is that for us, the isolation used to be an impediment to selling second homes. People just didn't see themselves making that flight when they could go to La Paz or Puerta Vallarta. Now distance is a selling point."

"How do you mean?"

"So many of our clients are looking for a place to go if the worst happens."

"The worst?"

"You know, climate, nuclear, pandemic, of course. Our clients like to know they can get away from all that."

"You do know all our food comes on ships."

"People lived here for thousands of years in harmony with nature. We can do it again!" Samantha said these words with a well-practiced snap of optimistic certainty. They were turning into Princeville's ornate gateway. Neptune gleamed atop the Italian fountain at the center of the traffic circle.

Nalani didn't want to be impressed by the infinity pool.

She'd wandered outside while Sam led the client and his team through the house. But the granite expanse of the lanai, the twelve-person dining table under a redwood pergola, the hot tub pouring a smooth sheet of water into the heated pool, its edge precisely engineered to disappear without interruption into the blue of Hanalei Bay: the effect overwhelmed all resistance, just as it had been designed. It was a space so exquisitely arranged for entertaining, it gave Nalani the uplifting buzz of being at a party even though she was alone. She couldn't help but feel that as long as she inhabited this space, life was truly good.

When they arrived, she'd helped Sam arrange bouquets of tuberoses in key regions of the house. The client—an extremely good-looking haole with tousled gray hair and a neatly trimmed goatee, the white hairs gleaming against his deeply tanned skin—arrived with a small entourage of women in business casual. Sam introduced Nalani as "my associate, Nalani Kanahele Winthrop," and for half an hour, she'd smiled obligingly as Sam showed off handmade ki'i masks, inlaid canoe paddles, oversize prints of Duke Kahanamoku surfing at Waikiki and a Hawaiian family standing picturesquely by their thatched hale, and what looked to be an authentic hand-carved fishing canoe suspended from the ceiling of the great hall.

"All Hawaiiana comes with the house," Samantha explained. "This is a one-of-a-kind opportunity to purchase a property that embodies the spirit of the 'āina. I understand you've come to feel a powerful connection with this culture. We have a term for that here: *Hawaiian at heart.*"

The producer stared up at the canoe, grinning possessively, his hands deep in the pockets of his loose slacks. This was when Nalani slipped away.

Sam found her half an hour later.

"How did it go?" Nalani asked.

"Hard to say. I'm showing three more properties tomorrow. None as nice as this, but in communities that are a bit more exclusive."

"It must be nice," said Nalani.

"These people are miserable!" Sam laughed. "Most of them." She covered her mouth. "Just a minute." She disappeared into the house and came back with two wineglasses and a bottle. She set them on the table and gestured for Nalani to join her. "This is a *great* sauvignon blanc, from my favorite place in Napa."

She filled the glasses with two generous pours and raised hers to Nalani. "So, did you enjoy it?"

"Some of it."

"I can tell, you're a natural in sales. What is it you do now, for work?"

"Help out at my friend's boutique."

Sam smiled. "Sales. See? I knew it."

The wine was good. The sun was setting over the water. White crescents were sweeping over the reef. "The thing is," said Sam, "you don't want to be these people. Trust me. You don't. You just want to be near them. I mean, professionally. I don't want to be crude, but they shed money like our Lab sheds hair. This client, this producer, he's going to buy this week. Eight million. Nine, maybe. When he does, I make three percent. I know you can do the math on that!" Sam laughed. It was the first time she'd come close to referencing their last conversation.

"Why are you telling me this?" Nalani asked.

Sam reached for the bottle and poured the rest of the wine. She leaned back and looked at Nalani over the edge of her glass. "You impressed me. And I like you. I'm at a phase of life where you start thinking about your legacy. Not to mention a vacation in Cap d'Antibes now and then! I'd like to take you on as a mentee, and, eventually, a partner. Maybe I'm overstepping. But I can read people, and something told me: it's been a long time since anyone offered you much help."

The last thing Nalani had expected from that afternoon was to watch the last red shimmer of the sun disappear into an infinity pool through a prism of ugly, uncontrollable tears.

23

Dalton and Erin didn't see each other as often as they had in the first crazy years of building the company. She spent most of her time in the New York office and owned a place in Malibu. It was obvious she avoided Menlo as much as possible.

Dalton thought she preferred LA to the Bay because meritocracies didn't suit her. Silicon Valley was the only place where intelligence and charisma weren't enough to elevate a beautiful woman to the pedestal of attention and deference she was used to receiving. Though he *could* admit some of her resentment was justified. No matter what she contributed to Sokoni, in the Valley, she would never be a founder. And for a simple reason: she didn't code.

Of course, the fact that he owned 51 percent of the company played a role in that perception, too. When the time had come to divvy up control, Dalton had held the leverage, and he'd used it just as his lawyers had advised.

The truth was: she wasn't avoiding Silicon Valley. She was avoiding him.

Not that she would ever admit it. Even if the breakup had been his idea, he'd always felt she'd gotten what she'd wanted (as usual) without having to ask for it. Or take responsibility. So why had he done it? The eternal question. It had always seemed just a little impossible that *she* could be in love with *him*. He'd felt it then and felt it even more now. Sometimes he suspected she'd simply seen his potential before he had. She'd groomed him for everything that followed. If true, did it mean she got less than she deserved, or more? Had she made him what he was, or ridden his coattails?

These were the types of problems people like her created. You couldn't be around them without getting sucked in. Sometimes he blamed her for it; sometimes he saw her as a victim, too. But he always resented it.

So, the uncertainty on her face when she showed up on his deck gave him pleasure. In Kenya, she'd worn loose shirts and pants or travel dresses designed to be washed in a hotel sink. Practical Chaco sandals on her mud-stained feet. Today, she wore a flower-print power suit. She was more beautiful than ever, that was objectively true. Just as tan. Fifteen pounds lighter. She removed her pink-mirrored aviators, banished the uncertainty from her features, and gave him her typical, cool smile.

"Can you still enjoy this view, or is it like the showers?"

"I enjoy watching other people enjoy the view."

She stuck her hands into the hidden pockets in her slacks, thrust her hips at a jaunty angle, and let him enjoy her enjoying the view.

What was in his heart right now?

She unfolded her aviators and slipped them back over her eyes. "Is this where you fire me?"

He stared at his warped reflection in the pink lenses.

"Actually, this is where I agree with you."

She pursed her lips, almost imperceptibly. Her hands were still in her pockets.

She couldn't even give him this.

He filled the silence. "You were right."

Now, she was smiling. He'd made her happy. And she was generous enough to let him see it.

"What changed your mind? If you don't mind my asking."

"Did I ever tell you what I did with my cell phone in my first months at site, before we met?"

She tilted her head. "I don't think so."

"I used to go for those long walks. You know. Twice a day."

She smiled. "I remember you almost got me trampled by a herd of zebras."

"They were just startled. Anyway, I always took my phone, at first, in case my parents called." He hadn't planned to tell this story. He kept his gaze on the ocean. "But I stopped."

"Why?"

"Because I couldn't keep walking back to an empty house, and if I left my phone, there was a chance a message might be waiting when I came in. Was that crazy?"

She shook her head.

"That's why we created this company, right? So no one has to feel that alone?"

She was nodding. They still understood each other. So what if this had been her idea? She'd given it to him because he could type the words and symbols that would make it exist. "I want to get back there," he said. "Get back to that vision."

"Is it even possible?"

"Once I convince Dhillon, anything is possible."

"What can I do?"

"Work your magic on the rest of the board."

She gave him that smile again, the real one. He stood.

In public, they had no trouble hugging hello or goodbye, exchanging pecks on the cheek. But in private, their whole history tumbled out into the empty space between them. They would grin, acknowledge it, and separate without touching, a moment of pure awkwardness that was the closest thing they had to intimacy.

"I'll never forget," he said, "the first time I found my phone blinking with a message from you."

24

Carlotta left Janice Diaz at a folding table with a plate of food while she checked in with some acquaintances. Someone tapped her on the shoulder: a jittery young Hawaiian with wired red eyes, dressed in a pair of torn board shirts and tan leather work boots.

"Aunty," he said, "sorry for interrupt, but you stay friends with that haole lady?"

Carlotta turned to the table where she'd left her, but Janice Diaz was gone. The Hawaiian shifted his eyes, and Carlotta saw her speaking urgently with some other young men. Men who were trouble.

"What do those men want?"

"They sent me for tell you she been asking for something. She not even sure what it is she like. But she trying offer pilau kine things for it."

"Mahalo," said Carlotta.

"Shoots, Aunty. I just thought maybe you like know."

When Carlotta arrived, the men looked at her with relief.

"Janice," she hissed, grabbing the other woman's arm and steering her away. "You must be feeling better."

"I'm dying," said Janice Diaz. "Tell me what I need. Is it meth? What do they call that? Those men were looking at me like I'm speaking a foreign language."

"They understood you, all right. We're getting you out of here."

Janice Diaz yanked her arm back. "Whatever I was taking, I need it."

She held up her hands. They were shaking. Then she sank onto the ground.

Carlotta waited to make sure she wasn't faking, then said, "I'm going to find us some bus fare."

In the warmth and sway of the bus, the softness of her seat, it was hard for Janice to remember the desperation she'd felt half an hour earlier. She was about to ask Carlotta if they could ride all the way to the end of the line, when she saw her reaching for the cable.

The bus turned off the highway and left them standing by a mowed field. It was the height of afternoon. The field was bright and dry.

"Come on, then," said Carlotta irritably. "We aren't there yet."

"I don't know if I can."

"You had the energy to pimp yourself out for ice. You can walk a little."

"It was only a negotiating tactic."

Carlotta slung her bag over her shoulder and stepped onto the grass expanse.

She smelled the ocean and, a minute later, heard it. They passed a gate protecting a row of two-story condominiums with ocean views. Carlotta turned in the opposite direction, where the road swung parallel to a narrow beach. The wind drove the waves across a shallow brown reef that came right up to the edge of the sand. She saw tents set up in the sand, with tarps to block the wind and spray. There was a public bathroom surrounded by a broad mowed lawn. The lawn was covered with tents. Most looked like they had been there a long time.

"You stay close," said Carlotta.

They wandered up an alley between the tents. She caught glimpses of battered pots, paperback books, sleeping bags, inflatable mattresses.

"Where is everybody?"

Carlotta gave her a look. "It's a weekday. They're at work."

They reached the end of the row. Ahead was a picnic table in the shade of an ironwood. The table was stacked with papers. A woman with a pair of reading glasses on her nose was peering intently at a notebook.

"Hey, Leilani!"

"Sister Carlotta. How you stay?"

Leilani raised herself from the chair, and the two women embraced.

"This is my acquaintance, Janice. She's new to the island."

"Good to meet you, Sister Janice. Call me Aunty Lei. You need one tent, we get 'em over there. Plenty kine stuff people drop for us. Soap? Shampoo? Tampax?"

Janice Diaz smiled politely.

"You going like this place," said Aunty Lei. "What you do in your hale is your business. We only ask you keep your space clean and no make no pilikia for anyone else."

"She won't be staying," said Carlotta. "Not yet."

She and Leilani exchanged a look. Lei took Janice's arm. "Hele over there to the shop. Take whatever you need. I going talk a little story with Sister Carlotta."

Janice Diaz walked where she'd been told, to an area covered by a broad tarp. Inside were plastic tubs of hotel soaps and shampoo. Deodorant. Tampons. Baby wipes and diapers. Cans of fruit and beans. Granola bars. Cookies. Jars of peanut butter. Blankets and towels. Janice Diaz started crying.

A few minutes later, Carlotta found her holding a small bar of soap and two granola bars.

"You been here three days," she said, "and you still don't understand."

She pulled a reusable shopping bag from a pile and filled it with toiletries and food, neatly folded underwear, a clean pair of jeans, and a T-shirt. She jammed a towel and a blanket on top and handed it to Janice Diaz.

"You are who all this is for."

They walked back up the road, through the field, and down a concrete sidewalk by the beach. The wind pressed their clothing tight against their bodies. It was getting cold. Janice did not feel right but wasn't sure what right was supposed to feel like. She'd grown used to the present moment she'd inhabited since waking on the plane, building a new history minute by minute. Now a memory existed: the other woman, a face, discrete moments that elided together confusingly—her thigh pressed tight in a crowd that smelled like vaping and sex. A sleeping body curled tight on a sheetless mattress. Was this how it would be? Her life coming back ten seconds at a time? Were these memories even real?

The path ended at a wide bay. Waterlogged tree trunks lay piled on smooth black rocks. Sticks churned in the eddies where a fast brown current met the green ocean. A river flowed under a bridge. Traffic passed loudly overhead. They climbed an embankment and crossed the bridge. Janice Diaz followed Carlotta down to the beach on the other side. A hut made of branches leaned against one concrete pillar. Somewhere, a bonfire was burning.

On the banks of the red, muddy river, six long canoes lay in the sand.

Carlotta led her up a quiet street that ended at a chain-link fence. Three black-and-orange signs read *Private Property: No Trespassing.* Nailed to a tree, a painted board read *Kapu Aloha: Property of the Hawaiian Kingdom.*

After just a few dozen yards, the fence ended in a forest of coco palms and shoulder-high grass. A gust rolled across the grass and sent the tall palms swinging. Dull impacts sounded around them. *Thunk thunk thunk.*

"Eyes up." Carlotta pointed at the clusters of dry yellow coconuts. The women pushed through the rustling blades until Carlotta parted a curtain of grass and disappeared into a burst of light. Janice Diaz found her beside a pond rimmed with cut volcanic rock. The concrete skeleton of a gutted building carved trees and sky into blue and green cubes.

"Is that where we're going?"

Carlotta shrugged. "Lei said they'll tell us where to go."

The water in the pond was emerald with algae.

They followed a concrete path. The air rose thick and hot. All they heard was the hum and chirp of insects. Then a sound. *Chockchockchock.* A blade or an axe.

They stepped into a blackened field. The ash left faint black marks on Carlotta's strong, bare calves. Raised rock beds were scattered on the blackened ground. Broad-leaf plants sagged in the heat. Under a shelter of thatched fronds, two men squatted. Both were brown and shirtless. Both had long black hair. One struck a machete quickly and precisely against something on the ground.

"Excuse me," said Carlotta. The men looked up, startled, then rose stiffly.

"I'm Carlotta and this is Janice. We're friends of Aunty Lei."

The man with the machete nodded. The other smiled.

"We heard you was coming. You like coco water?"

The ground was covered with green coconuts. Hazy liquid nearly filled a five-gallon bucket.

"Yes, please," said Carlotta. "But we need to find some shade. This one's not feeling well."

"I show you where you can rest."

He led them to a canal that separated the ruins from the fields. "Wailua fishpond," he said as they crossed a bridge over the dark water. "Had stay here long before they ever get one hotel. Going be here long after we all gone."

They passed under a carved wooden arch into a room walled in stone and mildewed wood. The man turned down a side passage, then up a flight of stairs.

"We reserved one suite for you. Ocean view."

Janice Diaz was falling behind. "We're almost there," Carlotta told her.

"The air more fresh up here," the man called down.

They were on the fourth floor, which was literally a floor, with here and there a concrete wall or column. One side framed a view of steep green ridges, the other, palm crowns and turquoise waves. The wind across the damp concrete raised a chill. Carlotta waited for Janice at the top of the stairs, wrapped a towel around her shoulders, and helped her across the long floor to where the man stood by a wall creating shelter from the wind.

"You can build one fire." He pointed to a stack of cut wood. "The wind takes the smoke." A few blackened pots were lined up neatly beside two jugs of water, purplish paste in a clear plastic bag, a hand of short bananas. "Sorry just poi and banana. All we had when Aunty Lei called. We going pull crab traps later. You like us bring you some?"

"Thank you," said Carlotta. "This is all we need."

"Shoots, Aunty. Oh, here come Ka'ili."

The other man balanced a green coconut in each hand, pale coir showing where he'd chopped their tops. He smiled as he set them carefully against a wall. "Anything you need, just find us. Someone always around."

Janice Diaz pressed her body against the bare concrete. She was shivering badly. The drain wanted everything now. She felt something bristly at her lips, sweet liquid on her tongue.

"Drink it all," said Carlotta.

The water trickled into her mouth and down her chin. Carlotta held it to her lips for a long time.

25

The dark outside the cube was total. The only light came from his screen. Dalton had spent two hours on the phone with Dhillon. Both had lawyers listening in. It had not been pleasant. Or productive. He was exhausted, and the real work hadn't even begun.

The twins must be asleep by now. Madeleine had texted him a few updates. *Bath. Story.* He'd asked her to do this whenever he was working late. Sometimes it worked.

He'd always been capable of disappearing into projects. When he was eleven, he'd read *The Lord of the Rings* and *The Silmarillion* in one glorious week. Ten years later, in his first months in the Kenyan town where he would spend the next two years, when unexpected loneliness had crushed him flat and almost broken him in ways he still didn't like to think about, he'd survived the days by reading for hours at a stretch, only the sunlight moving in the bare rooms, until it was time to take his long evening walk on the bone-white savanna.

Erin denied it, but he knew she'd been put off by his ability to concentrate so thoroughly, even though her own self-containment was arguably more powerful. Madeleine accepted him. Maybe because they'd met in a more mature phase of life, their late twenties, after the IPO. It didn't hurt that she framed her requests for attention as opportunities to work on his mindfulness practice. The Dalai Lama had told him the same thing.

It was only after the twins arrived that family time became something he genuinely craved. The hours he spent with them felt like the most important of every day. They shone when everything else seemed gray. So why was he still in his office, scrolling the internal network? He glanced into the darkness and saw his own pale reflection staring back at him.

While he'd been indulging in other priorities, his company had become something he barely recognized.

· · ·

Madeleine had unpicked her braids. Her brown curls fanned her pillow in a messy Afro. It always felt intimate to see her this way. He thought she looked her best the less she did to herself. She said that was only because it reminded him of sex.

They'd met at a promotional shoot. She was one of the models. It wasn't until their second date that he learned she was in Berkeley to get her PhD. At parties, she always joked he'd married her despite that revelation. "Un mec de base."

She paused whatever she'd been watching and looked up.

He crawled on top of their handmade quilt. They kissed.

"How was work?"

"Fine," he said. "Most of it was meetings."

"Et Dhillon?"

He shook his head. "Still working on him."

"But Erin, elle était heureux?"

"I think she was in disbelief."

Madeleine laughed. "I'm sure you were . . . *maladroit* in your presentation. I'll get the story from *her,* next time I see her. Is she coming to the hospital tomorrow?"

"They want to keep the focus on our family. Make it personal."

He hoisted himself off the bed. Madeleine was convinced he was still in love with Erin. Fortunately, she was from a francophone culture. She expected everyone to be in love with someone else. "I'm going to check on the boys."

Both were in Marc's bed that night. Lionel was on his knees with his butt in the air, his face pressed to the mattress, pursed lips pushed to one side. Marc slept on his back, right arm pointing straight out toward his brother. Their pudgy fingers interlaced. It still amazed him that a glimpse of his sons' fingers could stir more epic feelings than all of Tolkien.

Dalton brushed his teeth and took his pills. Madeleine didn't pause the TV when he slipped under the covers. On-screen, one of their Telluride friends was driving a garbage truck at high speed through rush-hour traffic as robots the size of high-rise buildings deployed beams of light to vaporize more timid drivers.

"Can we watch something else?"

"It has a happy ending."

"Not for that guy. Or her. Or them."

"He saves his kids and his dog."

"Against all odds."

She pressed a button and the screen went blank.

"You don't like watching an apocalypse you haven't prepared for?"

"I'm more worried aliens *don't* exist."

"You think they'll come and save us?"

"If there's really no advanced life in the rest of the universe, the math suggests that any civilization that reaches a certain technological capacity will inevitably destroy itself."

"Maybe an escape pod will crash-land in the ocean and a family will climb out and tell everyone they were the richest beings on their home planet. Would that cheer you up?"

"A little, yes."

"Bien. Beaux rêves." Madeleine gave him a peck on the lips.

Dalton lay back on his pillow. He struggled to believe anyone with children, especially anyone with *his* children, could watch anything in which a kid was endangered or the continued existence of humanity cast into doubt. No one ever identified with the countless workers in the collapsing buildings or thousands of rush hour drivers trapped in flaming cars. They never questioned whether *their* dog would survive. Their brains just didn't go there. As if helplessness was a form of happiness, an irony of human nature Dalton no longer found amusing.

He was all too aware of the random chance that had given them a good life. If they'd been born in medieval times, he and Madeleine would have lost one or both boys by now. If they'd lived in 1840s Ireland, 1930s Ukraine, North Korea, or northern Kenya, they could have literally starved to death. And this thought experiment didn't even consider that Madeleine and the boys were Black. What if they'd been Polish Jews, hiding in a woodshed, and if Marc had started crying? Would Madeleine have smothered him, or let them all be discovered by the Gestapo and marched to a pit in the forest?

These were Dalton's thoughts at night. And what if the boys did survive and thrive, as the odds were good they would? What would happen to his happy young men when the ocean acidified and the bottom of the food chain floated up from the depths?

He envied ordinary people. If the worst actually happened, they would wish they'd stockpiled a few months' worth of food or learned to make a rabbit snare. But until then, they got to live with the knowledge that they had done—more or less—all they could. Unlike him.

If he failed to protect his family, he had no excuse.

And he was failing. The security of the entire project was at risk from one family of stubborn locals. Someone with a grudge against his company had actually come to this island. And the people paid to protect them had no idea who he was or where he was hiding.

He found himself reaching for his phone. His fingers tapped the app open and began scrolling his commons. Madeleine already had her phone propped sideways on her pillow. The two screens bathed the bedroom in a soft blue glow.

26

Janice Diaz was in a small apartment. She knew it intimately. Every object. A kitchen and a living room divided by a partition with just enough space to fit a tiny table on one side of the wall and a tiny fridge on the other. Framed concert posters from obscure clubs. Small items placed carefully on floating shelves. Two pans hanging against the kitchen tiles. A teapot on a two-burner stove. She knew exactly where each thing belonged, which made her proud, as if someone might give her an award. Was this how she was: a perfectionist? If so, she was a long way from being herself.

She was walking through the apartment. Afraid. The type of fear you felt in a dream. A foreboding that emanated from the matrix of the place itself. But this fear had a source. Someone else was in the apartment. And there was nowhere to go except in a circle from the living room to the kitchen to the living room to the kitchen. Around and around. As she went, she took the things so carefully placed on the shelves and flung them behind her.

She was tangled in something. She opened her eyes. The orange glow of a fire. Carlotta beside it. Damp blankets twisted tight around her legs. She took a deep breath, coughed hard. Woodsmoke. The drain had closed, just a dull ache marking where it would reopen.

"How are you feeling?" Carlotta asked when she sat up.

Janice Diaz didn't answer. She shrugged off all but the innermost blanket and crawled closer to the fire. She watched the wind lift the smoke into the darkness. "I had a memory," she said. "I mean, a dream. But it was real. I was in an apartment. My apartment, I guess. It was nice. It made me happy."

"You had a home. What do you remember about it?"

"It was small. Everything was . . . selected. Carefully. Like, the person didn't have much space, so everything mattered. There was a teapot. And little cups for tea. And a record player and a box of LPs."

"It was an apartment for a single person."

"Yes. Definitely."

"No husband looking for you."

"I guess not."

"Probably for the best."

"But someone attacked me. I had to throw my things at her."

"Her?"

"It was a woman. I think, I know, I knew her. I can see her face, looking at me with so much love. But she wanted to kill me. It was like someone crazy was chasing me."

"Love will do that."

"I was trapped in that tiny apartment. I couldn't find my way out."

"How did you escape?"

"I didn't."

They stared into the fire.

"So, we know you were attacked," said Carlotta. "And we know you were an addict. And from those messages on your phone, it seems like you were part of some kind of team. Unless that's not really your phone."

Janice Diaz slipped the phone from her pocket and stared into its black surface.

"You had a nice place. You weren't living on the streets. So maybe you weren't just buying. Maybe you were selling. Or you were involved some-how."

"Involved how?"

"I've only seen it on TV. The ladies who swallow those bags. Condoms, I suppose. Mules."

Janice Diaz looked down at her body. The idea that something foreign could be inside, something that belonged to someone else, was unbearable.

"Relax." Carlotta laughed. "They'd have found it in the hospital. One way or the other. You weren't a mule. But you were part of something. And you couldn't have been in too deep. If your apartment was as small as all that."

The two women fell silent.

Carlotta set two larger sticks into the embers. In a few minutes, the fire blazed again. The light played across the stained concrete. The ocean sounded far away.

"Sinatra," said Carlotta, looking across the long black space. "Elvis. Now us."

A gust funneled through the concrete; the flames went sideways, disap-peared, then reemerged, one by one, from the underside of the log, dancing small and blue. Not enough to cast a light. Darkness filled the floor of the ruined hotel.

A small light glowed beneath Janice Diaz's blanket. A message.

Tomorrow, it said. *10 a.m. Lihue Hospital.*

DAY 4

27

Dalton's heart rate was rising along with his rage, which extended to every-one involved in the unfolding crisis. He wasn't used to feeling this way and was slightly freaked out by the thrill of allowing it to build beyond his con-trol. Not that he was *allowing* it. He had no choice. The emotional reserves that usually absorbed his dark feelings had been drained to zero.

But he couldn't scream at the boys. They were only toddlers. It was nat-ural for Lionel to go dashing through the house in just his shirt and Marc to writhe and thrash as Dalton wrestled with the tabs of his diaper. And he couldn't snap at Pilar; she was their employee.

"Are you going to help us here or not?" he hissed at Madeleine.

She appeared from the kitchen, holding two tubes of organic puffs. "Quoi?"

"I said, can you please help us get these boys dressed!"

Lionel raced past them, now completely naked and on the wrong side of the glass.

"Goddamn it, who left the door open?" Even as he said it, he knew he had.

"The boys can't travel without their snacks, either!" Madeleine reminded him as she plucked the squirming Marc from his grasp and raised him so his legs swung helplessly and Dalton could finally wrestle on the diaper. He opened the pair of pants Pilar had laid out, and Madeleine dropped the boy into them.

He was yanking the collar over Marc's enormous head when his earbud chimed. He ignored it, trying to force his son's elbow through the sleeve without hyperextending his arm. Pilar emerged with a tearful, naked Lio-nel propped on her shoulder. The earpiece chimed again.

He stood, held up a hand as if calling time-out, and ignored Madeleine's exasperated look as he let himself onto the lanai.

"I'm on the way out the door to our charity thing," he said.

"You haven't been checking your email?" Dhillon asked.

He pulled his phone from his pocket. Fifteen notifications and a news flash. *Sokoni whistleblower out with new allegations. Social media giant accused of abetting genocide in Indonesia.* From the other side of the glass, Dalton witnessed a tableau pulled straight from a Renaissance painting of a scene from Greek myth: his wife restraining each son with one arm while Pilar, on her knees, forced a shoe on a bare foot. It was obviously allegorical, though he couldn't imagine what the meaning would be.

"There are documents," Dhillon was saying. "We need to talk about what this is going to mean in Washington."

"How soon can we get everyone together?"

"On my boat in an hour. People are arriving already."

"For your party? You know I can't make that. I have this thing at the hospital. It's our big—"

"You're the CEO, and this is a crisis. You can't put personal stuff—"

"Okay. I'll talk to Maddy and tell them to prep the helicopter."

"Sorry, no helipad, remember? It's just a rental. I'll send the tender."

Madeleine was staring at him through the glass.

"Have your guys arrange it with mine. I gotta go."

Three identical black Suburbans were lined up on the gravel.

"I'm sorry," he told Madeleine. "This is very serious. We're being accused—"

"You are accused tout le temps. Aujourd'hui nous . . . Today we have something very important to our family. You were the one who—"

"I know. But things are in an extremely delicate place. We have to get ahead of this. And if I appear, all the questions will be about these accusations. The whole point of what we're doing—making the biggest charitable donation this island has ever seen—no one will even remember. You need to go. Bring the boys. You're more popular than I am, anyway. People love you."

Madeleine had her own phone out. Two members of the security team were helping Pilar buckle the boys into their seats. "C'est vrai? You have four content moderators in a country with six hundred different languages?"

"I don't know," said Dalton. "I haven't read the article yet."

"Can't we just cancel?"

"That will look worse. We want people to see who we really are: ordinary people trying to do their part to help the island. We can't have them think a scandal with my company will change that. You were going to do most of the talking, anyway. Just show off the boys, give your remarks, and smile."

Madeleine was about to say something else when a driver edged into their presence. "Mr. Dalton?"

"Yes?" He realized he sounded more impatient than he wanted to.

"Your plans have changed?"

"I'll be traveling north, to get on Mr. Dhillon's boat. My family is still going to the event at the hospital."

"Understood, sir. We just need to reassign the vehicles. It will only take a minute."

"The boys are already buckled in," Madeleine interjected.

The driver took in her expression, nodded, and stepped aside to speak into his earpiece. "We've got the pride loaded and Nala is ready to go. Can we send Simba with . . . okay . . . okay . . . ten-four." He turned back to them. "Sorry for the wait. We don't usually like to send these without the motorcade. But we've cleared it to go to the hospital. We'll just squeeze someone in the rear, if you don't mind. Mr. Dalton, please take the second vehicle there, and we'll have your number-three escort up momentarily."

"*Thank* you," said Madeleine, glaring at Dalton as if security protocols were something he'd invented. She pecked him on the cheek and climbed into the back seat, between the boys.

Dalton looked down the road toward the motor pool. No sign of the third vehicle. He dashed over and opened a door. Lionel yelled, "Daddy!" and reached for him. Madeleine looked surprised. "You'll do great," he said.

Madeleine finally smiled. "You remembered to tell them no giant check?"

"No check. Nothing like that. Just a banner with the name of our foundation."

He heard the grumble of tires on gravel, kissed Lionel on the forehead, and shut the door.

28

Nalani had never been on a boat like this. She was used to friends' fishing boats, with a cabin barely big enough to keep their bags dry, a Bimini capable of shading one or two people, and a cooler that smelled like fish guts. She couldn't help running her hand over the perfectly polished teak. Besides Sam, there were about a dozen other people on the long benches of the launch. A few were families. Kids who looked as excited as she was. Teenagers less impressed. Some of the youngest women might be her own age. Most were older. Most were white. A few were Black or Asian. None sounded local, except for the crew members in their blue polos.

The women chatted across the heads of their children, ignoring the boat as it skipped across the flat water of Hanalei Bay. The men had managed to extricate themselves from childcare and were standing by the open hatch at the back, surveying the launch, the yacht ahead, and the entire landscape of beaches and mountains with apathetic entitlement.

There was one exception. A man balanced on the highest step, clinging to a chrome rail and talking eagerly with a crew member squatting at the stern. He was tall, skinny, and pale, but his unruly brown hair was cropped into a decent haircut. Maybe if she'd seen him anywhere else, she'd have paid no attention, but in present company, his unguarded enthusiasm could pass for charisma. She wanted to protect him from all these California people with their perfectly calibrated boredom.

She felt the boat throttle down and looked through the porthole at the yacht. Everyone on the North Shore had been talking about it. Here, from the water, its bulk simply obliterated any sense of proportion, like standing at the base of a hill. The launch puttered around to the stern, where a small dock floated. Samantha beckoned her aboard.

Within minutes of reaching the main deck, Nalani had a bright cocktail in one hand as Sam dragged her along by the other. It was the middle of the morning, but the guests seemed to have been partying for hours. They sprawled across leather sectionals and pressed shoulder to shoulder at what appeared to be a craps table. When they left the cabin, she heard screams and splashing. She rushed to the railing to see a two-story inflatable slide with a bouncy island off the starboard side.

"I was wondering what happened to the kids," she said to Sam.

"We can go down later if you like. Did you bring a suit?"

On the next level, Samantha found her producer hemmed in by an entourage of the most beautiful people Nalani had ever seen in one place. Though, it wasn't that they were beautiful, exactly. To her, no one could be more beautiful than Aunty Haunani with her long silver hair. These people were the kind of beautiful you saw on TV or in the backs of magazines. The angles of their cheeks, noses, chins, and shoulders were so perfect they seemed askew, creating effects that were almost unnatural and deeply hypnotic.

Nalani could not stop staring. Somehow, she felt these people—ignoring her as completely as it was possible to ignore anything—were also performing for her, as if she were secretly the center of their universe. She looked around to see if anyone else was responding the same way, but they were all either chatting about business as if in a convention center ballroom or posing for selfies against the rails, expertly turning their smiles on and off as they checked each result.

Without seeming to, Sam had oozed herself to the producer's elbow. "Help me close this," she whispered. Nalani nodded, but the alcohol was getting to her head. She hadn't been drinking much recently, and apparently dragon fruit juice could mask a significant amount of vodka.

"That's why you can't think of it as your fourth vacation property . . . Sorry, of course, your fifth. This is your insurance policy . . . No, the house won't protect you from nuclear fallout, not yet, but . . . yes, sea level rise, but the beauty of this property is the elevation . . . I *know* the food is better in Amalfi, but . . . Look, it's more of a *Both/And* situation, in my opinion. Nalani!"

Nalani dragged her gaze away from a couple dressed in matching mauve togas with his-and-hers gemstones around their necks on silver chains.

"Nalani," said Sam, pulling her forward by the elbow. "Maybe you can explain this island's commitment to sustainable living?"

"Ummm," said Nalani. "Since the Costco opened in Puhi, a lot of people, they just make one trip for everything instead of going Foodland every time they need one small kine thing."

Samantha and the producer shared the same look of confusion.

"Tell them about making poi," said Sam, "and the ahupua'as."

"Well it depends if you like sour poi or—"

"We're *all* inspired by the Hawaiian spirit of self-sufficiency."

Sam expertly claimed the space Nalani had been occupying. She heard the Realtor's voice fading into the din. "You know that's why Franky is building his compound here . . . Well, I'm not allowed to say. But yes, it does . . ."

A server passed with an enticing tray of bright yellow drinks. Nalani helped herself. She was standing by the rail, surveying the festivities on the deck below, when she noticed a Zodiac approaching the yacht at very high speed, its prow planed high above the water. The speedboat skipped across the gentle swells like a smooth gray rock. Its dual outboards droned. Directly below her, a team of men in dark shirts emerged on deck, tightly knotted around someone in their center, almost carrying him. They slipped through the crowd like an axe splitting a log. By the time the guests realized what had happened, the team had moved on. They practically threw the man at the center down to the swimming platform, and he was yanked aboard the Zodiac, which roared off with a wake that rocked the yacht hard enough to throw people off balance.

It happened so fast, the Zodiac was halfway across the bay before Nalani realized who the man at the center of the circle had been. The billionaire founder, Franky Dalton.

29

Janice Diaz woke to the smell of damp embers. The last smoke from the fire hung above the concrete floor. Her lungs felt scratchy. Her side was cold. Her neck ached. It was a minute before she realized these discomforts were the worst thing she was feeling. The drain was closed.

She shook Carlotta. "We need to go to the hospital."

Carlotta didn't try to talk her out of it. And she didn't offer to come along. She told Janice Diaz the bus schedule and helped her pack her things.

"I hope it works out for you."

"Thank you for helping me."

"If you get in trouble, find Aunty Lei. She'll care for you better than I can."

As Janice climbed onto the bus, she felt grateful to Carlotta for making it so easy. But before the bus had crossed the river, gratitude slipped into something else. Had Carlotta really been that eager to get rid of her? Maybe she was more of a liability than she realized.

Or maybe Carlotta just hadn't liked her company.

This possibility felt even worse. The only person in the world who knew her had just spent her last two dollars to buy her a bus ticket.

"Hospital coming up," the driver said.

He left her standing in the same traffic circle under the same enormous tree from her first moments of release. She was ashamed, deeply ashamed, of course. The shame was constant. But she was also proud. She patted the heavy bag slung over her shoulder. Whatever happened next, she was infinitely more prepared than she'd been that distant afternoon.

A black Suburban pulled off the highway. It was moving twice as fast as it should in a hospital parking lot, but there was nothing reckless about the way it approached, circled the tree, and drove off along the side of the building. She had the same feeling she'd had on her first night, when an empty industrial lot uncannily resembled something from her past. This, too, was familiar. She'd watched the eyes of the driver and seen her own reflection in the tinted windows. She'd known men like this, and she'd watched people just like her with the same expression.

She hitched her bag up her shoulder and walked after the Suburban. When it turned the corner, she walked faster.

She sensed another motion in her peripheral vision and knew she'd been expecting it. A white van driving even faster than the Suburban. Recklessly fast. It, too, went around the corner. She dropped the bag in the bushes and began to run.

When she came around the corner, she saw the Suburban parked by a long blue awning. The driver, in a dark polo, was walking around the vehicle. The man who'd been riding shotgun, dressed identically, was holding a rear door open as a tall Black woman leaned in for something.

The driver lowered his shoulders when he saw the white van, but only made it to the passenger door when the van stopped with a shriek of rubber. Whatever the driver and the other guard now held in their right hands, they didn't raise them. The woman had frozen, looking over her shoulder, still leaning awkwardly into the vehicle.

A man in a black mask leaned out the van window, pointing a rifle. The door slid open, and two men in olive masks and tan fatigues tumbled out, aiming their own black rifles. "Bring him out!" one of them screamed.

"Oh my god!" This was the woman. English wasn't her first language, Janice noted.

The men in green took different sides of the Suburban. The closest one kept his rifle aimed at the two guards in polo shirts. The man in the black mask was out of the van now, aiming his rifle toward the rear windows of the Suburban. "In back! In back!" he screamed. "Get out! Get him the fuck out and no one else is hurt."

The driver was trying to say something.

"Set it down and raise your fucking hands! Raise your fucking hands!"

So many things were happening at once. The men in polos were kneeling, the driver still talking, both looking at the gunman's boots. Someone she couldn't see was releasing loud, shrill screams. The woman was sobbing. "Oh god. Please don't hurt them," she said. "S'il vous plaît. Don't fucking hurt them."

French, then. Or West African.

"He's not fucking here!" someone shouted.

The screaming rose and fell like a tornado siren. Janice finally made sense of it. The guards were standing with their hands raised. The man in the black mask was walking toward the woman and the open door. She shifted her body to shield it. "Don't you touch him!"

By the time Janice Diaz saw the little boy's curly hair spilling between his mother's fingers, she was running again.

"Take them. Take the family and let's go!" someone shouted.

The man in the black mask kept moving toward the mother, sighting down his rifle, finger extended over the trigger guard. He shuffled closer, slowing, until his muzzle touched her forehead. She flinched, whimpered, pulled her son tighter.

"You want me to take this kid?" screamed the gunman she couldn't see.

The mother's eyes shot in the direction of her other child. But she froze. The touch of the gun made her afraid. Then something new came into her eyes. She turned her face toward the man who threatened her. The skin of her forehead bunched against the black muzzle. She met his eyes, and he stepped back, breaking contact. Another moment, and the muzzle drifted downward, toward the small head in her cupped hands. She looked down, submissively.

The driver with his hands up saw Janice Diaz first. Just a flick of his eyes. But the man in the black mask noticed. He swung in her direction. Her chest tickled furiously where the black muzzle licked toward it. She braced herself, but she didn't stop running.

The man abruptly wheeled his rifle back toward the guards. "Where the fuck were you?" he said, softly, to her. "Leave them," he said loudly. "Fall back! Fall the fuck back. Leave them."

She was at the van now. She felt a forearm gather up her collar and shove her sideways. The man in the black mask was backpedaling. With his left arm, he forced her back. She hit her shin on the lip of the door and ducked her head as he shoved her inside. The others fell in behind. The van jerked forward. Janice Diaz lay squashed beneath men's weight, engulfed in the stink of adrenaline sweat and acrid smoke from the straining engine.

30

Franky Dalton found the twins in their high chairs, covered in pureed mango. A car had been dispatched for a child psychologist, and a young female sous-chef had been deputized to supervise the boys until Pilar could be given a mental health evaluation. Madeleine had told him all this on the phone. And he hadn't questioned her decisions. Though he wasn't worried about the boys. Their days were already studded with so many periods of intense distress, he doubted this would stand out.

Madeleine had said nothing about her own mental health. He'd imagined striding up and wrapping her in a supportive hug as she cathartically sobbed on his shoulder. But when he found her in the bedroom, she could barely hold still long enough for him to get his arms around her rigid shoulders before she burst free and resumed pacing.

"J'ai regardait dans ses yeux. Et il me regarde sans humanité."

"I'm sorry," said Dalton. "You looked in someone's eggs?"

"His *eyes*," said Madeleine, shutting hers. "They were without humanity." She wheeled around. "Who were they?"

"We don't know yet."

"They came after our *children*."

"We're going to find them."

She stopped in the center of the french doors overlooking the reef, wrapped her arms around herself. He went to her and held her, felt her body shaking, not trembling but shivering, like she had a fever.

"You know there's nothing that matters more to me than your safety. Whatever it takes, I am going to protect you."

She spun her slim body around in his arms and dropped her head on his shoulder. He felt her full weight, what there was of it, sink into him. He wasn't ready when she coiled back and shoved him in the chest. "Allez-y," she said. "Go parle avec your little men. Find these people. Kill them. I don't care."

. . .

All week, the weather had been perfect. Seventy-seven degrees. Trade winds bedazzling the turquoise water, rustling the palms, reminding Franky Dalton he wasn't in Fairfax County anymore, or Kenya, or Palo Alto. He was in paradise, listening to his badass head of security and his spooky ex-spy explain how some sort of group had almost kidnapped, or killed, his family under their watch. "We've worked with the hospital to get security footage," Hart was saying. "Unfortunately, we weren't able to pull any distinguishing pictures."

"What about the vehicle?"

"It was for sale online three days ago. The seller gave us a description of the buyer. But there was nothing actionable. Paid cash. Mainland accent. People around here think all white males look the same."

"What about the weapons? Are they even legal?"

Hart shrugged. "ARs are harder to get here. But they're perfectly legal. We're trying to get a better image of the magazines. But—"

"Was it Phoenix?"

"It's one possibility."

"Why does it sound to me," said Dalton, "like you think none of this is your responsibility?"

"I'm sorry?"

"You're giving a report as if it's your job to fill me in on an investigation. But I pay you to do the investigating. Actually, I pay you so no investigations should ever be necessary. Your security measures for my family were inadequate. My wife is traumatized. Our nanny is traumatized. My children are god knows what. And your men were useless."

"I understand your frustration. But we don't know they were useless."

"Just tell me who these people are, where you'll find them, and how you're going to make my family safe."

"We do have one group of suspects."

"We do?"

"The Phoenix whistleblower had . . . associates."

"Excuse me?"

"We are working on verifying their locations. It's possible they are on island."

"You said all he cares about is embarrassing us, pressuring our company, getting media attention. You never said anything about *associates*."

"We do believe his motivations are disclosure-oriented, and he has no personal agenda against you, except in your capacity as CEO. However . . ."

"Yes."

Hart looked extremely unhappy. He turned and glared at the consultant, who until that moment had used his powers of mediocrity to remain overlooked. "Mr. Raz should be the one to brief you."

Raz allowed the two men to watch him gather his thoughts and put them ever so carefully into words, as if precision was of the utmost importance. "Our intelligence indicates the whistleblower may have been assembling a support team."

"Support for what?"

"We aren't sure yet. His goal is publicity. He's a classic attention seeker. However, his associates have been known to express opinions that are more . . . extreme in nature."

"Extreme."

"Some of their views would be quite compromising for Phoenix, if he were associated with them."

"What are they, Nazis?"

"Nationalists, you could definitely call them. Accelerationists, possibly, seeking to jump-start the next civil war. Some have expressed views closely linked to white supremacy. Replacement theory. We have extensive files."

"They're shit talkers," Hart broke in. "According to what I was told," he hurried to add, "they like to wave flags and post videos of themselves shooting pumpkins with PKMs."

"PKMs?"

"Russian machine guns."

"Russian machine guns."

Hart nodded.

"Where?"

"Wisconsin, primarily."

"So are these people machine gun enthusiasts, or . . ."

"They seem to enjoy firing a wide variety of calibers."

"Like the ones pointed at my wife today?"

Hart nodded.

"What am I not understanding?"

"What do you mean?"

"I mean, what am I not understanding? Why did you begin this meeting by telling me you had no idea who these men were, then follow up by telling me someone you *knew* was here on island and you *knew* wanted to get media attention and you *knew* hated me and my company had recruited a group of *machine gunners*? He has a white supremacist militia, and a militia just tried to kidnap my Black wife and kids. It all seems perfectly clear. So what am I not understanding?"

"To be clear," said Raz, "these people may *call* themselves a militia, but most have no tactical training or experience. Their beliefs are severely out of step with mainstream American views, so Phoenix's association with them, once revealed, would essentially disqualify him as a legitimate critic of—"

"Shut up," said Dalton. "Shut up and tell me everything you haven't told me. Beginning with why you didn't mention your intelligence about these guys *yesterday,* when you told me I had nothing to worry about."

"This is frustrating for you," said Raz. "I'm sorry. You see, in my world, we are very precise about these terms. You pay me to bring you intelligence. I offered all the intelligence I have. If you're asking me for the information I base my intelligence assessments on, then this is going to be a long conversation. And of course, if you're asking for raw data . . ."

Incredibly, Dalton was still calm. His thinking was clearer than ever. He was seeing it now. "Stop bullshitting me," he said. "I cannot be bullshitted. You think you are superior to me. But you screwed up. And are trying to cover up your screwup and screwing up even more. So tell me, now, what you haven't told me. Because this conversation has already taken too much of my time, and I'm supposed to be on a call to Washington right now."

Raz offered a look of alarm. Dalton couldn't tell if it was genuine. "We can't answer anything definitively until we reestablish contact with our source."

"Is your source here?"

"Our source has disappeared."

"Disappeared from you."

"Disappeared completely."

"Is that your official intelligence assessment?"

"That's information."

"So give me the data." Raz was rattled. Dalton was sure of it. "Mr. Raz."

"After we lost contact, I visited the source's apartment."

"What did you find?"

"Nothing."

"Just because someone isn't home doesn't mean they've disappeared."

"Her normal patterns had ceased abruptly."

"So you went inside and looked for clues."

"More or less."

"And you found nothing."

"The contents of this apartment were completely undisturbed."

"You said that."

"This woman had been living in the apartment, using it daily. It should be disturbed. Even if she'd cleaned. There are always things you miss, things you don't have time for, things you've grown so used to you don't even notice they aren't right. They leave uncashed checks on the bookshelf. A dirty mug in the bathroom. This place had no dust."

"She was a neat person."

"Someone had gone through it."

"So what?"

"I don't know. I don't have any intelligence on it. I'm working it."

Dalton turned to Hart. "You hired these people. Is there a reason we shouldn't terminate their contract?"

Raz spoke up. "We're going to make this right, Mr. Dalton. We are bringing in a team. Some old colleagues of mine. They specialize in situations like this. There will be no more bills. No paper trail. Our work will be completely pro bono and off the record."

Dalton looked at him skeptically.

"They can arrive in two days."

Dalton looked to Hart, who shrugged.

"The satisfaction of our clients," said Raz, allowing a tiny hint of assurance to creep back into his voice, "is our highest priority."

31

In the minutes after it happened, Nalani wondered whether she'd actually seen Franky Dalton rushed away in a huddle of security guards. No one around her had noticed. The party carried on. She fell into conversation with a man and woman dressed in the same gray shorts and V-neck shirts, their hair cut close on the sides and brushed across their foreheads. They were cofounders of a dating app. They were also a couple. The app had matched them with each other. They described their compound at Burning Man, complete with an animatronic panther that matched burners' sexual compatibility based on their repressed fantasies.

"How do people know them, if they're repressed?"

The couple giggled.

"The panther asks three questions."

"Algorithms do the rest."

When they offered her a pill, she took it.

Samantha grabbed her arm. "Did you hear what happened? Franky Dalton had to leave. Some issue came up with his family. I'm *so* sorry you won't get to meet him. He's an amazing person. So inspirational. Are you ready to go swimming?"

On the deck where the slide had been set up, clothes were piled everywhere. A steward was trying to pick them up and fold each one before another dripping swimmer ran across them. Men and women chased each other screaming. Two deckhands stood at the edge, trying to prevent anyone from sliding down face-first or falling over the railing. When one of them bear-hugged a silver-haired Asian man trying to mount the top rail, a brown man in a turban and a pair of shiny board shorts began yelling at him.

"I'm sorry, sir, but the captain—"

"Don't worry about the captain. I'll handle the captain. Fukuyama-san's performance art has filled a pavilion at the Biennale. If he wants to dive off my boat, all I ask is that you record it for posterity. And be ready to go in after him."

The turbaned man then pulled up his own phone, eagerly, and trained it on the gray-haired man, who didn't seem to have noticed the discussion. He gazed off toward the mountains, then wandered into the crowd.

Nalani observed all this with wonder.

"What are you waiting for?"

It wasn't until Nalani saw Samantha standing in her underwear that she realized almost everyone else was in their underwear, too. The men in clinging boxer briefs, the women in every possible iteration of panty and, usually, bra. Most, like Samantha, wore something relatively sensible; there was no lace in sight, though quite a few thongs. For a moment, the spectacle of intimacy and carelessness stopped her slide into wherever the pill was taking her.

She tried to detect shame, or at least self-consciousness, in the faces of the people whooping, sprinting, and splashing into the water. But when she saw none whatsoever, she felt a knot release. She pulled her shirt up, the sun going dim and purple for a moment, then pushed down her jeans, enjoying the feeling of her thumbs against her strong, smooth thighs.

She wanted these haoles to see her.

She was in the water a long time, diving as deep as she could, watching the blue go dark and kicking onto her back to see the shimmering glare of the sun high above, feeling the silky caress of the current. She had to remind herself to surface, draw the most incredible lungfuls of air. It was intoxicating to dive into freedom and darkness, surface into noise and light. It was like passing between life and death. She had no fear.

When she was tired, she pulled herself onto the warm surface of the float, closing her eyes and lying there for calm eternities, not caring whose limbs slipped against hers in the tangle of people making the rubber tilt and bounce. Part of her knew she was staying in the ocean to avoid the party. But she was able to squash that thought and hurl it into a hazier part of her mind. She fluttered her feet and felt the ocean kiss her heels. She was squirming toward the edge, immersing feet, then calves, about to slide on her back into the blue, when someone said, "Hey."

It was the guy from the launch, leaning his elbows on the float. His hair was darker, wet, but still curly. Beads of water sparkled on the hairs of his forearms. His freckled shoulders were getting pink. He was smiling at her, but not too confidently. He was nervous. She liked that.

"I think I saw you on the boat."

"Shoots."

"*Shoots.* That's funny. What does it mean?"

She laughed. "I don't know. I never thought about it. It's like, you know, *shoots.*"

He tried it out again. "Shoots."

She laughed at him. "Shoots, brah."

"Are you from here?"

"Born and raised."

"So you're actually Hawaiian?"

"Yeah. Hapa kine."

He grinned. "That's so cool."

"This your first time here?"

"I've been coming here my whole life. Well, to Maui. Every summer."

"What's your name?"

"I'm Michael."

"I'm Nalani."

"So, are you having fun?"

She kicked her legs and slipped into the water, letting herself go under, then rising, reaching her arms onto the float beside him, shaking her hair. For a moment, she remembered she was in her underwear.

"Yeah, I guess."

"You must swim out here all the time."

She looked around at the mountains. "In Hanalei? Not so much."

He looked at her strangely. "Isn't this the best place on the island?"

"Too much traffic, I guess."

"Too many tourists?"

She gave him a goofy smile. "Um, yeah."

He grinned, embarrassed. She liked that, too.

"Anyway," she said. "Usually I surf."

"I surf, too. In the Bay Area."

"Cold, the water."

"Yeah, nicer here. But I don't really know the breaks. I hear the locals are territorial."

She cocked her head. She usually didn't act this way. In fact, she hated girls that acted like this. She threw that thought away. Kicked her legs, felt her foot brush his.

"I'll take you sometime. An' I won't let the local braddahs fuck with you."

"That would be awesome."

"Shoots," she said. "They're nice guys. Most of them. As long as you stay respectful."

Michael nodded eagerly.

Nalani shoved off from the float. "I'm starving," she said. "Let's find something to eat."

32

Janice Diaz couldn't see where they were going but could feel the van swerving through traffic. If she hadn't been pinned between two large men, she'd have been thrown violently from side to side. Instead, she felt the hard edges of whatever these men were wearing—ammunition clips, radios, the flat stifling weight of their body armor. When they bounced, she tried putting her hands in a new place, hoping to touch something she could use as a weapon: a baton, a knife. But she didn't want to draw attention, not before she had a chance to think.

Someone whooped. Someone else said, "Fuck yeah."

The driving had become a little less erratic, and she could feel the man to her left vibrating with energy. His right leg pumped up and down.

"That was so fucking heavy."

"Well executed, boys."

"Shut the fuck up," said a new voice angrily. It was the man pinning her beneath his weight. "Was *that* what you came out here to do?"

There was silence. The van was driving normally now. She heard the ticktock of the blinker. A moment later, they stopped, turned, bumped onto an uneven road. She smelled dust and heard the crackle of gravel.

The man on top of her spoke again. "Sorry, boys. It was fucked. But you all did good. You remembered your training. Now we just gotta convince this pussy to give us another shot at it. Maybe *you* can help us with that?"

She felt the weight slide off. A pale, middle-aged man with a thick black beard was looking down on her. "By the way," he said, "where the fuck have you been?"

They were driving down a red dirt road with bright fields on either side. The road dipped into a valley, and the fields were replaced with dense trees. Janice Diaz was thinking as hard as she could about how to say as little as possible.

She'd told them she'd landed four days ago, that she'd been taken to the hospital because of an assault, that her memory was foggy. She felt strangely sure of herself as she selectively revealed her story. Somehow, she knew exactly what to leave in and what to omit. It was an exhilarating feeling. When she'd imagined getting her mind back, it had always been concrete thoughts, ideas, memories. But this was different. It was a way of being, habits of thinking. She had the uncanny realization that she could be herself without even knowing who she was.

Two items of knowledge did seem clear, though. She was used to operating in situations like these. And whatever was going on, these men didn't seem like they were selling drugs.

Fortunately, they were distracted. The one who'd been sitting on her was typing on his phone. "I'm telling him we need to come in."

"What do you think he knows?"

"Nothing. I told him the press conference got canceled."

"What does he say?"

"He's being a cuck. Wondering if we should all walk away. *Fuck no.*"

"You think we'll get another shot?"

He didn't answer. Obviously, he was Alpha. The cuck must be P. The van had turned down an overgrown track. Abandoned vehicles, couches, and appliances rusted away amid decaying leaves. The trees grew thick. The air smelled of rot and mold.

The road ended. A four-door pickup was parked in the dusty grass.

The men climbed out of the van and began unclipping slings, belts, and body armor. All four were white. Two were skinny. One had a belly that hung over his pants. All had grown what facial hair they could, though only Alpha's could accurately be called a beard. They were filling a pile of black duffel bags. First with weapons and equipment, then with clothes as they stripped off their shirts, unlaced their boots, and removed their pants. Janice Diaz turned away.

"You got to change, too. This is all we got."

She felt something flop against her back and fall at her feet. A cheap aloha shirt, a pair of board shorts that said *Poi Pounders.* She walked around the van, crouched, began unbuttoning. Her bare skin was sensitive to the stagnant air. She buttoned the shirt, its short sleeves hanging below her elbows. It felt even worse, pulling her jeans off, but she kept her head up and watched through the windows of the van. All four men were tossing duffels into the truck bed.

She had to fold the waistband of the shorts several times. Fortunately, the shirt was long enough to cover the bare skin where the shorts sagged.

Alpha met her as she came around the van. He had a drab T-shirt in his hand. "You were the only one who didn't have gloves. Wipe down anything you might have touched."

By the time she was done, the truck was running and the men were all inside. To her relief, they'd left the front seat open for her.

Alpha was driving. "He's bringing us in. I'm going to let you do the talking."

"What do you want me to say?"

"How fucked up are you?" Alpha asked.

She shrugged.

"And you don't know what happened?"

She said nothing.

He let out a long sigh. "Just tell him we were ready to do his protest, just how he wanted, but we never got a chance 'cause the thing was canceled. We were worried we might have been blown in the van, so we switched out vehicles."

"What comes next?"

He looked at her again. "We convince him we got to try again." He opened his mouth to say something more, then shut it. Shook his head. "Fuck it," he said. "Let me do the talking."

They left the forest, then the fields, and pulled onto a major road. Alpha was a good driver. He waited patiently for opportunities to overtake other cars without drawing attention. The truck was quiet. The adrenaline had worn off, and the men were deep in their own heads. She looked at their faces in the rearview mirror. None of them were sure they wanted to go through that again.

They drove for a long time. She recognized places she had been. The government center, the beach down at the harbor, the bridge and the ruins of the resort. She thought she might see Carlotta walking on the sidewalk, a hitch in her stride from the weight of her bag.

Now they were passing places she'd never seen: restaurants, strip malls, gated resorts, neighborhoods of run-down wooden houses. They passed a fire house, a graveyard, then a long beach facing the open ocean, pastures, and overgrown fields. Dramatic green peaks rose in the distance, filled the windshield, then were gone. For miles, there were only scattered roads and buildings. Eventually, they turned right on a narrow road. Alpha was holding the wheel with one hand and his phone with the other. He kept glancing at it, muttering. They turned onto a series of gravel roads, each narrower than the next, passed a field of evenly spaced coconut palms, then a smaller field where banana trees sagged in clusters. Finally, they stopped at a long metal gate.

While they waited, Alpha turned to look at her. "Anything you want to say?"

She shook her head. He stared at her for a moment, then flicked his eyes around the van before bringing them back to her face. "We don't know this guy," he said. "If he's smart, and he is, he's going to try to split us up, get us to break our operational discipline and give up information we don't even know we're giving. Don't tell him anything. Leave the debrief on this op to me. If he learns what really happened, he'll call the whole show off. Understood?"

A small engine clattered, and a long bicycle chain began pulling the gate to one side. They followed a concrete drive surrounded by a trimmed lawn. A house appeared, roofed in green tile. Alpha parked the truck in front of the carved double doors. All five climbed down, uncertainly.

For the first time, Janice Diaz had a chance to see the men in their new outfits. They were dressed like she was—in poorly fitting aloha shirts and shorts or jeans. It was hard to believe these men had successfully ambushed a team of security professionals. They looked like a tour group waiting uncertainly for the next stop on their itinerary. Even Alpha had lost some of his taciturn calm.

She caught her reflection in the glass windows by the door, her baggy clothes more ridiculous than anyone's. But there was no trace of anxiety on her face.

The door cracked open. A man slipped out. He wore black cowboy boots, black jeans, and a black T-shirt. Receding hair, cropped to stubble.

His nose was narrow, cheekbones high and pronounced. His eyes were gray and oddly pale against his brown skin. He fixed them in his gaze, so it seemed he was speaking to each of them alone when he said, "I can't trust you."

33

Dalton had nights like this. Doomscrolling. He'd told Madeleine he had to wrap up a few things regarding the Phoenix leak. He couldn't believe he'd been so stressed that morning about something as insignificant as corporate PR. Though of course it was more than that. His plan was on the verge of unraveling. Apparently, in Washington, even some Bay Area representatives were going wobbly.

He'd spent a few minutes going through the leaked documents. Multiple HR complaints from Indonesian content moderators about watching videos of rape, beheading, mass shootings, and other flagged content for up to nine hours a day, with no mental health resources, for about fifty cents an hour. What had gotten most of the attention, besides the descriptions of graphic content, wasn't the moderators' well-being but how few of them there were. Sokoni employed four Javanese speakers responsible for ten million posts a day. Hundreds of other languages were unaccounted for, including everything spoken in Papua, a place he'd never even heard of, which was apparently the site of organized violence against indigenous people occupying forests that at least one presidential candidate wanted to turn into palm oil plantations.

It was a familiar pattern. A tragedy happened in a developing country, and the good liberals of the Western world blamed the Internet.

Involuntarily, he clicked back to the email from Hart with files on the men who'd tried to kidnap his family. Personal records—addresses, phone numbers, credit cards, mortgages, magazine subscriptions. Criminal records showed nothing but speeding tickets, drunk driving, misdemeanor possession of a banned substance. There were a few business liens and small-time bankruptcies. The taxes they'd paid seemed paltry. If these men weren't out-and-out losers, they definitely weren't winners. A few had run for local office on platforms you'd expect from rural areas like these—Wisconsin, Minnesota, Michigan—a total blank to Dalton, except for a week on someone's private island on a lake in the Upper Peninsula, which had been delightful.

Most of the content on the men was from Sokoni. A team had already been assigned to scrape, summarize, and analyze every trace they'd left on the platform. The files contained years of unedited conversations compiled from Barua, Sokoni's semi-encrypted messaging service. He'd grown bored with the banal cascade of softcore pornographic GIFs, coded memes, and running commentary on what he finally realized must be Green Bay Packers games.

Their videos, on the other hand, were mesmerizing. The men loved machine guns. But they also loved dynamite, large-caliber pistols, tracer rounds, modified AR-15s, hatchets, and historic weaponry, especially from the Wehrmacht. In one video, somewhere outside Vegas, they took turns firing a gun mounted to a tank turret. There were some politics, of course, mostly hovering around the idea that any limitation to the Second Amendment was a step in a plan to disarm true patriots, which itself was part of the plan to overthrow the American way of life.

"If you want to strip my rights away," one man said, "you'll have to disarm me first. And let me give you a preview of how that'll go." The camera zoomed in on a group of mannequins dressed in army surplus jackets leaning against a stack of hay bales at the far end of a field. It swung back to the speaker, who was kneeling by an orange plastic case with an antenna coming out one side. "Point it that way," the man mumbled, jerking his head. The camera swung back to the mannequins. A bang and white flash. The camera jerked chaotically. Dust. Then laughter. "Holy fuck," someone said. "You all right?" A moment of black. A new video began.

Dalton had surrounded himself with professionals in matters of personal security. And yet. These amateurs had been allowed to *touch* his family with their weapons. Hart and Raz had known about them, had known about the videos, and said nothing to him. It was an oversight they still hadn't properly explained. Had it been a conspiracy? His anger was everywhere: at the men shooting watermelons in the videos, at the men he paid to protect his family, and at the men and women he paid to run his company so he would have the time and energy to make informed decisions about his family's absolute most basic need: their physical safety from danger.

He paused the videos, moved the cursor, and returned to his commons. For the second time in two nights, he was too overwhelmed to do anything but scroll mindlessly until he was calm enough to return to his family. He noticed Gideon was active. When had they last talked? He vaguely remembered another birth announcement but had lost count of how many children that would be. He knew Gideon had transferred at some point, closer to his home area. He had no idea if he was still there or not. The Ministry of Education could be fickle.

                                                              Habari yako?

There was a long pause. Then the pulsing dots.

mzuri sana
samaki kubwa :-)
and you?

                                                              Fiti sana

habari ya jamaa?

                                                              They are well

praise god

                                                              And yours?

our eldest completed her kcse exams
our youngest had a small fever but is recovered
praise god
We received the funds you sent for the school fees
asante sana

                                                    I am glad to hear
                                       My own family was in great danger today
                                           They were almost kidnapped
                                              But they are all right

He hadn't planned to write this. But the words gave him relief. Now that it was something that could be shared in a chat, it lost one tiny edge of its menace.

There had been a pause. Now the dancing dots.

the crime here is also very bad
last week in nyeri a family was burned
in the home

                                                    By thieves?

yes
the father refused to pay them
now he is in hospital and left with nothing

                                                    That is very sad
                                        Does your house need more security?

this man's wall was very high
I think this is what brought the wezi
The gang was caught praise god and burned with tires
They have also caught the ones who did this to your family?

                                                    Not yet

i know you will find those men
and then you will no longer fear

                                                    I hope so

Bubu alisema juu ya uchunga wa mwanawe

                                                    ???

you have forgotten your kiswahili
lol
this means
even the dumb mother speaks to save her son
i know you will stop at nothing to protect your family
Class is starting
I must go
Tutaonana rafiki yangu

Dalton stared at the screen, then brought the cursor up to the corner and put it to sleep. His reflection looked back at him from the dark monitor. He realized this was the reason he'd been procrastinating. There'd been a choice he had to make. He could steer his company through this crisis or he could protect his family. But he couldn't give his best to both.

The screen had come back to life. He must have moved the cursor. His commons had populated with a whole new genre of content. With a few keystrokes, he pulled up the back-end labels to see which micro-category he'd been sorted into: *Educational—Personal Security—Patriotic*.

The first few videos it tried to show him were genuinely educational. But the algorithm filtered his preferences with impressive speed, and soon he was being offered a stream of videos and group invitations indistinguishable from the ones Hart had sent. Their constant theme was the need for every patriot to wake up, stockpile weapons, and prepare for the coming war over the soul of the country. Their message was urgent: the longer good men slumbered, the stronger the enemy became.

34

Somehow, it was evening. Nalani and Mike had lined up at the shower, and she'd felt his eyes on her as fresh water streamed down her stomach and thighs. The servers with the plates of fancy pupus had disappeared, so they had a few more bright drinks instead. They moved to the railing to stare at the sun, a pink ball settling toward the black and silver ocean. The crew had cast off from the mooring. The ship was moving smoothly toward the cliffs at Lumaha'i.

"We're going up the shore?" Nalani asked.

"I heard there's going to be a torchlight dinner. On a sacred beach?"

They passed the streams at Wainiha. Nalani pointed out the surf break at Tunnels and the shadowed valley of Manoa. The sun passed through a golden cloud. Mike took her shoulder and turned her for a selfie. Their faces came out dark. The sun was just a blur. The yacht swung wide around Ke'e and passed under Makana. Nalani was about to tell Mike he'd been wrong about the picnic. Napali was protected land. Then she saw torches flickering on a sandy beach.

The yacht stopped. Mike and Nalani moved with the crowd toward the stern, everyone inching forward, the outboards thrumming and buzzing until it was her turn to climb down the steep fiberglass stairs and be passed from hand to hand by a chain of crew members, then take one long, awkward step over the round bulge of a Zodiac, clutch someone's hand on the other side, let herself be drawn to a spot on a wooden bench with handles to grip as the bow lifted and the boat skipped across the dark water, the pale crescent of the beach growing wider, the torches glowing brighter, the peaks looming darker above the dimming sky.

She didn't like watching Mike step into the arms of the two local guys waiting knee-deep in the waves and let himself be transferred to the sand. She liked it even less when it was her turn. But it was nice to have dry pants.

She stepped onto a beach transformed by torchlight. Figures moved among white tables like characters from legend. People who'd been so shameless a few hours earlier now seemed mysterious and gracious. She realized she was finally seeing them as they saw themselves. Mike was something called head of product at a company she'd never heard of. The way he'd said it—so modestly, so obviously eager to move on—made her sure he made a lot of money. She'd known people did it, of course, but had never thought about it for herself. Strange, since it was so easy. All the plans she'd made, all the anxiety and exams and degrees she'd imagined getting, and all you really had to do was fall in love with someone rich. It could be as simple as that.

She'd lost track of him in the shadows. And when someone slipped an arm into hers, she was disappointed to realize it was Sam.

"There's someone you need to meet." Alcohol floated off her breath. Nalani took one last look for Mike, then followed Sam toward a table floating like a lily by itself at the edge of the darkness. The sand was cold on her feet. She dug in her toes, trying to wake from this dream.

The most beautiful woman she'd ever seen was waiting at the white table. She stood and came into the light as Nalani reached out a hand. On island, everyone hugged and pecked each other's cheeks. But over the course of the day, she'd gotten used to shaking hands, even with other women.

"I'm Erin," the woman said.

"I'm Nalani."

"Thanks so much for coming to this party. I've been wanting to meet you."

"Meet me?"

"Sam's told me about you."

Nalani couldn't stop looking into Erin's eyes. They were black and gold until a flame shifted and they were green and blue, the color of the deep water when you dove off your canoe a mile out, an endless blue she had seen nowhere else.

At some point, the panther couple had given her another pill. It must be kicking in, she thought. But it couldn't be just that. No one else had looked at her like this.

"You're really beautiful," Nalani said. Then she clutched her mouth. "Did I just say that?"

Erin laughed. "I was about to say the same thing to you."

"Who are you?"

"I work with Franky and Dhillon, at Sokoni."

"Oh my god," said Nalani. "I saw you on *Oprah*. You are *so* beautiful."

Erin said nothing. The light of the torches moved across her face. How can she just sit there, Nalani wondered, and *let* me look at her? She was getting confused. The pill really was kicking in. What was happening? Were they flirting? Of course not. But why was she getting warm?

Erin took a long drink from a tall glass. Something shifted. A moment ago, Nalani had felt the other woman drawing her in, a magnetic pull as if she wanted nothing on earth except Nalani's attention. Now there was nothing. Nalani was still staring, but it was as if a pane of glass had been raised between them.

"We used to date, you know," said Erin, "me and Franky. We were in the Peace Corps together. In Africa. Before any of this." She waved her hand, banishing the tables and torches to oblivion. "Can you believe that?"

Nalani had a vague memory of a poster in her high school guidance office. "You were like a volunteer or something?"

"The government sends you to another country for two years. It's actually really good. I always put in a good word for them with the Appropriations Committee. You meet the most interesting people. It's lonely as hell, though."

"What were you doing there?"

"I was working with local government. Helping them set up their IT. They didn't have Internet when we came. They did when we left. Not that we deserve credit for it."

"That's really great, though."

Erin didn't appear to be seeing her. Nalani had figured out she was extremely drunk, or high, or both. She wasn't in such great shape herself. But she felt protective of the other woman. Erin blinked, and Nalani felt herself seen again.

"Was it great? I don't know. It never felt that way at the time. I mainly felt guilty. We talk about strong women over here? We go to conferences? *Those* women are strong. You know what they told us in training? If you ever feel in danger, find the nearest mama. And it was true. And not just for us, for the men, too. *Especially* the men, honestly. That's what all of them did. They found the nearest mama. Do you want another drink?"

Erin lifted her hand. Within seconds, two fresh drinks appeared. She said something to the server, and a moment later, the man set down two shot glasses. Another local guy. Nalani might even have known him. She felt him trying to catch her eye. Erin raised her shot, and Nalani mimicked her. They tapped glasses. Tequila, the best Nalani had ever had, thin and clear and barely sweet, like something poured from the mouth of a flower.

"Near the end of our tour. Me and Franky took a trip up north, to the desert. There weren't any buses. We had to ride on top of trucks. And there weren't roads. Just tracks in the sand. The trucks traveled at night, so the engines wouldn't overheat. Sometimes we stopped and walked through sleeping villages, like a fairy tale. It never rained, and everyone slept outdoors. Moms and dads and kids all snuggled on these big beds in the sand. These were places that had never seen foreign aid. People just raised their camels and lived their lives. We bathed in oases. Then we reached a place where men carried rifles and everyone shat on the ground. There were empty boxes from the UN everywhere. Franky made us turn around. He thought I'd get raped and he'd get shot. I was so mad at him. But he was probably right. I remember on the last long ride back to Marsabit, we were lying in the canvas on the top of this truck. It was the most comfortable ride we'd had yet. At sunset, a cheetah ran beside us through the red rocks of the desert. The stars were so close, I thought, *This is as close as I'll ever get to being an astronaut.*"

"That's beautiful."

"Turns out, I'm flying into space next year. So."

"Wow," said Nalani. Meaning it.

"It's just men's bullshit. Do you code?"

"I'm thinking of getting my MBA."

"Good for you. Wharton? Stanford?"

"I'm not sure. I'm just trying to take care of my family right now."

Erin gave her a look of interest. Nalani thought she might actually melt. She touched her face, discreetly, wondering whether it was as hot as it felt. Maybe it was the tequila.

Erin lifted her glass. "They fuck you up. Families."

"My mom's an addict."

Erin reached across the table and grabbed Nalani's hand. Her palm was incredibly warm. Soft, but not weak. Nalani tried to say more, but she couldn't.

Erin kept holding her hand.

"I'm sorry," said Nalani. "I just realized I've never actually said that, to anyone."

"You've never talked about it?"

Nalani nodded, though it wasn't true. She'd talked about it plenty, with aunts, uncles, cousins, teachers, her dad of course, her friends, the cops, family services, a judge. She'd just never said those words. Everyone she'd ever met already knew her mother was a junkie. "She's living on the land now," Nalani said. "The land *he* wants. He's offered her a lot of money."

"*He?*"

"Your boyfriend. Um, Franky?"

"My *ex*-boyfriend."

"She says it's helping her get better. The land."

"Is it?"

"I don't know. She's said that so many times. That she's getting better."

"And now she doesn't want to give up the land?"

Nalani nodded. "She says it's our family's. It's always been our kuleana. She doesn't want to sell out." She badly wanted to cup Erin's hand in both of hers. To rub her thumb across the other woman's knuckles. But she held back. Afraid to do anything that might break the moment.

Erin's face turned dark. "You have dreams, right? You have a future. To me, it sounds like your mom is being . . . selfish."

Without thinking, Nalani did take the other woman's hand in hers. She clung to it like a swimmer caught in a rip current. And Erin squeezed back.

"You're a beautiful person. You have an effect on people. I can tell. Don't be afraid of that. People want to pull you down to their level. They can't stand to see someone get everything they want. You owe it to yourself to tell them to go fuck themselves. No matter *who* they are."

Abruptly, Erin pulled her hand away, stood up, and walked around the table. She took Nalani in her arms, a sisterly hug. "You fucking shine," she told her.

She took Nalani's cheeks between her hands, stared hard into her eyes, and kissed her on the lips, a crushing softness that was gone before Nalani had a chance to respond.

She was almost beyond the torchlight, when she paused, turned back, and told Nalani, "All he wants is a place where he can keep his family safe."

Mike found Nalani in the crowd moving back to the boats. He wrapped his arm around her without asking, and she rested her weight on him, comforted to have someone simple and solid to lean on. Someone ordinary.

"I saw you talking to Erin Bogosian."

She felt no need to respond. It was chilly, by the water. She felt warmth radiating off her, as if the torches had been baking her and now the stars were casting cool white light to blow the heat away.

"She's pretty amazing, huh?" he said.

"Yeah."

"She founded Sokoni, you know. Alongside Frank Dalton. People say it was her idea. The whole online village thing? When they still talked about the company that way? They dated. In Africa. She got her MBA to do the business side. He came to California to build the platform."

They'd stopped in the hard sand at the water's edge. She felt the ocean sizzle against her toes. She twisted in, kissed him on the mouth, and didn't stop. She wanted him to shut up.

The swell had risen, and the ride was bumpy. The outboards thrummed, powerful and slow. She gripped the handles on the seat beside her and let her head hang back, staring up at the pale streak of their galaxy whipped crazily across the darkness of the universe. She felt Michael's knuckles gripping the handle beside hers. She slid her hand over his, then guided it onto her stomach. His fingertips pressed into the soft skin of her waist, then under her waistband, carefully probing the elastic of her panties. She tightened her grip and shoved his hand past the seam, felt it passing warmly down the smooth skin in the crease of her thigh, bending the short hairs, then finding her. She stopped him, exactly where she wanted, still staring at the stars. She moved against him, and he slipped his fingers deeper, the thrill of contact, exquisite, unbearable, so intense she had to grip the handles harder to avoid pushing his hand away. She let the feeling wash over her in sets, feeling the sway of the vehicle, lost in the stars, the steady hum of the engines carrying her past sleeping villages, a cheetah running beside her through the night.

As she muffled a groan, she made a resolution. She would do whatever it took to remain in this world. And she wouldn't be content with sweeping up the hairs they shed, or whatever Sam had called it. She would fucking shine.

DAY 5

35

Janice Diaz was warm and comfortable. She felt the crisp tension of tucked sheets and the soft friction of a mattress. Dewdrops trembled on the windowpane. Hemlocks stood black in the fog. The nearest paved road was two miles off.

She turned on her side and bicycled her legs. The mattress was real. She curled around herself in the center of the king bed, knowing where she was now. A rental house, micro bottles of shampoo and conditioner on the bathroom counters, bars of soap sealed in plastic. The kidnappers were sleeping a few rooms away. After the man in black cowboy boots had let them in, they'd taken over one wing. She'd chosen a room as far away as possible, deciding to trust the man who didn't trust the men who'd kidnapped her, even if he didn't trust her, either.

She'd taken a long shower, locked her bedroom door, pulled on the shapeless, detergent-scented underwear from Carlotta's camp, and slipped into the sheets in the afternoon sunlight. At some point, hunger had woken her. The light had mellowed, but it was not dark. She lay still and listened for a long time. She didn't remember falling back to sleep. And now it was morning.

The microwave clock said 5:15. She opened the cabinets and made a pot of coffee. Such routine activities—walking into the kitchen, brewing coffee—shadowed with such elemental fear. What could one of those men do to her if he walked out and found her alone? Light was rising outside the glass doors. She pulled a blanket off a couch. Slid the door shut behind her.

There was a concrete patio and a small pool. A yard ringed with fruit trees and flowering bushes. She heard frogs peeping and a few trilling birds. She tucked her feet under herself and wrapped the blanket tight. The smell of coffee helped. For a moment after the first scalding sip, it was impossible to be anything other than an ordinary woman greeting a pearl-gray morning.

She heard the door slide behind her and pulled the blanket tighter.

It was P, still in his cowboy boots. He stood in the doorway and looked across the yard. Then he sat in the chair beside her.

"How are you feeling?"

"Better."

"They said you showed up unexpectedly."

"I wasn't able to make the rendezvous."

"Or respond to our messages?"

"Something happened. I'm not sure what. I've been in a daze."

"Were you poisoned?"

"Possibly. I don't know. I was able to see incoming messages. But I couldn't unlock my phone. I saw the location of yesterday's . . . event and showed up."

"And what did you see?" A new edge in his voice.

She shrugged. "The guys spotted me and picked me up."

"That's what they said." She heard the disappointment. "There was a press release last night. The Dalton Family Foundation made their donation to the hospital. It was the top story in today's local paper. It didn't say why the event was canceled. The Bali revelations are already sinking out of the national news. I think we missed our chance."

"Mmmmm," said Janice Diaz. She had no idea what he was talking about.

"When was the last time you saw Agile?"

Something folded over in her mind.

"This is important."

"I can't remember." The evasion came naturally.

"And you have no idea who tried to poison you?"

"I'm sorry."

"It's all right," he said. "You wouldn't know. Not with these people."

The light rose gradually. The sky was filled with heavy clouds.

"I haven't heard from her," he said. "No one has. Not for days."

"I wish I could remember."

"I'm worried she . . ." He stopped himself. Gave her a long look. No sympathy now. "I think she was taking drugs again. She swore she'd never jeopardize our mission. But I could tell she was getting careless. I even wondered if someone had gotten to her. You didn't see any sign of that, did you?"

Janice Diaz shrugged as noncommittally as possible.

"I convinced myself I was being paranoid. Now you show up, beaten and drugged. We have to assume the worst."

"Who do you think they are?"

He looked at her with a question in his eyes. She realized she needed to be more careful.

"You mean, specifically? We'd never know. Sokoni has so many layers of security. Something like this would be indirect. Contractors. Scary people. But official channels, too, of course. Agencies. *Anyone* could be helping them. I told Agile to make that clear to you. I guess she didn't."

"I think I knew what I was getting into."

"You couldn't. Even Agile didn't. With Sokoni, it goes way beyond data collection or screen time. They're happy to let everyone think they're too cheap, or incompetent, to fix their algorithms and find all the evil stuff. The truth is, their algorithm is trained to promote the evil stuff. They're turning ordinary people into extremists—connecting moms with anti-vaxxers, turning gamers into white supremacists, introducing gun rights advocates to accelerationists. The crazier their users get, the more time they spend on the platform. That's why what we're doing is so dangerous. We're not just threatening their reputation, we're threatening their market cap."

The details were hard to track, but Janice Diaz instinctively understood the stakes: They were fighting a system with the scale to multiply collective suffering to a level that made isolated acts of violence almost inconsequential in comparison.

"So that's why you're willing to go so far."

It was daylight now. The clouds were thinning fast, revealing pale blue sky.

"Everyone thinks they'll do it," P said. "The right thing. But when I actually had to take the step, everything in me said, *Walk away.* I had to shut it down. I had to shut a lot down."

"I know what you mean," said Janice Diaz.

"That's why I believe they turned her," the man said. "I don't want to. But I do. They find your weaknesses. They find them and they pry them wide open. Then you're done."

"I'm sorry I can't remember more." She meant it now. This story had made her strong.

"I know you tried to help her," the man was saying. "She made that crystal clear. Like she knew she wasn't strong enough, so she was sending you instead. I think, by the end, she trusted you more than she trusted herself."

They sat in silence. A question had occurred to her. Something she couldn't believe she hadn't thought of earlier. And as she considered its implications, she worked very hard to prevent any hint of her feelings from showing on her face.

If she wasn't Agile, who was she?

He misunderstood her expression. "It'll come back," he said. "Whatever they tried to do to you, they failed."

She was about to ask the man his name and tell him just how little she remembered and how damaged she had been, when she heard the door slide open behind them.

Alpha stepped out, sipping from a coffee mug and surveying the scene with a look of profound satisfaction. "Nice place, Phoenix. I told the boys to be ready in thirty. Should we meet poolside?"

36

Dalton was literally tugging his wife by the hand, out of their bedroom, toward the lanai. The twins were practicing phonics with Pilar. He could hear their eager babble in the other room.

"It's only a stand-up," he told her. "It's only ten minutes."

In fact, he was supposed to be on a call with a United States senator in ten minutes, so he needed the meeting to be even shorter than that. He'd asked Hart to stop by in hopes that a rational discussion of safety measures with an experienced security professional would help Madeleine in a way that the visit from the child psychologist and multiple teleconferences with her own therapist had not.

In the hours after *the attempt,* as Dalton had been calling it—to emphasize the reassuring fact that it had failed—he'd been impressed with Madeleine's absolute commitment to making sure the boys would be all right. But there'd been little to do. When the psychologist asked what they remembered, they'd spoken only of the random details they usually recalled from their parents' efforts to enrich their lives: treats they hadn't been allowed to eat, construction equipment they'd passed on the road. Madeleine wanted the psychologist to push past the gently probing questions and uncover the hidden trauma that would cripple their future selves. But it was only when Marc mentioned "the angry man" that she seemed to be getting somewhere.

"Who was angry?" the psychologist asked.

Marc pointed at his father.

"We got a little flustered," he said, "on our way out the door."

Before leaving, the psychologist assured Madeleine she could resume her routines with the boys. But she had avoided them the rest of the day. He tucked the twins in by himself as she stood outside the door, silent and tearful. She'd spent the night curled rigidly on her side of the bed. He lay on his back, listening to her wakeful breathing, following the dark paths of his own 3:00 a.m. thoughts.

. . .

Dalton was counting on Hart's sensitivity to the dynamics of the situation. His security lead did not disappoint. His attention to Madeleine was pitch-perfect—sympathetic, stern, and confident. He offered a vague and optimistic summary of the state of the investigation. The suspects had been confirmed on various flight manifests five days earlier. Return tickets had not been booked on any of the airlines. When she asked about the police, he was vague.

"So, what are we doing," she asked, "to make sure this never happens again?"

Hart nodded. The question he'd been waiting for. "To begin, you and your children will be treated with the same protocols as your husband. You will never move without two vehicles in support. It will be more conspicuous, I'm afraid."

"Je m'en fous de ça," Madeleine said quickly. "I don't care."

"Tout à fait," said Hart. "We're ordering several up-armored vehicles and exploring the logistics of keeping two helicopters on standby."

"Whatever it takes," Dalton broke in. "The budget is unlimited."

Madeleine ignored him.

"We're adding more full-time personnel," Hart said. "Screened by me, of course. That will take a few weeks. In the meantime, we're hiring locals, doubling their pay and their shifts."

"Are these people vetted?"

"Most of them are off-duty law enforcement. All have pristine records. We're bringing them in from Oahu and Maui, too."

Madeleine still seemed uncertain.

"We also have a team of contractors flying in tomorrow," Dalton added.

"How many?"

"Eight," said Hart, looking uncomfortable.

"Ce n'est rien," said Madeleine.

Dalton waited for Hart to explain why these particular contractors were not nothing.

Hart changed subjects. "Once the team's built out, we'll double personnel at every entry point and have a quick-response team on twenty-four-hour readiness." He turned back to Dalton. "Which brings us to our primary security concern at this time. We still lack full operational control of our perimeter."

"What does that mean?" Madeleine asked.

"Due to legal issues, a family residing on neighboring land has an easement granting full entry and egress privileges for themselves and their guests."

"You mean anyone can drive onto our land?" She turned to her husband.

"Only across it," he said lamely.

"To reach the beach our family still cannot use?"

"Just seal off the land along the beach road until this is resolved," Dalton told Hart.

"That would take nine months," said Hart, "increase your security perimeter by seventy percent, cut your property in half, and interfere with your excavations."

Dalton looked at Madeleine. She seemed more alarmed than ever.

"I've spoken to your legal team," said Hart. "Apparently, we have forty-eight hours to lock down ownership, or the process becomes much more complicated."

Dalton turned from glaring at Hart to find Madeleine glaring at him.

"While you are busy with your lobbyists," she said, "your family is sans défense."

He glanced at his watch. There were five notifications. He was ten minutes late.

Madeleine was staring at him with an expression he had never seen before.

"I'm going to fix this," he told her.

Erin was waiting for Dalton at the top of the stairs.

"He's just sitting there. Waiting for us to connect."

"So why didn't you get started?"

She looked at him blankly. "He's a *senator*. This was your meeting."

"How did it go with that woman last night?"

"Woman?"

"The Hawaiian woman. Cannoli?"

"Nalani?" Erin was trying to adjust. "We hit it off," she finally said. "She's a smart one. Listen—" She had him by the elbow and was dragging him toward the video room. "Do you have your talking points for this—"

"So, she's in?"

In the tiny delay before Erin responded, Dalton's mind went to a dark place.

"I told her to own her power. She's ready."

"She's ready? Or she's in?"

Erin scowled. "I laid the foundation. She's ready to say yes."

"You were supposed to be the closer."

Erin stopped tugging on him.

"Did I miss something?" she said. "Are we cooling off a United States senator now? Because I don't think—"

"We're not cooling anyone off. I just have other priorities. My *family* comes before this company. *Always.*" He watched to make sure the subtext of that comment had been received. "Now I need to make a call."

"That's what I'm say—"

"Not that call. You need to cover for me. I need to arrange something."

Erin was staring at him with real surprise. "This is the future of the company. This is everything you and I have been discussing."

He gave her his biggest, fakest smile and clapped her on the shoulder. "Just use your charm."

She didn't smile. "It's not that simple."

"I thought that's what people like you get paid for," he said, "to make things simple for people like me."

37

It was almost dawn when Sam dropped Nalani at her apartment. She woke a few hours later, feeling surprisingly good. She stared at the surfboards stacked in the corner. Then her phone dinged, and she lay down on the couch. Mike asking to join her village. She lazily scrolled his photo album. Then she looked up Erin Bogosian.

Getting off the couch became increasingly difficult as the morning passed. She wondered what she had consumed the night before. Parts of her brain had gone disturbingly silent. Thank God it was a Sunday.

Her phone buzzed. Sam. "Hello?"

"Oh my goodness, girl, how was that party?!"

"It was something."

"Wasn't it? And it's only the beginning. Listen. We want to move forward, with the deal. The one we discussed? Conveying the land to a nonprofit for protection and study? I've got an appointment set up to go over the details."

"I'm not feeling—"

"I heard about your conversation. With Erin? It sounds like you two really hit it off. She's an amazing woman. You remind me of her, actually. There could be a possibility, you know, for mentorship? She's on the business side. Just like you."

"Wow. Really? I thought you—? I mean—"

"Great. They've sent a car. It should be there any minute. Aloha!"

Nalani stared at her reflection in the phone's black mirror. She looked better than she felt. Things had regressed. It took all her energy to make it to the bathroom. She was still waiting for hot water when her phone rang. She tried to make the shower quick, but she wasn't tracking time too well. Once she started scrubbing, she found she couldn't stop.

As she approached the black Suburban, a man in a blue polo stepped out and opened a door. There were two leather captain's chairs, but she couldn't resist the chance to sink across the enormous rear bench seat. She helped herself to a bottle of alkaline water and watched silvery clouds and black sky pass above the sunroof. Soothing instrumental synth played over the speakers. She was falling asleep and didn't try to arrest the slide.

Her door opened. In the guard's mirrored glasses, she saw two tiny versions of herself sprawled on the cushions, her face imprinted with the armrest stitching. The man's expression was exquisitely blank. She tried and failed to imagine what it would take to draw a reaction. This was his expertise: giving his clients the illusion of privacy.

They were at the house she and Sam had shown the producer. Two men, dressed in black body armor and carrying small rifles or large machine guns, she wasn't sure which, flanked the ornate doors. One of the men in blue polos opened the door, and she entered, alone, walking uncertainly through the dim living room toward the blinding panorama beyond the glass. On the lanai, she felt the breeze from the ocean and the humid air from the yard. Franky Dalton was sitting at the head of the long table.

Nalani had never been interested in mainland celebrities, definitely not Frank Dalton. But the cognitive dissonance of meeting a stranger so familiar was oddly transfixing. It was different from meeting Erin Bogosian, who was extraordinary, which had made Nalani feel extraordinary too. Frank Dalton was ordinary. But his ability to be so ordinary while being one of the richest people in the world gave him his own weird mystery. It was the opposite of charisma, but could be mistaken for it, if you weren't paying attention.

He grinned and held out his hand.

"Thanks for coming, Nalani." He said her name very precisely. "Have a seat. Would you like anything to drink?"

She was still clutching her bottle of water from the car. "I have this."

His smile was appropriate, pleasant, and just the slightest bit irritated.

"Sam and Erin have said amazing things about you. I'm so glad we're finally meeting. I'm in awe of the stewardship your family has shown over your land."

"Thanks?"

"I know Samantha has told you how special we feel Momona Bay can be. And the plans we have to learn from it. But I wanted to address it with you myself. And to make clear how much we recognize its value."

Any confusion cast by his celebrity had worn off by that last word. "Tell me again," she said, "why you want this land so badly?"

"The Dalton Family Foundation is one of the world's largest funders of oceanic research, particularly littoral zones. Coral reefs support more marine life than any other part of the ocean. All we need is a pristine area to study. Momona Bay has remained untouched for centuries. It's the perfect candidate."

Dalton swiveled toward the vista of Hanalei and gestured at the fan of brown coral just visible below the cliffs. "Some say reefs as degraded as these can never flourish again. I'm going to prove them wrong. At Momona, we will build an internationally recognized oceanographic facility capable of deploying an array of spectrumming capabilities—lidar, multiband, 4D spectrography—to map every millimeter of the reef and its biome. Our AI will analyze the habits and patterns of marine life for an unprecedented understanding . . ."

Nalani was trying to sort her thoughts. She knew he was full of shit, but she didn't think he was lying. His presentation was far too slick and practiced to be trusted, but all that practice had been for her. It was all right to feel flattered, she decided. She could still keep her guard up.

On cue, he shifted to a more intimate tone. "It's amazing, really." He chuckled softly, for reasons unclear. "We've depended on these reefs so long yet know almost nothing about them."

He met her eyes, as if challenging her to disagree. She challenged herself to bite her tongue.

"I hope it doesn't sound hyperbolic to say I believe the survival of our species depends on projects like this. We must gain new understandings of the natural world and its systems, so we can predict catastrophic dysregulation events."

"So, you think that's going to happen, catastrophic . . ."

"Dysregulation."

"Your technology tells you that?"

"Let me put it this way," said Dalton, "in every self-regulating feedback system, there are tipping points. They could be changes to the ice caps, acidity levels, jet streams, ocean currents. They're not necessarily *likely* to happen, but their consequences would be immense. We have to prepare for them."

"And try to prevent them?"

"Of course. *Of course.* That's our number one priority. Prevention."

"And that's why you want to study Momona Bay."

"Exactly."

"So why here? Why not go to Florida? Aren't you from there?"

"No, no. Virginia. It's on the same coast. No coral reefs there. I have to be honest, there *is* a bit of selfishness when it comes to choosing a site. We feel connected to Hawaii. My wife and I. My whole team. We're inspired by Native Hawaiians. I think we share a respect for living with nature. And being self-sufficient. We want to make self-sufficiency possible again."

"Who said self-sufficiency became impossible?"

"The average person," said Dalton, "has no idea of the systemic complexities they take for granted." He spoke rapidly now, almost robotically. "The food supply chain. Farms all over the world relying on inputs all over the world to produce food transported regionally by road and rail then transferred to ships—which rely on *ports,* obviously—*then* back onto local intermodal networks. If one port can't off-load, ships wait at anchor. Soon there are no empty ships to pick up other cargo. Everything stops. And all of these logistics are *completely* reliant on the electrical grid, and Internet, I mean the DNS system alone, most people have no idea how vulnerable . . ."

He stopped—possibly noticing Nalani's expression—and skipped to the end. "TLDR, our food supply is more fragile than people want to know, with many points of systemic failure."

"You think we need to understand nature better, so it won't kill us."

Dalton nodded uncertainly. "I brought you here to reassure you, we want the same things you want."

"Remind me again, how much . . ."

"I believe Samantha explained that the center wants to offer you three million dollars to act as its representative?"

"She said two million."

"Oh, well. Three million seems reasonable. And we understand your family will need a place to live. The board of directors decided to purchase this house in your name. Sam thought you liked it?"

Nalani was quiet. "I'll need to think about it," she said.

"Of course." He offered a smile, then his hand. "No pressure at all. Take some time to explore the property. The car will wait to take you home. Or you can stay if you want. The beds are made. We can bring anything you need. All we ask is that you make your decision tonight."

Nalani sat on the lanai, looking at the ocean. She remembered the certainty she'd felt the night before and was ashamed. Everything she could remember about that night was shameful. Everything she couldn't remember was even worse. But the most shameful thing of all was that, when she thought about the decision that had seemed so blindingly clear on the Zodiac, she wasn't sure it had been wrong.

Her uncle Richard would be disgusted. His voice still came into her head. He would say ancestral land defined and bound you. Nothing could excuse giving it up; anything could be justified to keep it. Because of him, the land on Namahana Mountain still belonged to that side of her family.

She tried to picture the property after two years of neglect. The island worked fast on empty houses. She'd seen photos with police tape strung everywhere; she doubted anyone had come to take it down. Uncle Richard had only been missing six months when the family sold his horse. Her own, Emma, was stabled on the westside now. She drove over sometimes, but it was hard to watch Emma gallop two or three times around the paddock just to settle enough to come and nuzzle her hand. Nalani knew how much loneliness it took to create that much joy. She told herself when she was in a better place, she would see her horse more often.

All that should make this simple. Her uncle *had* justified anything to keep that land. He'd cooked meth. He'd murdered people. She could take a better path.

Horseshit, she heard him say, and he was right. If she was going to do this, she would look at it squarely.

She stood, walked past the table—the longest slab of koa she had ever seen—through the french doors, under the canoe. She passed through bedrooms with vistas of mountains, bathrooms with showers the size of her condo's living room. Housing was the biggest problem for every local family she knew. Solly and Maile could spend the rest of their lives here. The family would be set for a hundred years, forever, if she set up the estate correctly. She'd taken enough accounting to know that nothing was more powerful than compound interest.

She'd circled back to the koa table. Now she placed both hands on it. She'd always known there was an offer she could not say no to. She'd just been hoping no one would make it.

38

Janice Diaz knocked on Phoenix's door. He opened it a few inches and peered out.

"Can I borrow a laptop?"

He stared at her. "I think I have a clean one."

She brought it back to her room, lay on the bed, entered *Sokoni leaks* in the search bar. Hundreds of pages populated. Fortunately, the first was a Wikipedia entry. There had been four releases going back fourteen months. The first was a cache of internal complaints from content moderators employed by a contractor in Arizona to view the most disturbing images and videos imaginable for eight hours a day. A reporter had dubbed these *the Phoenix Leaks,* and the name caught on. A Sokoni spokesperson categorically denied the complaints and, a few weeks later, announced all content moderators would be eligible for free subscriptions to a mental health app.

The next two leaks focused on user data. The leaker, now calling himself Phoenix, claimed the Sokoni app was harvesting the entire contents of any device it was loaded on. If someone gave it permissions to share one video to their commons, all their image files uploaded to company servers. CFO Erin Bogosian was quoted explaining this was an engineering hack to help the app run faster and improve experience for users. *We are sorry for any unnecessary concerns this completely misleading abuse of proprietary information may have caused,* she wrote. *We promise to do better.*

There had been a campaign to *#ExitSokoni,* but it had petered out after a few weeks. The company went on to have its best quarter ever.

The fourth leak had been two days earlier. It was about content moderation, again, and obscure languages, and Indonesian politics, and possibly genocide, but that was debatable. She'd only been reading a few minutes, but her mind didn't seem to be functioning at what she hoped was its highest level. She was sinking deeper into the mattress, letting her eyes close.

There was a tap on the door. "You coming?" Phoenix called.

They sat around a table with a large umbrella rising through the center.

"Tell me again," said Phoenix, "what happened at the hospital?"

Alpha leaned on his forearms. He glanced at Janice Diaz. "We followed the plan. Took up a strategic position near the dais and waited to initiate the action."

"Which was going to be what, exactly?"

Alpha rolled his eyes. "The plan was . . . dynamic. We were hoping there would be a giant check. Something we could throw paint on as he was handing it over. That moment you could turn into a Jeff, like you asked for."

"Did you say Jeff?" Phoenix asked.

Alpha stared blankly at the other man.

"Or *GIF*?"

"The thing you wanted," said Alpha.

Vulnerability flashed so quickly across Phoenix's features, Janice Diaz wondered if he'd even felt it before he set his mouth in a thin, grim smile. "And then?"

"He never showed. So, we aborted."

"That's it?"

"That's it."

Phoenix looked at her. "And you . . . just wandered up to them?"

At least she could answer this question honestly.

"Yes."

"Can you brief us," Phoenix said, "on everything you remember of the last few weeks?"

"I landed four days ago," she said, ignoring the look between Phoenix and Alpha. "First responders met me on the plane and took me straight to the hospital. I couldn't—I can't—remember anything from the time before."

"How far back?"

"I'm not sure," she said. "It's still vague. Days, weeks." Years.

"You have no idea what you were doing?"

She shook her head.

"What have you been doing since?" Alpha asked.

She shrugged. "Surviving."

"When was the last time you saw Agile?" Phoenix now.

"I was hoping you could help me piece things together."

"You aren't aware that none of us have ever met?"

"I'm not aware of a lot of things."

"It was part of our operational security. We had a communication tree. We—"

"You can explain it to her later," said Alpha. "We need to plan next steps."

"You have the exit plan. We'll put it into effect tonight."

"You're saying we abort?"

"What's the alternative? You think it's a coincidence Agile disappeared and they canceled the event?"

"You think your girl tipped them off."

Phoenix shook his head. "Whether it came from her or not, they're spooked. They won't give us any more opportunities to make news at their expense. Not on this island. We follow our exit plan and wait to see what develops."

"There *is* no exit," Alpha said impatiently. "They're hunting us now. Doesn't matter how good our OPSEC has been. They'll ID us all, if they haven't already."

"Why would they be hunting us?"

Janice Diaz couldn't tell if the question was as innocent as Phoenix made it sound.

Alpha answered hastily, "If they got tipped off, I mean. Whatever else you're sitting on, it's time to get it out."

Phoenix put his hands in his lap. "I'm sorry," he said. "I know you've given a lot to this. But the stakes aren't the same for you as they are for me. None of you have done anything illegal yet. I can't afford any risks."

Janice Diaz found herself speaking. "In an asymmetric situation, caution can be the riskiest option. You can't be predictable. They're expecting us to run. They're ready for it. We need to get surprise back on our side."

"You have more to leak," said Alpha. "Right?"

"I do," said Phoenix, "but I don't see how it will be any different. We need an incident to capture people's attention. Otherwise, they just skim the headline and keep scrolling. They already know they hate Sokoni. But they still get their news *on* Sokoni. That's the problem."

In the last few days, Janice Diaz had been making peace with the idea that she was what she appeared to be: an addict and a loser, someone who'd failed to achieve the most basic levels of success or self-care. Today, she was learning there was nothing to be ashamed of. She'd been beaten down and beaten up in a desperate fight for a worthy cause. She was part of a team trying to take down one of the most powerful corporations on the planet.

"What would we do," she asked, "if we did decide to seize this moment?"

Alpha answered first. "It's like he said. Statistics don't go viral. We need to make it personal."

39

Pastures and ridges rolled past the window to a soundtrack of synth tones and bass bumps precisely calibrated to make reality feel ever so slightly—and productively—askew, allowing Dalton to momentarily forget the stakes involved and simply savor what had just occurred.

These karmic opportunities were his favorite part of being wealthy. Like most Hawaiians, Nalani and her family had experienced some tough breaks. He'd had some lucky ones. Now the world had a chance to be a little bit more equitable.

And his least favorite part? He wasn't sure he had a word for it. His therapist did: *narcissism*. But that diagnosis seemed too simplistic. There *were* things that mattered to him more than his own well-being. His family, obviously. And his company. What his therapist didn't understand—how could she?—was that the more attention he gave the things he cared about, the more it all looped back on him. He was the father and the founder, with unlimited resources at his command. What was he supposed to do, abdicate those responsibilities? That would be the most narcissistic move of all.

He pressed a button over the door. "Just drive awhile."

The driver nodded. Dalton watched him through the glass, mumbling the new plan into the radio. Then he called Erin.

The senator had rescheduled. "He needs to hear it from you personally." She was off the phone in less than thirty seconds.

They left the North Shore behind. No more fenced estates on old plantation acreages. Just humid jungle in the muddy river valley below Kong Mountain. He knew it was sacred somehow, that it had a Hawaiian name. But the peak was shaped uncannily like the head of a gorilla, and that's what everyone called it.

They passed a dirt road cleaving an overgrown field. Six kids on three four-wheelers emerged from the grass and tried to keep pace with his motorcade. The Suburbans smoothly gained speed. To the men up front, everything was a threat.

Maybe they weren't wrong.

Everyone warned you about Anahola. On his first visit, it had reminded him of Kenya. The plastic chairs in the yards, the dilapidated general store and quaint post office. Sam had laughed when he asked if there were any properties nearby worth looking at. And now he'd been around long enough to laugh at that too. The beaches were nice, supposedly, but only clueless tourists ended up there. To locals in the know, the whole place was a stay-away. You could get carjacked, or worse.

He knew it was historical injustice. He'd even asked about giving them all broadband. The Sokoni Native People's Initiative had laid high-speed fiber-optic networks in over thirty reservations already. But there was something about the way Hawaiian land was designated, federally. It hadn't qualified, according to Initiative bylaws, and he hadn't followed up.

He called DC next. As his VP of public policy went down an endless list of legislators he would need to contact the next day, he passed the waves at Kealia, the headstones in the Catholic cemetery, the tents and tarps of what seemed to be a homeless camp up in the trees. They took the Kapa'a bypass, skipping the depressing sight of run-down hotels, shabby T-shirt shops, cheap oceanfront condos. They hit a red light at Wailua River. He stared at the eerie concrete skeleton of the old Coco Palms Resort. How had the county let it stay like that so long? He made a mental note to get an estimate to tear it down and build a park, something the community could use.

He called Hart as they swung through Lihue. On Rice Street, he saw a woman facedown on a bench, a little white dog alert beside her. A man biked past with a rooster on his handlebars. Still no progress in tracking down the kidnappers.

He wondered if the men up front were on the team that had almost lost his family. He began putting together his own list of people to call. Men who'd been living these realities longer than he had. A few heads of state. People who could help him find a new security lead. Anyone who might have a reference for Ariel Raz. He pushed the button over the door.

"Take me to the hospital."

It was enough to see the building. The day had turned gray. They circled an enormous tree that whipped its black leaves back and forth. There was still so much for him to do.

"Take me home."

They stopped at a red light beside a man at the bus stop, hospital bracelet still on his wrist. He was screaming at a streetlight, veins standing out from his neck.

Dalton had read somewhere that psychologists were having to change the definitions of paranoid psychosis, now that everyone really was being spied on.

That was the problem with all these diagnoses. They didn't take circumstances into account. Of course he had grandiose thoughts. Everyone did. Almost everyone. No one seemed to appreciate just how hard he worked to maintain the fiction of being an ordinary guy, a kid from NoVA, a coder, a business owner, a dad. He appreciated his therapist's candor. But you had a disorder when your thoughts didn't fit the facts of your life.

Trying to keep believing in his own normalcy, that was the definition of insanity.

40

Nalani didn't know what to do with herself. She'd barely walked into her own apartment when Sam called with a list of things she'd need to do in the next two days. Now she paced the tiny unit, trying to decide where to start. She grabbed a bag and began filling it: bathing suit, rash guard, toothpaste, change of clothes. She realized she was packing for a night in Momona Bay.

Uncle Solomon was on the lanai, mending a pale blue pile of monofilament fishnet, each knot hand-tied. Her mother sat at the picnic table under the false kamani. She had a magazine in front of her but ignored the flapping pages. The trade winds were bringing a storm. A big one. The weather guy on Oahu was on the news every ten minutes predicting when it would make landfall. Not that he ever got those things right.

The storm was days away, but the landscape was already in motion. Waves bunched and hollowed as they crossed the reef. Leaves on the kamani fluttered, shuddered, and went spinning off the branches. Green nuts thunked into the sand. Coco palm fronds clashed overhead. When the wind gusted, stinging grains of sand streamed across the table. Ocean plastic went tumbling over the dunes. Her mother sat perfectly still.

She finally looked up when Nalani sank onto the rough planks a few inches above the drifted sand. She smiled, but still seemed far away, as if her daughter were part of a dream she hadn't escaped.

"How you stay?"

Her mother shrugged.

"You no like get out of this wind?"

"I like 'em. S'how it used to blow, before times. When I was a girl."

"Still blows like this plenty. I no can surf on days like this."

Her mother smiled. She still hadn't looked at her. "I'm sorry, you know. For how I was. For how I made you be."

"How's that?"

"You had grow up too fast."

"I never knew nothing different."

"Maybe I stayed away because I was afraid of what I'd do to you."

"I know you wish that's how it was. But you weren't afraid of nothing. You were drunk or high. Or trying get drunk and high. You never cared about being one bad mother. You forgot you were a mother."

"I never beat you."

Nalani shook her head. "Congratulations."

"Your great-grandfather. You know how bad he used to beat my tūtū Maxine? She died before you were born. One car accident. Straight into a pole. They said she was drinking, but I know she was just trying for get away from him once and for all. He was full-blood Hawaiian. Came up in the foster system. Plenty of them had get taken away before times. Their parents never spoke nothing but Hawaiian language; the children was beaten for saying one word. He had go fight in two wars. Came back mean. But Maxine gave it right back. Threw a pan of frying oil at his head once. My mother and my uncles, that's the house they was raised in. No wonder they had raise us how they did. Your grandfather, he was one gentle man. Too afraid of my mother for protect us kids. The lickings she could give. Flyswatter, bottle brush, bare hand, coat hanger. She thought she was being easy on us."

"I'm sorry," Nalani said. And she was. She had seen how angry her tūtū could be. And she could picture the little girl, always smiling in the few photos she had seen. But she felt no sympathy for the woman in front of her, telling the same old manipulative stories. Excuses for her own failures. "I know how hard things were for you. But why are you telling me this again?"

Her mother's black hair whipped across her cheekbones, creased by lines that made her one of the only Hawaiians Nalani knew who looked older than her years. She stared at her daughter without speaking. Nalani watched her trying to form the next words.

"Is it true," she finally said, "I never hit you?"

Nalani nodded.

"You sure?"

"You never," said Nalani.

Her mother's eyes were glassy.

"It was here I used to come," she said. "Momona Bay. Solly would pick me up. He's really my mother's cousin, you know. His faddah did pilau kine stuff to him. He went jail for what he done to Solly. By then, the boy stay like he is now, quiet. He got bullied at school. He move down here before he even get one chance to graduate. My aunties and uncles never like him use the main house. He built himself one camp, up the valley. When the police try take him back school, he hid. Easy for get lost up there in the forest. He still know every inch."

Maile turned to watch the ironwoods tossing in the valley. Her hair curtained her face. She turned, and it whipped behind. Nalani saw her eyes again.

"He was the one looked out for me. Just a few years older, but he knew how to live off the 'āina. He tried pass what he had learned from our kupuna. About the fish houses that stay out in the moana"—she pointed at the horizon—"about po'ina kai, where the waves first break. An' everything that happen right up to 'ae kai, where the water washes on the beach. He brought me opihi, he'e, ula off the reef, never mind what season it was. I never bring him nothing but pilikia. When I was older, I had boyfriends call him māhū, donkey, retard, right to his face. Saying he one pervert, just like his faddah. But I was using then and never said nothing."

Her mother lifted her hips and slid a flattened pack of Winstons from her jeans. Her hair hid her eyes as she flicked the lighter, shook it in exasperation, tried again. Finally, she turned back to her daughter, shielding the cigarette with her hand, smoke streaming beneath her fingers.

"When I came back to this place, I never knew if he would take me in. The way I'd let people treat him. Not just my friends but our own family. The old-timers. Til the day they died, when they saw him, all they saw was shame on our family. You don't remember. You loved it in the old days, when you was just one girl. The parties they used to throw. Holiday weekends, everyone camping. I saw how happy you were, running wild. Maybe you don't remember."

"I remember," said Nalani. "You taught me to surf."

Her mother glanced at her, so quick she almost missed it, then looked toward the ocean, took a long drag, still shielding the cigarette, her hair streaming back from her face.

"You taught me," said Nalani. "Right there." She pointed toward the break, blown out now by the wind. Small barrels collapsing into foam before they could fully form.

Her mother was looking that direction, too, but she had her hand across her eyes. Her shoulders tensed and released. The cigarette danced in her fingers. The wind had blown it out.

As Nalani watched her mother, she searched herself for something she could offer. But that was dead. Whatever it was that allowed a mom to hurt her kid, whatever allowed a parent to make their child rotten inside, so rotten they passed it on to their own children, whatever that was, it wasn't in her. She had turned a blowtorch on herself and burned it out. The way they burned the heartwood from a log of koa before they carved a new canoe. Whatever had passed through generations of her family, it would end with her. She had decided that a long time ago.

That was why she had the strength to do this. To give them all a new start.

She knew what had burned. And sometimes she grieved it. In the bargain she had made, there would be things she'd never feel. She would have daughters, and she would love them. But there'd be certain things she couldn't give them. And they would feel the lack, even if they never understood what it was. They might even hate her for it.

And if they did hate her, it was because they'd been protected. She would never tell them what her mother had done to her, and what her mother's mother had done, and what her mother's mother's mother had done. All so that when her girls had daughters, they would be able to love them with everything inside them intact. And it would be those girls who started the family line anew.

And those children *would* love her. Her mo'opuna. Even if they sensed the hollowness inside her. Even if they heard the stories of how tūtū had betrayed the family and sold the ancestral land, their one hānau. They would love her, and they might even forgive her, but they would never understand her.

They would never understand what she had done for the sake of her family.

41

Janice Diaz spent the rest of the afternoon by the pool, ready to get up and leave if any of the men came out. But they stayed inside.

The weather was strange. Cold breezes died suddenly, allowing warm air to settle like a blanket. Then winds bent the trees again. High overhead, the clouds were streaming. Lower in the atmosphere, wisps and tattered ghosts hung motionless, scabs across the blue sky.

She knew Phoenix was in his bedroom, at work on the next phase of the plan. He was going to release something; Dalton would respond, and the team would be ready. For the *action*. Whatever that meant.

She watched the light wobble like mercury on the silver surface of the pool. She couldn't forget the woman's face as she leaned over her child. She'd been afraid of the men, of course, of what they would do to her children. But she'd been afraid of herself, too, of what she would do if she had to. Most people never face what they're capable of. And they're never the same once they have. She wondered how she knew that.

The action, whatever it was, would not be pleasant. And whatever was happening in Indonesia, that wasn't pleasant, either. Those women loved their kids, too. What was this hesitation, then? Weakness. That was all. If she believed in this cause, which she clearly did.

An idea shivered through her. If she could remember her own home—or at least the hemlock forest outside her window—the apartment must belong to someone else. The woman with the knife. Agile.

So, she'd been in her house. And something had happened. Something bad.

Should she share this intel with Phoenix? Eventually. But not yet. Not until she'd given herself a chance to understand the implications. There was no urgency, operationally. He was already acting under the assumption Agile had betrayed them.

She had to admit, it was invigorating to navigate such terrifying uncertainty with such sure instincts. She had no idea where this confidence came from, but it fit her like a tailored suit. It was who she was.

There was another decision. A harder one. Alpha was lying to Phoenix about what happened at the hospital. Backing him had bought her time to assess the situation, but it would be malpractice to move forward while ignoring that her teammates' objectives might not be aligned. She would have to make a choice.

Her instincts told her the answer was obvious. But she forced herself to think it through.

Darkness arrived too soon, a cold, gray curtain drawn across the dusk. She turned to look through the glass into the dim, empty rooms.

It took Phoenix a minute to answer her knock. He opened his door wider when he saw it was her. Three laptops sat on his bed, their screens all turned away. "Yes?"

"The action we're planning," she said. "What exactly is it?"

He grimaced. Then smiled, kindly. "That's your area of expertise. Or *was*, I guess. The plan was always to get in his face, rattle him, try to force him off script. On camera, of course. Create something attention-grabbing, something people will click on."

"You want to make a meme?"

"That's always been the plan," he said, wounded by her skepticism.

"Can I come in?"

He stepped aside. She shut the door behind her.

"If that's the plan," she said, "why bring in *this* team?"

He looked at her strangely. "I don't know anything about civil disobedience, live protests, media relations. I'm a coder."

"And that's what these guys know?"

"Supposedly."

His look was wary, as if he thought she was trying to make him the butt of a joke.

"So, no violence," she said. "No guns? No kidnapping?"

"Kidnapping? What good would that do?"

"What do you know about these guys?" she asked him.

"What do *I* know? I don't even know their names. What do *you* know?"

This was the moment she should walk out. Out of his room. Out of the house. Out of this mess. But then what? She'd made her decision. Whatever doubts she had about Phoenix, she was sure his objectives were the same as hers. When it came to Alpha and his team, she had no idea.

"There were inconsistencies," she said, "in what Alpha told you about the hospital."

"Fuck," said Phoenix. "Fuck. Fuck. Fuck." He began pacing in a circle.

She realized she would have to take a firmer hand in this operation. "Calm down," she told him. "You and I can sort this out. We'll start by working backward. Pull yourself together and tell me, who brought them in?"

Phoenix stopped pacing and raised his eyes. "You did."

DAY 6

42

In her dream, Nalani rode Emma through familiar pastures ringed by green ridges. Mist rose from the valleys and faded into the clouds. It was a place she had not been in a long time and would never return to. She was painfully happy.

Someone was touching her shoulder. She rushed from the green valley into the darkness of the house on Momona Bay. A man's hand was on her. A soft voice.

Her uncle Solly.

"Akule running."

"What?"

"I been watching for 'em. You like help?"

"Help with what, Uncle?"

She could hear him moving away. "One fish ball stay in the bay. Your maddah going be the kilo. I need someone for help run net."

"Shoots," said Nalani. "We go."

The wind had died overnight. The water inside the reef was calm enough to mirror the brightest stars. The beach was a pale band. There was a faint rim of blue in the east. Her mother and her uncle stooped over the kayak. "You coming with me," said Solomon. "Your maddah going look 'em right here from the beach and tell us where for go."

The net shimmered as they walked the kayak into the water. Solomon handed her a paddle, and she hoisted herself onto the seat in the bow. He held the plastic gunwales as she braced her feet in the notches cast in the deck. He gave her a shove, and she felt the kayak wobble as he hopped onto the seat behind her.

"Kaukau," said her uncle. She set her blade. The sky was pearly gray. All but the brightest stars had faded. Each time she raised the paddle, cold lines of water ran across her knuckles and down her arm. She felt the warmth rising from the ocean into the cold morning air.

"Lawa," said her uncle.

She set her paddle across her lap. Drops from each blade left interweaving rings across the surface. Her uncle trailed a blade to spin the kayak as it drifted. The clouds were glowing high above the shadowed island. The hills that ringed the bay showed faint touches of green. On the beach, her mother stood motionless.

Her uncle pointed toward shallow water, where small pinnacles made the surface quake. "These small-kine reefs," he said, "choke fish in there. Plenty he'e, manini, weke, 'āweoweo, sometimes kole, even kūmū. Your ancestors, they ate plenty fish from there. Me and your maddah, too, when we was young. But only when the waves too big for take from the reef outside. Cannot go too often to those holes, or else no more."

"You shoot 'em with one spear or what?"

Her uncle laughed. "Sometimes. Your great-grandfaddah, he just reach in and take 'em with one hand. He's the one taught me every puka and how to know where moray eel like stay. Get plenty tricks, the old Hawaiians. Chew up coco meat and spit 'em on the water for see where Mr. Octopus stay hiding. The he'e very smart, he never like get caught. But he curious, too. If you put one stick, the buggah going reach one arm around it. Then you just yank 'em out and bite the eye before the fackah grab you. Ho, spahk your maddah."

On the beach, Maile was signaling. They paddled slowly in the direction she pointed, toward a slight disturbance on the surface, a mist of tiny splashes.

"Start feeding net," said her uncle. The end lay neatly on top of the pile, foam floats and lead weights drawn together. She slipped them over the side and saw the float bob to the surface while the weighted end released a few small bubbles as it sank. She felt her uncle paddling silently behind her, the kayak swinging in a wide arc around the pile.

Her uncle spoke. "Once it set, I like for you go in and move the pile."

She made sure the net released cleanly, looking over her shoulder to watch the floats. The last filament slipped from her fingers, and she could see the full arc in the water.

"I get mask and fins right here. Go when you ready."

She reached back until she felt the rubber straps, then set them carefully between her feet. The sky was alight, and the water reflected the brightness back at her. She flipped onto her belly and slid over the bow, feeling the kayak rock as her legs slipped into the world below. Then she let go, and for a moment she was under, looking at the shadowy bulk of the hull and the dim blue night below the surface.

She kicked and thrust her head into the silvery morning, reached for the fins, and let herself sink back as she pulled the straps behind her ankles. The silver surface of the water danced around her face. She grabbed the mask and pulled the straps over her wet hair. She rested her hands on the round edge of the kayak, breathing deep through her nose, inflating her lungs until she felt them stretch against the inside of her shoulder blades. The water slopped quietly against the hull. She slipped into the silent world.

Ahead, something pale and silvery. She looked for the net but couldn't find it. The sun was still too low to cast much light this deep. She came up and looked across the bright surface until she found the dark bumps of the floats and the gap where they ended. She knew she wasn't the only thing hunting the akule. There could be ulua, 'ōmilu, shibi, monk seals. And the manō would be hunting them. But she trusted her uncle to watch for those.

She took a few more breaths, then doubled over and let her upper body sink with as little effort as possible. She scissored her fins, moving in slow motion toward the silver mass that morphed ahead of her, a tight ball one minute, a long finger the next, reaching into depths she could not see. The school sensed her approach. A tear opened.

Shit, she thought. She stopped and watched the shape re-form. She kicked once, sending herself through the water at an angle to the mass. It compressed in the opposite direction, tightening and going smooth. Thousands of fish weaving themselves together. Against the rest of nature, this was their protection. An akule separated from the smooth shimmering mass could be picked off by the predators that probed the flanks. But against her and her uncle, their cooperation was their downfall. The tighter they whirled, the more would be entrapped.

The faint lines of the net emerged from the blue.

She hauled herself back onto the kayak, tireder than she'd expected. Her uncle was pulling in the net. Drawing it around itself. She hooked her fingers and began pulling with him.

The net kicked and wriggled as it came over the side. Akule flipped their tails and flopped against the plastic hull. More and more silver fish.

Everywhere she felt the slick monofilament lines, the friction of their tiny, hand-woven knots, the flickering quiver of the life departing the akule with each flare of bright red gills. She saw their wide lidless eyes staring back at her, thick as stars.

As they passed over the small reef heads near shore, her uncle spoke for the first time since they'd pulled the net. "This place called pu'ulima, 'cause it looks like a fist. And this one called pu'u'oi'oi because it just one sharp point. That one called pu'uwai."

"What are you talking about, Uncle?"

"Those are names your great-grandfaddah had teach me. All these small 'apapa get one name. Every puka, too."

"You're saying every hole in this reef has its own name?"

"Most been lost already. Some I name myself."

"Did you write them down?"

Her uncle didn't respond. The kayak bumped against the sand. Her mother was running down to meet them. Nalani hopped off. She grabbed the handle at the bow, and the three ran up the sand as far as they could, the kayak dragging heavy with their catch.

They spent half an hour unhooking akule from the gill net and tossing them in coolers. The wind rose with the sun. Soon, clouds were sprinting across the sky, strobing the morning with light and shadow, gradually thickening, first at the center of the island, then spreading to the coast, blotting out the blue day, spitting rain on the Hawaiians as they worked.

Finally, the coolers were full and the nets were empty.

Nalani took a long, cold shower under the tap beside the house.

When she came out, her uncle was waiting. He gripped her hand in both of his and smiled. Then he stopped smiling, but didn't let go. "I remember," he said. "When you were one young girl. You was serious then, too, trying for take care of everyone. Just like you trying now."

When Nalani used her free hand to hide her face, she remembered how her mother had hidden hers the day before.

Her uncle gave no sign of noticing. He pointed to the sea, beyond the waves breaking on the outer reef, toward the next point. "One ko'a stay out there," he said. "One fish house. Very important, for the fish to live in that place. Make babies. Most of the i'a on this reef come from that ko'a. Used to be plenty ko'a li'dat up an' down this coast, each the kuleana of one family. Now all them pau already. Only this one stay. Us families, the ones stay makai, our kuleana the 'apapa, the reef, and out there, too, moana. I go feed 'em now. Make sure the fish like stay, make plenty babies. Your great-grandfather had done it. Now I do it."

It was the most words she had ever heard him speak on land. She looked in the direction he was pointing, an indistinguishable point in the wind-whipped open ocean, the moana.

"I show you, one day," her uncle said, "if you like learn."

Nalani went in to get her things. She was supposed to meet Sam and the lawyer in town. If she hurried, she'd have time to stop at home and change. When she came out, her uncle was gone. The two coolers were loaded in her truck. Her mother was waiting for her.

"Your uncle asked you to pick up ice at the country store and drop these off at the camps. You got time for that?"

She looked at her daughter closely, almost coldly. When Nalani hesitated, she said, "No matter what kine things our kupuna done, they remembered they was blessed with this kuleana. We always mahele what we cannot eat. 'A's how we make sure the fish going come back."

Nalani nodded, slammed the door, and headed up the hill.

43

In the stillness and darkness, Janice's body spoke to her. It said no wonder she was struggling with so many things. She was missing something extremely important. Until she found it again, nothing would be right. These other details. The questions. The conversations and schemes. They were distractions. No matter what the answers, the need would still be there.

She thought about getting up and crossing the dark house, knocking on the door of the room where the men were sleeping, asking whether any of them had anything that would offer relief. She knew the kind of men they were. She knew one of them would.

She pictured the marble counter in the kitchen. White chemical lines. The high before the high. She could remember how it felt to hold a pill in her palm. She remembered the clatter of a plastic case in her pocket, rattling around in the console of a car, or, best of all, nestled, safe and silent, in the drugstore's crisp white paper bag.

She'd never been on meth. She knew that. She knew a lot of things. Knew them without knowing them. She wasn't that kind of person. An ice head. A tweaker. It had been legitimate. A prescription from her doctor.

This was worse. To lie in the darkness, knowing what she needed was just a call away. But a call to whom? Some things still weren't clear.

Her phone was dead on the nightstand. She saw no point in charging it.

Things were coming back. But nothing like that. Codes and numbers. Names.

She saw people. Places. Office buildings. Army bases. Ruins. There were certain streets she could drive for blocks, as long as she never tried too hard to remember. As long as she simply lay in the dark. She knew that if she wanted to remember how she knew those men, she should absolutely, positively, under no circumstances, try to remember how she knew them.

She lay still and drove the familiar roads, and when she opened her eyes, it was daylight.

Alpha was in the kitchen, on a stool at the island, arms crossed on the marble counter, a mug of coffee square between his hands. She moved toward the coffee maker.

"It's cold," said Alpha.

She poured herself a mug and put it in the microwave.

The microwave dinged.

She removed her coffee. Took a sip. Overheated, bitter, stale. But a tiny jolt of the thing she was looking for. A shadow of it.

"So," said Alpha. "You remember how to make a cup of coffee, but you don't remember your own fucking name."

She said nothing.

"What is this amnesia shit, anyway? I've only heard of it on TV."

She shrugged. "Ask the doctor who diagnosed me."

The house was silent. She glanced around to see what she could use to defend herself. Nothing in sight. Only the mug she was holding. Maybe the coffee wasn't overheated.

He was following her eyes. "It's recon day," he said. "You and me. The officer and the chief."

"What about Phoenix?"

"We never worried about Phoenix before we got here. But I guess you don't remember that."

"And the rest of the team?"

"Don't worry about them. Everything has been arranged."

She had the mug clutched to her chest. Fuck him. She wasn't afraid. She set it on the counter. "Good," she said. "And we can stop for a decent cup of coffee on the way."

He gave her a trucker cap and a pair of sunglasses and put on a pair of his own.

They took a series of narrow roads past tropical orchards, pastures, and gravel drives. She looked for landmarks and memorized them. They turned left on the highway. There was a fruit stand at the intersection, closed. Alpha drove fast; windows down; wind whipped through the cabin. He seemed more relaxed. That made sense. He was an action-oriented person. He'd been cooped up too long.

They came up on a black Tacoma with a huge decal in the rear window. Two crossed carbines with the phrase *Defend Hawaii.*

Alpha crossed a double line into the oncoming lane and accelerated past. She didn't turn her head, but glanced at the other driver: a large brown man with long black hair, looking startled. They pulled in front of the truck, which accelerated to catch up, hanging just a few feet off their bumper. Alpha didn't seem to notice.

"You see that shit?" he said. *"Defend Hawaii?"* He didn't wait for her to answer. "I admire these people. I really do. They understand sovereignty. I mean. Hawaiian islands for Hawaiian people? I can't disagree with them."

The man was still riding their bumper.

"The thing is," said Alpha, "what the fuck are they doing about it? Besides putting stickers on their trucks. I hear you, bro. Defend your island. Let's see you defend it from assholes like me."

He threw on his turn signal and hit his brakes at the same moment, coming almost to a stop on the highway before turning onto a road she hadn't seen until the last minute. He didn't accelerate after the turn, just coasted down the side road as he watched his rearview mirror. The truck slowed a moment longer, then sped up and was gone down the highway.

Alpha smiled. "Yeah. They're fucking defeated, all right. Check this out."

Ahead was a long black fence and a guard post, a black SUV parked beside it.

"You saw that?" said Alpha, after they'd passed.

"The Suburban?"

He nodded. "How many, you think?"

"Four or five?" she said. "But they can get a lot more, quick."

"The fence doesn't look like much. Seven feet. Steel?"

"Probably aluminum, because of the salt."

The fence went on over a mile. It wasn't overtly hostile. No razor wire. But every pole ended at a subtle, sharp point. Beyond the fence were pastures and fields, stands of trees in the ravines.

"They must have cameras, sensors, something."

"Drones?"

Ahead, they saw another gate. This one larger. But the setup was the same. A guardhouse and a black Suburban. Now the fence was covered by green fabric, obscuring the view of the landscape beyond.

"See those roofs? What are they, barns? Sheds?"

From the road, she could see two long roofs and the tops of what looked to be sheet-metal walls. "They're huge."

"Got an armory in there. I'm sure."

The fence extended a few hundred more yards, then they were driving past neglected barbed wire and overgrown pastures.

"What do you think?" said Alpha.

"It's a big perimeter."

He looked at her. "You're starting to sound like yourself again."

"How's that?" she said.

"Professional."

The road dipped down a steep hill. Neither said anything for a long time.

"I won't ask what you're planning," she said, "if you don't trust me."

He snorted. "The plan hasn't changed. Send up the flare. Launch the rev."

She said nothing. She could sense he wanted to talk.

"The boys are good," he said. "They're good with that shit we pulled two days ago. Sticking up a mom and her kids. Getting the jump on a couple of rent-a-cops. They're ready to pack it in and start telling everyone back home what badasses they are."

He fished a tin of dip out of the console and tucked a wad into his lip.

"They like stroking their fucking pieces and firing them down at the range. They like making videos and talking shit about what they're gonna do when it gets lit."

He spat out the window.

"They're just like that fucking pussy back on the highway. To be honest. But I'm not gonna let 'em back out of this. I won't lie. This guy Franky wouldn't be my first choice. But sometimes you have to take a target of opportunity. And this is the opportunity that came along. Thanks to you." He grinned at her. "And it's not like he didn't marry a fuckin'—"

He let the thought go unfinished. The road was narrow and he whipped around the hairpin turns as it descended deeper into the jungle.

"All these people saying they're ready to go to war. For the big boogaloo or whatever the fuck they think it's going to be. But no one has the balls to kick it off. They keep giving a little more and a little more. They watch their rights get taken piece by piece and keep saying, *Next time, we're gonna fight*. And they buy more ammo, and more ARs, and post more videos of all their shiny hardware. And they don't do shit."

He reached between his legs and fished a plastic cup off the floor. She heard the tap of a well-aimed stream.

"Meanwhile, the other side is *organized*. They're systematically defining *our* values right out of existence. They tell you genders don't exist. Love, peace, and equality? That means hating the right people, rioting in the streets, and moving *privileged* groups to the back of the line. They tell us *we're* crazy, *our* ideas are hateful, *our* means of self-defense are a danger while *they* burn police stations. They want to bring us to the point where we don't believe our own fucking eyes. And they're still just *testing* to see how far they can push us. Well, they haven't found a limit yet. We just keep folding."

They'd climbed out of the valley and were driving down a long straight road. She could see the ocean beyond a bluff to their left. She wanted to ask where they were going but didn't want to interrupt him. He wasn't talking to her anymore. He was psyching himself up.

"There are twenty-five thousand of us who stand ready. I've seen the list. We got people in every state. Ex-military, ex–law enforcement. We got SWAT, Special Forces, psyops, ICE. We got doctors and lawyers. All organized. Plans in place. Just waiting for the signal. And for every one of them, we got a hundred quiet patriots. People who'll do the right thing once they see the situation.

"The thing is," he said, looking at her for the first time in several minutes, as if reading her thoughts, which she certainly hoped he was not, "people get uncomfortable. With the violence. Even a lot of people in the movement. They're ready to defend themselves and their families. No question. But when it comes to starting the fight, their knees go wobbly. It's human nature. They *understand* that anyone *participating* in an injurious system is just as guilty as someone who injures you directly. But they can't bring themselves to follow that logic to its conclusion. And that is exactly what *they* are fucking counting on! Our civility, the Judeo-Christian code endowed to *us* by *our* ancestors. Look at me, I'm not a violent man. I love peace. I love *life*. All lives. But I'm a patriot. And that carries obligation. I won't stand by and cling to life, mine or anyone else's, when liberty is threatened."

They were back on the highway now, still driving south. Away from where they'd come.

"Take the fucking opioids. The opioid epidemic. Who gets prescribed painkillers? Workingmen: soldiers, firefighters, miners, loggers. The men—and women, too—who would naturally be on the front lines in defense of liberty. And, I'm sorry, but who invented that stuff, Oxy, fentanyl, all those German pharmaceuticals? Jews. Look, it's a fact. And who's making the heroin? Mexicans. And who's selling it? Blacks. Oops, now I said it. Now I'm fucking canceled. Now I'm the racist."

They passed the ruined resort and crossed the bridge. They passed the turn for Aunty Leilani's camp. Now she wanted very badly to know where they were going.

"So maybe I am. Or maybe I'm just being honest. I want my shot. You want your shot. Europeans took this country from the Indians. Now these others want to take it from us. I can't sit and whine about it. I'm no hypocrite. Let them take their shot, fair and square, right? What I'm saying is, we aren't going down without a fight. And you know the funny thing? I've met a lot of Blacks, a lot of Mexicans—online—who agree with me. They love America. They love the opportunities this country gave them. They believe all men are created *equal*."

"Where are we going?" she asked.

Alpha leaned his elbow on the open windowsill. They were on the outskirts of the city. A helicopter passed overhead and descended toward the airport.

"They go about it in a very clever way. See, I *did* my research. But I'm also lucky. I was exposed to the right sources of information. You know, thanks to Sokoni, honestly. I'd have no problem with this guy, Dalton, if he'd just let us share our facts on an even playing field. But that wouldn't fit their agenda. They pull the classics off the shelves for being racist, then call us book burners if we don't want our kids reading groomer porn and atheist propaganda. They know once our generation is gone, there won't be anyone left who knows the truth of history. In that sense, what we are living through is an attempted genocide. The complete eradication of a four-thousand-year-old culture. Now, if you could kill just one person to prevent a genocide, don't you think someone would be morally obligated to do that?"

"Where are we going?" she asked.

"And what if you could bring back a little justice, a little sanity, while you're at it? Put someone on trial who *deserves* judgment. There are people who think we need a false flag op. They want to dress as Antifa and fire on our own people at a rally, even assassinate a politician who supports our cause. They think that's what it will take to launch Day X. And maybe they're right. If that's what it takes, I'm down for it. But first we need to exhaust all other options."

"Where are we going?" she asked again. But now she knew where they were going.

They dipped down a long hill. Janice Diaz glimpsed the abandoned building where she'd met the Micronesians. Then they were passing the harbor, the beach, warehouses, and oil tanks. The road climbed out of the valley into a long stretch of forest and fields. Without signaling, Alpha turned onto a dirt road. The trees were tall and gray. Their leaves were coated with dust.

"I can't blame you," he said, "if you're having second thoughts. This is some rough shit. I always wondered why a person like you was involved in it. You never seemed like the type. But I checked you out. I heard how you operated. I figured you had seen some shit that clarified your thinking."

The road ended. There was the white van. Alpha turned the ignition, rolled his shoulders, looked at her with an expression she assumed he thought was sympathy.

"If I'm wrong," he said, "I'm sorry. But this amnesia shit. This disappearing. Showing up in the middle of a blown op. Those late-night talks you're having with Phoenix. You understand the position I'm in."

He got out of the car. "I've got to check on something. You sit tight."

He made a point of turning his back as he walked to the rear of the van. But she could see the tension in his shoulders. She could sense him listening. He wasn't armed, yet. She felt fairly certain. So, it was a calculation. Every step took him farther from her, but closer to the weapons.

He'd parked the truck on the far side of the turnaround.

Cocky asshole.

She let him get all the way to the van before she opened the door and took off running.

44

Outside the glass walls of the cube, light overtook the landscape. The green slopes had never looked so inviting. The ocean was settling into a profound blue. Dalton was supposed to be on the phone with the first name on a very long list of members of the House of Representatives. But he'd had to push it off. Hart had requested an emergency stand-up.

The delay had given him an unscheduled moment to appreciate sunrise on his estate. He was relieved he could, given how far off the rails his plans had almost gone. In less than twenty-four hours, the last issue with his land would be settled for good. Everything the sunlight touched would officially belong to him.

He'd been up since 4:00 a.m. Erin had rescheduled his call with the senator for 10:00 eastern, which was 5:00 Pacific standard. She hadn't conferenced in, and her assistant was intercepting all her calls. At least all calls from him.

The senator, *his* senator, their closest ally in Washington, grateful recipient of tens of millions in campaign support, had been noncommittal. The rest of Dalton's day was booked in fifteen-minute increments, an agenda painstakingly assembled by the collective efforts of dozens of schedulers, ruined before he'd made the first call. He tried to remember the last time he'd called a House rep individually. Apparently, his DC team believed the only way through this crisis was to grovel.

A quiet knock. Hart, hugging a crisp manila envelope, and unexpectedly, Raz.

"The report's come back on the Kanahele family," Hart said. "The older woman, Maile Kanahele Winthrop, you already know. History of misdemeanor arrests. Possession of controlled substances. Multiple visits to rehab. Investigations from CPS. Some new information did turn up, sealed records indicating she was charged with conspiracy to distribute. The charge was dropped. We suspect she became a cooperating witness. The investigator is still working on that."

"Is this what you called the meeting for?" said Dalton. "The mother is out of the picture."

Hart nodded, but carried on. "The daughter, Nalani Winthrop, turned up in local police files in connection with a methamphetamine ring that seems to have been organized by her paternal uncle. There was a violent altercation with multiple murders, still unsolved. Her uncle disappeared. She has not been connected to the events, as far as we know."

Dalton was staring very hard at his security lead.

"Finally, the cousin. Solomon Kanahele. Very little on him. He disappears from the system during high school. He has never paid taxes, taken out a loan, or signed a lease."

"I'm sorry," said Dalton, "are you updating me on this man's credit history? You know I could have done this myself in ten minutes for seven ninety-nine?"

"Obviously, sir. There *is* more. Solomon's father went to prison. Sexual abuse. Names redacted because the victim was a minor, but our investigators acquired filings indicating Solomon was at the center of the case. They followed up and uncovered certain claims—unsubstantiated at this point— that he himself may have inclinations . . ." Hart clasped his palms together.

"Inclinations of what?"

Hart pursed his lips. "The accusations are vague."

"*This* is why you called a meeting? To share *gossip* about someone who is less than twenty-four hours away from permanently vacating my life?"

"Um, no."

In this moment, Hart looked so miserable, Dalton found himself feeling sorry for him, which immediately filled him with rage. He'd hired someone who'd intimidated him, a Special Forces officer who'd killed terrorists. Where had that man gone?

"And what the hell is *he* doing here?"

"We completed our deep matrix of the assailants," said Hart. "Mr. Raz was extremely helpful in developing the profiles. It seems the videos we've already viewed on Sokoni were only the content that passed community standards for hate speech, racial and religious discrimination, calls to violence, et cetera. There is a significant archive of material, some available on our servers, some from more . . . marginal social networks, that paints a more disturbing picture."

"More disturbing than the picture of my family held at gunpoint while your men did nothing?"

"A poor choice of words, sir." Hart offered a moment of silent penitence. "The good news is that three of the suspects have no tactical training in military or law enforcement, as far as we can tell. They are simply amateurs with a strong ideological motivation."

"What ideology is that?"

"Difficult to summarize. Their oldest activity on the Sokoni platform was apolitical, though there are indications of broadly conservative beliefs, typical of their user profile. It escalated in the last few years, beginning with a focus on election integrity and Second Amendment issues, which seem to have been a gateway to virtual communities with more extreme views on national identity and racial grievance. The apocalyptic thinking was the most recent development, within the past six months."

"I assume you're not talking about climate change?"

"No, sir. You can read the analysts' full report, but they essentially believe the country is in the midst of a cold civil war, which their own side is currently losing against people of other cultures, religions, races, coastal elites, technocrats, billionaires, liberals, globalists. It's a fairly long list of categories, many of which you and your family fall into. They judge society to be in a state of extreme emergency and are preparing for survival while also attempting to wake their side to the urgency of the situation and provoke an effective response."

"What type of response?"

"An armed uprising."

"You said, three of the men. What about the fourth?"

"The fourth is a man named Charles Sutton. His background is . . . varied—brief military career, undistinguished, at least some affiliation with several sheriff's offices, time as a private security contractor. He worked as a self-defense instructor and was briefly certified to offer firearms safety clinics in North Dakota."

Dalton rubbed his eyes. "I'm trying to connect the dots here. These men sound like polar opposites of everything you told me about Phoenix. Are you telling me your profile was wrong?"

Hart stared into the distance. "We're asking ourselves that question."

"So, you called this meeting to inform me this investigation has taken a step backward."

Hart slipped a hand into the manila envelope.

"We're hoping you might recognize this woman."

He handed Dalton a glossy printout, a still from a security camera. It showed a short procession in a white tiled hallway: a young woman in scrubs pushing another woman in a wheelchair, her face tilted away from the camera. A pudgy man in jeans and a floral shirt walked beside them. Dalton looked at Hart and raised his eyebrows.

"The woman in the wheelchair."

"Where did you get this?"

"We developed a description of the woman who interrupted the assault and cross-checked it with airline records, police bulletins, first-responder reports. This woman had an incident on a plane inbound to Lihue on the same day the other suspects arrived. She was met by emergency responders and released from the hospital the same day."

Dalton shrugged. Her face meant nothing to him. He was about to hand the image back to Hart when he noticed Ariel Raz staring at it with an unguarded expression.

"You recognize her," said Hart.

"It's Rebecca Hunt," said Raz. "My partner."

45

The churned red mud was slicker than she'd expected, and for a horrifying moment, Janice Diaz felt her feet go out from under her. Then she found her footing, pushed thin branches aside, felt a spongy layer of leaves beneath her shoes, and was in the forest, quiet and gray.

Most of her training had been in urban situations, where blending with a crowd was more important than speed. But she knew that in the forest, you had to run.

The trees were spaced apart, the underlayer thin. She had no idea how far back Alpha was, but she knew he could see her. The only priority, in these first vital moments, was to get off the X: put time, distance, and terrain between herself and her pursuer.

She'd let him reach the van not only to get the longest head start but because she knew he'd be tempted to unlock the vehicle and grab a weapon. Those few seconds were more precious to her than the prospect of facing him unarmed.

He knew that, too, of course. But she was confident he'd go for the guns. He was cocky. He would want to feel in charge. So he would take his time. Confident in his tracking. And in her panic.

But she wasn't panicked.

She took a hard right, away from the paved road. If he followed his training, he'd try to guess her destination and cut her off. So he would head for the road, then he would remember she was trained, too. He would second-guess himself and double back to look for a sign. When he did, he wouldn't have trouble finding it.

A fallen log lay across her path. She swerved and maintained momentum. *Don't go over obstacles; go around them.* They kept the lessons simple.

She let her eyes unfocus, looking for avenues between trees. Her lungs were starting to grate now. She would have to stop soon, but not as soon as her body wanted.

All things being equal, she would have gone uphill. The high ground offered more advantage—sight lines, defensibility, optionality. You could traverse just below the crest and slip over the ridge if you needed to. But she was headed down.

She hadn't looked over her shoulder yet. The risk of falling outweighed any advantage that could come from that.

Her breathing, heavy and loud. Her lungs were raw now. Ahead, another fallen tree. This one had taken its roots with it. She slid into the muddy hole below the root ball, flopped onto her belly, pushed leaves up to the rim of the shallow crater, and finally looked back.

The sound of her breathing filled the forest. She expanded her diaphragm, trying to satisfy her heart with deep lungfuls of oxygen, to stop the earth from jittering at the pace of her adrenaline. Finally, the trees went still.

This was an ugly forest. Leaves hung limply from gray trunks strangled by vines. There was no understory, which meant good visibility, which was bad. But there was no sign of Alpha.

As she watched the forest, her hands were busy scraping black muck from the sides of the hole and spreading it down her cheeks and across her forehead. She used each arm to slather the other and squirmed in the mud to cover her clothes. She rolled over and mucked up her backside. Then she gathered the crushed and rotting leaves and pressed them to her body.

She could stay here. Watch him walk right past. Wait for nightfall.

That was a fantasy. She hadn't even doubled back to throw him off. He'd be looking for her hole-up site. This one was too perfect.

She had to move.

She didn't move.

She watched the forest. Gray and still and ugly.

She had to move.

Would he guess where she was going? Unlikely. He had to assume the road was her only landmark, and she'd have to go back eventually. He didn't know what she knew. That was her only advantage.

She stood and slipped behind the fallen log, waited, listened. Instead of looking for aisles now, she looked for cover. She stepped deliberately, each foot squarely up and down. She did not want to kick any leaves, overturn a clump of dirt, snap stems, or scrape a streak of exposed green wood from a softened root. She took care to look up, too, ducking under spiderwebs and low-hanging limbs. Her breathing was regular now. At least maintaining noise discipline was easy. If you had nothing to carry, you had nothing that could bump or clatter.

She fell into a rhythm: looking, stepping, finding cover, listening, always listening. She hadn't heard the scurry of an animal. She hadn't even heard a bird-call. It was a still and silent forest. It was easy to imagine dying in this forest.

She heard the sound she had been hoping for. The trickle of water.

This would take her to the river.

For a minute, she gave herself the luxury of walking in the open by the high bank of the stream. She was at least a mile in: Alpha's search area had expanded massively. It should have given her comfort. But it seemed worse, knowing he could be anywhere. As if the chance he was a mile away increased the odds he was a few feet ahead, hidden in his own cover, watching her look back over her shoulder as he waited for a shot.

He *would* shoot her without warning. And if she was still alive, he might say something shitty to her before he made sure he got the kill. Or he might not even bother. It was only in movies that people knew what to say right before they did something like that.

No, he would put two more bullets in her, then he would take a moment to orient himself, and he would walk out of the forest with that glow you got from executing a plan that had gone to shit. This little complication would be a win for him, an opportunity to take her down in action, getting to think of her as a worthy adversary, not someone he'd just . . .

She stopped that line of thinking.

She took a right angle, away from the stream. She wouldn't make it that easy.

Finally, she reached the river. Its banks were choked in a maze of mangroves, brown water slopping between intertwined roots. The river was narrow here. Thirty feet wide. She crouched, balancing on the roots, thinking things over.

Upstream, a commotion, the swish of leaves rubbing together. Then a broad gray wing, a heron taking off in what passed for a hurry, beating its wings once, twice, swooping low across the river, trailing its long yellow legs.

She watched the trees where it had been, then crawled backward across the roots, staying flat. She lowered herself into the water without making a splash. The river was warm and greasy red. Green leaves and cupped yellow flowers spun down its center. She held the slick black roots and watched the bank upstream. A branch shook.

She pushed off, toward the current in the center of the river, felt it gently gather her. She barely felt the motion, but the spot where she'd gone in was already fifteen feet behind her.

She floated with her nose and toes above the water, swiping her arms to stay afloat. She saw a flash of something. He was there, she was sure of it. He wasn't trying to hide. He'd found her trail, then, and figured she'd be heading for the river. He would assume she was trying to reach the harbor and was running to catch her before she arrived.

· He hadn't seen her yet. But he would soon.

Something bumped against the back of her head. A line wrapped around her arm. She was tangled. The current pulled, winding the line tighter. For a moment, panic, then she felt an anchor release and begin to drag. She unwrapped the line from her arm. Its end was twisted around a rough block of foam. She pushed it away and saw another block floating up ahead.

She kicked wide to avoid it. But she could see the disturbance in the water. The ripples spreading from where she'd splashed and struggled. He would have heard it.

She listened hard for any sign of someone in the mangroves. And she heard something. *Bump, bump, bump,* barely audible. She spun onto her side so she could see ahead and stroke if she needed to. A sharp bend was up ahead.

The bumping was louder. The sound of a rifle on a sling, bouncing against someone's back. So he had spotted her back there, maybe even before she'd gotten wrapped in whatever that thing was. This was the perfect spot to ambush. The river swung wide, and he could cross the point, set up on the other side, completely concealed, until she came sweeping around and it was too late. She could dive into the red water, but she'd have to surface eventually.

She grabbed a slick mangrove root and hung in the current. The sound was even louder now. There were higher tones, complicating it.

She realized what it was, let go, and drifted around the corner.

A blue plastic hull sat low in the water, floats lashed on each side, sheets of plywood laid across them. A shirtless man stood on the deck, poling against the current. A pile of wire traps were stacked at his feet, each attached to a foam block. Bob Marley sang from a cheap speaker.

She raised a finger to her lips. The current was fast. She grabbed at one of the lines lashing the deck to the plastic float. The man kept poling, eyes on the river ahead. But he was listening.

"Manny," she said. "I need help."

46

Nalani stopped for ice at the Anahola general store but didn't have time to drop the coolers, much less shower and change at her apartment. She didn't care about keeping Dalton's lawyers waiting, but there was someone else. She'd called the firm that had advised her father's family for generations. They were sending their new associate, Kalani Ho'okano Chong III.

She hadn't seen Trey since sixth grade. He'd gone to boarding school off island. Had it been Punahou? His family could afford it. No, he'd gotten into Kamehameha. She remembered the day the kids got their letters. She'd tried to apply, but the forms were too much for a thirteen-year-old without her parents' help.

There he was, waiting in the shade of the building. She'd wondered if she'd recognize him. He wore perfectly fitting pants, narrow cuffs ending above slim ankles. His aloha shirt funneled from his wide lats to his narrow waist. A line of diamond spearheads marched out of his left sleeve down one golden-brown tricep. She was suddenly very aware of the red dust coating her truck, the chili spice odor under her arms; the smell of fish scales and blood she hadn't been able to rinse from her fingernails.

If Trey noticed, he made no sign of it when they hugged and kissed cheeks.

"What's this about?" he asked as they walked up the stairs in the lava-rock interior of the three-story office building.

"Real estate stuff."

He waited for her to elaborate, then skillfully guided them out of the awkward silence. "I don't know this lawyer personally, but I made some calls. He's a managing partner with a firm on Oahu. They had a hand in most of the big resort developments back in the '70s and '80s. A lot of political families hui'd up with them to invest. The guy's got choke experience, and he's connected to everyone."

It was chilly in the deep shade. Nalani clutched her arms as they walked up the stairs.

"It shouldn't be complicated," she said. "I just need to sign some paper-work."

"Whatever you need."

She hesitated. "This isn't Winthrop stuff, okay? It's on my mother's side."

"Shoots," he said, dismissing the anxiety in her voice.

"So I don't know how it works," she went on. "With the billing."

Trey laughed in a way that was obviously meant to set her at ease. Was that genuine, Nalani wondered, or something they learned in law school?

Probably genuine, she decided sadly. Trey was exactly what he seemed to be: a beautiful, kind, respectful Hawaiian guy. The kind of guy she never dated.

He probably surfed, too.

A receptionist led them to a corner office with a long conference table and a view of Kalapaki Bay. Sam was standing beside a tall Japanese man dressed identically to Trey, except his pleated slacks showed no ankle and puffed where they cinched to his thin frame, and his aloha shirt hung baggy from his shoulders. He introduced himself as Mr. Shimabukuro, smiling broadly but speaking at a volume barely above a whisper. They all shook hands.

"Before we begin," said Mr. Shimabukuro and swept his hand down toward the table. Nalani noticed two crisp sheets of paper and two blue pens.

Trey picked one up and scanned it. "If you sign this, you agree not to share *anything* discussed in this meeting. It's very broad and maybe not enforceable. But it would be very expensive to find out."

"What if we don't sign?" he asked the other lawyer.

Mr. Shimabukuro shrugged. "You knew these mainland clients. I never write the document. They just give 'em to me and say, 'Tell 'em sign or no talk.'"

Trey looked at Nalani.

"It's okay," she said.

They signed. Mr. Shimabukuro bowed his head, collected the NDAs, and they all sat down. It would be very simple, he explained. Quiet title suits were resolved with an auction on the courthouse steps. This one happened to be set for tomorrow. In the morning, Nalani would arrive at the court-house to file her claim as a stakeholder in the property. She would designate him as her representative. At the appointed hour, the land commissioner would gather all registered claimants and gavel in the bidding. Mr. Shimabukuro would handle all that, until it was time to convey the deed, which would require her signature.

"Will you be there?" she asked Sam.

"Of course."

"Who else will be bidding?"

The lawyer shrugged. "A quiet title can only be resolved by someone with a preexisting claim to the land. It's possible someone else could step forward."

Nalani looked at Trey. He met her eyes and raised his eyebrows. His look told her that although he didn't know what was going on, since she'd chosen not to tell him, nothing he'd heard so far raised any red flags. He raised his eyebrows higher. Did she want to step outside?

She shook her head. There was a question she wanted to ask, but it took her a moment to recall it. She was still thinking about her attorney's eyes.

"Um, out of curiosity," she said, "if I didn't make it, to the auction. What would happen?"

Mr. Shimabukuro glanced at Sam, then Trey, then back to her. "Well," he said, looking at her in a very steady way, like an animal he was trying not to startle, "Hawaiian Kuleana Law goes back almost two hundred years, so the process is not so simple to explain."

Trey spoke up. "Can try, though, yeah?"

Nalani reflected for a moment on how nice it was to have a lawyer.

Mr. Shimabukuro smiled. "Of course. Like most land originating with the Kuleana Act, title for this property can be traced to the tenant farmers who first asserted ownership rights in 1850."

"Tenant farmers?" Nalani interjected. "They had lived there hundreds of years already."

"As tenants of the king." Mr. Shimabukuro smiled.

"I know the history," said Nalani.

Mr. Shimabukuro nodded cheerfully. "Of course. Since parcels were, by law, just three acres, and families tended to view them as a collective responsibility, in many cases ownership was never precisely defined beyond the first generation. Most family trees grow significantly in one hundred and seventy years. That's why we're extremely fortunate to have quiet title as a method for converting underutilized lands with indeterminate title into useful properties under consolidated ownership. It allows a title-holder motivated to use the land productively to buy out those who have failed to maintain it."

"So you're saying it's my responsibility to make this land productive by outbidding my family?"

"Exactly!" Sam broke in eagerly.

Mr. Shimabukuro grimaced. "It's a very fair process, in that it allows the person who cares most about the land to express that commitment in a concrete and quantifiable way. If someone wants it more, or has a more profitable plan for it, they can demonstrate that."

"And you've settled a lot of quiet title suits over the years, Mr. Shimabukuro? It must be very satisfying to help so many Kānaka Maoli turn their land to such productive use."

"We do have some experience in this field, and I take great satisfaction from that, Ms. Winthrop."

Now it was Sam's turn to look pained. "I know this all feels a little rushed, Nalani. We're all on a very unforgiving timeline. And these decisions can bring up big emotions. I'd love to help you process that. I'm free all afternoon. There's a *great* spa in Poipu. I can check their openings now. When was your last facial?"

"I've got to deliver some fish," said Nalani. "What time is the auction?"

"Bidding starts at 8:00 a.m. We ask that you arrive at 7:00 to go over the documents." Mr. Shimabukuro reached for something below the table and lifted a stack of crisp white papers.

Trey raised a finger off the table. "Counselor, you never answered my client's question."

The lawyer smiled weakly. "What was that?"

"What will happen if she doesn't appear?"

"Well," said the lawyer, glancing again at Samantha, "if no one with a valid interest in the land offers a bid within one hour of the auction being gaveled in, the judgment defaults to the plaintiff's claim of adverse possession. Now . . ." He began to gather the papers on his desk.

"And who is the plaintiff?" Trey asked.

The lawyer cleared his throat. "Maile Kanahele Winthrop."

Trey glanced at Nalani.

"My mother."

"And what would that judgment entail?"

"Ms. Kanahele Winthrop would have the opportunity to purchase the property at its assessed value and take sole, fee simple ownership."

Nalani stood abruptly. "All right, then. I guess I'll see you at seven."

The lawyer looked surprised. "We have the documents here for you to sign."

"I thought that was happening tomorrow morning."

"These are agreements with the foundation. The first is a standard NDA, affirming in perpetuity that you will not disclose anything you see, hear, or discuss pertaining to the AinaKai Alliance, the Sokoni corporation, or the Dalton family and its interests."

"That sounds like a lot."

"It's actually very simple. The second document is an agreement between yourself and the AinaKai Alliance to convey the title to the property located on island four, zone five, section one, et cetera et cetera, commonly referred to as 'Momona Bay, Lot Three,' within twenty-four hours of purchase."

He glanced up, then continued. "And the third document is a contract between yourself and the AinaKai Alliance, with compensation of five million dollars and a property located on Punahele Road." He gave her a warm and genuine smile. "Congratulations. I just wish my work could always be so mutually beneficial for everyone involved."

Sam, who'd been edging around the table, took Nalani's arm. "I'm *so* excited for you!"

Nalani stared at the neatly stacked papers. Trey asked permission with his eyes, then reached across and began scanning. Everyone froze while he read. Samantha kept one hand on Nalani's arm. Mr. Shimabukuro sat with his shoulders hunched, arms stretched across the table, staring at his clasped hands. Nalani watched out the window as a tug pulled the weekly Oahu barge past the breakwater. Trey licked the tip of his thumb and turned a page. He was reading more slowly now. She found that reassuring.

The barge was passing the lighthouse on the point.

Finally, Trey looked up.

"Can we have a private room?" he asked.

47

Dalton lost count of the members of Congress he spoke to that morning. He had a bullet list of talking points—to be repeated *precisely,* he was constantly reminded—but his primary goal was ephemeral: to convince each member that, this time, when he said Sokoni would change, he really meant it, without, of course, admitting he hadn't really meant it all the other times. But sounding convincingly sincere became more challenging with each repetition. And when he tried to go off script, he was chastised by his handlers.

The bullet-pointed portion of his call addressed *a few minor clauses* (the phrase double underlined) in the proposed legislation that might cause Sokoni's extensive network of political action committees to reconsider the generous contributions they'd been making to So-and-So's campaign. He was only a few names down the list before he started losing track of which MoC he was speaking to. Fortunately, his staff noticed his slowing cadence—"Thank *you* . . . so much for . . . *your* . . . time"—and rescued him. Eventually they assigned an intern to hold a sheet of paper with the member's name in all caps. But after a frighteningly long pause at the end of a call with the ranking member of the Appropriations Committee—Dalton staring blankly at the paper pulled taut between the terrified intern's quivering hands before finally screaming, *KAY!* and immediately hanging up—they told him to take thirty minutes and get some fresh air.

He dutifully set off down one of the paths landscaped into the hillside. He could have crossed the lower pasture, but the wind was flattening the grass, and he was tired of sea, sky, and rushing gray clouds. The forest was inviting.

He noticed a footpath winding into the trees.

In the forest, he could think. These calls, he knew, weren't going to resolve the issue, not in the short term. They were the first step in a process that would take months, maybe years. He should get his family on the jet and off this island. The house in Woodside would be out of service two more weeks until the floors had been redone, but their estate in Panarea could be ready in forty-eight hours, and the New York place much quicker than that. She could stay with her parents in Paris. Or his, in McLean. He pictured how she would react when he suggested an eleven-hour flight (minimum) with the boys (and without him) because they weren't safe on the property he'd spent five hundred million dollars (so far) supposedly transforming into the ultimate refuge.

It had been a few minutes since he'd noticed the trails in the forest weren't as obvious as the ones he was used to. But that hadn't stopped him from pushing ahead. He was beginning to think this may have been a miscalculation.

Overhead, leaves rustled: an almost soothing sound beneath the rising, falling roar of wind. The ground was covered in orange needles. He looked back for the trail that had brought him here. Aside from a few patches of bare red dirt, there was no sign of it. He pressed a button on his watch, checked his phone. No signal. It occurred to him he might not be on his own land.

With no alternative, he kept walking. How long had he been on this thirty-minute break? Forty-five. They'd be missing him. Soon they'd initiate a code. Which would be embarrassing. He checked his phone again. Even a text message wouldn't go through. He remembered the place outside Erin's village where the residents lined up to use their phones, a spot of dirt two meters wide that got a single bar of service.

He thought about the situation logically. Any direction he walked would lead somewhere eventually: a field or a beach, a stream or a road. There was nothing to do but choose a direction. He started walking and for the next few minutes thought of nothing but shadow and light, the scuff of dry leaves, the stillness of the forest, the rushing wind.

It was the stream he found first. Smooth boulders furred in green moss jeweled with clear drops of water. Bright ferns hanging by short, tumbling falls. He followed it uphill. His distracted thoughts resumed. But an unexpected sound broke through. The clink and thud of a rock dislodged, up where the land rose steeply, and the stream went out of view in a ravine.

Dalton stepped carefully through the underbrush that grew thicker in the damp earth. Erosion had torn off sections of the steep bank. He was looking straight down into a black pool where a man's dark and naked back floated facedown in the water.

Not floating, Dalton realized: standing thigh-deep, face under the surface. The man shuffled forward, his shoulder sweeping back and forth, occasionally twitching. An impossibly long time passed. Dalton began to wonder if he should keep moving. Then he wondered if he needed to go down and rescue the man. Then the man stood up. With his left hand, he pressed a dive mask against his eyes. With his right, he held a net. A pouch hung from the bottom of the webbing. It bulged with slick, dark things. The man lowered the mask as he turned his back and upended the net into a five-gallon bucket. Dalton saw flapping flat tails and fat, waving claws. Prawns. Dozens of them.

The man turned back toward the pool, and Dalton recognized him. *Hunt Fish Dive Survive*. Solomon Kanahele.

He wore board shirts, torn and stained, loose enough to reveal the white hairs above his groin. He was skinny but fit. A little more mass in his pecs, and his body would have rivaled Dalton's trainer's, who'd been a starting shooting guard at Stanford just three years earlier.

Dalton watched the man press the mask to his face and go down again. He looked around the forest. Among the shiny leaves of a tall tree, he noticed pale green mangoes. He saw black mud where wild pigs had rooted. He thought of all the things that had filled his head in the last few hours: the fears and anxieties and endless to-dos. This man Solomon had woken that morning and decided he would dine on prawns. He lived according to the weather. He met with no advisors. And the worst that could happen? A branch fell on his head or a boar gutted him with its tusks, and he died the same way he had lived.

Dalton questioned every decision he had ever made. Then he remembered his children. It was one thing to lie on the leafy floor of the forest, staring into the branches as the life eased out of you, it was another to lie there knowing your kids were waiting for a meal that would never come. This was why we had society. Because living by nature meant dying by nature. The direction of history was to shield us from such consequences. You could pound your hands against your bubble, but only because you'd never for a moment had to live outside it.

Modern survival called for another kind of knowledge, not the messages of trees and clouds and birdsong but of geopolitics, logistics, and primary energy accounting: mastery of a system so complex it was a path to madness for the average person.

All he wanted out of life was to see his boys thrive.

His world was impossibly complicated. But this goal was simple. And spending his day calling members of Congress wasn't bringing him closer to it.

Solomon was looking at him.

Dalton rose to his feet and ran upstream, through the trees, toward what he hoped was the refuge.

48

Mr. Shimabukuro sent Trey and Nalani down the hall to a windowless room lit by one long fluorescent bulb, barely large enough for a counter with a microwave and coffee maker, a mini fridge, and a table with two plastic chairs. When they sat down, their knees touched.

"So?" Nalani said.

"There's nothing tricky in the paperwork. It's as he described."

"All right."

She reached for the papers. Trey, looking alarmed, placed a hand on them.

"Do you want to consult at all, about the general situation?"

She stared at him blankly.

He misunderstood the hesitation. "We're protected by attorney-client privilege. You won't be violating any NDAs."

"It's probably pretty clear?" she said.

He laughed. "Maybe I'm just slow."

She felt her cheeks flush. When was the last time someone had made her feel like this? She could remember precisely: a table at a coffee shop across from a pet store. It hadn't ended well, to say the least. And the guy had ghosted her.

She shook her head. This was a consultation with her attorney. "Sorry," she said. "There's just a lot going on. A few days ago, I got served with a lawsuit, or something, I don't know. The quiet title with my mom's name on it. Like they said in there. She was working for them, but she changed her mind. She's living down there, on the property. She's a junkie, basically—I mean, she used to be. Anyway, we don't know each other that well, honestly. But when she backed out, they started coming at me. They kept offering me more and more, and at some point, it was obvious I should take it. But I didn't want to just sign anything they handed me."

"You wanted to do your due diligence."

"Exactly. Someone in my family had to take this seriously. So I called you—I mean, your firm. And they sent you. You're on Sokoni, right?"

Trey blushed. "I have an account . . ."

"I just mean, you've seen what everyone's saying about the families who already sold their land to the Daltons. Easy for all them to talk stink. If *they* were the ones getting offers like this, they'd take it in one second. Like that bitch Leleihua with her big mouth. Remember? She was one year ahead of us—"

Trey raised a palm. She took a breath. "What I'm saying is, according to them, I'm supposed to spend my life caretaking my family's bones."

As she stared expectantly across the table, she realized she needed Trey to tell her she had made the right decision.

He stared at the stack of papers, then looked up and met her eyes. "As your lawyer, I'm here to offer counsel on whatever course you choose."

She remembered why she'd never dated nice Hawaiian guys. "Then advise me."

Trey smiled. A little condescendingly, Nalani thought. Maybe he had gone to Punahou.

"Is there anything you could be unaware of, pertaining to the value of the land? Have you had it appraised recently?"

This was the part where the mainland lawyer patiently lectured the local girl on all the steps she'd missed. She took a deep breath.

"All this happened in six days," she said. "So no, I haven't had the land appraised. And if they were offering me what they originally offered my mother, I would do that. But you and I both know there is nothing they could tell me about the land that would value it at what they're offering now."

"Do you know why your mother changed her mind?"

With relief, Nalani thought of an actual legal question she wanted to ask him. "Yesterday," she said, "Frank Dalton offered three million. Now the lawyer said it's five?"

Trey paused to process the question, then flipped back through the contract. "That's correct. Five million. Do you have any concerns about that?"

"It's just so much money."

"It is. That's why I'm asking—"

Nalani rolled her eyes. "Look, if you were on Sokoni more, you'd get it. This is all local people are talking about. The guy just paid two hundred million for all this land and fenced it off. But he never knew my family has a right to drive through whenever we like."

"So he has a unique interest."

"Yeah. Almost as unique as mine."

"Right," said Trey. "Sorry. Look, I get it. I mean, sort of. Not really. Our only land is in Wailua Homesteads. It was a nice place to grow up, but it's just property, you know? My parents bought it in the '80s."

"It's home, though. Yeah? It must mean something."

"I guess. It's not why I came back. Have you been to the Bay Area?"

"For a week, years ago, to visit some MBA programs."

"Oh yeah?" He sounded excited for a moment. "But you never . . ."

"No, I never."

"It's nice. Lincoln Park. The Presidio. That's where I used to live."

"So why did you leave?"

"I don't know. To please my grandfather? I guess that would be *my* family's kuleana, the firm. I mean, when my great-grandfather started it, his parents were still working for the sugar plantation. Not many Chinese lawyers then. There's pride, you know? But no one pressured me. They know it's not an exciting practice. Property management, mostly. Contract disputes. Old families with old land and old money."

"Like mine," said Nalani, "except for the money part."

"Things got pretty interesting, from what I hear." He said it carefully.

She felt herself tense up. Was he fishing for gossip or inviting her to talk?

"Not that I heard anything about it from my dad guys," he said quickly, "and I'm sorry about your uncle. I knew him a little bit."

It was the first time she'd heard him sound uncertain. She liked it.

"You don't have to be sorry. He made his own choices."

Trey was silent, giving her space. *Fuck* these nice Hawaiian guys.

"He's dead," she said. "He's not in hiding or anything like that. Whatever people say. He's not living on some island in Tahiti. They took him into the forest and killed him. Or they gave him a gun and let him do it himself. And he deserved it."

She'd pictured it so many times in every possible way. On a fishing boat miles off the coast. In daylight or darkness. But she'd settled on the scenario that made the most sense. The forest reserve was right there, and it was vast, and you didn't have to worry about currents. The pigs could eat a body as well as any shark. They wouldn't have delayed it. It had happened in the same rain that had been falling when they said goodbye. She saw her uncle stumbling up some nameless valley. The familiar scowl as he looked over his shoulder. She saw him kneel and wait.

She'd forced herself to imagine it until she was numb, not just to it but to everything, until, when she did try to stop seeing it, she couldn't. Every time she closed her eyes, he was there, on his knees in the forest. She saw it that way even after she'd decided this wasn't even how it happened.

The people who'd taken him wouldn't shoot him from behind, no matter who her uncle had taken from them. And no matter how delusional her uncle had become, some part of him still knew what justice had to look like. She was sure of that. So he had asked for the gun. Or they'd simply untied his hands and given it to him. The police had never found his old 1911. The one he'd taught her to shoot cans with, clasping his hands around hers until she was strong enough to hold it on her own.

It wasn't much better, thinking of it that way. But it allowed her to imagine looking up one day and meeting the eyes of the man who'd taken her uncle into the forest. And that meant imagining a time when she could go somewhere on this small island besides her friend's shop, Foodland, or Kealia Beach at dawn.

Something touched her hand, and she jumped. Trey was holding out a folded handkerchief. Pale yellow. Who carried handkerchiefs these days, she wondered as she scrubbed her cheeks. Maybe that was something else you learned in law school.

"I'm embarrassed."

"It's all right."

And it was.

"I'm just not sure," she said, "that I'm making this decision with the proper mindset. I've been struggling."

"It's one small island," said Trey. "It fucks you up. That's why I never wanted to come back."

"I just wish he'd never made the offer," said Nalani. "I know that seems crazy."

"It's not crazy," said Trey. "Not for you, or for him. If you had money like he does, it would be crazy *not* to overpay for something you really wanted. Money is meaningless to those people."

"What is meaningful to them?"

Trey shrugged. "Privacy, I guess. It doesn't really matter. People like this get what they want. He isn't used to someone having leverage on him. I guarantee he's sweating. You are the one with the choice to make. You can ask for anything."

"Is that supposed to make this easier?"

He laughed. "I'll tell you what I tell all my clients in situations like this. You have to ask yourself what *you* want."

"I've had my whole life and I haven't figured that out. Now I need to know in the next fifteen hours?"

He sighed. "Okay. Look, as a resident of this island, and as a Hawaiian, I want to say fuck that guy. But as your attorney, I have to advise you signing this offer would be very beneficial. You won't get a better one. And things could get a lot worse. If you cross him."

"Okay." She found herself smiling.

"Okay?" He held the contracts under his palm.

"Okay."

He waited another moment, then slid them across the table. "They marked all the places you're supposed to sign."

She took the smooth brick of expensive paper between her hands.

"I don't have to sign them now, though, yeah? Can let him sweat a little longer?"

Trey considered this. "You like me tell 'em?"

Nalani smiled gratefully. The purity of what she felt toward her lawyer in that moment made her bashful. She stared at her hands as she pushed the papers back across the table.

She stood up, and so did he.

"I'll say goodbye for you."

"Mahalos." It was time to go. "So, just, send me a bill, I guess?"

Trey shrugged, looked at his watch. "Honestly, I'm on my lunch break. No charge for helping out an old . . . classmate. You want me to be there tomorrow?"

"I can't ask you to do that."

"You got my number. Call if you want."

Nalani had only been driving a few minutes when her phone began buzzing across the stack of papers she'd tossed on the seat beside her. *Haole Realtor.*

"Nalani!" said Sam, her voice more cheerful than ever, but pitched to a level of strain Nalani had never heard before. "So sorry I missed you on your way out. I think it's *totally great* you are taking a little time to think things over. Listen, if you have plans for tonight, you need to cancel them. I just got you an invite to a party you *cannot* miss."

49

Janice Diaz wasn't sure whether Manny recognized her from the night she and Carlotta had spent on his raft, but it didn't matter. He'd helped her without hesitation, poling back downriver as she hung on the side, hidden from the bank.

He brought her to a boat ramp in a muddy channel behind a marina, showed her a spigot where she could rinse off, then wandered off to request a clean pair of clothes from one of the aunties who moored her raft nearby. When he returned, he gave her two dollars and offered to walk her to the bus stop. She took the money but told him she could go on her own.

The aunty had passed along a pair of sweatpants and a hoodie, well worn, but clean. The sweatshirt was a man's XL. Perfect. Leaving the county park, she passed the stench of rotting meat from a trash barrel buzzing with flies. She hauled out the black plastic bag, knotted it, and hoisted it over her shoulder: camouflage for the long, exposed walk down the harbor road. She stared at her feet, hunched her shoulders, transformed herself into someone invisible.

There were two other people waiting at the bus stop. Everyone grinned with relief when she dropped the bag on the sidewalk before boarding the small island bus.

She got off beside the big green field. Only when she reached the beach did she flip back her hood. She heard waves on the sand and smelled salt air. The tides were small here. There was none of the pleasing, rotten smell of kelp exposed at low tide. For a moment, she remembered slippery rocks on the bank of a canal, city lights sliding across oily black water. But she refused that memory.

She reached the first small cluster of tents. At first, there was no one in sight. But as she walked deeper down the orderly rows, she saw more people: women absorbed in solitary tasks around their tents, children running full speed. It was late afternoon. School was out and work was over.

Aunty Lei was sitting at the same picnic table. "You're back quick," she said. "What, Carlotta acting lōlō again?"

"I'm sorry?"

"Carlotta. She a nice lady. But she not right, you know."

"She seemed fine when I left her. We just . . . split up."

Lei raised her hands. "I never like dig in no one's business. All that matters is you ready for be here now."

"I guess so."

"How long you been living outside?"

"Six days?"

Lei laughed. "Right on schedule. No one comes their first day. They'd rather sleep on the street than admit they need a more permanent situation." She rose from the table. "Everyone here was like you once. None of us thought we belonged in a place like this."

Janice Diaz said nothing.

"I'll show you around, get you set up with whatever you need." They walked back through the encampment. "We try make it so everyone feels comfortable. That means trying to put people together who want to keep themselves in the same way, more or less."

They were on the sandy access road that split the camp in half.

"Down there," said Leilani, pointing at a cluster of tents, "those with mental illness. They're nice people, but we try keep 'em away from the kids and those who gotta go work in the morning, what with the screaming and all. Over here"—she pointed at a larger neighborhood—"those the people still using. Plenty of 'em here 'cause the shelters won't take 'em. If all you doing is smoking pakololo or keeping quiet in your tent, no need stay down there. But we never like the keiki see none of the rougher stuff, and don't want the cops coming through, either."

They walked back into the largest area. "This where the working people stay. And families. Kupuna, too—that's our elders. I never like say we got rules—just keep your eyes open and you'll learn how things go—but there are a few things I can say, for save you some time. First thing is, keep Aunty and Uncle happy. Our kupuna are the head of this family. You bring something to them, they going settle it their way, and nothing you can do about it. Second, no stealing. Can happen, we understand. And we never like shame you. If you take something, best for just give 'em back an' no harm done. But if you going be one donkey, then we handle it, Hawaiian-style. Third thing is, if you like fight, take it outside the camp. We never like call the cops. Fourth, keep your area clean. That's a tough one for the new people. They think just 'cause they get no more hale, they going live in dirt. But if you like live li'dat, we get one big forest you can have all to yourself."

"Thank you. But I won't be here long."

Leilani laughed and gave her a one-armed hug. "You and everyone else."

A man's voice interrupted. "Ho, Aunty! Go spahk da kine. I heard they was telling my wahine bullshit about me."

"What I tell you?" Leilani shouted back. "No bring *me* your pilikia. Go to the horse with the source unless you like be one jackass making noise." She rolled her eyes. "Anyway, we got a few spots just opened up, away from the beach where it's quiet. You like see?"

Janice Diaz watched the man walk away, shaking his head. He hadn't made eye contact with her. Hadn't even looked at her. No one had. They were going out of their way to ignore her. A customary courtesy, she thought. But that didn't mean they hadn't noticed. It sounded like most of the residents scattered daily across the island, to their jobs or whatever else they did to make the days go by. If Alpha started asking in the parks about a white woman fresh from the mainland, he wouldn't have much trouble getting word of her.

"I shouldn't stay," she said. "I came because Carlotta told me to find you if I was ever in trouble. But I don't want to bring that trouble here."

"You got someone looking for you?"

"Yes."

"Plenty wahine hiding out here. Their men stay in their house, or at the shelter, so where they supposed to go?"

"It's not like that."

"Police?"

"Not that, either."

Leilani nodded. "We got zero tolerance of violence here. Someone starts trouble, we get guys ready for handle. And wahine, too. Opportunity knocks, you know?"

"This isn't something I can ask anyone to handle."

Aunty Lei looked stern now. "I like help you. But I don't know what you asking. If you like stay, stay. If you no like stay, no stay."

"I'm sorry. I guess I don't know why I came."

Aunty Lei stared at her for a few seconds without speaking, then she took her by the elbow and steered her through the tents, onto the sandy road. They turned away from the camp and walked into a grove of ironwoods. Sunlight came in shafts between the trees. The fallen needles glowed orange on the ground.

"I know you're just passing through," said Aunty Lei, "and maybe I said too much already. But, one thing I know about this place is that by the time a person gets here, they have zero level of trust in anyone, including themselves. You been bouncing around awhile now, I see that. You showed up with nothing; we sent you away supplied. Now you show up again with even less than what you had before. It ain't easy. We all know that. Every person here did everything they could *not* to be here. But here they are. I don't know your secret, but I do know Aunty Carlotta told you to find me for one reason."

"Someone tried to execute me today. Shoot me in cold blood."

Leilani seemed unfazed.

"I ran away. He tracked me through the forest. I jumped in the river, found a man on a raft. He gave me bus fare. That's how I got here."

"We got a group," said Aunty Lei. "Meets once a week. You think it won't help, talking about it. But it does. I served on a submarine. I was attacked. I reported it and nothing happened. Spent three more months underwater with my rapist."

"Just tell me where people go when they need to hide. When they really need to hide. If someone killed a cop, where would you put them?"

"You're asking me to trust you now."

"I guess so."

"We've got one more place. We call it the pu'uhonua. It's set apart."

"All right."

"No one there gets turned away. You understand? Whatever you done, whatever they done, once you enter that place, you agree not to bother nobody and not to tell no one what you seen. You may find the man tried for kill you this morning. But he can't touch you, and you can't touch him."

Aunty Lei had left the road and was leading her down a narrow trail between the ironwoods. "We get some tough braddahs and sisters back here," she said. "And you going be here on your own. But I no let no one forget rule number, even in the pu'uhonua. No one fucks with Aunty. I make sure of that."

50

As soon as he got off the phone with Hart, Dalton called Raffi Garcia.

"What's up, man?" Raffi's breathing was audible. Dalton was staring straight up his nose.

"Am I on your watch?"

The view shifted. Trees and a green mountain, a glimpse of a wide red trail. "Two-mile walk. Doctor's orders. How's it going with Congress?"

"I've been making calls all morning. But I can't get my head in it."

"Sometimes you've got to eat shit."

"There's other stuff going on. With my family."

Raffi stopped and brought his wrist up to his face. "I heard about that. It's ugly stuff. I hope everyone is coping okay?"

"The boys are fine," said Dalton. "I'm fine. Just furious. Distracted, like I said. Madeleine, I'm not so sure."

Raffi nodded. He was walking again. Dalton looked at the screen long enough to get mildly nauseous from the sway of trees and trail before he looked away.

"I don't think I can do this. Not right now. I need to focus on my family."

"Do what, exactly?" Raffi gasped.

"Go through with this negotiation. The realignment. I've got too much on my plate."

"You mean, security-wise?"

"Yeah, with my family, and this attack, pushing the refuge across the finish line. That's what needs my focus right now."

"Don't you have a team for that?"

"I thought I did until a few days ago. Now I'm realizing I need to handle this myself."

"Risk is part of life, you know. No one can control everything. Not even you."

Dalton glanced down at the screen, hoping Raffi could see his expression.

But it was still only swinging trees, blurred now by what must be a stream of sweat across the glass.

"I understand probabilities."

Raffi's eye appeared in the screen again. "A yellow dwarf," he said, panting every few words, "has about ten billion years. Until it becomes a red giant." He paused to draw a long, raspy breath. "No matter what you do, or I do, or anyone does, this solar system's about halfway through its life span before our star eats everything. That comforts me, you know?"

"This isn't about my ego, Raffi." Dalton was regretting this call. "Or passing on my DNA, or whatever. There are trillions of future lives at stake based on the choices we make. We're developing approaches at the refuge with a chance to positively alter more lives than have ever been lived."

"I think you're missing my point, man."

"*No one* is forgetting the age of the sun. If we survive the next few centuries, anything is possible. All we've got to do is get to Proxima Centauri, and that will buy us three trillion more years."

Raffi managed to channel his next exhalation into an exasperated sigh. "You know I love you, Franky, but you're only using half your brain."

"Raffi, I didn't call you to debate effective altruism. I'm trying to tell you I would *love* to be the weak link in all this. But every time I try to let someone else take the lead, they fuck it up. My family was almost killed the other day. They were surrounded by security, and they were still almost *killed*. What am I supposed to do? Bury them underground already? The refuge isn't even functional yet. Nothing I do is working."

Finally, finally, finally.

He made no effort to control his voice or his tears. He let it all come through. This was why he needed Raffi in his life. This was why everyone needed a Raffi. Eventually, the sobs stopped shaking him. They rose one by one from the black place and popped like bubbles. And that place wasn't black anymore. It was hollow and light. He felt strong again.

"Have you checked in with your therapist?" Raffi asked gently.

"I paused that months ago. Micro-dosing was more effective."

"Maybe you should call him."

Dalton laughed. "I have you, Raffi. That was all I needed. Thank you."

"I think you might be having a nervous breakdown."

"It looked bad for a second there, huh? It's okay. I just needed to let it out."

"I'm not talking about that. I'm talking about everything you've been doing this week."

"We're in crisis mode, Raffi. We're at war. We need to be decisive. And bold."

"It's just been a little erratic, man. From what I hear."

"From Dhillon? You know you can't trust him about this."

"It's not from Dhillon. I just want to make sure you're thinking clearly. Is there anything you want to share? I can help, you know. This isn't my first rodeo. I was there with Steve through everything. I don't want to see you make the same mistakes."

"Is that a threat?"

"Of course not."

"I learned what I needed from Steve. No one can fire me."

"No one wants to, man. That's not what I'm saying."

"I'm giving them Falkor."

"What?"

"No more of this negotiation, this *begging*. I don't have time. They need to understand who they're dealing with and what we're capable of. I'm cutting out Congress, going directly to the administration, and offering them Falkor."

"Shit."

"You knew we'd have to use it eventually."

"It's your company, man."

He tried to read Raffi's expression. He'd been ignoring the notifications steadily dinging his phone, but a new one caught his attention.

It was from Samantha. Three words. *She didn't sign.*

"Fuck," said Dalton. "I've got to go. Are you okay with this?"

"I don't even know what this is, man."

"I'll get you the details once we have them. Thank you, Raffi."

He was already typing.

                                                          She's out?

Sam responded instantly.

Not out
Thinking about it
has a lawyer

Where is she?

Home?
I'm getting her
Later

Getting her?

Taking her to Michael's thing

I'll get back to you

Whatever doubts he'd had about this path were over. Crisis clarified everything. There could be no going backward. No weakness. Dhillon had been right, but for the wrong reasons. He thought of everything in terms of market cap. He didn't understand power. Maybe Park and her drone company, or whatever it was, would be as successful as she thought. But when she reached that level, she would find him there already. It was time to unleash Falkor.

The permissions associated with the Sokoni app had allowed the company to collect quadrillions of data points over the years. Not just packet capture and net flow. Not just where people shopped, the websites they visited, the politicians they voted for. And not just their secrets—sex tapes, illegal porn, admissions of criminal conduct. There was metadata from every photo ever snapped on ten billion devices correlated with GPS locations, web searches, audio recordings, notes and emails archived and deleted, shopping lists, plus the heart rate and blood pressure of anyone wearing a fitness tracker as they were doing any of those things.

This data set wouldn't have mattered if he hadn't had the foresight, years ago, to build out a rig that could handle it. When the first 5D torus networks were coming out, he'd dug an underground facility outside Tahoe for a massively parallel cluster of twenty-five thousand water-cooled CPUs. For over a decade, Falkor had been lying in its cave, digesting every data point, making predictions, checking results, ceaselessly revising its algorithms. By now, even its operators had no idea how it made its calculations. All they knew was that it was becoming uncannily accurate. It could predict whether a parolee would re-offend. Whether an American was flying to Turkey for a vacation on the Adriatic or to cross into Syria. Whether a few errant keystrokes meant a future diagnosis of Parkinson's. It was constantly streamlining the data points it needed and broadening the predictions it could make. Fewer than fifty people had even a rough understanding of its capabilities. Dhillon only thought he knew. Erin had no idea it existed.

At some point, its liabilities had become clear. Possibly when it could diagnose heart conditions with 95 percent accuracy. Definitely after it began identifying adolescents who would attempt suicide within three weeks. At least, due to the nature of its data set, it was limited to predictions on a case-by-case basis. It could foresee a human's destiny, but not humanity's.

Regardless, he had enough access to DARPA and NSA to know how far DOD or any of the agencies were from these capabilities. If he offered Falkor to the government, they would drop their witch hunt against his company and track down the people trying to hurt his family. And they would finally begin treating him as he deserved. An equal partner.

51

There was a version of her life, Nalani thought, where she had zero interest in a haole party on some gross North Shore estate. But this was also the version where she would never sell her family's kuleana lands. The version she would have chosen with absolute conviction just one week ago. Which made it the version of someone hanging out alone in her apartment.

She was tired of the version of her life where she said no to things.

She was ready to start saying yes again.

And of course, as soon as she had said yes, Sam immediately got weird about it.

"What am I supposed to wear?" Nalani asked.

"Whatever makes you happy!"

"I'll be happy if I'm wearing whatever everyone else is wearing!"

"Well, I can't tell you what that will be. Everyone is going to wear what makes *them* happy, too."

"But they'll be happy because they know what to wear, and I have no idea."

"Don't be silly. You have incredible taste. You look stunning in anything."

"Literally no idea. They didn't say *anything* on the invite?"

"You know what they say for all these parties. Island style."

"Like, *island* style? Or island *style*?"

"*Your* style."

"But—"

"Relax. It just means be yourself."

"But does it mean, be *my*self?"

"Of *course*. You're so funny."

"It's not funny to me, Sam."

"It's just aloha, Nalani. People bring their aloha. No one will be judging you."

Nalani gave up. It wasn't like she had that many options, anyway. She picked out a romper from her friend's boutique. It was something she would never have chosen for herself, which she figured made it her safest bet.

This decision took most of the afternoon and left the contents of her closet strewn across her bedroom. The akule were still in her truck. But Sam insisted on picking her up, even after she explained they'd have to make a stop.

"Oh my god, you look fantastic."

Sam was wearing jeans, a flimsy V-neck, and so many twisted strands of pink Tahitian pearls, Nalani knew they must have cost over ten thousand dollars.

"So do you," she said. "That necklace."

Sam laughed. "It's just fun. You ready?"

"Back up to my truck," said Nalani. "Easier to load that way."

Sam's smile grew extra wide. "We're really doing that," she said.

Nalani stepped into view of Sam's mirror, raised a hand, waggled her fingers to guide her back, and made a fist when the bumper of the Range Rover was two inches from her tailgate. By the time Sam was out, Nalani had slid the first cooler halfway into the trunk.

"Help give it a push. I got forty pounds of ice in here."

Sam looked apprehensive.

"It's just akule," Nalani told her. "Fresh this morning. I told my uncle I'd deliver them."

"He sells them?" Sam asked.

"He never sells. These are for the beach camp. Aunty Lei guys?"

"Doesn't ring a bell!"

"She's a good person to know," said Nalani. "You got four-wheel drive?"

Sam smiled wider than ever. "If she's a friend of yours, I can't wait to meet her."

"You really never been here?" Nalani asked.

Sam gazed attentively at the tents.

"No," she said. "I definitely never have."

"What do they say?" said Nalani. "It's all about location?" Now that the stress of choosing an outfit was over, she was enjoying herself.

"I specialize in North and South Shore properties."

"Ho! There's Leilani." Nalani rolled down her window. "Hey, Aunty! I get something for you from Uncle Solly."

A large woman in an XXL T-shirt and knee-length board shorts walked up to the Range Rover. "How you stay, Nalans?"

"Good, Aunty, I stay good."

"And your maddah?"

"She still staying down Momona with Solly."

"Nice place that."

Nalani nodded. "Akule going off right now. I get some fresh for you. Two coolers."

"Shoots. We t'row one party tonight! No need get out the car. I call some of the boys for unload 'em. I going see if we get coolers."

"No need, Aunty. We gotta hele. Just take 'em, and I get 'em back another day."

"Shoots. I get someone for drop 'em then. I like get your number."

"Tell me yours," said Nalani. "I send you one text."

She punched the number in her phone while Sam looked nervously in the mirror at the teenage boys who'd opened her trunk.

Lei's phone chimed with the message. "I get," she said. "You tell Solly big mahalos, yah? And your maddah, too. Your family always been real good li'dat."

"Shoots," said Nalani.

"How do we get out of here?" Sam asked.

Sam turned off the highway on the road to Kalihiwai. They dropped into a valley of ragged goat pastures, then climbed to a stretch Nalani had passed hundreds of times, where grassy banks were topped with dense privacy hedges, interrupted by tall gates with security cameras and electronic pass codes.

Her friends in landscaping had stories about the celebrities they saw on these estates. She waited eagerly to see which one was their destination. But Sam passed gate after gate. Soon Nalani could see the bend where the houses ended and the road descended the steep valley to Kalihiwai Bay, one of the best breaks on the island. Sam slowed. There was one more gate.

"Perfect," she said. "Just in time for sunset."

The entrance was flanked by lava rock pillars. Gas torches released smoking jets of flame. Two dark brown men in matching black-and-white print shirts stood inside the open gate. Sam showed them something on her phone. They looked familiar. She'd probably shared a lineup with them, maybe the break below this cliff.

They drove on, past a white KPD SUV with two officers inside, down a curving avenue lined with royal palms, each at least sixty feet high, white trunks round and smooth as marble. Every few yards, they passed another pair of torches, the flames glowing and gusting, releasing curling whips of smoke.

They dipped into a small valley, crossed a stone bridge beneath the arching white limbs of two enormous monkeypod trees, and climbed onto a dome-like lawn, acres wide. Nalani saw towering orange clouds and their vast reflection. She saw Kilauea Lighthouse on a long point of land, the stony island Moku'ae'ae rising beyond the point, the high green rim of the crater. She felt a red glare and looked at the pink ball of the sun just as it dipped into the water.

Now she could see the house. Two houses, or three. The aqua-blue glint of a pool between the buildings. Sam shifted into park, smiled at Nalani. "I'm ready for a drink. Are you?"

A valet in a black-and-white shirt opened Nalani's door. "Aloha," he said. "Right this way." He swept his arm toward the gap between buildings, where long chains of pink plumeria were draped over ornamental bamboo.

The valet was her own age. Maybe a year or two older. He looked fantastic, the muscles of his smooth brown chest rising square beneath the wide collar of his shirt. His black hair, brushed behind his ears, grazed the top of his collar. Was it a sign that the universe was suddenly throwing these guys in her path?

"Aloha, Hawaiian," Nalani said. "How you stay?"

For a moment, a sweet grin broke across his face. His brown eyes danced to hers. Then the wide, professional smile froze his features, and his eyes moved to a point in the distance. "Enjoy your evening," he said. "Aloha."

Three thin, young Filipino women stood in a row holding trays of champagne. Nalani took a glass, returned their smiles, nodded thanks. Flat, smooth stepping stones were set into a bed of polished pebbles. Statues sat in grottoes illuminated by flickering tea candles. Buddha laughed. A six-armed goddess smiled coyly. At each corner of the building, strings of little bells hung from green copper gutters and disappeared into stone barrels.

Beyond the narrow passage, another line of torches flickered against the dark ocean, their flames making long, bright fingers in the water of a swimming pool. She could hear music, slack key guitar. She stepped into the open and could see everything: the lighthouse, like a bright white candle catching a final beam of sun, the dark clouds moving unnaturally fast in the brighter sky above, the long white stripe of Anini Beach, the low, dark bulk of Princeville, foam breaking at Queen's Bath. She could even see the gray spire of Makana, all the way up in Ha'ena.

She was standing on an enormous lanai divided into platforms of teak and polished concrete. A rectangular swimming pool was illuminated by invisible lights, morphing from one color to the next as she watched. There were lines of chaise lounges, cabanas, dining nooks and bars, a long table that could seat at least twenty, a hot tub almost as large as the pool, steam rising in the cooling air, and everywhere she looked, the most beautiful people she'd ever seen.

At least that was her first thought, which she immediately realized wasn't true, since some of them were definitely models she had seen in magazines or surf wear catalogs. Here and there, faces even more familiar flickered in the crowd. They seemed to sense her interest, and when they looked up and met her eyes, they held her gaze. She got a chill of déjà vu. The feeling, she finally figured out, of smoking too much pakololo and going out in public.

"Pretty great, huh?" Sam asked.

"Whose house is this?"

Sam named an actor who'd filmed three movies on the island. "He's not here, though. He's shooting somewhere in China. Come on, let's mingle." She hooked Nalani's arm in her own, but felt her resisting. "Don't be nervous," she said. "I'll introduce you to some other locals. They love the beaches, love to surf. You'll have all sorts of things to talk about."

They moved into the crowd. Sam expertly inserted Nalani into a group of three women, introduced her, and slipped away. The women welcomed her with hugs and kisses, and told her their names, which Nalani immediately forgot.

"So, anyway," one woman said, "I know three liters *sounds* like a lot of water, but after a few days, you wonder how you ever drank less. And it's *so* worth it, once you finally go in for your treatment."

A second woman held up a hand in warning. "But don't expect it on the first session. I was all fired up, you know, to see what would come out? And sure there was, like, green mucous going through the tube. But it was honestly a little bit of a letdown. Even though Devyn had warned me? I just *knew* I was carrying around such gnarly stuff in there. Then I came in the *next* morning, and it was like, whooosh." She threw her hands apart.

"Whoosh *what*?" said the third woman.

"*Everything*," said the first woman.

"*Chunks*," said the second.

"Like, years' worth of chunks."

"Black tar."

"Imagine all of that *stuck* to your intestines?"

"And it doesn't hurt, when they put it *up*?"

The other two shared a glance.

"Well, it turned out I was, like, *impacted*? So—"

"Devyn is so gentle," the other woman cut her off. "I know three fifty sounds like a lot. But for what you get—"

"Her equipment is really state-of-the-art. Lane read up on it for me."

"And she leads you in a guided meditation, to open your root chakra?"

"I found it . . . so healing."

"Oh my god, sister," said the other woman. "So did I."

"My niece, Naia, is turning thirteen next week. I'm getting her three sessions. I just wish I'd had something like that when I was her age."

"Devyn does *everyone* on the North Shore."

Abruptly, all three women turned to Nalani.

"Have you had your colon cleansed?"

"Uh, actually, I haven't."

"Go to Devyn. It will change your life. Where do you live?"

"Kapa'a."

Silence.

"So how do you know Sam?" the first woman asked.

"Through work, I guess?"

"She is so great. She sells *all* of my houses."

"I love your romper," the second woman chimed in. "Where'd you find it?"

"My friend makes them, actually."

"It is so important to support local businesses. I'll have to find her on Insta. Where does she source her cotton?"

"I don't know."

"Hmmm. It looks so good with your complexion. Sorry, but I have to ask, are you Thai?"

"No. Just hapa."

"Oooh. What's that?"

"Haole, Hawaiian, some Filipino, Japanee, a little Portagee on my dad's side."

"Oh my god."

"You must surf."

"When can."

"*Us,* too," said one of the women. "Well, we paddleboard."

"Don't you just *love* Hanalei?"

"I actually don't make it there that often."

"Oh," said the second woman, "you *really* should. It *is* the nicest beach. And such a great community. We have a house on Weke Road."

"We practice yoga in front of her house every Sunday morning."

"Rain or shine."

"You must know our teacher, Koa Palekana? He's Hawaiian, too. Well, not *Hawaiian* Hawaiian. He was born here. Then his parents took him to Brazil, Bali, India, all over the world. But he was called back to this island."

"I don't think I've met him."

"Oh my god. You have to meet Koa. He was just here."

The woman turned toward the pool. Nalani started looking for the bar.

"There he is. Babuji! Babuji!" She waved frantically. Nalani followed her gaze and saw a middle-aged white man in a flowing garment not quite loose enough to hide his prominent belly. He was talking with a couple she recognized from the yacht. They were dressed in royal-blue togas with gemstones hanging from their necks. Koa Palekana did not look up. The woman turned back to Nalani.

"He was the meditation consultant for the cast of *Glee*? But he gave all that up. Now he runs a yoga retreat and healing center."

"Are those his disciples?" Nalani asked.

The woman glanced back. "That's Miles Schneider. The founder of Xintic? His company was just valued at eighteen billion dollars."

A haole with his head shaved walked up with a tray of champagne flutes. "Here you go, ladies. Don't ask what I did to liberate these. Those ladies acted like I wanted to take their job! I told them their tips aren't *that* good."

"Lane, this is Nalani," the second woman said. "She surfs."

He gave her a hug and a peck on the cheek. "Nalani, howzit?"

"All right," said Nalani.

He squinted at her. "Where have I seen you in the lineup?"

Nalani shrugged. "Kealia?"

"Nah. Never go there. Always so messy and too many kooks."

Nalani considered this.

"I stay in Haena mainly. Cannons? All the local braddahs know me there. Kaipo Owens. Lefty Cabral. Makana Ali'i . . ."

Nalani kept nodding. Was he asking if she knew them? Obviously, she did. She wondered how many names he planned on listing. Now he seemed to be waiting for her to say something.

"I usually just stick close to home."

"Right on. Nothing wrong with knowing your limits, yeah?"

He flashed her a shaka and turned to his wife and her friends, redrawing the circle without her in it.

Dusk was slipping into night. Since she'd stepped out of Sam's car, Nalani had been scanning for Erin in the crowd. She found herself alone at the small stage where no one was listening to a brown man with thick white hair leaning over his guitar, lost in the fluid precision of notes he laid so unhurriedly the song seemed always on the verge of drifting away. But it never did.

Sam found her again.

"He is really good," said Nalani. "Like, really good."

Sam glanced at him, then took Nalani's hand and led her a little farther into the shadows, where it was quiet enough to hear the ocean far below.

"Are you ready for tomorrow?" Sam asked.

"I guess so."

"To be honest, you made us a little nervous this afternoon."

"Sorry."

"But you're ready for tomorrow, right?"

Nalani didn't answer.

Sam sighed. "I sense your hesitation. We all do. To be perfectly honest, between you and your mother, this has been very difficult for me. Professionally. I'm trying not to take it personally, but . . ."

She gave Nalani the opportunity to break in and reassure her.

Nalani had turned her back on the ocean and was looking toward the island. She saw ridge upon ridge running down to the sea, black and silver in the moonlight, and strung across each ridge were the lights of other estates just like this one, like dew on a spiderweb or pearls on a knotted strand, neighborhood after neighborhood she had never known existed, hidden from everyone except each other.

"All right," said Sam. There was something new in her voice. Sternness. Exasperation. Anger. Her face was illuminated by the screen of her phone.

"I have to tell Franky about this. I didn't want to. I was hoping it wouldn't be necessary."

A moment later. A soft chime.

"He wants to see you," she said. "Right now."

52

The ironwood forest was open and airy. Black branches shook in the sea wind. Tiny, sharp cones lay scattered underfoot. She was supposed to be finding a campsite, but her head was too full to do anything but wander among the gray trees.

She heard an electric whine below the wind. A golf cart coming up the path. Aunty Lei with a pile of supplies. "Sorry we no more cookstoves. But no need worry about tonight. There going be one small kine party. Come down once you're settled."

She waited by the pile until Aunty Lei was out of sight, then walked until her feet touched sand. The wind raised white foam on the gray ocean. Clouds streamed in ragged rows. She sank onto a salt-white log half-buried in the sand. She sat there for a long time. Once, she stood and took a few steps backward, looked up and down the beach, sat down again.

Finally, she returned to her pile and pitched the tent Leilani had brought her. It was cheap, designed for family camping. The wind bellied its tall sides and strained its two curved poles. There was nothing she could do but drop everything inside and hope the weight would hold it if the stakes pulled loose.

She walked down the sandy road. Faint smell of woodsmoke and hot oil. A crowd had gathered in the open field. Picnic tables she'd seen scattered through the camp were now dragged end to end, anchoring a row of pop-up canopies, their legs duct-taped together. People were cooking over grills, camp stoves, woks with propane burners. Four-wheel-drive trucks lined the beach, tailgates down, coolers out. She heard the thrum of a small engine and saw three four-wheelers coming along the sand. Two kids on each. Young children played in the breaking waves. Rods were planted above the surf line. From each one hung a metal bell.

There had to be at least a hundred people watching the rods, leaning against the trucks, sitting at the picnic tables, tending grills and stoves. Most were brown, but enough were white that she could blend in. She didn't see Leilani, so she headed toward a group of aunties arranging aluminum trays on the tables.

"How can I help?" she asked a pale white woman with coarse black hair, dressed in a flowered blouse and crisp white culottes.

"You know how to make fly whisks?" the woman asked, pointing at a pile of long green leaves, then picking one up and using her thumbnail to slice a strip down its length, repeating the motion—rip, rip, rip—and knotting the strips together at one end. "Like that."

She sat on the bench with her feet in the sand, making whisks. It wasn't quite as simple as the woman made it seem. She hadn't realized how ragged her fingernails had become. But she improvised, pinching each side of the leaf and ripping it apart.

There was a moment when the sun painted the undersides of the clouds. From a boxy speaker, country bands sang mournfully about Tennessee whiskey, whiskey glasses, the color blue. The songs were all familiar. It wasn't the first time she'd heard them playing over the sand.

The women arranging food trays had gathered by one of the pop-up canopies. She heard them laughing. A few raised small plastic cups and tipped them back. Someone close to her own age, a short brown woman with Asian features, walked toward her, a bottle in one hand and a stack of plastic cups in the other. "We finally catching up to all the men. You like one shot of Crown?" Without waiting for an answer, the woman set two cups on the table and sloshed in the golden liquor. "'Ōkole maluna."

She took a long sip. There was an instant flare of adrenaline, the way she felt after an injury. She took a few more, smaller, until the cup was empty. It fumed inside her skull, settled warm in her empty stomach. By the time the woman thanked her for her help and walked back to the group, it had spread throughout her body, dull and calming. The craving that was always there suddenly wasn't.

She was sure she had plenty of whisks. But there was something satisfying about the long, clean tear of the waxy lengths, now that she had the hang of it.

Her bench sagged under someone else's weight.

"Look at you. Right at home."

Suddenly, the whiskey warmth felt like a blanket wrapped too tight.

"Hi, Carlotta."

"You *look* better. How are you feeling?"

"The bar was set pretty low."

"I'm glad you're safe."

In front of them, three men used tongs to lift golden fish from a wok. Hot oil crackled. The fish were split open and cooked whole. Another man sliced thick sausages with a long knife, then used the blade to scrape the greasy chunks off the cutting board into a foil pan.

"What's this party for, anyway?"

Carlotta shrugged. "The fish are running. Someone had a catch to share. No one shows up empty-handed. That's how these things happen."

"And you always come to these?"

"Leilani got word to me that you were here."

"And I needed help?"

"She didn't say that."

The beach was in shadow. The kids were coming out of the water.

"You got your memory back," Carlotta said.

She watched the children run up the sand, the youngest dancing impatiently until their parents wrapped dry towels around their skinny shoulders. They shivered happily, staring at the trays of food packed tight across the tables.

"You were right," she said, "I was involved in messed-up stuff."

Carlotta was silent.

"I need to get clear of it. But I don't think I can."

"Well, you're clear of it here," Carlotta said. "You're clear of it tonight. Why don't you eat a good meal and worry about all that in the morning."

"My name isn't Janice. It's Rebecca."

"It's nice to meet you, Rebecca."

"It was my job to be someone I wasn't. But I got confused."

"That's very common in this fallen world."

"The people I went to meet? It was me who brought them here. They almost did something terrible. I don't know if I prevented them, or what. But they're going to try again."

"Do they know where you are?"

"No," said Rebecca Hunt. "They're looking for me."

"Stay here, then, as long as you can. You won't find a better place."

"Those people are going to kill someone. They think they're going to start a race war."

Carlotta nodded. "The signs are there. The twelfth octave is close at hand. If they really are agents of the Nephilim, all the more reason to keep your head down. You don't want to get mixed up in that."

A woman came and took the whisks. The aunties were lining up behind the serving trays.

"I wouldn't mention it to anyone else," Carlotta added.

"I won't."

"Of course," said Carlotta, "it would be better to prevent it. If we could. For Black folks, especially. I've got cousins in Houston."

53

Dalton spent the rest of the afternoon with the heads of Legal and Public Policy, penciling in the framework of their offer to the administration. As they envisioned it, teams of Sokoni employees would embed at the Pentagon and DHS. They would offer access in tiers, with some databases searchable directly by military or law enforcement, some reserved for internal access by Sokoni but available by individual request from the agencies, and a final tier available only with a warrant from the Foreign Intelligence Surveillance Court. It had been a tedious session, a dance between his political and national security lobbyists and the lawyers making sure everything they offered would be legally defensible under the terms of the user agreements.

Falkor had been renamed the Spectrum Mass Assessment Database. Its team was given an urgent, but fairly routine, assignment: to deliver a report with the identities and geolocation of a group of migrants planning to cross the southern border in the next twelve hours. This would be the initial proof of concept to get the attention of the administration.

The form of their offer was the final sticking point. Dalton assumed he would bring it directly to the president and was hurt by how decisively this idea was rejected by his DC team. They wanted Erin to present it to the attorney general.

This meant he had to brief Erin.

Which was something he was not looking forward to.

She entered, looking wary. "Legal's been camped in your office all afternoon. Is this about Indonesia?"

The question took him by surprise. "That's been dealt with."

She leaned back, amused. "So easily?"

"We suspended all political advertising until the election and pulled the sales rep who'd been working with the rogue candidate."

"The genocide candidate is rogue now? Last week, he was our biggest Asian account."

"You know genocide is a word that gets thrown around too easily. And those are meaningful steps."

"A real feather in our cap."

"I need to brief you on something important. We're making an offer to the administration. Data sharing. We let them access some of our capabilities. They stop treating us like just another corporate entity."

For the first time, he saw something in her face he didn't think she'd chosen for him to see.

"Are you saying we're going to start *giving* user data to the government? That is a fundamental violation . . ."

"Of what? Not our user agreement."

"Two days ago, you said we were going back to basics, rebuilding *trust* with our users. Are you okay? Mentally?"

She was looking at him with genuine concern. This was absurd.

"Of course. It's the situation that's dynamic. We can't afford weakness right now. We have very powerful enemies. Not just in government and not just against our business. For some people, this is personal. We are the faces of this company. *You* and *me*. We have vouched for it countless times. They will *never* trust us. It was nice to imagine we could make Sokoni a quaint little village again. But that ship sailed years ago."

Erin was shaking her head, still refusing to believe what he was telling her. "I'm sorry about what happened to your family. I know how scary that must have been. But this is billions of people you are affecting."

"They agreed to the UAs. They made their choices. I have to make mine."

"We made the choice to build this thing. And we had good reasons. We can't lose touch with those."

"I think you should look at it," he said, "as a testament to the power of relationships. People have gladly entrusted us with their private information in exchange for the opportunity to connect with each other. Now we're going to use that information to make them safer."

Erin looked past him through the glass. It pierced his heart to see her like this: unguarded. It took him back fifteen years, to the bed with the pink mosquito net, the bright little room where they'd spent so many bored, blissful hours.

"People want to connect," he said. "There will always be a dark side to that. No matter what we do. At least this way, we can catch the worst ones."

Now she was looking at him. No matter how bad their arguments had gotten, she had never looked at him like this. And it came as a relief. He'd accused her of this feeling so many times, and she'd always denied it. Now she'd finally let her guard down. He wasn't crazy. She did hate him.

"You don't get to tell *me* about this company," said Erin. "I fucking invented it. All you did was write the code."

Dalton laughed. Genuinely laughed. He felt decades of misery lifting from his chest. How had he ever let someone like *her* make him feel so bad?

Erin watched him, the corners of her mouth twitching. Then she was laughing, too. "God," she said, "you've always been such a prick."

"I never pretended not to be."

"I'll give you that."

They looked at each other.

"It sucks," said Dalton. "I know. I never wanted this to happen."

"You kinda did."

"I am curious to see what happens next."

She couldn't put on a brave face anymore.

"So that's it?"

"I need you to sell it to the attorney general."

"Of course you do."

"The call's set up already. Tomorrow morning. You'll do it from here."

They sat in silence.

"It's funny," said Erin, "I was just telling someone about that village. The one in the desert, where everyone was sleeping."

"Where we were going to buy drugs?"

Her mouth twitched again. "Just khat," she said. "To stay awake. You were scared we'd fall off the truck. But seriously, have you ever looked at it?"

"What do you mean?"

"Have you ever pulled the geotags?"

"I think I looked at a satellite view. Years ago. I don't know. Houses in the desert."

"They're falling down. The families we saw sleeping together in the big beds? They're gone. Those kids grew up and left."

"We could pass that on to Research. Run a survey. Ask them why."

"Leave them alone," said Erin. "Who knows what kind of stuff they post. I don't want them popping up in any databases."

54

Sam kept Nalani moving through the crowd, one arm linked through hers. When Nalani hesitated, Sam pulled her forward, like the impatient parent of a naughty child. She told Nalani to stay put while she spoke to one of the staff, then brought her through the main doors of the house. They wound through dimly lit corridors and ended in a theater with three rows of shiny leather recliners facing a wall-size screen. A low hum filled the room. A pale glow appeared on the screen. There was a moment of jittery static, then Franky Dalton's face. Ten feet tall.

His lips were set. Then he raised them into a smile, pinched and dry.

"Hi, Nalani."

She could hear the spittle smacking in the corners of his mouth. She looked over her shoulder. Sam was gone. When she turned back to the screen, he'd pulled back his lips, revealing his teeth.

"Tomorrow is the big day. I can only imagine all the emotions you're feeling."

"Can you see me?" she asked.

"I was just thinking back on our last conversation," he said as if she hadn't spoken. "I realized there was an oversight. I never explained what this land means to me and my family, personally. You can probably imagine that we rely on elaborate security measures. I accept that my work entails personal risk. I'm a mission-driven person, and I'm seeking something far more important than my own safety. However, I do fear for my family. And earlier this week, our worst nightmares came true. A group tried to kidnap my wife and children. Fortunately, they were unsuccessful."

"I'm sorry—" she began.

"I'm sure you suspect this process has been motivated by more than scientific discovery. And you're correct, of course. I do believe in the profound importance of our littoral zones, but I intend Momona to be a sanctuary for myself, our family, and those we love most, a place where my children can feel completely safe. You understand?"

Nalani nodded, still uncertain how, exactly, she was being observed.

"I'm telling you this because I know you care about the health and safety of your family, too. Maybe you're wondering whether you're betraying them with this arrangement. I want to lay those fears to rest. What we're building is not just secure from the threats of today. We're constructing a compound for the threats of tomorrow, with enough food and fuel to sustain every resident for at least five years with no outside inputs. We have aquaculture, fungiculture, and hydroponics fueled by renewable power and a plan for equitable communal thriving based on NASA research."

Since the moment he'd come on-screen, he'd been staring at a point five feet above her head.

"I want to extend an invitation. The compound can sustain thirty-two people. Should it ever be necessary, you and two companions of your choosing—assuming they pass the standard vetting—will be among those thirty-two."

"Oh."

Dalton grinned. "Amazing, right? Whatever anxieties you have about climate change, ocean acidification, super volcanoes, pandemics, bioweapons, nuclear war, the singularity—from this moment on, your worrying can stop. You and your loved ones will be safe. That is my guarantee. This land sustained your family in the past; now it will guarantee your family's future."

"I honestly don't know what to say."

"This is my gift to you. Tomorrow, you are going to help me keep my family safe. I want to do the same for yours."

"Well, it's very thoughtful."

Dalton's smile eased gradually from his face.

"You'll be there, tomorrow morning. You are feeling good about everything."

This felt like a command, not a question. But it seemed important to respond. Until now, she'd been able to maintain the luxurious idea that her decision was still unsettled. Now it was time to lay that luxury to rest.

"Yes."

He was still looking somewhere over her head. But his face relaxed. For the first time, a real grin broke out. Suddenly, he seemed lighthearted.

"You know I lived in Kenya, Africa, for two years? They used to call the Peace Corps the toughest job you'll ever love. It's corny, but it's true. And I learned a lesson that's guided me ever since: that in the end, human connections are all that matter. That's something people don't really appreciate in America, the mainland, I mean. I think it's why my wife and I love island culture. On Big Island, we visited the pu'uhonua, the village of refuge? A place where anyone could claim sanctuary and be safe from harm. We found that really inspiring. Of course, our Momona pu'uhonua can't take in *everyone*. It's not designed to. But when I had the idea of inviting you and your family into our 'ohana, it just felt so pono, we knew it was the right decision."

Nalani was still in the moment of calm before the lip of the wave began to curl. She noted his impeccable pronunciation, and when he smiled, she smiled back. But something dark and powerful was rising.

"Goodbye," said Frank Dalton. "And aloha."

She started to repeat the word by force of habit, but it stuck in her throat, and then the screen went dark. Nalani sat perfectly still, then reached for her phone. Sam walked in as she was slipping it back into her pocket.

"So, it's settled?" Sam asked, her face naked with anxiety.

"Definitely," said Nalani.

55

He was in his cube, cantilevered into the darkness, staring at the blinking cursor of the command line. He used to do this more often, logging in as a low-level engineer on the infrastructure resolutions queue. It was like playing the slots: you might get a simple bug and an instant hit of dopamine, or you might get a problem that took all night and pushed the limits of your self-control.

A knottier problem did have its rewards. Nostalgia, most obviously, for the years when he had all night and day to stare at the cursor, wrestling frustration into submission, loading the codespace into his mind until he could see the logic of the structure, how its functions branched and injected, how data traveled through the variables, until he'd smelled the problem and could begin to tease it out, testing, failing, trying again, his understanding getting clearer, until he slipped completely into the parameters of the code, unconsciously following its unique logic and forgetting all others, performing shotgun surgeries, eliminating freeloaders, tidying data clumps, disentangling object orgies, losing himself in the work and resetting his own neural pathways in the process, emerging hours later, cleansed and refreshed.

He told himself this was good leadership. It kept him humble, to log in and do his part repaying technical debt. But there was no shame in acknowledging he craved that state of flow. Even the smelliest code rewired his brain for the better, which wasn't exactly reassuring. And when he did have to leave a problem unresolved, he could pass on responsibility, certain it would reach someone who could handle it more capably than he could. This was singularly unlike every other problem in his life.

There was the contractor, Ariel Raz, and his partner who'd so thoroughly fucked up the op. The full dimensions of it still weren't clear. All Raz had told him was she had infiltrated the group within one degree of Phoenix, everything according to plan. She was highly reliable, Raz had told him. Ex-CIA. She'd operated in war zones and only left government when she hit the glass ceiling. She was talented, supremely ambitious, perfect for private sector work. When she went dark, he'd assumed she must be dead. Instead, she'd shown up with the men who'd tried to kidnap Dalton's wife.

None of this would have bothered Dalton, necessarily. He was glad to learn he employed *someone* whose sense of urgency matched the gravity of the problem. But why hadn't Raz given them more warning? When he asked, the man repeated how bad all this would look for Phoenix, as if it were still a PR problem for the company, not an urgent matter of personal security.

He was dealing with a god object. Instead of assigning classes cleanly, each with intuitive and well-defined responsibilities, someone had packed a single object with an obscene number of procedures, one of which was causing a cascade of broken functions across the program. The easy fix would be to find the broken line, repair it, and let the object keep running. But the situation offended him. He knew the malevolent little knot in the code base would keep reappearing in the queue. He needed to fix it for good. And that meant getting his head inside it.

As a young coder, he'd believed the perfection possible in a closed system could be shared with everyone. *People deserve clean code* had actually been written on the wall in the little second-floor rental they'd moved into after their first round of funding. Yet Erin could still tell him, all these years later, with a straight face, that he had *only coded* Sokoni. As if the code wasn't the thing itself. *Anyone* could have an idea. But no one had ever coded an app like that, where every user was a potential saboteur and every line had to be bulletproof.

Building a viable public network changed your view of human nature. You learned that people, as a group, were wicked and relentless. If there was any weakness in a system, they would trigger its worst consequences through some combination of laziness, incompetence, obtuseness, and spite. Only the most cynical engineer could possibly design a system robust enough to survive. Relying on the good behavior of your users was the path to destruction.

If he was going to streamline the object, he needed to understand the methods it contained. But the deeper he scrolled, the less order he could find. He typed his notes on another screen, trying to group methods into coherent responsibilities, getting more and more enraged with their refusal to make sense according to any logic he could discern. Finally, he stopped himself. It was pointless.

You could not argue with code. It could not be persuaded and would never change its mind. The only way forward was to accept its premises—no matter how nonsensical they seemed—and see the situation through whatever chain of reasoning guided its functions. If he threw himself a pity party, he would get exactly what he deserved: failure.

This was what he loved about coding. There was no hiding from its judgment. In the midst of fear, uncertainty, and doubt, your nature was revealed. A coder had the temperament to persevere and solve the problem, or she didn't. Failure was weakness. Most coders refused to accept this. And each of them failed their way to the status they deserved.

This was what he hated about the outside world. The metrics were elusive. People failed their way up. Take Hart, whose talents, the more he dug into them, seemed to consist primarily of knowing the right people, presenting himself advantageously, getting assigned to good missions, and avoiding accountability.

And what about his own failure to choose the right protector for his family? It had been a problem of time—he hadn't familiarized himself with the domain well enough to make an informed decision—which was more accurately defined as a problem of prioritization. He'd put the growth of his company ahead of the safety of his family. And now he was in a mess of smelly problems.

He needed clean solutions. He was getting bloated plans with no redundancy and countless vulnerabilities: relying on a broken local family to convey a key piece of his security, treating a murderous militia as a corporate PR problem. All systems experienced deadlock, overflow, instability, infinite loops. Sometimes you could upgrade and replace. Usually, the best you could do was a kludge: secure your priority functions and ruthlessly eliminate the most catastrophic vulnerabilities. Simple code made all of that easier. Elegance wasn't just something you did to show off. It was objectively more effective, less liable to fail, easier to fix.

And sometimes the simplest solution wasn't elegant at all. Sometimes you had to kill a project so the rest of the system could run smoothly.

Phoenix and his team were bad actors, taking advantage of his profoundest vulnerability. You couldn't just release a patch for malware that vicious. It had to be attacked on its own terms. Raz wasn't trustworthy. But he offered a solution. His team was on island. These men weren't bureaucrats, like Hart. They were operators. On their missions, success was always measurable. And according to Raz, they'd never failed.

His list of functions was still growing. The object really was beginning to look omniscient: entangling with every process, capable of bringing down the entire system. He copied and pasted the notes he'd taken, created a ticket. Wrote *WTF? This code stinks—FD* and hit *Return to Queue*.

He had bigger problems, and he needed to prioritize.

DAY 7

56

Rebecca Hunt lay on her back, watching the darkness folding on itself, listening to the humming nylon as the tent walls sucked and swelled. It had been raining for hours. If Aunty Lei had brought a ground cloth, it was still lying in the pile of stuff she hadn't sorted. She felt the tent floor lift and slosh beneath her, cold water soaking through.

The shift had been instant. One moment she'd been gazing at the ocean, about to walk down to the party—a tourist on vacation from herself—then a memory arrived. And another. A trickle became a flood, and the empty spaces were full again. She was Rebecca Hunt, all other possibilities foreclosed.

She'd stood, in the moment of shock, and tried slowly backing away from this version of reality, as if there was still a chance to catch the next one instead. But she'd always been good in a crisis. She soon sat down to reevaluate her options.

How long had she and Raz been working this particular op? Three months? Four. An incredibly short time to develop a source so thoroughly.

Agile.

Alex.

And how long had she been an addict? Years. A lot of years if you included the trammies she'd been getting off the SEALs in the SMU assignment that had set her career back ten years.

And what had triggered the memory loss? Something traumatic.

That one was easy.

She'd sat on the log and methodically worked through the steps that had brought her to this spot. Then she walked down the beach and joined the party.

Now, in darkness, with the tent walls breathing like overworked lungs, and the rain seeping up from the ground into her cotton sweatshirt, she walked through the events again.

She'd seen the possibilities from the moment Raz outlined the contract. An op like this was the reason she had finally quit the public sector: one of the most powerful clients in the world and all the opportunity you could ask for to rise or fall on your own merit. No political appointees or years of service. She'd tightened things up, physically, mentally, asked her doctor to bump her Adderall prescription five milligrams. Then done the best work of her life, if she was honest with herself.

All Raz had known was that Alex existed. Finding her had been a feat, but any good agent could have done it with the right connections and a few lucky breaks. It was what she'd done afterward that had proven Hunt's value.

The first obstacle was something she hadn't trained for at the Farm—though she was sure they taught it now: how to approach someone who never removed their headphones. Alex would have been a challenge even without them. She was always barely there. Hiding in a black hoodie, gravitating to the corners, darting through traffic, disappearing behind her laptop. Surveilling her had been a pain in the ass. She went everywhere by bike, shapeless messenger bag hitched tight over her shoulder, recklessly asserting herself in downtown traffic the way she never seemed to do in any other area of her life.

But the longer Hunt watched, the more she realized even Alex's most reckless acts were calculated. She never rode with headphones on. She always knew what was coming up behind. Once Hunt noticed that, she knew everything about Alex she would ever need to. First, she had to buy a bike. She did her research, found a used LeMond, a little rust on the frame but pristine aftermarket components. When the two just happened to lock up on the same rack at the same time, Hunt took the opportunity—before Alex slipped her headphones up from her neck—to comment on the other woman's classic black Cross-Check. She was new in town, Hunt mentioned. One thing led to another.

The thing about Alex was that once you got to know her, you learned her mind moved as fast and fluidly, as fearlessly, as she weaved between lanes on her battered Surly.

The thing about Alex was that—no matter how many chat windows she had open on-screen—she was lonely. She'd never figured out how to be in the world. She kept her hair chopped, invested in three-hundred-dollar headphones, and buried herself in sweatshirts. There was a whole generation of kids like that, Rebecca knew, and now she had to wonder how many of them were like Alex.

None. The answer was none.

The thing about Alex was that she and Rebecca had a lot in common. The world had taken a lot from each of them, but they hadn't let it have their confidence. They were both idealists. The only difference was that Alex believed freedom meant releasing information, and Rebecca Hunt knew freedom depended on keeping some things secret.

Alex was a tough nut. She'd spent her last year of high school living on friends' couches. For months, she never, not once, even hinted to Hunt about what she was involved in with Phoenix. There were times Rebecca wondered whether she was even with the right person at all. Their security really had been incredibly tight. Everyone knew only what they needed to know.

Of course, Hunt didn't try to coerce Alex into sharing her secrets. She'd let Alex coerce her to share her own. After they slept together the first time, Hunt stopped texting. She'd already made sure Alex knew where to find her. And when Alex slid, a week later, onto the bench across from her at the coffee shop, silent and angry, Hunt reluctantly explained she hadn't been completely honest about why she'd come to Seattle. She'd been deeply involved in direct action for many years, quietly lending her expertise wherever it could be useful—Seattle, Zuccotti Park, St. Paul, Ferguson, Waukesha. She wasn't violent, but she did believe in diversity of tactics. She'd wound up on a watch list in Portland and come north to let things cool down. She didn't want to get Alex involved in anything like that. She cared about her. She was trying to protect her. The relationship resumed, but another month passed before Alex vaguely revealed her own activities and asked whether Hunt had any connections she could recommend.

Thanks to Raz, she did.

He'd predicted Phoenix would be desperate to generate attention for his next leak and might finally expand his circle of trust in ways they could exploit. Hunt didn't want to know how Raz knew Alpha, but she couldn't deny he was perfect for this op: obscure enough to be misrepresented to Phoenix, but easily linked—with a few helpful tips to the media, when the time was right—to a long and damning archive on white supremacist message boards. Alpha was genuinely scary—Hunt saw that immediately—so when she described him to Alex as an old colleague from her Occupy days with deep experience in nonviolent action, she promised herself she would ID Phoenix long before she let Alpha and his men near any of them.

Unfortunately, Alex had been disciplined. She'd trusted Rebecca to recruit the team for the action in Hawaii, but in the weeks that followed, she didn't bring Hunt any closer to Phoenix or offer any clue to his identity. The night before their flight to Lihue, Hunt panicked. She'd been upping her dosages, seeking the keyhole that would make everything fall neatly into place: deliver Phoenix's identity to Raz, report his new white supremacist connections to a few favored journalists, help Alex disappear.

She'd been surprised how easy it was to convince Alex to drop a dose of MDMA and go dancing. They'd grinned as they chewed the pills and washed out the taste with shots of Suntory.

And they had fun.

Those last hours remained hazy, but at some point, Hunt left the mattress where they'd passed out, walked into the kitchen of Alex's tiny apartment, slipped the woman's laptop from her battered messenger bag, entered the twelve-digit, randomized code she'd captured, key by key, after weeks of careful observation, and logged on.

It didn't feel as desperate as it was. Everything, at that point, had felt desperate for days. She was on the razor's edge. Pushing her tradecraft to its limits. Revealing to herself what she was capable of. Traversing further and further on a ridge there was no backing off from.

She'd been almost there, in the deep archives, when something made her turn: Alex, in her favorite pair of boxers, staring at her with sleepy affection, gradually changing to confusion, then, rapidly, understanding. Then she was gone. And when she came back, she was holding the Japanese chef's knife she kept on a magnet above the sink.

The thing about Alex was she'd been dead for a week.

It was unfortunate, what had happened. Phoenix had recruited her into something out of her depth. Not that she couldn't have excelled in the role, with the right training. She'd been an extremely talented person. It was a shame all around.

And now Raz's plan had jumped the tracks. She assumed he was on island by now, trying to contain the situation, probably with his team on call. If she could just contact Raz, and they could prevent Alpha from doing any more damage, they could reveal Phoenix's connection to an attempted kidnapping by a violent militia and completely discredit him. The operation, incredibly, could still be a success.

The walls of her tent were still bellying in slow motion, but now she heard only the occasional tick of a raindrop. She unzipped the door and poked her head through the gap. Gray sky and black, thrashing trees. She pulled on her hoodie and stepped into the wind.

Aunty Lei was walking the aisles of the family section, checking on people.

"Your tent still standing?" Leilani asked.

"Barely."

"What you need?"

"I know this sounds strange, but I need to find Frank Dalton's house."

Lei gave her an appraising look. Then laughed. "Shoots. You like catch one ride? Last night, I get one text from my friend Nalani. She say the akule running, and everyone invited."

57

It was 7:45, but there was no sign of sun. The palms along the road were bent, fronds streaming like the flags in front of the courthouse. The auctioneer was sheltering with his lectern under the foyer. Mr. Shimabukuro was beside him, outlining how they planned to proceed.

Samantha stood on the steps in the wind and bursts of rain, holding a venti latte in both hands, absorbing the final hints of warmth still seeping through the cardboard. Her gaze went back and forth from Rice Street to the parking lot. She took out her phone again. Quadruple-checked that her last message to Nalani had gone through.

The sound of tires made her look up, hopefully. An azure Jeep Rubicon. A golf umbrella unfolded first, obscuring the driver, until he straightened out and she recognized the Hawaiian lawyer with the preppy name. She watched the passenger door. But the headlights flashed, and the lawyer made his way through the rain alone. At least no other bidders had shown up.

"Any word?" she asked as soon as Trey had climbed the steps.

"From Nalani?"

"She isn't here. Were you meeting her? You're late."

He smiled tightly. "I had some business at the county building. I just thought I'd—"

"Can you call her? Right now? The auction's about to start."

Trey considered this, then nodded. He took out his phone and poked at it. "Straight to voice mail."

"Fuck," said Sam.

The auctioneer looked glumly at the sky, hefted the metal lectern, and began walking it down the steps. Shimabukuro caught Sam's eye but didn't leave the shelter of the building.

The auctioneer raised a black umbrella. A curtain of gray rain swept across them. The flags snapped and the palm fronds rattled. The park was completely empty. Samantha wondered where the homeless went on days like this.

The auctioneer rapped his gavel. He was looking at Sam. She looked at Shimabukuro. Reluctantly, he walked down the stairs, unfurling his own umbrella. The rain was falling steadily now. Sam hadn't brought an umbrella. Shimabukuro stopped three feet away.

"No word from your client?" he said.

She was tempted to correct him. Frank Dalton was her client. She only shook her head.

"I'm supposed to report to Mr. Dalton on the status of our transaction once it's secure."

This, at least, made her smile. Thank god that wasn't her job.

"How long do we have?" she asked.

The auctioneer checked his watch unhappily. "Fifty-eight minutes."

"I'll check her apartment," said Samantha. "We should call the hospitals. And the police. At least we can tell Franky we tried everything."

She turned to Trey. He'd been keeping a respectful distance. Now he stepped closer and raised his umbrella over her. "Is she your friend?" Sam asked. "Maybe you should look for her. She could be in danger."

"I can ask around," said Trey, clearly not sharing her sense of urgency.

"As someone with a fiduciary duty to your client," said Sam in the tone she used with Realtors who were being particularly intransigent or obtuse, "I would urge you to do everything within your power to prevent her from making a big mistake. Mr. Dalton can be very litigious."

Trey looked at the rain falling past the edges of the umbrella. "Be careful driving," he said, "in weather like this."

She left her Range Rover running in the middle of the lot and ran up to Nalani's floor. It seemed impossible that seven days ago she'd stood right here, pulled together her brightest smile, and knocked politely on a perfect Hawaiian morning. She'd been prepared to do whatever it took. But it had been easy. She genuinely liked Nalani. Admired her. And pitied her. She'd imagined they might really have a future together. Professional. Personal. That was all a bit confused in the real estate business.

She knocked on the neighbors' doors for good measure. Then sat in the car, considering her options. Thirty-two minutes remaining. Only one other place she could think to go.

There was no way they would be back in time, even if she found her. But she had to do something. And she really didn't want to face Mr. Shimabukuro again. She didn't want to face any of them ever again. She turned north on the highway. There was no point speeding now.

She almost missed the turn, accelerating to pass a line of pickups and vans before realizing they were going the same place she was and pulling up to the back of the line.

But the line wasn't moving. She checked her phone. She studied the clouds, stared at the truck ahead of her. On its tailgate was a decal of a dog snarling at a charging boar. *Run your dogs,* it said, *not your mouth.* Below, on the rust-eaten bumper, was a smaller sticker. *No forget for go home.*

The line began to move. Men in black ponchos clustered around the gatehouse. Most held the kind of military armaments she'd only seen on police in foreign airports. A black Suburban was parked down the dirt road inside the fence. The vehicles passed through one by one and re-formed in a line behind it.

One of the guards waved the truck ahead of her through. She rolled after it, and the guard lifted his hand to wave her, too, when he noticed what she was driving, then looked at her, then at someone over his shoulder as he hurriedly opened his palm in a signal to stop.

She watched the truck roll ahead and join the others. The gate descended.

A guard was at her window. Thankfully one of the ones without a machine gun.

"You have an appointment?"

"I'm Samantha Rittenheimer," she said, pleased with the casual self-assurance she could hear in her voice, "Mr. Dalton's *personal* Realtor? I'm sure I'm on a list somewhere . . ." The last sentence had come out with a little less confidence.

The man stepped back and consulted with someone through an earpiece. He leaned down.

"We don't have authorization," he told her, stepping back and swinging his arm toward the highway. "Now if you'll just proceed that way . . ."

"Wait," said Samantha. "I can't get in, but *they* can?"

The guard's face snapped into an extremely professional expression. "They are guests of an . . . occupant."

"The Kanaheles?" said Samantha. "Wait, I'm a guest of the Kanaheles! That's who I'm going to see. I am on my way to see Nalani Kanahele Winthrop. You need to let me through."

The guard stared at her very sternly, as if she were being naughty and he was giving her the chance to stop before she faced the consequences.

She stared right back.

He said something into his earpiece.

The gate began to rise.

The guard glumly waved her through.

She pulled into her spot behind the pickup.

The pickup's passenger door opened and someone hopped onto the ground.

Samantha wondered if they were going to be here awhile. She checked her rearview mirror just in time to see the black SUV lurch from the gatehouse and accelerate across the grass. It was either heading directly at the pickup, or the skinny stranger in the baggy hoodie, or at her. Samantha tightened her grip on the steering wheel and braced herself.

A streak of mud splatted her windshield as the SUV rocked by, sucking the stranger's hoodie in its slipstream before sliding on the wet grass to stop inches short of the truck. Doors opened. Men with machine guns leaped out, making him look even smaller and more vulnerable.

Assholes.

At first, Sam thought it was a teenager they were screaming at, then realized it was a woman, a white woman her own age, bruises showing on her pale face.

Sam had known this property when there was nothing but a cattle gate padlocked with a code half the island seemed to know. Now a lady, clearly someone down and out, was being treated like a deadly threat for stepping foot on a cow pasture.

Not that the woman seemed intimidated. She hadn't flinched when the truck nearly took her out. And she wasn't backing away now. She was calmly showing her empty hands, speaking fast and urgently. At least they'd all stopped shouting. But they were still aiming their machine guns at her.

Sam really didn't like the attitude of these mainland guards.

No forget for go home.

For a second, she wondered where she could get one of those stickers.

58

Three yellow Wranglers were lined up on a narrow causeway covered with tall grass. On one side was a square pond, ten acres wide, its water blooming rusty red. On the other side, the dam sloped steeply to a vast construction zone of red dirt. Two bulldozers were parked in a pit of red mud and pooling tread marks, long scrapes visible where they'd pressed fresh dirt against the original slope. From a concrete pipe, frothing red water poured into a ditch running through the construction zone and into the forest. Long braids of rain twisted across the land, spattering the raw earth and raising a red mist across the surface of the pond.

A man in a black poncho climbed from the front of one Jeep, opened a wide umbrella, and held it over the passenger door. Dalton was never comfortable with stuff like this. Asking a man to cover him with a rifle was one thing; asking that man to cover him with an umbrella was something else. But it was a nasty day. And now he faced the choice of taking the umbrella and leaving the other man with nothing or allowing him to continue sheltering them both.

His engineer was waiting for him patiently. "This could be a one-hundred-year event."

"Isn't that what this is designed for?" Dalton asked.

"Hypothetically. But, as you know, this is not the optimal method of reinforcing a one-hundred-fifty-year-old structure."

"It's an earthen dam. Doesn't more earth make it stabler?"

The engineer grimaced. "Under the right conditions. It can."

"And under these conditions?"

"There could be sloughing if we get enough flow. The new material might sheer away."

"You said it yourself." Dalton raised his voice above the rising wind. "This dam has held for one hundred fifty years. It's survived storms like this before."

"If the pile sheers, it could compromise the spillway. And if the spillway is compromised, we'll see water buildup on the other side. And if anything gives, it will give catastrophically."

"We knew there were risks. That's why we didn't build here in the valley."

"We can minimize this risk. There's an overflow channel we can open up to divert the pond and relieve pressure."

"Great. Why haven't you done it?"

"It will affect our schedule."

"The schedule?"

"For completing the refuge."

"How's that?" Dalton was shouting even louder.

The engineer pointed to a mild depression on one side of the dam. "If we bulldoze that channel, the flow will go directly into the pit. We won't be able to dump there until we repair it, and we can't excavate without a dump site. Installation of essential systems will pause."

Dalton surveyed the massive red pile of displaced earth that interrupted the green walls of the narrow valley. As dramatic as this situation was, and as potentially annoying, he couldn't muster the will to get worked up about it. If anything, it felt like a relief to put his energy toward something as simple as an engineering problem. Any minute, his lawyer would be calling to tell him the Momona parcel was finally his. They had a judge on standby, ready to issue an injunction to immediately evict all unauthorized personnel from the property. Hart was coordinating personally with the chief of police.

"How long a delay?" he asked, hating himself for getting the slightest amount of enjoyment from the other man's anxiety.

The engineer shrugged. "Weeks? Maybe. Months, more likely."

"So you're saying if we open this channel, there is a one hundred percent chance of a significant delay on a project that's already significantly delayed. But if we do nothing, there's a slight chance of having the same delay?"

"There would be other consequences. The emergency generators could be affected. And there are environmental factors."

"Why are the emergency generators located in a floodplain?"

"You asked us to relocate them. I believe the noise was audible from the house?"

Dalton needed to be back at the office. Erin was calling the AG in forty-five minutes. "By the way," he said, "we're not calling it the refuge anymore. It's been rechristened. Now it's *pu'uhonua*. No need to write that down. We'll have the new branding soon."

"What's your call, sir?" The engineer was beginning to look very damp.

"How long can we wait?"

The engineer looked across the landscape, where isolated puddles were coalescing into a single, shiny orange pool. "We do it now, or we don't do it."

Dalton was about to end the conversation when something caught his attention down the valley. Headlights. He stared through the rain. A black Suburban. One of his. But more headlights kept coming behind it.

"Can I see those?" He gestured at the binoculars the engineer had slung around his neck.

Dalton twisted the knobs until the caravan came into focus. A line of trucks, mostly. A few SUVs and minivans. Driving slowly. All construction crews had been told to stay home, because of the storm. There was no reason for anyone to be authorized on the road to Momona.

He spun around and speed-walked back to the Jeep, his body man rushing to keep the umbrella overhead. He opened the door himself and slammed it, forgetting to return the binoculars, forgetting to give his engineer an answer.

"Get Hart on the phone," he said. "Make sure the homesite is fully secured. Tell him if my family isn't already under protection, he's fired as soon as this is over. Wait. Don't tell him that."

Hart was fired no matter what.

59

Rebecca Hunt was tired of men with guns. But she hid her impatience as she coached the nervous security guard through the steps that would take her to Ariel Raz.

She felt bad about the holdup. No one was moving until they sorted this out.

Finally, another Suburban rolled over the hill and pulled in behind the first. A rear door swung open, and a familiar, tanned hand extended from a crisp white sleeve.

She nodded to the guards, who'd finally dropped the muzzles of their MP5s and were looking disappointed.

Raz was alone in the spacious back seat.

He offered a grin, trying to turn her appearance into a joke they could share. But she'd registered the disgust he hadn't been able to hide in time. She glanced at the driver and the man riding shotgun. Both were bearded, dressed in flannel shirts and baseball caps. They weren't Dalton's, that was certain.

"I guess the client still trusts you," she said.

Raz grinned, waved a hand dismissively. "Whatever our misjudgments, they are nothing compared to the incompetence this freier surrounds himself with."

She didn't bother asking why his opinion of Dalton had fallen so low. When Raz was speaking frankly, he used *freier* the way most people used *him* or *her*. It reflected his outlook on life. Everyone was a sucker. She sank back into the seat and watched the landscape roll past tinted windows. Rebecca Hunt was in her element, bumping across a field with a team of operators, discussing how to salvage a situation gone wildly sideways.

"When did they get here?" She nodded toward the front seat.

"Last night."

He was doing her a courtesy. They both knew she wasn't the one who needed to be debriefed.

"Agile is dead," she said. "I sped up the timetable, trying to get ahead of the situation. Took a calculated risk. She caught me going through her computer. Unfortunately, she assaulted me."

Raz was shaking his head. The picture of sympathy. "In the apartment?"

"I cleaned it up."

"I know."

Of course he did. She'd been too thorough. She hadn't had time for anything else. Of course, she'd also never told him the location of the apartment.

"Has she been found?"

He shrugged. "There's no indication."

"I left her bike on the Aurora Bridge. I left her in the Fremont Cut. There's an asphalt plant downstream where you can access the river. No IDs, of course. But she does have some tattoos."

Raz looked bored. Paying her a compliment by taking her professionalism for granted. But she knew his mind was working fast.

"There'd be bruising around the neck. Detectable, if they found her in time."

For a moment, everything familiar about the situation dropped away, and she was back on top of Alex, the familiar narrow hips pinned beneath her thighs, their bodies slick with mingled sweat, a stream of it running down her forehead to her cheekbone buried in her lover's short black hair, small gasps growing fainter as she slipped her elbow deeper under Alex's jaw, straining to lock everything tighter despite the pain of the C2 vertebrae digging into her forearm, desperate to be merciful in these final moments, to release her lover from fear and pain.

"Hunt."

"Sorry."

His eyes were on her. Somehow summoning even greater depths of sympathy. If she hadn't been certain this was an interrogation, she was now.

"Why the silence?"

Now it was her turn to shrug. "The ER doc called it a psychogenic fugue. I woke on the plane under one of my old identities. We'd been doing a lot of party drugs. I was trying to put her out for the night. I misjudged the dose. All I had was a phone I couldn't unlock. It took me a few days to contact the team and get back on track. They went rogue. Tried to kidnap Dalton, almost took his family. You didn't warn them."

"And where are they now?" Each word carefully enunciated.

She met his eyes. No trace of sympathy now. "They're on a compound with Phoenix. Less than ten miles from here. North. Put me in a vehicle and I could find it."

Raz nodded. Looking out the window again.

Wherever they were going, they hadn't taken the directest route.

"We have an assignment," said Raz. "To clean up this mess. You understand?"

She said nothing. He knew she understood.

60

Dalton had never been in his cube during a storm. He discovered he liked it even better than the postcard days of green mountains, blue sky, and turquoise sea.

On any list of the most powerful people in the world, his name showed up. But being powerful and feeling powerful were two different things. It was easier for him to get people on the phone. And he could walk into any restaurant in the world and get a table. But grilled salmon was grilled salmon. Whatever chefs did to justify their prices rarely improved it. The body men, the machine guns, the motorcades—all that was how they moved prisoners, too. It was the showers all over again. The more comfortable your life became, the harder it was to enjoy.

But standing in a cube of silence as endless sheets of water sluiced against your walls of glass, listening to the sound of your breath as the island writhed with snapping crowns, watching sea and sky churn toward you and pass without stirring a hair on your arm, *that* felt like power.

Erin was with a team of lawyers in the conference room. Her call with the attorney general was in ten minutes. They would patch Dalton in once it cleared the switchboard at Justice. His phone buzzed. Shimabukuro. Finally, an update on the auction. It was beyond time to resolve that situation. The commander on duty at the police station had six squad cars on standby, just waiting for authorization to proceed.

"Is it done?" he asked.

There was a long silence. Then a voice so quiet he could barely hear it.

"What?"

"The auction was . . . inconclusive."

"Is someone trying to outbid us? I told you, offer whatever it takes."

"There's no one."

"Then who are you bidding against?"

"No one. No one is bidding. Ms. Winthrop never showed up."

Dalton looked at his watch. "You waited an hour to tell me this?"

"We waited to see whether she would come. Ms. Rittenheimer is searching for her. I haven't heard back. In the meantime, the auction closed, so it passes to the plaintiff, by default."

"I'm sorry?"

"The plaintiff in the suit, Ms. Kanahele."

"What does that mean?"

The room was blinking dull red from a tiny light on his desk phone. Erin was speaking to the AG.

"Maile Kanahele will be declared the owner of the land by default."

"The sole owner?"

"Yes. She was the sole plaintiff in the suit."

"What can we do?"

"We can put together an offer," Shimabukuro said hopefully. "It would be a very simple transaction now that ownership has been successfully consolidated."

"Successful? If she wanted to sell, she would have kept her contract. Tell me, who is in control of this process? Who do we appeal to?"

"The judge controls it, of course. But he'll be guided by the law. And the statutes are clear."

"You're telling me we did everything right, followed every rule and by-law, set up a nonprofit foundation to steward the land. We were the only ones to show up at the auction. And the state is about to hand over title to a convicted drug dealer?"

Shimabukuro was silent for a long time.

"Are you still there?" Dalton checked the network bars on his phone.

The voice, quieter than ever. "Is there any illegal activity occurring on the property?"

"I have no idea," said Dalton. "Probably. Her cousin might be some kind of pedophile, supposedly. And the girl was caught up in some scandal. There are a hundred people down there right now throwing a hurricane party. Most of them look like they're living out of their cars."

"Hawaii has a very broadly worded statute when it comes to asset forfeiture."

"What?"

"Asset forfeiture. It allows the police to seize property associated with criminal activity."

"So?"

"The forfeited property is put up for sale and the proceeds are used to fund law enforcement."

"Put up for sale to whom?"

"It depends. There is some latitude as to how, exactly, an asset is disposed of. An arrangement could be made to ensure it goes to a suitable buyer."

Dalton considered this. "But if there was a crime, it would have to go to trial. It would be in the media for months. It would give that family a platform to make all sorts of accusations."

"It doesn't have to go to trial. No one even has to be formally charged. Everything is at the discretion of the police and prosecutors. And we have connections in those departments."

"The police can't just take your property and sell it."

"It's the law, as written. It's certainly not unique to the state of Hawaii. A forfeiture of this value would be desirable for the department. Of course, such a high-profile seizure might also cause them some hesitation."

"But Ms. Kana—the lady hasn't taken ownership, right? Not officially?"

"That is a bit of a gray area," said Shimabukuro. "The judge overseeing our suit *is* quite sympathetic to law enforcement. In the case of an unclear claim to the land, he might view an asset forfeiture as a win-win for all sides: the cleanest way to resolve a contentious issue. That is speculative, of course."

"Of course," said Dalton.

"I could make some inquiries," said his lawyer. "With the relevant offices. Would you like me to call the judge's chambers and present our questions?"

"Absolutely not," said Dalton.

He hung up the phone.

Dalton thought of the rusty pickups caravanning across his land. He thought of the clan hiding out in that falling-down shack: a child molester, a drug trafficker. And Nalani, involved somehow in a dozen unsolved murders, who'd accepted all his generosity, the ultimate generosity, and lied to his face—the behavior of a deeply disturbed person, a sociopath. He thought of Madeleine and the twins, in hiding *at this moment,* under guard. He thought of Raz and the men he'd flown in the day before.

The red light was blinking on his landline.

He'd have to be briefed on it later.

He had a more important call to make.

61

It was a shitty day for fishing. But the akule were running. A row of trucks stretched down the beach. Some early arrivals had tried pitching a pop-up tent and anchoring it with coolers. Eventually, the wind had sent it cartwheeling down the beach, coolers dumping ice and fish until they tumbled empty across the sand. Now people sat cheerfully in the rain, soaked through their shirts. There was no point taking shelter. The steel bells on the tall surfcasters tinkled constantly. No one could remember a run like this.

A bird pile had gathered over the bay. Blue-footed boobies cranked back their wings and dove a hundred feet into the water without a splash. Great 'iwa birds swooped down to maraud successful hunters, chasing boobies and shearwaters in corkscrewing spirals across the sky.

Nalani scowled when she saw the Realtor walking across the beach, dangling a pair of strappy heels in one hand.

"What happened?" Sam asked. She had a strange expression on her face.

Nalani was ready to find out what was behind Sam's professional smile. When it came, she would give it right back. But Sam was just standing in the rain.

"I couldn't," said Nalani.

"How long did you know that?"

"Not until last night."

"At the party?"

Nalani nodded.

"Fuck," said Samantha.

"It wasn't the party. It was him. Frank."

Finally, Sam was angry. But not at her. "I tried to tell him."

"Did you know he was going to offer me a place in there? In his bunker?"

"He did what?" Now Sam was very angry. "That asshole. I've spent years . . ." She trailed off. "Look," she said, turning back to Nalani, "you have really screwed me over here. You embarrassed me. I vouched for you. I thought—"

"I would have sold him the land," Nalani cut her off. "But our culture isn't mine to sell. Pu'uhonua is a place where all are welcome, safe on pain of death, enforced by kings. If he wants to build a bunker and hire soldiers to keep our people out, he needs to call that what it is. He cannot take our sacred names."

"That's it? You screwed me because you didn't like the branding?"

Finally. "Don't give me that attitude, you haole b—"

Nalani felt strong fingers on her arm.

"Would you like to come inside?" Maile asked Sam. "We get one nice fire going in the woodstove. I made tea."

62

The storm felt less exciting now that the gusts were pressing Dalton's soaking shirt against his back. A stream of water slipped past his collar and tickled his neck. Liquid mud squeezed from his shoes each time he stepped. He'd left the office without an umbrella or a jacket. Raz had told him not to draw attention.

He kicked off his shoes and stooped to roll his cuffs. Red mud squelched between his toes and splattered his calves, but it was an improvement. In ten minutes, he reached Barn One. The access door looked tiny in the windowless gray wall, tall enough for an excavator to clear the hydraulic door and wide enough for a dump truck to circle the main pit. He tested his card. The light blinked green. He pressed the access door open and stared into the darkness.

Raz pulled up in one of Dalton's black Suburbans, another trailing behind. He had initiative, that was for sure, requisitioning these vehicles and motorcading around the property with his team as if someone had already given him all the authority he needed.

He got out alone, indifferent to the rain soaking his gray suit. Dalton opened the door and was about to slip into the vast shadow beyond when Raz held up a hand and stopped him. Dalton froze and watched Raz lean back and scan the exterior. He found what he was looking for and tilted his head. Dalton looked up at a tiny camera mounted high on the wall.

Raz turned so that his back was to the camera and nodded for Dalton to do the same.

"It's better out here."

The two men stood shoulder to shoulder, staring into the rain.

"We have new intel on the Phoenix team's location. We can resolve it tonight."

"There's something else now."

Raz waited.

"A situation on the property. There's going to be something called an asset forfeiture. Because of the drug dealing going on down there. But—"

"There must be drugs," said Raz.

Now Dalton waited.

"It's a simple thing. Whatever you need."

Dalton felt his shoulders relax.

"But it won't solve your problem, even if we do it perfectly. There are still too many ways it can backfire on you. Unless you do it clean."

"Clean?"

"No case in court. No one to charge."

Dalton felt Raz's eyes. Reluctantly, he turned to meet them.

He could have what he wanted, the man's eyes told him. But he would have to face what he was asking for.

Dalton watched the rain slide off the black windows of his black Suburbans and thought of Nalani at the table where he'd offered to change her life forever. He thought of Solomon looking up at him, thigh-deep in the stream. What if it had been the boys who'd come on him like that in the forest? And what if he had slipped through the screening and actually been allowed inside the refuge?

Dalton had done everything he could to make things work for everyone. He'd offered those people his most precious invitation and given away his company's greatest asset to the government. And it wasn't enough. They were going to force him to make a decision that would haunt the rest of his life.

He brought his eyes back to the other man's and nodded.

Now Raz looked into the storm. "The three from Hart's report?"

"Yes."

"Your timeline?"

"Today."

"In two hours, call the police."

"Two hours?"

"I know you've got unwanted visitors. You're going to say they're causing a disturbance. When the cops show up, you'll send some of your men down with them. Things will get a little rowdy. We'll make sure the three stay onsite. The rest will go. Your men and the cops go with them. No one can be near the valley after that. Hart and his men will have to stay at the gates. No locals anywhere on-site. Anyone who works for you—security, caretakers, house staff, whoever—send them home."

"What about Phoenix and his men?"

"I'll post some of my guys at your residence. Two of them are better than a dozen cops."

Dalton nodded.

"Listen," said Raz. "Clean doesn't mean quiet. No one is disappearing. They're going to find things. Drugs, porn. They're going to find bodies. It will be an ugly scene. You'll be in the spotlight for a while. Can you handle?"

Again, Dalton felt the man's eyes. Again, he nodded. This time, it was easier.

"Okay," said Raz. "Then it will be no problem."

Raz stepped into the rain. Dalton watched his shoulders tighten, almost imperceptibly, under the first cold drops. He watched Raz climb into one of his Suburbans and both vehicles roll slowly down his gravel road.

This, too, was what power felt like.

63

For the second time in a week, Rebecca Hunt was trapped in a vehicle with a mysterious team of paramilitary operatives. At least no one was sitting on her. She was on the wrong side of the vehicle to see who Raz was talking to in the rain, so she evaluated the other men. Their eyes flickered alertly out the windows every few seconds, settling into long, straight-ahead stares in the interim. Conserving energy, keeping senses open and minds clear. Anyone with the résumé to work for Raz had been operating long enough to be stripped of all but the same essential traits.

That changed, of course, off duty, when the masks came off and the personalities—often extreme—emerged. But she wouldn't be getting to know any of these men. She could tell that as long as she was in their presence, none of them would be off duty.

She sat with her back against the door, her feet drawn up on the seat, lost in the folds of her oversize hoodie, thinking about how the hell she was going to get out of this.

Raz opened his door and slipped back into the seat across from her, his suit a shade darker—ruined, probably—his posture, even in the soft leather captain's chair, impeccable.

"Take us back to the motor pool," he told the driver. "Phoenix is on hold. We've been tasked with cleaning up another problem. It won't be pleasant. I'll brief you all when we get back to the bay."

All four men gazed out a different window as the vehicle bumped over the muddy trails in the gray curtain of rain.

Somehow Raz had managed to requisition a garage. The men had turned it into their locker. Plastic strongboxes and black duffels were spaced in neat, even piles around the bays.

There were eight men in the team, plus Raz. Rebecca Hunt was allowed to move freely, but she couldn't help noticing every door was shut. Whenever she wandered near one, the same two pairs of eyes—men on opposite sides of the room engaged in completely unrelated tasks—moved in her direction. So she made sure to keep wandering, establish a pattern of having no particular pattern, just in case.

A few of the operators had unzipped their duffels and were sorting rolled and folded items of clothing like any experienced traveler during their first minutes in a new place. But most of the men had opened the black plastic cases. The room was filled with the soothing ratchets and clicks of firearms being assembled and inspected. She felt a pleasant uptick in her own adrenaline, a Pavlovian response to the familiar sounds. Raz came through the door carrying a large cardboard box. He let it thud on the concrete, getting everyone's attention, then opened the top and held out a navy-blue polo, identical to the ones she'd seen on the men at the gates.

"Here are your uniforms," he said. "Huddle up for a briefing."

The eight wandered closer. Raz met her eyes. An invitation? She shrugged. Fuck him. He shot her a dark smile, then turned to the men around him.

"I shared earlier we have a new priority. There is an unwelcome gathering in the valley. In the next few hours, the police will be called to remove a group of locals. There are three residents who must remain. They are our responsibility. Doc, what is our status on heroin and fentanyl?"

One of the men walked over to a case, unsnapped, and sorted through. He held up two ziplock bags of white powder.

"We'll use all of the heroin. All three are going to overdose. We'll stage on-site whatever we don't use. That part is very important. First shift of surveillance starts in fifteen. I'll let squad leaders come up with the specific game plan."

He clapped his hands. "This is a simple op. All civilians. Two women and a man in his seventies. No need to be too gentle. We'll get in, get out, make sure it looks good. Keep the client happy. Now let's do it."

The men broke the huddle and returned to their activities with a sharper sense of urgency. Two disappeared and emerged in polos and black pants. They left by one of the exterior doors. Raz wandered over to Rebecca Hunt's corner.

"Real estate is such a cutthroat business. It's why I prefer renting."

"Who are those people?"

Every person had a tiny window in their eyes that let the light of life shine out. Raz was the only person she had ever met who could close it at will.

"Civilians," he said, "always causing so many problems. But for us it is— what do the Americans say?" He answered his own question. "Job security."

He turned abruptly and left her alone.

Civilians. When was the last time she'd spoken that word without irony? And not just irony. Bitterness. How long had she resented everyone who complicated her life by meaning no one any harm?

Rebecca could remember the detachment she'd experienced on countless briefings just like this. But she couldn't feel it anymore, not quite. She'd slipped so comfortably into her old identity. Only now was she noticing Janice Diaz had lingered. She examined this new terrain of thoughts and memories the same way she'd explored the island in the past six days.

Missions were nasty. That's what made them missions. It was a mark of professionalism to achieve the objectives without sentimentality. She'd slept with people and betrayed them, ordered killings, and witnessed many more. So what was this tide rising inside her? Remorse? Or shame? Rebecca Hunt was ashamed—of this entire line of thinking, irreconcilable with her profession. Janice Diaz—or whoever this person was, this other voice, this pair of eyes staring so judgmentally at her own life—Janice Diaz still couldn't believe she'd killed someone she'd—

The noises had stopped. The men had finished prepping and were undressing indiscreetly, changing into Dalton's security uniforms. Rebecca Hunt was as invisible to them as Janice Diaz had been to the people driving past her on the street.

Suddenly, it was completely clear. She wasn't part of this team. She was another one of its targets.

64

It didn't seem possible, but everyone agreed it was raining even harder. At least the wind had eased. They'd raised three pop-up tents, so everyone had shelter as they watched the line of rods. Now and then, someone used a stick or spare paddle to poke the sagging awnings and push off pools of water before they grew too heavy.

Sam and Nalani were in the shack, where the heat from the fire in the old iron stove and the press of bodies filling the two rooms was fogging the windows and making everyone a little delirious. Bottles of Crown Royal had been produced. Sam declined the first that found its way to her, but Nalani brought the next one herself, along with two Solo cups. She carelessly poured generous shots and insisted she take one.

"Is he going to fire you?"

"Probably," said Sam.

"But you already made plenty money, yeah?"

"Yeah."

Nalani grinned and tapped her flimsy plastic cup against the other woman's, hard enough to slosh a few drops onto her hand. "'Ōkole maluna. You know that one? Bottoms up."

Sam raised the cup, felt the sweet burning on her tongue, forced herself to swallow, coughed a little, swallowed more, felt herself gagging, pushed the cup as far from her nose as she could. Her chest was warm, and a white balloon was floating in her head, relaxing the tense band of anxiety that had been tightening all week. She *had* made a lot of money, even without this final closing.

She looked around. There had to be thirty people in there, oblivious to all the deferred maintenance. A cheer broke out from one corner. Nalani had her arm around the shoulder of another woman, shouting into her ear, both of them laughing. Suddenly, it was too much, the heat and the steam beading on the windows. She slid through the room and swung the door into the shock of drenching rain. Water pooled over her ankles and opened wide brown channels in the sand. Through the gray haze of rain, she could see the bay was a bright and opaque brown.

A light caught her attention. She turned to see the first police cruiser creep through the shallow ponds around the house. The cruisers kept coming. By the time the fourth had pulled up, it occurred to Sam to tell Nalani.

The police had come with helmets and clear shields. They formed a line across the sand, backed by a mass of blue-shirted security guards. An officer had a bullhorn. But only fragments slipped through the downpour. "*Trespassing . . . illegal gathering . . . Private property. Vacate immediately.*"

Nalani found the man with the bullhorn.

"What the hell are you doing?" she asked. "This my family's land and these our guests. How you going tell them they cannot stay?"

"We've had complaints of trespassing and excessive noise," the officer said. "Also, reports of possession and promotion of controlled dangerous substances."

"Who reported? The only noise I hear is your loud-ass bullhorn."

"We're just here to restore order. Please step back and let us do our job."

He lifted the bullhorn back to his mouth. Nalani was about to grab it out of his hand when she felt someone dragging her away.

"No use," said her mother. "They going do what they like. Believe me."

Nalani saw two men in blue polos leading police to a white pickup. One of the officers held a short leash attached to a German shepherd, its ears perked cheerfully, despite the rain. The police pulled the door open and let the dog rear up and sniff the teenagers crammed inside.

"They searching Ron Ron's truck," she said.

Her mother waved her hand. "I could smell those boys' pakololo from here. Nothing they can do now. Going have to work it out with the judge."

Nalani watched people running anxiously from the beach, clutching rods and folding chairs. She heard shouting and whirled around. Police officers with raised batons were piling onto a group already rolling in the sand. They jerked someone to his feet, a large Hawaiian with a cop in riot gear on one arm and a private security guard on the other.

"Looks like Uncle Maleko."

"This a violation of sovereignty!" Maleko shouted. "What right you have for do this?" A cop smashed him in the mouth with a baton. He spat a mouthful of blood and shouted, "Kapu aloha!" before he was shoved into one of the white vehicles.

Nalani reached the cruiser a moment after the door swung shut. She pounded on the window. "Arrest us all, then!" she shouted. "Arrest us all for trespassing if this no more our land." Two officers used their shields to pin her against the vehicle. She screamed and tried to grab the smooth edge and hurl the cop back. She felt hands on her, and she was on the ground, being pressed into the muddy water, the pungent smell of wet rubber in her nostrils. Then her face was in the water. Someone was kneeling on her.

Suddenly, she was being lifted. The officers still kneeling below her looked up in surprise. She bumped over someone's back, then traveled rapidly backward through the crowd. A few people were still battling the officers and guards. A larger group had linked arms to chant at the row of shields faced off against them. She heard Aunty Lei crying, "Shame! Shame!"

She was away from it all now, still moving backward. Over her shoulder she glimpsed the navy shirts of private security. They brought her to the beach shack, still warm from all the bodies that had just been there, its emptiness making it feel, for a moment, as big as it had in her earliest memories. Her mother was there already. Sitting rigidly in one of the cracked chairs at the small kitchen table, a strange, blank expression on her face. Two more security guards stood behind her.

Nalani found herself in the chair beside her mother, rocking on its uneven feet. The rain pounding the windows concealed whatever was happening outside. They were back in the quiet shack on a very rainy afternoon. She and her mother. And four men. Four very scary men.

She flicked out her hand and felt her mother's fingers wrap hers and squeeze.

The noise of the rain got louder. Someone had opened the door.

Sam poked in her head. She looked at the two women seated at the table. She looked at the four men standing in the shadows behind them. Her head ducked back the way it had come. The door began to close.

Sam's face reappeared.

"Is everything all right?" she asked so quietly they could barely hear.

No one spoke.

"Is everything all right, Nalani?"

Nalani looked at her mother. Maile's eyes seemed far away.

Sam stepped into the room. "Do you want to come with me?"

"They're staying." Whoever had spoken, he had an Australian accent.

Sam ignored him. She took another step, lifted her chin, and summoned all the haole attitude in her entire being. "You're both coming with me now."

"Get the fuck out of here," the Australian said. "They aren't going anywhere."

Sam turned and shut the door behind her. "Then I'll stay, too."

"Lady, you need to listen to that man."

Maile had finally spoken. Nalani looked at her in surprise.

"Find Aunty Lei," Maile said. "Tell her what you seen."

The Australian took a step toward Sam.

"Leave now!" Maile shouted.

Sam ran to the door and disappeared into the rain. The Australian reached the door a moment later. He looked out indecisively, then shut it firmly and turned back to the two women.

"Where is Solomon?" he asked.

65

The trucks emerged every few seconds from the ironwood trees and curtains of rain, all spattered in fresh orange mud. Raz had positioned his Suburban at the top of the bluff, a few yards from the road. The engine was running and AC blasting. The driver and another operator were up front. Rebecca Hunt and Raz had their seats in the middle. Two operators sat behind her.

She turned sideways to ease the prickle between her shoulder blades. She didn't bother trying the door handle. She knew it was locked.

The vehicles rolled past, their tires sucking in the red clay of the disintegrating road.

"Yes?"

Raz was speaking into an earpiece.

"No sign of him? Are you looking?" . . . "All four of you?" . . . "Wait, who saw you?" . . . "Koos emek," Raz swore. He stared into the rain with an irritated expression. "You have to leave," he said. "And be seen leaving. The police are still there?" . . . "Good" . . . "Don't worry about that. We'll get eyes on them. Just get out" . . . "Roger that."

She watched him shake his head, then make eye contact with the driver in the rearview mirror. "Someone saw them with the targets. We've got to go down and sub them out."

The driver shifted the Suburban and rolled forward. He let an aging Explorer pass, then swung onto the road. Tiny chunks of mud speckled Hunt's window. The road narrowed in the ironwood forest. The first vehicle they encountered pulled aside. Rebecca Hunt caught the blank stare of a young woman and held the curious gaze of the toddler in a rear-facing car seat. Ahead, a pickup was climbing the hill. It did not move over. Their driver moved his palm to the center of the steering wheel. A long honk and two shorter ones. The other truck stayed in the center of the road, barely rolling now, but not making room. Their driver finally braked. The front bumpers were nearly touching.

The driver glanced back at Raz, who was staring rigidly ahead. The man in shotgun sighed and grabbed his door handle. The driver shifted into park and opened his own door. Rebecca Hunt stared at the truck through the windshield. She recognized it. A brown elbow popped out of its passenger window, followed by a familiar face. Aunty Lei.

Uh-oh, thought Rebecca Hunt.

Both operators ignored Leilani and converged on the driver side. She could see them exchanging words. Hunt glanced at Raz, who was looking conspicuously bored and impatient, staring out his window toward the dripping forest.

She hadn't buckled her seat belt. And she'd already done the calculations. The Suburban had an extra-wide center console between the front seats. And now that the idea was in her mind, she had to act. So far, she'd shifted nothing but her eyes, but that was enough. Her adrenal glands were dumping. The air was filling with pheromones. In another moment, all three men would be on alert, and a moment after that, they would guess why.

She hinged forward at her waist and pushed off the floor with both feet, sending herself tumbling onto the console between the front seats. She didn't care how awkward it looked, or felt. She just wanted to get her body clear of the men behind her as quickly as possible and get the seat back between herself and Raz. She tucked her shoulder and rolled, ending on her back with her feet on the dashboard. She reached across with her left arm, searching for the door latch. Raz's tan wrist snaked through the gap, a heavy silver watch sliding down his arm. Her hand was on the latch. She used it to lever her shoulders up and roll into the front seat, just in time to pull her face beyond the reach of the man lunging over the back seat. She pushed the door open and fell face-first in the mud.

When she pushed herself up, she saw one of the operatives wedging himself into the space she'd just vacated. Raz's furious face pressed against the window. That was satisfying. She'd never seen anyone get a reaction like that out of him.

The two operators getting soaked beside the truck were both staring at her, trying to calculate what Raz would want them to do in view of witnesses.

"Lei!" she screamed.

"Ho! Haole lady!"

Doors were opening in the Suburban. The driver and the other were coming toward her now, blocking her path to the truck. Something had changed. The noise, she realized. A vehicle was revving, and it wasn't the Suburban.

The next moments unfolded slowly but inevitably. The pickup struck the driver behind his knees, dropping him, and rolling on until it banged the Suburban's pristine chrome, trapping the second operator on its far side. Rebecca Hunt stepped on the truck's rear tire and launched herself into the bed, among the coolers and fishing tackle. She felt tires spinning as the truck tried to reverse, then Rebecca Hunt, the coolers, and the fishing rods went sliding toward the cab, stopped abruptly, and slid back toward the tailgate. They all bounced into the air as the truck went halfway off the road, climbing over tree roots, picking up speed.

She poked her head up in time to see Ariel Raz standing helpless in the rain.

Her hoodie was soaked through, heavy and cold. She pulled it off, wrapped her arms around her knees, and felt the rain sting her bare back.

She'd expected to see the black Suburban pull up behind, was already game-planning what she would do when the driver used a precision immobilization technique to spin them out. Instead, she saw a pearl-gray Range Rover, hugging their bumper, covered in the same orange clay as the other vehicles coming up from the valley.

66

The men left a few minutes behind Sam. The Australian was the last out the door. "We're not going far," he said. "And we're not the only ones watching you."

Nalani and Maile didn't speak or move.

Then Nalani got up from the table, leaned her forehead on the window, and cupped her hands against the cold glass. She stepped onto the lanai and watched the last taillights disappear into the ironwoods. The only vehicle left was her own.

She ran through the rain and climbed in the cab. The key was where she'd left it under the seat. She turned it in the ignition. Nothing happened.

Nalani sat for a long moment in the cab, watching the water pour down the windshield. It was only afternoon, but darkness had arrived. She checked the bars on her phone. Nothing.

She dashed back through the rain.

Whatever was happening, it was a small relief to be back in the warmth of the hale, with the familiar smell of smoke and the dull glow from the fireplace, with her mother.

"Truck won't start."

Maile sat with her arms stretched across the table, her fingers tented as if she'd tried praying, then let them collapse. She didn't look up.

"I'm sorry I went behind your back," said Nalani.

"What?"

"I told myself you only wanted this land because you needed it to get sober."

Maile stared at her hands without lifting her chin. "You were right."

"I had a house for us. And a lot more. I drove a tougher bargain than you."

Maile looked up, met her eyes, and smiled. "You always was akamai li'dat."

"But I should have trusted you. You and Solly."

"Trust us? Your strung-out maddah and your lolo uncle Solly? At least I try for raise you with more sense than that."

"I don't know why I thought I could do any better." She sat back down across from her mother. "I had this idea I was going to have my own daughters one day. And I've always been terrified they would end up as fucked up as me."

Maile patted the center of the table, then turned both hands palm up. Nalani reached out and took them. They had the same hands. Wide palms and strong fingers. Good for pulling kalo. Good for pulling water.

"Momona Bay is your kulāiwi," she said. "Our family's bones are part of this land. You cannot separate one and the other. My great-grandmother used to say, '*He lani i luna, he honua i lalo.* She meant as long as we stood strong on our land, we had everything we needed, heaven and earth. That's how it was beforetime. Maybe no more. To give your daughters one chance, you had to make a choice. That's where *your* kuleana stay, not to the land, or to the bones."

"I wish you'd told me that before I skipped the auction."

She heard her mother laugh. "You as kolohe as ever. 'As why we here?"

Nalani nodded. She couldn't look at her mother.

"Listen," said Maile. "No matter what we do or where we go, we always kua'āina. We born with this land on our backs. I spent my life running from that kuleana. You seen how that turned out."

Nalani stared at their clasped hands. Neither woman said anything for a long time. They listened to the rain on the roof and the quiet crackle of the fire.

"They are coming back for us, aren't they?"

Maile squeezed her daughter's fingers. "Yeah. They coming back."

"Mom?" said Nalani. "I'm so sorry."

She felt her mother's hands leave hers, but left her arms outstretched across the cold boards. Her shoulders shook against the wood. When she tried to stop, the crack inside her opened wider. She felt her mother's arms wrap tight around her shoulders. Her mother's fists pressed hard against her collarbone.

"Listen," Maile told her. "When I was in jail, I had to look at what I done with my life. An' what I done to you. I knew I'd lost you, and it was what I deserved. I never wanted to get out. I been chased, beaten, shot at, OD'd. The only thing scared me was trying to live straight. I never done it. My last week in jail, I was going find some way for end it. But I heard one voice telling me for live. All night I hear my na'au talking. Going on so long I got annoyed. So finally, I said, 'Ke Akua, *why* I got to live?' And soon as I asked, I had the answer."

Nalani reached up and gripped her mother's hands.

"So I came here to Momona, and your uncle Solly took me in. I tried for stay sober. Then you came. An' now I more scared than ever. 'Cause now I get something for lose."

"We need to get out of here," said Nalani.

"You know they're watching."

"We could take the kayak over the reef. Or go through the woods."

Maile released her daughter's shoulders and walked to one of the windows. "These kine people, their guts so dark inside, they never know how blind they stay. They going get what they want, whether we run or not. Those men getting paid too much to let us walk out this valley."

"You don't want to try?"

Neither woman moved.

"I'm sorry, Mom," Nalani said. "I'm just so sorry."

"Listen," said her mother, almost angrily. "You got to listen. It don't matter what happens tonight. I've seen what's on the other side. There's nothing for fear. I already met my mo'opuna, the grandkids you was going give me if you could. I know you going meet them, too. And they are so beautiful."

67

A line of men in black ponchos stood beside the raised gate arm, watching the mud-spattered caravan pass through. Sam's truck didn't slow until it was miles clear of the compound. When they finally pulled over, Leilani cracked her door and beckoned Hunt inside. The Hawaiian wrapped her arms around the other woman's bare shoulders.

"Guess you found your friends," she said.

"Whoever is down there," said Rebecca Hunt, "they're going to kill them."

She felt Aunty Lei's grip tighten.

"Whoever is down where?"

"Wherever you were coming from. Three people. One man and two women. The men I was with have been hired to keep them there and kill them, once everyone else is gone. They're going to make it look like an overdose."

Leilani looked at the man driving. His silver hair went past his shoulders. He looked bored, but he didn't take his focus from the road. Visibility couldn't have been more than ten feet, and he was driving eighty miles an hour.

"Who are these men?" Lei asked.

"Professional killers. Eight of them. I only know the man in charge. He hires the best."

"How do we stop them?"

Rebecca Hunt shook her head. "You can't. Not directly. Not in a fight."

"Then we got to get them out."

"They'll have it all under surveillance. The road. The dwelling. That's where they were going when you found me."

"You're saying we cannot stop it?"

"Do you know anyone in the police? Someone you can trust?"

"I know plenty cops. But none I can trust, not after this. I never seen 'em like that before. Not here. Oahu maybe. They getting orders from the very top, guarantee."

It was an old truck and the cab was small. Aunty Lei had to press her legs tight against Hunt's when the driver shifted into fifth. Lei felt her shivering.

"I going bring you to Carlotta," she said. "Get you dry and warm. No worry about this little pilikia. We going fix 'em."

68

Dalton stepped out of the steaming shower onto the heated tiles of the bathroom. In the bedroom, his skin chilled pleasantly. He glanced through the windows. Incredibly, the rain was still coming down. How long had it been, twelve hours?

A team had found him on the road as he was walking back to the residence. He hadn't even tried to explain himself. He'd just told Hart to call the mayor's office and the police chief. Hart pushed back when Dalton explained their local security needed to leave. He'd done more than push back, he'd threatened to resign, claiming it would be a dereliction of his duty to leave the compound without enough men to control the perimeter or protect the family. Dalton told him Raz was a professional, too, and this was his plan. At this point, Hart *had* resigned. Dalton said he would accept it in twenty-four hours, along with an exit package he could permanently retire on, but they needed to get through this day. Hart, the good soldier and enterprising private citizen, had agreed.

Dalton dressed for comfort. Runners and a black fleece. He wouldn't need to appear on any screens that day. The AG had been amenable, his lawyers had reported. Negotiations would commence. He hadn't spoken to Erin yet.

He was about to go find his family when he noticed something on the floor-to-ceiling windows. Condensation. They definitely weren't supposed to do that. He would have to have a conversation with the contractor when all this was cleared up. He pressed his hands to the window and peered into the dusk. He'd been out there, in the rain. He felt more exhilarated than he had in weeks. He couldn't remember the last time a shower had felt so good.

He tried to think about the valley. But it wasn't possible. Despite the orders he'd just given Hart; despite the conversation with Raz, anything that might be happening out there in the rain was unknowable. He tried and failed to believe any of it could have anything to do with him.

69

Aunty Lei wrapped Hunt in a towel and led her through the rain-beaten encampment. Water was flowing everywhere, over their feet, under the tents. Tarps sagged and poles buckled under the weight of pooling water. Tents had collapsed in the downpour, draped over whatever they still held. Everything drenched. Everything ruined.

There was no one in sight. But many of the tents were glowing.

"Ho, Carlotta, we coming in!" Lei shouted.

Leilani unzipped the door, poked in her head, backed out, and pushed Hunt toward it. "Tell her what happened. Get warm. An' be ready for go any minute. I'll bring you some clothes." She looked the shivering woman up and down. "Something that fits this time."

Hunt slipped through the unzipped door.

Carlotta was sitting cross-legged on an inflatable mattress near the center of the tent, away from the sagging, wet walls. Several candles burned on a low table. The floor squished as Hunt stepped carefully across.

"You can sit there." Carlotta pointed. "It should be dry enough. And take that blanket. How do you keep losing your clothes?"

"I'm sorry about the mud."

"Did you find who you were looking for?"

"I did," said Hunt.

"But it wasn't what you had hoped?"

"I guess it was what I should have expected."

"Has the war started?"

For the first time in hours, Hunt thought of Alpha and his team.

"I don't think so. But there's something else. The person I was looking for has plans to hurt the people living on that land. Lei knows them. It's going to happen soon."

"So, the person you were running from has plans to hurt someone, and the person you were running to has plans to do the same thing. Have some tea?"

Carlotta leaned forward and crawled a few feet to a wooden crate set on its side. She unscrewed a thermos cap and poured something into a travel mug. "I'm sorry it's not hotter. I made it this morning."

Rebecca Hunt took the mug in both hands and pressed it against her breastbone, beneath the blanket. It was warm enough. There was no operational need to explain any more than she already had. She was surprised to hear herself talking.

"The man who plans to kill those people is my partner. We went into business a few years ago. I had a career with the government, but . . . things stalled. And I knew I had more to offer. When Raz called, I said yes. We took on a client, Frank Dalton. Someone had stolen documents from his company and was releasing them. They needed us to find out who. The techs we hired scraped something off . . . something, I don't know, a file they posted. It gave us a lead. A woman. My job was to turn her, convince her to lead us to the source. Classic tradecraft."

She looked up to see whether Carlotta was following, but it was impossible to tell. She was gazing into the shadows. Hunt realized it didn't matter.

"There are all sorts of ways to do it. Money is the simplest; most people take it. Or you compromise them, learn something you can blackmail them with. But you need to develop a relationship. Everything comes from that."

She took her first sip of tea.

"I figured out pretty quickly, if anything was going to work with Alex, it would have to be the relationship itself. So that's what it became. A relationship. I guess that was the problem. I was out of my element. It's not an approach I was very familiar with. Not professionally."

The tea was lukewarm and bitter. She took another sip.

"Or personally, actually. Things got pretty intense. I had a prescription for a drug to help me focus. I was feeling a lot of pressure. Spending way too much time undercover. All my time. Raz created a legend for me, a background in what they call *direct action*—protests and stuff. Alex asked me to help find a team that could help them get attention. The people I brought in aren't activists; they're a white nationalist militia. The goal was to bring them together—but not together, together, like physically—then expose the connection and discredit Phoenix."

"So, you found the men who are going to start the war."

"They were never supposed to get near Dalton, or anyone else. This was the biggest contract we've ever had. We had to exploit every vulnerability.

Secrecy was Phoenix's strength. No one in the chain knew more than they needed to. That meant trust was their weakness. Phoenix trusted Agile. Agile trusted me."

"She was in love with you."

Rebecca Hunt froze.

"What were you going to do," Carlotta asked, "when this was over?"

"I was going to get her out. No one needed to know she'd been a part of it."

"But she would have known you lied to her?"

They heard the tent unzipping. A plastic shopping bag bounced inside.

"Put these on," said Aunty Lei. "We got to hele. The word is out, and no one going wait for us."

70

The fire was dying. Maile had added the last log. A kerosene lantern hung over the table, but neither woman rose to light it. The old hale was settling into darkness that would soon be absolute.

The rain poured so loudly on the metal roof, they didn't hear the door-knob turn, even though they'd been thinking of nothing but what would be coming through that door.

It was only when Uncle Solomon slipped into the room, water puddling on the floor beneath him, that the women looked up.

He stared at the dim embers in the stove as he used his hands to sluice the rain from his arms. Then he noticed the two women at the table, staring at him.

"Cousin, you still here?" he said.

"We're here, Hawaiian."

Solomon immediately turned back toward the door.

"Men stay coming already."

"I rather meet them here. Stay dry at least."

Solly looked at Nalani.

"Can we take the kayak?" she asked.

He shook his head.

"What about the forest?"

"Men stay hiding there."

"But you can guide us."

"Ua noho au a kupa."

Nalani turned to her mother.

"He say he can get us through," she said.

71

A gray van was waiting, its headlights making the rain glow white. Leilani opened the rear door. Rebecca Hunt stared into the darkness. "Climb in quick," said Aunty Lei. "So we keep the samples dry."

"Samples?"

"Eddie owns one carpet business."

"Just look out the table saw," a voice called from the darkness.

"He do tile, too," said Aunty Lei.

Hunt hoisted herself in and felt her way forward, bumping a sharp edge she thought must be the saw. She found a seat on the rolled, prickly bundles that lined the floor. Then the door slammed and there was only the glow of the dashboard and a bright wedge of illuminated rain. Hunt listened to the *swish-slap* of the wiper blades.

Lei slapped the wall, and the van pulled forward. "You heard about Maleko?" she asked.

"What about him?" said Carlotta.

"Braddah go jail. He started fighting cops. Took six of them to get him in the wagon."

"This one handled him all on her own."

"I could see she had some tita in her."

"She's a professional spy," said Carlotta.

"Did you say a spy?" Hunt jumped at the sound of an unknown voice. She wondered how many more people were in here.

"I don't think we've been introduced," said Hunt.

"Oh, I'm Samantha Rittenheimer. Call me Sam."

"Sorry," said Leilani, "I thought you knew each other."

"Just because they're haole," said Carlotta, "doesn't mean they know each other."

"Sam seen the men who had kidnap Maile guys."

"I think they were professional soldiers."

"They're worse than that," said Hunt.

The headlights were picking up huge brown puddles. Impossible to tell whether they were two inches deep or two feet. Eddie the carpet-and-tile guy plowed through them all. Sheets of water rapped against the thin metal walls.

"Can't you hurry up?" shouted Leilani. "I no like miss."

"Miss what, exactly?" Hunt asked.

"Cannot say, *exactly*," Leilani answered. "That's why I no like miss."

They passed a sign for Anahola. The van slowed. There was too much traffic heading north. Four-wheelers buzzed up the shoulder, their drivers getting soaked. Now and then, a dirt bike buzzed down the centerline.

"Where are all these cars going?" Hunt asked, tired of feeling stupid but struggling to process what could possibly be happening.

"Same place as us," said Aunty Lei. "The call went out."

The rain abruptly glowed a brighter red. Hunt heard the tick of a turn signal. The headlights illuminated a familiar fence and gatehouse. As they passed through, she saw the place where the gate arm had been. A few feet farther in, she saw the arm and its tower lying in the mud.

"What happened?" she asked.

"Guess they wouldn't open up," said Aunty Lei. "You know how Anahola boys are, always like show off whose truck can pull more weight."

They were being observed, Hunt realized. Men in ponchos stood outside the guardhouse, watching the long line of headlights moving toward the valley.

72

Nalani stepped beyond the eaves and had the giddy sensation she'd had as a kid, when rainstorms were still something you played in. Now she only got this wet when a squall swept through a surfing session. She would sit on her board and watch the waves become an endless range of granite mountains, the kind she'd never seen, rising from a mist of droplets.

But now she was in darkness, and the rain felt inseparable from the darkness. She could not tell mauka from makai. She felt her uncle's broad, rough hand take hers. A moment later, her mother's hand found hers as well. Her uncle tugged. Her mother stumbled up the sand behind.

The rain fell differently in the forest. She felt roots and slick mud underfoot. They moved slowly, struggling to stay connected as her uncle wove between the trees. Sometimes, she felt cold branches brush against her. Gradually, she began to see.

She let go of her uncle's hand. Her mother gave her a squeeze and let go, too. The rain glimmered dully all around. Her uncle was a dark shape moving ahead, sure and confident.

73

When Eddie finally maneuvered the van to a stop, Leilani opened the door, and the women stepped into a beehive of roughly idling engines. The night glowed with the warmth of halogen high beams and the cool, blinding violet of aftermarket xenon. The crystalline spotlights of roof-mounted LED bars pushed long shadows into the ironwood forest.

Leilani found a bullhorn and began organizing search parties. There were over a hundred people, at least as many women as men. Some were dressed in hunting camo. A few carried rifles. Most wore whatever they'd been wearing that day: jeans or board shorts, rubber boots or slippers. It was the harsh light and soaking rain, Hunt tried to tell herself, that made so many of these people look so old or so young, so scrawny or so overweight. But none looked scared.

Maybe it was for the best, she thought. The more nonthreatening they were, the better it might go for everyone. Their only real strength was in numbers.

"We go already," said one uncle impatiently.

"Find these fackahs," said a woman.

"You explained how dangerous these men are?" Hunt asked Leilani quietly.

"Of course," said Aunty Lei. "'As why they're all here."

"Make sure to keep the searchers in big groups," said Hunt. "There's a reason the men out there have had long careers. They can fight their way out of anything, but if they think the operation's gone sideways, they'll walk. It's only a paycheck."

At least there aren't any kids, she thought just as a cluster of umbrellas approached.

"We was coming straight from Tūtū's house when we got word," a woman said. "Doreen and me like add our kokua, but we need someone for watch Kamalu and Malina."

Leilani glanced at Hunt and the other women clustered around her. "Shoots, Mahea," she said. "You know I like get both you ladies out there.

You can do more good than most of these buggahs I been sending out. We can watch the keiki. Just stay maka'ala. Don't take no chances. An' don't get in no fights. These fackahs stay dangerous."

"Shoots," said another woman. "I stay dangerous, too."

Hunt heard a shotgun being racked.

"Damn it, Doreen," said Mahea. "Not around the kids. Now go along."

Mahea pushed the two smaller umbrellas forward. "Mahalo nui," she said. "Kamalu and Malina, they good kids. But they can be small kine kolohe."

"More than small kine," said Doreen. "You gotta watch these two."

Before she sent them off, Leilani gave Doreen and Mahea a personal message to pass on to the killers, should they find them. The children giggled when they heard it. Hunt watched the women walk beyond the lights. Of all the searchers she had seen so far, these two seemed most capable of handling themselves, which made her even more worried for them.

"Take these aunties' hands," Lei said to the children. "And stick close."

Hunt felt a small hand slip into hers and looked into the brown eyes of a girl, ten or twelve, small for her age. The boy had taken Sam's. Hunt caught Carlotta watching her, amused.

74

When the water in the valley reached their ankles, Uncle Solly led them to higher ground. He'd held Nalani's hand until her eyes could find him, flickering and folding up ahead, moving like a flame in the wind. Whenever she wasn't sure where to go, she moved toward the darkest part of the night, and it was always Solly, leading her between trunks, ducking under limbs, stepping high over roots and stones. There was no one but her uncle who could do this—lead them through this forest in this storm. The cringing tension between her shoulders, the feeling a stranger was about to reach out and take her from behind, had eased.

A red light appeared. It danced across a stand of trees and went out.

She wondered if she'd imagined it. Then she bumped into Uncle Solly, lost her balance, felt him grab her wrist and keep her upright. She felt the stillness overtaking his body and tried to match it.

The light appeared, closer, probing across the long roots, reflecting dully in the puddles. She could see the length of it in the rain, stretching back into the trees. She'd almost traced it to its source when it went out again. She felt her uncle pulling her wrist toward the earth, very slowly, and bent with him, lowering her knees, holding her breath.

Then she saw her uncle clearly. Crouched among the roots of a pale *Albizia*. He was staring alertly at a point to her right. She saw roots forking across wet earth.

"Shit," said her mother.

"Stay calm," said a voice with an Australian accent. "Stay calm and stay right there."

The light was jogging, getting brighter. She turned and looked at her mother, hoping for a sign of encouragement. Maile just looked pissed.

Two men dressed in black were standing a few feet away. One held a rifle with a light on the barrel. The other reached up and toggled something on his shoulder. "We got 'em. All three. See you at the rendezvous."

The familiar accent, as upbeat as ever. "Let's get out of this rain now, yeah?"

The other man panned his beam down the hill, the way they'd come.

"Mind finding the trail for us, Solomon?" asked the Aussie. "We'll just sweep the rear and make sure no one gets left behind."

There was a moment when everyone was perfectly still. Then Solomon began moving through the trees. They came to a path, one of several branching through the valley, remnants of a network that had once connected the entire island. The light behind them made it hard to see. Their shadows obscured the trail ahead. Everything outside the light was pure darkness. Nalani heard trees thrashing and sometimes the groan and rustle of branches crashing from the canopy.

Now she saw her mistake. She'd misunderstood these people. They didn't seem to take anything seriously: their work, their money, or themselves. But it wasn't their own lives they didn't take seriously. It was hers.

She felt sick with anger at herself. But she was too cold and tired to maintain it for long.

They stumbled through the darkness.

75

Hunt looked up the valley. Small lights flickered, but the dark was huge. At first, her surprise at the scope of the effort had given her a surge of adrenaline and hope. These had both worn off. She understood it didn't matter how many people turned out. The forest at night, in a storm, would swallow them all. The odds of finding anyone who didn't want to be found, especially professionals, were infinitesimal. She looked down at the two children, still hovering behind Aunty Lei, and was glad about that.

She turned to the Realtor. "Show me where you last saw the family."

Sam started off. Carlotta followed. Lei was about to join when another beam cut through the trees. Hunt recognized the round headlights of a Jeep Wrangler. A lone man climbed out of the driver's seat. Hunt would let Leilani deal with him. She turned and followed the other women.

They walked to the end of the beach, then doubled back before they found the cabin. Only a few embers still glowed in the stove. Carlotta produced a flashlight, and after a few minutes, Hunt determined that if anything had already happened to the Kanaheles, it hadn't happened here.

They heard the door creak open.

"There you are," said Leilani. "I been looking all over. You got the kids with you, right?"

76

They'd been walking fifteen minutes when the Australian broke the silence. "Stop and hold tight."

They all froze. Then they saw what he saw. A light wavering in the distance.

It was just a small, pale dot at first. Nalani watched it slide over the ground, pausing for long moments then plunging ahead as if rushing to make up ground. The small light danced along in the darkness, just two or three feet off the ground, growing steadily closer.

The lights behind them went out.

The flashlight kept coming. Above it now, a pale, round shape, faintly glowing. The beam darted straight down into a bright circle on the ground, then played out down the path, nearly reaching Uncle Solly before diving back to its source and lifting, tracing the trunk of a tree just long enough to reveal the underside of an umbrella. A small brown hand. The sleeve of a yellow raincoat. It came back to earth, and now they could see the wide brown eyes and black hair of a girl, ten or eleven, her skinny legs emerging from a pair of blue rubber boots. Beside her, sharing the umbrella, was a boy, a few years younger, green jacket, same blue boots. The girl held the umbrella. The boy gripped the light.

He shone it across Uncle Solly and Nalani and her mother. Then he shone the flashlight on the two men dressed in black. They stood stiffly, gripping the handles of the guns in their slings, squinting into the light. The boy's face remained impassive, betraying just a hint of curiosity as he played the light over the bulky vests covered with pouches and clips of extra ammunition. He turned to his sister.

"You think these the dangerous men?" he whispered, loud enough for everyone to hear.

The girl nodded solemnly. She held out her hand. "Come, Uncle. Come, Aunty. It's not safe here." She took Uncle Solly by the hand and tried to pull him away. She beckoned to Nalani and her mother. "Aunty, Aunty. Come."

Nalani turned and saw one of the men touching his shoulder.

"Be advised, we've got, uh, two more civilians in the woods with us."

While he waited for a response, he adjusted something on his gun.

His partner reached over and touched his elbow. There were more lights in the woods. Beams of white and yellow, slicing between the trees, illuminating pale curtains of rain.

Nalani walked up the trail toward the children.

"Roger that," she heard the Aussie say behind her. "Aborting. Meet you at the fallback."

The little boy hadn't taken his light off the men. Maile stretched out her arms to herd him and his sister up. "Okay, kids," she said. "We go. Hele back the way you come."

The boy started to turn, but the girl stopped him. "Remember what Aunty Leilani said for tell them?"

The boy's eyes got wide. "You tell 'em," he said.

The girl turned toward the two men. She pulled her heels together and put her shoulders back. "Aunty Leilani say for remind you, *No forget rule number one.*"

"Rule number one?" A hint of confusion in the Aussie's usual cheer.

"He never know rule number one," the boy whispered loudly to his sister.

"You tell him, then," she whispered back.

"You think?" he said.

The girl nodded.

The boy stood a little straighter. "Rule number one," he said, loud and precise above the roar and drip of the storm. "Do not fuck with Aunty."

77

As soon as she realized the children were missing, Leilani headed for the tree line. She was gone before anyone could follow. The first groups of searchers were trickling out of the trees, covered in mud and shivering, sometimes limping. When Carlotta told them Malia and Kamalu were missing, they turned and headed straight back in.

It was Sam who noticed the thread of light, growing brighter as more and more beams wove themselves into the flow. Even before the kids and the Kanaheles emerged from the trees, horns began to sound. There was a crackle and fizz and a bright flare streaked off the beach, making the clouds glow red. Soon, Kamalu and Malia were standing shyly in the center of the crowd. Only their parents seemed unimpressed. "I already tell 'em," Mahea said to Aunty Lei, "you disappear li'dat again, you both get lickin's. Automatic. We no care who you rescue!"

The celebration was intense but short. The rain was falling as hard as ever. A red path of taillights was soon visible on the hill. Hunt studied the family that had caused this commotion. They were draped in beach towels. A girl in her twenties stared blankly into the darkness, her jaw clenched. The mother was prettier than her daughter—at a distance at least. Her eyes roved the night, never resting for long. The man was tall and thin, white stubble against his dark skin. His eyes were milky with sun damage. He stood with his blanket wrapped tight, one hand visible, obedient—as if patiently playing a role he planned to abandon soon enough.

A man walked up to Aunty Lei, the latecomer in the Jeep. His patterned button-down must have been tight even before he stepped into the rain. Now it seemed painted on. His white slacks were red with mud below the knee. His low-cut shoes were balls of mud.

"They're okay?" he asked Leilani.

She laughed. "Go ask 'em yourself. You her lawyer."

"I no like boddah 'dem," he said. "They never ask me for come. I only heard 'cause they was talking about it at the jail."

"You down there for Maleko guys? No need rush for get *him* out. Buggah needs—"

The roar of revving dirt bikes stopped the conversation. Two teenagers came skidding out of the forest. One had a long pipe resting across the handlebars like a lance.

"What you get there?" Leilani asked.

He shot her a scared glance. "'S only one tailpipe, Aunty."

"And where'd you get 'em, boy?"

The other rider pulled up. "We found their truck, Aunty, an' it's cherry."

"Kaleo Boy already had 'em lifted when we got there. He going put the tires on his Hilux."

Leilani laughed.

"Hele on outta here an' don't bend your pipe!"

The boy twisted his clutch, stamped the bike into gear, and took off.

Leilani called to Maile, "You three going ride with us in Eddie's van." She stopped, looked around with confusion. "Where's Solly?"

The two women looked just as confused, but only for a moment.

"He'll do what he like," said Maile.

One by one, the women climbed into the van. Leilani came last and slammed the door.

78

Dalton looked at his phone again. The network bars had disappeared forty-five minutes ago. That always seemed to happen in a heavy rain. But the Wi-Fi was still strong, thank god.

"Okay, guys," he said, "five more minutes on YouTube, then we watch something with a story."

Madeleine looked up from her own phone. "How about *Moana*?" she said with exaggerated enthusiasm.

Neither boy looked away from the screen, where two blond kids were about to unbox two hundred and fifty toy cars.

"Did you hear your mother?" Dalton asked. "She wants to watch Maui fight the sea monster with his fishhook!"

The boys did not respond.

"We're turning off the toy show in five minutes."

"No!" Marc shrieked. "No, Daddy. No!" He threw himself on his back, banging his head.

"Don't hurt my brother!" shouted Lionel.

"He hurt himself," Dalton answered. "Marc, are you okay?"

"No," sobbed Marc. "I need to see the Hot Wheels City."

"We let you watch *Hot Wheels* for half an hour," said Dalton. "Do you want to *play* with *your* Hot Wheels?" He held up an ambulance and a monster truck.

Madeleine took advantage of the confusion to pause the TV. But Lionel had seen her reach for the controller. His head swiveled to the frozen screen. "You said five minutes!"

Dalton and Madeleine locked eyes.

"Why did we have to send Pilar away?" she asked.

"Something about security," Dalton mumbled. "We had to clear all non-essential personnel."

Madeleine surveyed the two sobbing boys rocking helplessly on the floor. "When did we start considering Pilar nonessential?"

Just then, the doorbell chimed. A second later, his phone vibrated. He pulled it out and checked the live feed. Two men in tactical gear, their black caps pulled low against the rain. He glanced up. Madeleine was looking at him curiously. He should have told Raz to dress his men more discreetly.

"Just security," he said. "I'll get it."

He turned the knob. Felt the cold draft.

The door flung open from outside, knocking him back. The two men pushed their way into the room, aggressively scanning it.

"Who's with you?" one asked urgently.

"Just my family."

"No one else?"

"We sent them all home."

The man asking the questions smiled. He reached up and held a button on the small radio attached to a harness on his chest. "We're in," he said in a flat American accent.

79

They bumped up the road, tires slipping in the steep places, but Eddie never spun out. Hunt leaned against a quaking panel and watched the mother and daughter. Something heavy and dark had opened inside her as she scanned the beach shack for signs of violence. Now she had time to think about why.

A week ago, she'd inspected another room just as carefully for the same signs. That was after she'd spent half an hour on her hands and knees, shining a light across the floor to make sure she'd swept up every sliver of glass and ceramic. She'd dusted the shelves and rearranged the remaining items. She'd rehung the copper-bottomed pots, put the knife back on its magnet.

Alex had seemed impossibly light when Hunt folded her into a military surplus duffel. She was heavier on the long walk down the hall to the service elevator. Still, it had felt like any other busted op. There'd been no grieving. Only the taut wire of adrenaline that made effective action possible. The introverted thrill of one thing, then another breaking her way—beginning with the oversize duffel she'd found under the bed—until she reached that rare, euphoric point of knowing nothing would go wrong, like cruising down an empty street as red light after red light flips to green.

The apartment was just a few miles from the Fremont Cut. The Aurora Bridge was notorious for suicides. She chained Alex's bike to a barricade, took her lover into the darkness by the cement plant, held her for the last time as she lifted her across the rocks, and slipped her into black water wavering with long lines of copper light.

Alex was dead because Hunt had tried to end the op before Alpha and his team could board their plane. Now they were running loose out in this storm. Raz certainly wasn't going to be protecting Dalton from them. And from what she'd seen of his security arrangements, no one else was, either.

"Sam?" she said. "Do you know where Frank Dalton would be right now?"

"He's building something for situations like this," Samantha said. "Some sort of bunker."

Hunt let her head fall back against the vibrating metal. "That's good."

"But it's way behind schedule. They're probably just at home."

"Who's *they*?" asked Hunt.

"The Daltons? Franky, Madeleine, and the twins."

"Hey, Eddie," said Rebecca Hunt. "You got time for one more stop?"

80

There were four men in their home now.

Dalton was trying to understand. He'd been around hundreds of these people, protecting presidents, prime ministers, hotels, airports, embassies, him. They looked the part: Kevlar vests, cargo pants, ball caps, sunglasses. But something was off. He caught two of them smirking at each other then abruptly going stern when they noticed he was looking. It occurred to him even though he'd never seen men like this (and they'd all been men, except in Israel) actually doing much of anything, they always managed to do nothing with extreme professionalism.

These men just seemed aimless. Even the one who'd spoken, presumably their leader, didn't seem to know what to do next. The primal stab of absolute and overwhelming horror had worn off. He was still terrified, but he was already starting to feel something else. Annoyance.

Someone needed to take charge.

He raised his hand and said, "I don't want to frighten my children. Will you let me tell my wife to take them to the bedroom? After that, whatever you want, I will help you get it."

Three men looked to the fourth. The question seemed to snap him out of his daze.

"We're all going in there."

At least his kids had spent nearly as much time around men like this in their short lives as he had. Still, the dreamlike moment of coming around the corner and seeing the scene he'd left just minutes before—the two small boys mesmerized by the enormous television, his wife with her legs drawn up on the couch, staring at her phone—was the worst of his life.

It was really happening.

He'd imagined this so many times, it was almost confusing. Madeleine looked up from her phone, frowned in annoyance at the men who'd filed in behind him, then noticed whatever expression was on his face. She was a composed person. Being Black in France had taught her to control what she showed the world. But he'd never seen her demonstrate *this* much control. He was suddenly very grateful they were in this situation together. The twins still hadn't looked up. On the screen, the blond brothers were dumping hundreds of metal cars into a backyard pool.

The leader took control. He pointed two men to the windows on opposite sides of the room, the third to keep eyes on the boys. Then he pointed at Dalton and the kitchen door.

Dalton looked at Madeleine. She looked at Lionel and Marc, then back to him, and nodded. He turned his back on his family and walked into the kitchen.

"How do you turn off these lights?" the man asked.

"Nyumba," said Dalton. "Lights off."

The lights did not turn off.

"Nyumba. Lights off."

The lights did not turn off.

"Hello, Nyumba. *All* lights off."

"Isn't there a switch or something?"

"They're smart."

The man rolled his eyes.

"Are you going to tell me what you want?" Dalton asked.

"We're putting you on trial."

"Excuse me?"

"We are putting you on trial for seditious betrayal of your heritage and conspiracy to destroy our God-given constitutional system."

"Sedition? I love this country. Ask the president." He regretted the last sentence as soon as he said it.

"He'll have his turn, soon enough. And because we do respect the Constitution, you will both have the opportunity to defend yourselves at trial."

"Defend myself against whom?" Was it possible this situation was funny?

"We've convened a battlefield tribunal."

"What about my family?"

"Once the trial is concluded, and the sentence is carried out, they'll be free to go."

"And who are you? Where's Phoenix?"

The man grimaced. "Phoenix can do what he wants. If anyone cares after today. This isn't his show anymore. You can call me Alpha."

"Okay, Alpha. Why are you here? What group do you belong to?"

"We're an advance unit of a citizen army, patriots ready to defend their heritage and culture against the globalists trying to tear down what took thirty centuries to build."

"There are more than four of you?"

The man grinned. "As to our exact numbers, that's something you would know better than me."

"I'm sorry?"

"Only you can count the millions Sokoni has censored in your conspiracy to connect the planet while scattering your own people. I'm here to officially inform you that you've failed. We used your tools against you. And you will be the first example of our power."

Again, the dreamlike feeling. He'd heard all this before. Or some version of it. Was he in a simulation? It had to be considered. Was the rainstorm just a work-around to hide any telltale flaws in landscape rendering? If this was the latest iteration of their graphics card, the VR team had outdone themselves. He looked around for a tell, a glitch or faulty shadow.

He stared into the eyes of Alpha.

There *was* something uncanny about them.

"Pull yourself together. We don't have much time."

Dalton pulled himself together. This had been his nightmare for a reason. Because it was possible. And now it was happening.

"If you wanted to get my attention," he said, "you've got it. Now tell me what you want, I will get it, then make sure you enjoy it for the rest of your life."

"That's the thing about people like you," said Alpha. "Just when someone is ready to give you the benefit of the doubt, you open your mouth."

He reached behind the small of his back and pulled out a pair of zip ties.

"We didn't come to ask for money. We didn't come to make demands. We came to show our people their power. All I need to know is, are you prepared to die honorably, or am I going to need these?"

81

Leilani didn't like it. "That donkey tried kill these two wahine."

They were parked on the long drive leading to the house. Rebecca Hunt ignored Aunty Lei and tried to read the expressions of the Kanahele women.

"Please don't take this personally. It's a situation I created. I just need to resolve it."

"Do what you need do," said the mother. "We no going stop you."

Hunt was already moving toward the door.

"I know the house," said Sam. "I can show you."

"Just point me in the right direction, please."

"I'm going, too," said Carlotta.

"None of you are coming," said Hunt. "There are four of them, and they aren't pros. I don't know what they'll do."

"Last time I let you go off alone, my friend had to fish you out of the river."

Hunt had no answer to that.

"Go if you like," said Leilani. "We going wait fifteen minutes. If you ain't back by then, I coming for drag you all back. No one getting left behind on this one."

82

Dalton understood the situation now.

Alpha was keeping him in the kitchen, away from his family. He'd found the control board and turned the smart glass to full opacity. No one could see in. And there was no video inside the residence. Madeleine had insisted on it. Cell network was down, but the Wi-Fi was going strong, apparently. They'd never let the boys watch so many videos in a row. What would happen when their attention finally wavered?

Eventually, Hart would check in over the secure network. When he did, there was a word Dalton could use that would initiate a sequence of events. They had practiced the entire scenario.

Until then, he needed to delay.

Alpha spoke first. "This is what will happen. We'll need a few minutes to set something up. We'll let you back in to see your family. Say your good-byes. When we're ready, you're going to log us in to your Sokoni account using your phone. We'll get a live stream going and start the trial. It will have to be quick, obviously. We'll have the sentencing, say a few words, then carry it out. Got it?"

Dalton nodded.

Alpha had been looking at him with concern. Now he relaxed a little. "You're doing great. I can see you understand the situation. It's nothing personal."

"It won't work," said Dalton, hoping he sounded calm. "The AI will catch it. Or the moderators. They'll block the content."

"Not *your* content," said Alpha. "VIPs get special rules, right? I saw it in the news. And who's a bigger VIP than you?"

Two years earlier, Dalton had been heli-skiing in the Coast Range when a cornice gave way one valley over. He happened to be looking that direction, so he'd had the experience of seeing a mountainside collapse and feeling the thud a moment later, threatening their own snowpack. What happened inside him as he listened to Alpha's terse explanation felt exactly like that:

a sheering and a slumping. He thought of all the scenarios he'd imagined over the years, back to the long nights on the school compound when students and staff had gone home on holiday and there was no one to hear him call for help if a gang of thieves decided to see what the mzungu from America kept in his house. They would pry up a corner of his tin roof or lock his door from the outside and threaten to burn him. That was how it usually happened. He had tried to visualize exactly what he would do in each situation, the same way he'd imagined what he would do if he startled a lion on his long evening walks. In that scenario, he raised his shirt above his head and charged it, screaming. He'd always wondered if he would actually have the nerve to do it. Alpha snapped his fingers inches from his face. "You there?"

Dalton nodded. Despite himself, he appreciated the sympathy in the other man's face.

"It's time to see your family."

"How long will I have?"

Alpha shrugged. "Two, three minutes."

Dalton was relieved for this small mercy. He could hold it together for three minutes.

An urgent tone came from his phone, on the island where Alpha had told him to place it.

"It's my security."

Alpha looked unfazed. "You know what to do."

Dalton answered the phone and put the call on speaker.

"Hart?"

"Yes, sir."

Dalton had worried the anxiety in his voice would be obvious. But it was his security lead who sounded stressed. Hart reported that a caravan of civilians had shown up at Gate A, removed the barrier, and entered the compound. The skeleton staff at the gate had stood down.

As Hart spoke, Dalton was thinking about the choice he was going to make. If he used the word, responsibility would pass from him to people who'd spent their careers training for situations like this. He could end this agony of protecting his family and become a hostage just like them. Together, they would wait for the professionals to manage things as they saw fit. Whatever happened, he would know he'd done the prudent thing.

Hart was done with his report.

"Say that again?" said Dalton.

"Given the situation, do you want me to send any of my men to your living quarters?"

Dalton was silent.

"We are stretched extremely thin as it is."

Dalton was silent.

"Do you read?"

Time was up. He had to use the word, or not.

"We're all good here."

"Roger that." Hart signed off quickly.

"You're being invaded," said Alpha without curiosity.

"Apparently," said Dalton. Amazingly, he wasn't curious, either. Another fuckup from someone who was supposed to be the best at what he did. Raz was as useless as the rest of them.

This was exactly why he hadn't used the word. If he surrounded this building with cops, snipers, hostage negotiators, and whoever else showed up in these situations, anything could happen to his family. But if he did what he was being asked, his family would be safe.

At his middle school in Great Falls, they'd read a story about a man who was going to be hanged from a railroad bridge by a regiment of soldiers. The rope broke, and he fell into the river and made his way back to his family, but just as he was hugging his wife, the rope jerked, and you learned the whole story had taken place in the man's mind during the moment of free fall.

Sometimes at 3:00 a.m., he wondered if he'd ever left Kenya, if everything that had happened since the headlights pulled onto the road behind his matatu was just a gift from his imagination before the van overturned and caught fire or a tire burst and the thieves dragged him out and left his body naked on the Nairobi Road.

It would explain a lot.

Alpha snapped his fingers. "It's time to see your family."

83

Sam led the way up the long drive until Hunt saw windows glowing above the hill.

"Security should be parked here," Sam said. "And there are always men at the house."

Even in the downpour, it was clear no one was there.

"Where would the family be?" asked Hunt.

"That way."

Hunt stepped onto the dense, crisp grass. A narrow lanai ran the length of the house. The windows were frosted. She crouched and climbed up. Behind her, a noise. Carlotta.

"Stay low."

Thin strips of light shone on the water pooling the deck. They had left the louvers open.

Hunt went from her knees to her stomach. She crept forward until she could look up through the gaps between the slanting wooden bars.

A man with his back to them stood by a tripod with a phone mounted vertically. It displayed a tiny version of the scene laid out beyond. On the wall hung an American flag, upside down, the blue canton nearly touching the floor. Two men in familiar tactical kits and balaclavas stood stiffly at something resembling attention, cradling rifles. One of them was Alpha. Beside him was her client, Frank Dalton. It would have been easy to mistake his expression for anger. But she had seen it too many times not to recognize someone fighting to control a level of dread few people would ever know. Alpha was talking, but she couldn't hear the words.

"Looks like that war is coming any minute now." Carlotta lay beside her.

Hunt could see the tiny green dot in the corner of the screen. "It's going out live."

"You've got to get in there."

"And do what?"

"Spy stuff."

"These men have AR-15s."

"Well, you better do something, fast."

"We've got time," said Hunt. "That guy likes to talk."

She got to her knees and crawled to the end of the lanai. She wanted to find the fourth man. There he was, sunk into an easy chair, the tip of his rifle jutting up at the ceiling. Across the room, she saw the woman from the hospital. She was on a love seat with a young boy on either side. Their knees were up on the couch, their heads in her lap. She kept a hand on each of their short brown Afros. She was staring into the eyes of the man in the easy chair. Hunt had dismissed the idea of direct resistance. Now she reconsidered. If she could distract the man in this room, she had no doubt the mother would do her part: instantly, capably, eagerly.

But then what? Even if the mother did overcome one sentry, she wouldn't know how to fight off the three in the other room. She reviewed everything she'd seen, searching for the keyhole. Then she had it.

The pulsing green light in the corner of the screen.

The men's goal wasn't to kill Dalton, it was to mobilize an army.

84

"I'm confused," said Nalani. "How many different guys with guns are running around out there?"

Leilani shrugged. "You know haoles. They like make everything complicated."

"So the ones after me are different from the ones after them?"

"Those guys was working *for* Frank Dalton. *These* guys like kill him."

"And what do they have to do with that haole lady?"

"The ones looking for Dalton was chasing her, too."

"She got away already. Why is she going back?"

"'Cause she's the one had brought 'em here in the first place."

Nalani put her face in her hands, then looked up. "Okay," she said. "Whatever. But if he was in danger, why did he send all his men into the woods after us?"

"'As why I never understand why those wahine like go looking for trouble. Cannot help one guy who cannot help himself."

The rain fell on the metal roof.

"You think Uncle Solly is okay?" Nalani asked her mother.

Maile laughed. "More okay than us. The buggah probably dry and sleeping already."

"And what is my *Realtor* doing out there?"

"She's *your* Realtor now?" Maile asked.

"Maybe my friend, then."

"Real estate one tough business on this island," said Leilani. "Cannot let some buggah kill your best client."

Someone knocked on the window. Nalani banged her skull against the van. "Who's that?"

Eddie looked out, then lowered the window a few inches.

"Where I seen that guy?" Maile asked.

"It's Trey Chong," said Nalani, rubbing the back of her head. "My lawyer."

She ignored the look her mother gave her. "What are you doing out there, Trey?"

"I was following you and saw the van turn off."

"Were you just sitting in your car the last ten minutes?"

"Can I get out of the rain?"

"Come around," said Aunty Lei.

The dripping man slid onto a roll of carpet beside Nalani.

"Watch the samples!" Eddie called out.

"What are you doing here?" Nalani asked.

"Like I said—"

"I mean, what are you doing out here at all?"

"Oh, uh, Legal Aid asked me to come down to the station. A bunch of people were being processed for something that had happened on your land. I thought you might still be in trouble."

Nalani felt a little warmer than she had a minute before.

"So . . . What are *you* doing here?" Trey asked.

"Waiting on some friends."

"But you're okay."

Nalani pulled the towel tighter around herself. "Yeah."

"Can you tell me what happened?"

Nalani thought about what had happened. "Honestly," she said, "I don't really want to talk about it right now."

"Sure," said Trey. The rain on the van was very loud. "Um, could we talk some other time, over coffee?"

Nalani was wringing rainwater from handfuls of her hair. She looked over at Trey. "I'd rather get one Crown and Coke."

Now she was *really* ignoring her mother's look. Somehow, the rain was even louder.

85

Dalton kept his eyes on the trinity of lenses in the corner of his phone. He'd worked hard on his live appearances, but he still let Erin take them whenever possible. She had the rare ability to accept other people's attention as proof it was deserved. The more people watching, the more confident she felt. In this respect, he was like most people: exactly the opposite.

They'd given him a few minutes with his family. Lionel wanted to know if he could have pasta for dinner. Marc tried to tell him something about whatever they'd just been watching, but Dalton couldn't understand, and he finally went silent. Normally, this was where Madeleine would step in and translate. But she just stared very intently at all three of them.

Recently, Marc had become a hugger. He would raise his little arms, lay his head beneath his father's chin, and let his full weight rest, heavy and still, for seconds that felt fleeting and endless. But that night, Marc wasn't in the mood for hugs. Dalton squeezed his sons until they writhed and wriggled free, their cool little limbs slipping away. He stood, and Madeleine rose with him. When he discovered that he lacked the strength to lift his arms, she clutched him fiercely. She took two fistfuls of his shirt and stared into his eyes.

"I love you," he told her. "I love you all so much."

"Nous t'aimons toujours, mon chou."

She pressed his chest with both palms and released him, then held his eyes as he backed slowly toward the door, sending him the strength he needed to turn and leave. The boys, the future, those had become her responsibilities.

In some way, this was the easiest appearance he had ever made. All he had to do was keep it together, maintain his dignity, and tell these murderers to fuck themselves when the time was right.

"We are demonstrating to the world tonight that we have the courage to stand up to the status quo." Alpha was wrapping things up.

Things didn't feel so easy now.

His heart was beating extremely fast. Was he shaking? Could they see that? He glanced at his hands. He didn't know what to do with them. He couldn't put them in his pockets.

How long had he been staring at his hands?

He clasped them and looked up.

He realized he was starting to fall apart.

There was really nothing he could say that would change this? Nothing he could offer?

What did he have to lose by trying?

His dignity.

So that was it? He would die because he was too embarrassed to beg? He remembered learning in one of their tactical security workshops that if you ever saw someone get up abruptly from a meal, you should follow them. People choking to death try not to make a scene.

Alpha was looking at him now.

There was nothing he could give them. The time for that was over. They were live, and these men had their own dignity and shame to think about. He looked from Alpha to the other men. Their eyes were wide. They weren't ready for this.

He looked back at Alpha. The man was smiling behind his mask.

This was going to make him happy.

He felt as if he'd just been sprinting up a hill. He was going to puke. They were talking again, but he hadn't heard them. Was it time for him to speak? It didn't matter. It wouldn't be possible.

How long had it been since he'd held his two boys? Two minutes? Ten? It seemed like it had been years. And before that—a lifetime ago—when he'd made his decision on the phone with Hart, when he thought he was prepared for what would happen? He'd had no fucking idea.

So how much worse could it get? Would he look back in thirty seconds and think this moment, now, had been easy? Would he be alive in thirty seconds? Now Alpha was looking concerned. He had an idea about how this was supposed to look.

Dalton realized that up until this moment, he hadn't believed in any of this. It had only been as real as all the other times he had imagined it. He tried to put himself in the future, enter the infinite darkness and get it over with.

So that was it? He was going to try to skip these last precious moments of consciousness?

Alpha had definitely asked him if he had something to say.

And he had shaken his head. *No.*

"Wait." Where was this coming from? "I have a statement."

He did? What was it?

"You took this too seriously," he said. "No one really believes the crap you're saying. Not even you. You were looking for a distraction, and our algorithm fed it to you, until you forgot you'd ever believed anything else. But we could have given you *anything.* All you wanted was to stop feeling alone and useless. And now you're going to spend the rest of your life in prison, because one night you clicked a couple fucked-up memes."

He felt a little better.

Alpha was staring at him. Had it sunk in? He opened his mouth, then closed it again. He was looking at the other man. Were they having doubts?

Alpha was digging something out of his pocket. He turned to Dalton. "I forgot to ask. Do you want a blindfold?"

86

"I don't like it," said Maile.

"What's that?"

"Just sitting here while pilau things stay happening."

"Pilau is what that guy tried do to us," said Nalani.

"Our family always kept things kapu in this ahupua'a."

"Mom, no one's kept kapu on this land for a hundred years."

Maile hissed in the darkness. "All Solly tried for show you, and you still cannot see?" Her tone changed. "But you right, anyway. I just never thought I'd see two haoles and one pōpolo go regulate on this ahupua'a while our family sits on our 'ōkoles in the back of one van."

"Now that you mention it," said Leilani, "I was just thinking, Carlotta my only pōpolo friend. If something happens, who knows if I ever going find another one as good as her."

"What can we even do?" Nalani asked.

Maile shrugged. "What are four guys going do against all of us?"

"What guys?" Trey asked.

Leilani was already moving toward the door. Nalani felt a hand grip her arm. "If we going do this," said her mother, "no forget, these haoles all made choices. We ain't going to die for none of them."

"Which haoles?" Trey asked more urgently.

"An' if you got to scrap," said Maile, "remember, first—"

"I know," said Nalani. "Ears, eyes, nose, or throat."

"Then you kick 'em in the—"

"*I know,* Mom, you been telling me since I was seven."

"Could you repeat that list?" said Trey.

Leilani opened the door. The van filled with the sound of rain.

87

When Rebecca Hunt first told Alpha about Frank Dalton, he hadn't been interested. She'd had to walk him down the path: if they were going to inspire the uprising, they would need to reach as many people as possible. The traitor's identity didn't really matter, she'd explained, his platform did. And Frank Dalton had the largest platform in the world.

If the platform got cut off, they had no reason to go through with the murder.

"This way," she whispered to Sam and Carlotta, then crawled to the edge of the lanai and slipped into the darkness on the lawn. She ran around the corner of the house and found what she was looking for.

The electric meter.

The box was sealed with a wire lock. She slipped a finger in, tried to yank it apart, failed, predictably. She looked around the grounds for anything to snap it. There wasn't even a twig.

"Shit."

Now they were short on time. Hunt felt herself panicking. Someone shoved her aside. Carlotta. There was something in her hand. A long nail hammered through a piece of wood. Carlotta slipped the shank into the wire seal and snapped it open.

"Stand back," said Hunt. "Stand way back."

She thought of trying to wrap her shirt around her hands. But there was no point. Water was sluicing off everything. It would happen, or it wouldn't. Either way, the power would be cut.

Rebecca Hunt took a moment. She looked into the darkness. Then she looked at her friend, who'd taken her advice and moved several yards away.

She closed her eyes, curious about what she would see. There was nothing. No one. Then there was something, a movement, a feeling, someone's spine curving against her palm, the short hairs at the nape of someone's neck.

A deep and agonizing loneliness flooded through her.

She grabbed the smooth plastic of the meter box, hooked her fingers under the edge, and yanked it off. There was a blue flash and the smell of burning rubber. Pure darkness.

She felt the rain pouring into her eyes.

She covered her face with her hands.

88

The room faded to darkness. Digital appliance clocks lingered one tick and went out. The only light was the glow from the phone on the tripod.

Dalton took one breath. Two. He heard one of the boys crying in the other room. Lionel, probably. In his executive security trainings, one lesson had been drilled again and again. If the worst did happen, passivity would get you killed. You had to be alert for opportunities. And when they arose, you could not hesitate.

This was the moment.

But something had already changed. A dim light around the baseboards. Somewhere in the house, a device chirped. Then another. Soon there was a chorus of machines rebooting.

One by one, the lights blinked on.

89

Hunt felt warm hands on hers.

"Let me see," a woman said.

It was Sam, holding her palms up to the light. What light?

The windows, Hunt realized, were glowing. The backup generators had kicked in.

"Is she all right?" Carlotta asked.

"I don't see anything," said Sam. "Does it hurt?"

Hunt didn't answer.

Carlotta looked up at the windows shining cozily. "We've got to get out of here."

Hunt let herself be led back across the sopping yard. Once, she looked up and caught sight of the mother inside the house, framed in the window, a child's fat leg hooked tight over each hip. She was staring at something across the room.

It occurred to her a moment later that she shouldn't have been able to see through the window. The smart glass must have been reset.

There were changes to the situation that could be exploited. But her mind was moving slowly. The other women were already back on the driveway. The house was receding behind them. She didn't have the will to halt the momentum of whatever was unfolding.

She had murdered someone.

Now she was going to redeem herself?

That would never happen.

The van. Sam swung the door open, and a light illuminated mud-stained rolls of carpet. Eddie stuck his head out from the front seat.

"Where is everyone?" Sam asked.

"Fuck," said Eddie. "They're not with you?"

90

"Do we have signal?" Alpha asked.

"Nothing yet," said the cameraman.

Alpha paced to the window, cupped his hands against the glass. "Fucking rain."

"It's back."

"Okay. Okay. Get ready. But don't start yet. We'll arrange the scene."

"How many viewers did we have, anyway?"

"Five hundred thousand something?"

"Okay. That's great. We can't lose them."

He looked at Dalton. "Okay, no blindfold. Go stand against that flag, okay? Right up against it." He gestured with his rifle. Dalton looked at the flag, then took his place against it.

"Okay, we're gonna make this quick," said Alpha. "Charlie, get it all lined up. We're going to leave a place for you. Once you start the video, join us here and we'll do it together, so we're all, you know—it'll look better that way."

Alpha found a place squarely in front of Dalton and the flag. He looked over his shoulder to see whether he was blocking the camera.

"How's that?" he said. "Good? Okay, Delta, you can leave the family. It won't matter in a second. Just close the door behind you. All set, Charlie? Okay. Everyone check to make sure your safety is off. We want this to go without a hitch. Right, Mr. Dalton?"

He was grinning again. The other men looked nearly catatonic. But they followed orders.

Dalton wasn't sure why he'd followed Alpha's commands so meekly. He'd been ready to act, he was sure of that, before the lights went on. He could still charge them. Or throw something. He could ruin the spectacle these jackasses were trying to create.

Or he could be the one person to give this farce some dignity. He could honor his own final moments with the respect they deserved, even if no one else involved could do the same.

He braced his shoulders, looked away from the camera and into the eyes of Alpha. The man wasn't grinning anymore. But there was another eye. A dark one raised between them. Dalton closed his eyes. He felt himself shaking and ground his teeth together.

"You ready?" Alpha asked. His voice high and nervous. "Three. Two. Wuh—"

A sound obliterated Alpha's voice. The sound of the Coast Range collapsing all over again. Dalton thought he'd imagined it until he felt the tremor pass under his feet. There was the distant rumble of a train. The lights went out and didn't come back on.

91

Nalani was staring at one of the most beautiful women she had ever seen. A chubby boy was tucked under each of her arms. She was standing on the other side of a long glass window, looking away from them toward a closed door in another wall.

Maile stepped forward and rapped the window. The woman startled, then strained to see through the bright reflection. Lei pulled on the handle of the french doors. They didn't slide. The woman heard the sound. She stood, frozen, then moved her lips, and the glass doors opened.

"Qui es-tu?" the woman asked.

Silence.

"Who are you?"

"We the kua'āina of this place," said Maile. She held out her arms. Without hesitation, Madeleine shrugged one of the boys into her grasp. He clung to her as she cradled him onto her hip. Nalani couldn't stop looking at her mother with the child in her arms. She felt something shift inside her, but couldn't tell if it was cracking open or closing shut.

There was the sound of a collapsing wave. The lanai swayed, and the lights went out.

"Run," said Leilani.

For the next few seconds, Nalani heard bodies in motion. Then she was alone in the roaring silence of the rain. She waited for her eyes to adjust. But the darkness was resolute.

She thought about the last time she had seen her uncle Richard. The long road down Namahana mountain and the aimless drive that brought her to Kealia Beach. She remembered parking on the sand and watching the gray ocean, waiting for her phone to ring. She'd been waiting ever since.

Inside the house, rain echoed off the walls. She stood for a moment, listening. Then she reached out and touched the glass. In a few feet, she found the corner. She kept her hand to the wall and kept moving. This was the wall the woman had been staring at. The wall with the door.

"Shit."

She brought her finger to her mouth and tasted blood, then cautiously moved her hand back to the wall, tapped whatever had cut her, found its edges. She ran a finger from one serrated crescent to the next, all the way around the curve. Then she lifted it from its hanger. She wrapped both hands around the smooth wooden handle and held it before her as she edged through the dark. It didn't belong here, in these people's house, but she was grateful for it.

She used an elbow to guide herself, sensing the door before she bumped the frame. She could hear them calling to each other from the other side of the wall.

As she felt for the handle, someone grabbed her. She bit back a scream and whirled to swing.

"Nalani?"

"Trey? You fackah. I almost cracked you with one leiomano."

"You get one leiomano?"

"What are you doing here?"

"I realized you weren't with us."

"And you figured I was dumb enough to go inside?"

His silence lasted long enough for her to reach out and make sure he was still there.

"This land's been your family's kuleana one long time," he said.

She squeezed his forearm, the first part she found. It was reassuringly solid. "You don't have to go through that door with me."

She felt him close his hand around hers, hefting the weight of the shark-tooth club. "I just like get one of these."

"You're not getting mine."

He released her hand. She heard a bump in the darkness. "I'm ready."

"What you got?"

"I think it's a lamp."

"You can have the leiomano."

"Nah," said Trey. "You keep 'em."

She felt his hand on her shoulder, his body tucked behind hers. She found the doorknob for the second time. Then froze.

"Imua," Trey whispered in her ear.

"Imua," said Nalani.

The door swung open. Instantly, a band of light whipped through their room, illuminating a patch of the opposite wall before moving on. They waited. The men were still shouting at each other. They weren't like the men from the forest. They sounded panicked.

"Delta, I told you to close that fucking door."

"I did!"

Nalani poked her head around the corner. The beam of light swung erratically around the room.

"Turn on your goddamn lights already!"

She could hear Velcro ripping, the sound of mumbled cursing.

"This shit is fucked."

Another beam of light came on. Then two more, almost side by side. They all began playing wildly across the walls and furniture.

"Where the fuck is he?"

"Split up and start searching!" screamed the screamer. "Someone check the other room!"

One light started moving toward them.

Nalani took a breath and eased her body through the door. She scrambled to the far side of something, a kitchen island, she guessed. Trey's hand never left her shoulder. The man with the light was standing where they'd just been. She could see herself and Trey in the glow from his flashlight.

"The family's gone. The doors are open."

"Then go fucking find them!"

The man moved away. Trey squeezed her shoulder. It was time to do something.

"Frank," she said in a voice a little louder than a whisper. "Hey, Frank Dalton."

"Who the fuck is in here?" someone shouted.

"Frank," she said more urgently.

"Check the kitchen."

Another light headed toward them. She felt the muscles in Trey's thighs tense against her as he raised himself a few inches. The light played across the cabinets. It would be on them in a few more seconds.

The rain got louder. She felt a draft of chill air.

The circle of light was coming toward them across the floor. She felt Trey draw his arm back. She hoped he'd found a heavy lamp.

There was a thud, a groan, a crash. The light jerked away.

"Oh, fuck."

Something hit the floor and shattered.

Almost immediately, there was a sound from a different corner. Wood clattering on tile.

Objects were in flight.

"Find something to fly at them," she whispered to Trey.

She heard a drawer slide open.

"Who the fuck is in here?"

"The front door's open."

"This one, too."

"That's it. I'm outta here."

Nalani lifted her head in time to see a light illuminate the back lanai and then a bouncing triangle of rain, getting smaller at the speed of a running man.

Now there were two lights left in the room.

"Get the fuck out of that corner and find Frank Dalton!" the screamer screamed.

"I saw a woman."

"The fuck you did. Find Frank Dalton."

The screamer was moving methodically across the long room. The man in the corner wasn't leaving his corner. His light jerked from spot to spot. The room was full of whispers.

The screamer had stepped in front of the open door. She could see him silhouetted in the rain. A familiar figure rose beside him.

Oh, shit, thought Nalani.

He'd heard a noise behind him. His light was swinging around.

Nalani stood and screamed, "Ho, boddah you!"

Both beams converged and her shadow leaped in all directions. When Trey surged up beside her, shark's teeth and shadow figures filled the room.

"Fuck *this.*" One light went running out the door.

Through the glare, she glimpsed a large man covered in complicated gear, half shielding his eyes, and another, shorter figure with her arms raised on either side of his head.

He screamed.

"'As right, you fackah," said her mother.

A headlamp went whipping off into a corner of the room.

The screamer groaned.

"You no like me break your fingers?" said her mother. "Then drop 'em." Something clattered on the floor. "'As right. Now someone come and kick this fackah."

The man screamed louder than ever.

"Damn, haole lady, where you learn kick like that?"

Nalani ran to the headlamp. Her mother was sitting on a large man's back. She had his right arm twisted, each of her hands grasping two of his fingers, pulling them apart in a V and hyperextending his wrist. A mask hid his face, but his eyes were shiny with tears.

"Mom," said Nalani. "What'd you do?"

"I just clap 'em in the ears is all. This Realtor lady vicious, though. He'd better check his ala-alas once he get his hand back."

92

When Frank Dalton climbed out from under the American flag, there were six women in his house and a young man in a dress shirt holding a lamp. They were all soaked to the skin, and some of them looked homeless. The taller white woman had the zoned-out stare of a meth head. The other white woman was his Realtor.

He recognized Nalani and realized it was her voice he had been afraid to answer. She put the light on him. "You okay?"

He shielded his eyes. Unsure what to say. She moved the light back to the rough-looking woman sitting on Alpha. He must look okay enough.

"Damn, Mom," said Nalani. "You had to use the front door?"

The woman opened her mouth but never answered. Something sparkled in her eyes. Maybe she wasn't as rough as he'd thought.

Nalani let it pass. "Why you never do that with the guys in the forest?"

The woman gave Alpha's arm an affectionate twist. "Those guys was real killahs. I listened ten seconds to this donkey and knew he never killed no one. His gun not even loaded."

She released two fingers, reached for the large gun lying nearby, and pointed it toward an empty corner. There was a flash, bang, and clatter as the gun kicked out of her hand.

"Shit," said Maile. "Never even had the safety on. This fackah could have shot us all." She took his fingers back and gave them a hard yank. The man groaned.

"Where's my family?" said Dalton.

"They with Uncle Eddie."

"Who's Uncle Eddie?"

"Everyone know Uncle Eddie," said a large Hawaiian woman. "Menehune Carpet and Tile?"

Dalton stared at her. Sam touched his arm. "I'll take you."

"You one lucky fackah," the Hawaiian told him matter-of-factly as he stepped into the rain. "You could have been make, now you only going jail."

EPILOGUE

Dalton didn't go to jail. He didn't even go on trial.

Every news network in the world reported he'd been executed live on his own site. He'd gotten to see his *New York Times* obituary, which described him as a *visionary founder* in the first sentence and didn't mention any controversies until the fifth graf. There had been quite a bit of sympathy, those first few days. Until it came out that a breach of his illegal dam had destroyed an ecologically pristine reef and that a local man, Solomon Kanahele, was missing. Then the *Seattle Times* reported the police were questioning an ex-CIA employee who'd accused him of hiring a hit team to murder three people to acquire their land.

Fortunately, she had no evidence. Raz and his team had vanished. Dalton liked to think they'd been in the valley when the flood came through. But he would never know. The Coast Guard found one of his armored Suburbans, mysteriously missing all four wheels and most of its exhaust system, upside down on the reef. The state flew it off by helicopter and sent him the bill.

The trials were complicated. It turned out Hunt wasn't actually a meth head, but she *had* been addicted to its close cousin, Adderall; killed her lover while under the influence; and recruited the militia members who'd tried to publicly murder him, in a scheme he couldn't make sense of no matter how many times the federal prosecutors tried to explain it. Charles Sutton—Alpha—was sentenced to thirty years in prison. Bravo, Charlie, and Delta all got twenty-five. Rebecca Hunt—for reasons that remained opaque—pleaded to voluntary manslaughter and unlawfully disposing of human remains and got only ten. Throughout these proceedings, Dalton followed his lawyers' advice and took the Fifth at every opportunity. It was not a good look, from a public relations standpoint, but it was effective, from a legal one.

Dalton could not take the Fifth with Madeleine, unfortunely. She received the largest divorce settlement ever recorded. He fought harder against his board's vote of no confidence, until a long weekend with Raffi

Garcia at his place up in Mount Shasta changed his thinking pretty radically, on a lot of things.

He stepped down—on the eccentric condition that he could retain indefinite access to the debugging queue—and cashed out a few billion of his shares. His timing was excellent. Dhillon stepped in, fired Erin and the rest of leadership, and was photographed on the bridge of his new mega yacht for the cover of *GQ*. Then news leaked that Sokoni had entered a secret deal to share user data with the government, and the value of the company fell 70 percent in five days.

Phoenix, whose real name turned out to be Calvin Fish, took the moment to go public and offer the dramatic story of how a content-moderation supervisor earning fifty-five thousand dollars a year became an iconic whistleblower only to be infiltrated by an undercover security contractor, kidnapped by a militia, and locked in the bathroom of a Hawaiian vacation rental until the cleaners freed him two days later. Book rights sold at auction for six figures, but sales were disappointing.

Dalton saw the boys every other weekend.

It was hard going anywhere, with all the paparazzi. He spent a lot of time on Kauai. Madeleine had let him keep the refuge. The county had suspended his permits, so construction was on hold. He wasn't feeling much urgency to complete the project, anyway. He'd fired his security team and hadn't replaced them yet; there were plenty of off-duty cops willing to man the gates for the right price, and it wasn't hard to manage everything else on his own, with just his assistant, cleaners, chef, and grounds crew.

Now and then, he saw dust trails from the trucks going down to the bay. There was *Hunt Fish Dive Survive*—driven by the mother, now—Nalani's Tacoma, and a Jeep Wrangler he didn't recognize. Supposedly, there was a chance parts of the reef could come back once a few winter storms cleared out enough silt.

He spent a lot of time in his cube, which he'd cleared of every unnecessary item, leaving just his chair and desk. He'd hired a service to fill his e-reader with a bespoke library, each book hand-selected to suit his tastes and interests. But he never seemed to get to any of them. He spent most of his time on the command line, going deeper and deeper into the codebase, tidying and pruning. Sometimes he recognized lines he'd written himself, in another life.

The sunlight started high on the wall each morning, climbed down, crossed the floor. Then the shadow began its round and chased the light away. He hardly noticed. The smart glass maintained optimal brightness, regardless of the time of day. This wasn't to say he didn't appreciate the view. The feeling he'd had in the midst of the storm had never gone away. Even on days of light wind and blue sky, he savored the four-square silence inside the glass, the privilege of overlooking the world without having to be in it.

In fact, the more time he spent inside the cube, the harder he found it to leave. He'd been so busy for so long, the solitude was something he could almost enjoy.

ACKNOWLEDGMENTS

Thanks to my family: Liz, August, and Max. I'm sorry this book took so much of my attention these past fifteen months; I'm grateful for your love. Thanks to my brother George and my stepmother Juanita, always two of my first readers and most enthusiastic supporters.

Thanks to Danny, Teddy, Kevin, Luke, Evan, Chris R., and Chris A. for twenty years of friendship (and one or two stories that found their way into this novel). And thanks to Anna, Njoki, Alice, Julius, Mama Naomi, Washuka, Gideon, Joe, Samuel, Robert, Lampat, Hawa, Grace, and everyone else who helped me make a home in Kenya.

Thanks to my mother, for warming us with love and knitting. Thanks to my father for being the most joyful person in my life.

Thanks to Aunty Pua and Steve from Moloaa for sharing your experiences. Thanks to Sabrina Bodon, Caleb Loehre, Stephanie Shinno, Terry Lilley, Hank Soboleski, and the rest of the great writers at *The Garden Island* newspaper, and to Brittany Lyte and *Civil Beat* for all your reporting on homelessness in Hawaii. And John P. Rosa at the University of Hawaiʻi-Mānoa for his care and attention in reading the final draft of this book.

Thanks to my agent, Kirby Kim, and my editor, Robert Davis, for giving me the opportunity to keep telling stories. And thanks to the talented staff at Forge—Peter Lutjen, Greg Collins, Ryan Jenkins, Jennifer McClelland-Smith, and Libby Collins—for turning my stories into such a beautifully crafted book and helping it find an audience.

Thanks to my friends and family on Kauai. I miss you.

I could not have written this book without the extraordinary efforts made by countless people to preserve and record Hawaiian knowledge, history, and culture. The following books were particularly useful, and I'm grateful to these writers for sharing their manaʻo and recording so much wisdom with such skill, diligence, and love.

Kaiāulu: Gathering Tides by Mehana Blaich Vaughan
Ancestral Places: Understanding Kanaka Geographies by Katrina-Ann

R. Kapāʻanaokalāokeola Nākoa Oliveira
Hāʻena: Through the Eyes of the Ancestors by Carlos Andrade
Land and Power in Hawaii by George Cooper and Gavan Daws
Kauai: Ancient Place-Names and their Stories by Frederick B. Wichman

It's humbling to read these books and confront what a vast body of knowledge exists and how little of it I'm capable of comprehending. I'm grateful for the generosity of so many Hawaiians who share their understanding of the world with outsiders like myself. I've tried to honor that by being as accurate as possible. Any errors in this novel are entirely mine.

GLOSSARY

Note: Most Hawaiian words and phrases have numerous meanings linked by analogy, metaphor, and other poetic associations. It is an extraordinary and delightful language that rewards even superficial exploration, but its depths are bottomless. For complete and comprehensive definitions of the Hawaiian terms listed below, I suggest readers consult the *Hawaiian Dictionary, Revised & Enlarged Edition* by Mary Kawena Pukui and Samuel H. Elbert, as well as the excellent online resources provided by UH-Hilo and the Hawaiian Electronic Library.

A

'ae kai—(Hawaiian) zone where ocean meets land
ahupua'a—(Hawaiian) traditional land division
'āina—(Hawaiian) the land
akamai—(Hawaiian) wise, clever
ala-alas—(Hawaiian pidgin) testicles
allez-y—(French) go for it
aloha—(Hawaiian) love, but much more than that
'apapa—(Hawaiian) coral reef
aujourd'hui—(French) today
'āweoweo—(Hawaiian) *Priacanthus meeki*, Hawaiian Bigeye, a reef fish

B

beaux rêves—(French) sweet dreams
bien—(French) good
Bubu alisema juu ya uchunga wa mwanawe—(Kiswahili) Even the dumb mother speaks to save her son; a Swahili proverb

C

Ce n'est rien—(French) It's nothing
C'est vrai—(French) It's true

choke—(Hawaiian pidgin) many

chouchou—(French) pet, term of affection

E

elle était heureux—(French) she was happy

F

fackah—(Hawaiian pidgin) fucker

fiti sana—(Kiswahili) very fit; common greeting in Kenyan sheng dialect

freier—(Hebrew) sucker

G

grincheux—(French) grumpy

H

Habari ya jamaa?—(Kiswahili) How is your family?

Habari yako?—(Kiswahili) How are you?

hale—(Hawaiian) house, pronounced hall-ay

haole—(Hawaiian) white person

hapa—(Hawaiian) half, mixed race

'He lani i luna, he honua i lalo—(Hawaiian) Heaven above, earth beneath; traditional Hawaiian saying: if you have these things, you have all you need

he'e—(Hawaiian) octopus

hele—(Hawaiian) go

holo holo—(Hawaiian) go around

hoteli—(Kiswahili) small, simple café. Often a single wooden room with food prepared on a wood or charcoal fire outside

hui—(Hawaiian) group, collective; (Hawaiian pidgin) to form a group, work together

huli—(Hawaiian) flip, capsize

I

i'a—(Hawaiian) fish or marine animal

imua—(Hawaiian) move forward

J

J'ai regardé dans ses yeux. Et il me regardait sans humanité.—(French) I
looked into his eyes. And he regarded me without humanity.

je m'en fous de ça—(French) I don't care about that.

K

kai—(Hawaiian) sea

kalaka—(Hawaiian) juvenile fish

kalo—(Hawaiian) *Colocasia esculenta*, taro, Hawaiian staple crop

kama'āina—(Hawaiian) a person who belongs to a place

Kamehameha—Kamehameha I, Hawaiian king who conquered and united
the islands in the nineteenth century. A prestigious school for students
of Hawaiian ancestry is named for him.

Kānaka Maoli—(Hawaiian) Native Hawaiian

kanga—(Kiswahili) brightly printed cloth wrap

kapu—(Hawaiian) traditional code of ethical and spiritual conduct

Kaukau—(Hawaiian) command to begin paddling

Ke akua—(Hawaiian) god

keiki—(Hawaiian) child

khat—*Catha edulis*, a plant native to Africa that acts as a stimulant when
chewed

ki'i—(Hawaiian) sacred image, often of gods or spirits carved in wood or
stone, tiki in other Polynesian languages

kijiji—(Kiswahili) village

Kikuyu—Kenyan tribe and language

kilo—(Hawaiian) fish spotter

koa—(Hawaiian) *Acacia koa*, a tree endemic to Hawaii

ko'a—(Hawaiian) a place in the ocean where fish breed

kokua—(Hawaiian) help, assistance

kole—(Hawaiian) *Ctenochaetus strigosus*, also known as yellow-eyed tang
or spotted surgeonfish, known for symbiotically cleaning algae from
green sea turtle shells

kolohe—(Hawaiian) naughty

kooks—slang for a surfer who doesn't understand the culture or the eti-
quette

kua 'āina—(Hawaiian) Someone who cares for the land and sustains themselves from it, literally someone who carries the land on their back

kulāiwi—(Hawaiian) homeland, literally the land where an ancestor's bones are buried

kuleana—(Hawaiian) responsibility

kūmū—(Hawaiian) *Paurupeneus porphyreus*, Whitesaddled goatfish

kupuna—(Hawaiian) elder

L

lawa—(Hawaiian) enough, command to stop paddling, pronounced la-va

leiomano—(Hawaiian) war club, often lined with sharks' teeth

limu—(Hawaiian) seaweed

limu kohu—(Hawaiian) *Asparagopsis taxiformis,* a leafy, edible seaweed

lōlō—(Hawaiian) crazy

Luo—Kenyan tribe and language

M

mahalo—(Hawaiian) thanks

mahalo nui—(Hawaiian) big thanks

mahele—(Hawaiian) to divide, to share

māhū—(Hawaiian) gay

majengo—(Kiswahili) informal word for dense, lower-income areas of a town; literally, buildings

maka'ala—(Hawaiian) alert, vigilant

makai—(Hawaiian) toward the sea (opposite of mauka), directions useful on an island

make—(Hawaiian) dead, pronounced mock-ay

mālama—(Hawaiian) to care for

mana—(Hawaiian) power

manini—(Hawaiian) *Acanthurus triostegus sandvicensis,* Convict tang

manō—(Hawaiian) shark

matatu—(Kiswahili) a bus or van used for public transport

mauka—(Hawaiian) toward the land (opposite of makai), directions useful for on island

menpachi—(Hawaiian) *Holocentridae,* a red reef fish

moana—(Hawaiian) the deep ocean

moi aussi—(French) me too

mo'opuna—(Hawaiian) grandchild

Momona—(Hawaiian) fertile

mzee—(Kiswahili) old man

mzungu—(Kiswahili) white person

mzuri sana—(Kiswahili) very good

N

na'au—(Hawaiian) gut

Noho—(Hawaiian) manini (convict tang) grown to their biggest size

nous—(French) we

Nous t'amons, mon chou—(French) We love you, honey

O

'ohana—(Hawaiian) family

'ōkole—(Hawaiian) butt

'ōkole maluna—(Hawaiian) bottoms up

'ōmilu—(Hawaiian) *Caranx melampygus*, bluefin trevally, a predatory fish

one hānau—(Hawaiian) place where you come from, literally, sands of birth, pronounced own-ay han-ow

opihi—(Hawaiian) limpets

P

pakololo—(Hawaiian pidgin) cannabis

palekana—(Hawaiian) protect

parle avec—(French) speak with

pau—(Hawaiian) finished

peut-être—(French) maybe

pilikia—(Hawaiian) trouble

poi—(Hawaiian) pounded taro

po'ina kai—(Hawaiian) zone where waves break offshore

pono—(Hawaiian) excellence, rightness

pōpolo—(Hawaiian pidgin) Black

puka—(Hawaiian) hole

Punahou—(Hawaiian) private school on Oahu

pu'uhonua—(Hawaiian) place of refuge

pu'ulima—(Hawaiian) knuckles

pu'u'oi'oi—(Hawaiian) pile of stones, resting place

pu'uwai—(Hawaiian) heart

Q

Qui es-tu?—(French) Who are you?

Quoi?—(French) What?

R

rafiki yangu—(Kiswahili) my friend

S

samaki kubwa—(Kiswahili) big fish

sans défense—(French) defenseless

shaka—(Hawaiian pidgin) a hand gesture with pinkie and thumb extended, origins unclear

shibi—(Hawaiian pidgin) small yellowfin tuna

Si forte—(French) So strong

s'il vous plait—(French) please

Sokoni—(Kiswahili) market

spahk—(Hawaiian pidgin) see, look

T

Tita—(Hawaiian pidgin) tough lady

Tout—assistant on a matatu who takes fares and seats passengers

tout à fait—(French) Absolutely

tout le temps—(French) all the time

Tumesikia taarifa za wezi kwenye barabara ya Nairobi—(Kiswahili) We have heard there are thieves on the Nairobi Road.

Tunaenda wapi—(Kiswahili) Where are you going?

Tutaonana—(Kiswahili) See you later

Tūtū—(Hawaiian) Grandma

U

Ua noho au a kupa—(Hawaiian) I have stayed and become well-aquainted to this place, song lyric by Edward Nainoa

ugali—(Kiswahili) boiled cornmeal

ula—(Hawaiian) lobster

ulua—(Hawaiian) *Caranx ignobilis*, Giant trevally, a large, predatorial gamefish

un mec de base—(French) a basic guy

W

wahine—(Hawaiian) woman

wanasema nini—(Kiswahili) What are they saying?

weke—(Hawaiian) *mullidae*, goatfish

wezi—(Kiswahili) thieves

wiliwili—(Hawaiian) *Erythrina sandwicensis*, an endemic Hawaiian tree with light wood traditionally used for surfboards and canoe outriggers